IN NEED
OF THERAPY

By
Tracie Banister

Cover Art designed by Jeff Okerstrom.

IN NEED OF THERAPY

To all of my wonderful author friends, who've supported and guided me through the oft-intimidating, always exhilarating publishing maze.

CHAPTER 1

Patient's name: Lori Bryant
Age: 25
Occupation: Hair stylist
Diagnosis based on initial evaluation: Patient suffers from abandonment issues that stem from parents divorcing when she was 7. Looks to romantic partners for the love and devotion she never received from her absentee father. Patient self-destructively chases men who are emotionally distant or unavailable and sabotages all relationships with her neediness and possessiveness. Prone to dramatic, emotional outbursts and mood swings.

Goal of therapy: Build patient's self-confidence and provide her with the tools she needs to have a healthy relationship based on reciprocity.

"I just don't understand what I did wrong!" Lori wailed pitifully, tears streaming down her swollen pink cheeks.

I opened a fresh box of Kleenex and handed it to her with a look of sympathetic concern. She'd already worked her way through the packet of tissues she'd pulled from her purse at the beginning of our session and balled-up wads of soggy white paper now littered the couch where she was sitting.

"We were so happy! I thought for sure that James was the one, that we had a future together." She stopped to blow her runny nose, making a loud honking noise as she did so.

"I did everything to please him. He said he thought Cameron Diaz was hot, so I colored my hair blonde and started wearing stilettos to make myself look taller."

And lightening her hair had been a tragic mistake. Lori's curly red locks, which I'd always admired, were now a bleached-out, frizzy fright. She looked like she'd stuck her finger in a light socket. Surely, her new 'do was bad for business? If I were a potential client of Lori's and I walked into her salon and saw the mess she'd made of her own hair, I'd run screaming for the door.

"I did his laundry. I gave him foot massages. I made him a home-cooked meal every night. I even sent him love notes via text and e-mail every hour on the hour when he was at work. What more did he want?" She turned beseeching eyes on me as if I knew the secret to men's hearts.

"Well . . ."

How could I put this politely? 'Lori, you scared off James by smothering him with your so-called love? You'll never hold on to a man if you continue to act so clingy and desperate?' If I was honest with Lori, who was high-strung on a good day, I'd have to put her on suicide watch.

"He probably wanted some space." I opted for a truthful, but benign, answer. "You'd only been together for what? Three weeks?"

"Two weeks and three days. The happiest 403 hours of my life!"

She was now counting how many hours her doomed romances lasted? *Oh, dear.* I made a note on my steno pad.

"In terms of a relationship, that's not much time, and my guess is that James was feeling rushed, like things were getting too serious, too fast."

"That's exactly what he said! But I don't understand, Dr. Alvarez. James and I were so compatible. Why take things slow when our love felt so right?"

"But was it really love? You barely knew each other," I gently reminded her.

"Do you have to know someone in order to love them? What about love at first sight?"

"In that context, love is a misnomer. There can be lust or attraction at first sight, but not love.

What you feel for a man when you first lay eyes on him is

Sara stared up at me. "Do you want me to come with you?"

"No, I can handle this." I took a few steps away from the table, then stopped and went back for my Mojito. I had a feeling I was going to need it.

"Hello, Victor," I acknowledged the dark-haired man in the cream-colored designer suit who was conspicuously perched on the corner stool at the bar.

He swiveled around to face me. "*Buenas noches, mi amada.*" Victor was not bilingual, but he liked to pepper his conversation with Spanish words and phrases as though he was. It enhanced his Latin lover image, or at least he thought it did. "This is a surprise."

"I doubt that. You followed me here, and now you're spying on me and my date. Remember that discussion we had about boundaries? You're not respecting mine."

"But I am!" he insisted with a hurt expression. "I didn't come to your table. I was just admiring your beauty from afar."

"I don't want you admiring me *period.* We broke up, remember?" I kept using that word as if he suffered from amnesia. Selective memory was more like it. Most of what I said to Victor seemed to go in one ear and out the other.

"I don't accept that." Before I could stop him, he dropped down on one knee and took my free hand in his, clutching it to his heart. "I love you, Pilar. No other man will ever love you like I do. I eat, breathe, and sleep you. You are in my thoughts every minute of every day!" It was quite an impassioned speech, but then Victor had always been one for the big romantic gesture.

"You are developing an unhealthy fixation on me, Victor. Please, get up." I tugged on his arm, and with a plaintive sigh, he rose to his feet.

"You have no romance in your soul, *mi querida,*" he

22

business? If I were a potential client of Lori's and I walked into her salon and saw the mess she'd made of her own hair, I'd run screaming for the door.

"I did his laundry. I gave him foot massages. I made him a home-cooked meal every night. I even sent him love notes via text and e-mail every hour on the hour when he was at work. What more did he want?" She turned beseeching eyes on me as if I knew the secret to men's hearts.

"Well . . ."

How could I put this politely? 'Lori, you scared off James by smothering him with your so-called love? You'll never hold on to a man if you continue to act so clingy and desperate?' If I was honest with Lori, who was high-strung on a good day, I'd have to put her on suicide watch.

"He probably wanted some space." I opted for a truthful, but benign, answer. "You'd only been together for what? Three weeks?"

"Two weeks and three days. The happiest 403 hours of my life!"

She was now counting how many hours her doomed romances lasted? *Oh, dear.* I made a note on my steno pad.

"In terms of a relationship, that's not much time, and my guess is that James was feeling rushed, like things were getting too serious, too fast."

"That's exactly what he said! But I don't understand, Dr. Alvarez. James and I were so compatible. Why take things slow when our love felt so right?"

"But was it really love? You barely knew each other," I gently reminded her.

"Do you have to know someone in order to love them? What about love at first sight?"

"In that context, love is a misnomer. There can be lust or attraction at first sight, but not love.

What you feel for a man when you first lay eyes on him is

based solely on his physical appearance. It's a chemical reaction to aesthetics. Love is a deep and complicated emotion that grows over time."

"Soooooo," Lori slid forward to the edge of the couch, "you're saying that if I could get James to take me back, he would *grow* to love me?"

"No," I stated firmly, "that door is closed. James ended your relationship, and you need to move on."

"To another man?" The idea seemed to perk her up. "There is this cute civil engineer who came in for a cut last week. I think he was interested. He did wink at me a few times, or that might have been a nervous tic."

I resisted the urge to sigh impatiently. "I wouldn't advise jumping into another relationship so soon. You need time to recover from this latest disappointment."

Lori frowned. "How much time?"

"Let's say, a month. I want you to avoid any and all romantic entanglements for the next four weeks."

"A month!" She was incredulous. "I can't live without a man in my life for a month."

"You can and you will. You need this time for self-reflection. Think of it as a therapeutic exercise."

"What am I supposed to be reflecting on? Why nobody wants me? How I'm going to die alone? I can't do it! I can't be by myself for a month. I need someone to love, someone to take care of," she whined.

"Then get a puppy."

Lori's jaw dropped, and her heavily made-up blue eyes widened. "Are you serious?" she wondered.

"Absolutely," I enthused. "A pet will give you the unconditional love you crave. It will keep you company and give you something to nurture. Studies have shown that people who have pets live longer, happier lives."

Lori chewed on a hangnail while she considered my

suggestion. "There is a park near my apartment complex. If I had a dog and I walked it there every day, I'll bet that I could meet a lot of guys."

Freud, give me strength! Did this woman have to relate everything back to men?

"You may make new friends through your pet; animals do tend to make their owners more sociable. But don't forget your month-long moratorium on dating. I want you to focus on yourself and the new addition to your household, not men."

"Okay, I'll try."

"Good." I glanced over at the small crystal clock located on the end table next to the couch and was relieved to see that it was 4:49PM. "I'm afraid our time is up for today."

"Already?" Lori looked down at her watch as if she thought I was lying. "Wow! Time really does fly when I'm here." She stood up to leave. "Thanks so much, Dr. Alvarez. I feel a lot better."

"I'm glad," I replied with a smile as I stood and smoothed out the wrinkles in my linen skirt. "Let me walk you out."

I led her out the door of my office into the small waiting area, which was empty since Lori had been my last appointment of the day. Stopping at my receptionist's desk, I asked, "Margo, would you write down the number and address of the Humane Society for Ms. Bryant?"

"Sure thing." Margo lifted her reading glasses, which were attached to a gaudy red-and-purple beaded tether that hung around her neck, and placed them on the tip of her nose. She turned the knob on her rolodex until the F-tab came up, then spent a couple of seconds flipping through the cards in that section. She stopped when she found the one she wanted and scribbled a few lines on a fluorescent pink post-it note.

"Here ya go, honey." She handed the information to my patient. "Good luck."

"I'll see you next Tuesday at the same time, okay?"

"I'll be here," Lori assured me as if there were any doubt. I was confident that her appointment with me was the highlight of her week. In our first session, she'd told me that her girlfriends, as well as her mother, steadfastly refused to discuss her man problems anymore. And so, she'd had to turn to me, a paid professional, to listen.

"Poor thing," Margo remarked after Lori was gone. "She gets dumped more often than my garbage, and I have a twice-a-week pick-up."

"Hopefully, adopting a dog will bring some love and happiness into her life. Why did you have the Humane Society filed under the Fs?"

"Furry friends," she explained.

"Ah." My receptionist was what we in the psychology biz called 'an abstract-random thinker.' She was orderly in her own way, but things that made perfect sense to her left other people scratching their heads. If Margo ever quit and I had to figure out the method to her filing system madness myself, I was in deep trouble.

"What do we have on the schedule for tomorrow?"

With a few keystrokes, Margo pulled up a list of Wednesday's appointments on her computer screen. "A new patient in the morning, and the Ortegas and Mr. Campbell in the afternoon."

"Three appointments for the whole day!" I groaned and sank down in defeat on the corner of Margo's desk. "That's awful. I should be booking 7 or 8 sessions every day of the week."

"You're seeing 6 patients on Thursday."

"It's not enough."

Margo gave my knee an encouraging pat. "Honey, you've only been in this office for 3 months. It takes time to build a practice."

I looked down at the liver spots on the back of her 67-year-old hand. "I know, but I've got bills to pay. Maybe I should do more advertising? Of course, that would cost money."

"So, ask that nice father of yours to help you out."

"He's already done too much."

Not only had *Papá* found me a beautiful office in South Beach, he'd had it furnished and decorated by some trendy interior designer and paid the first month's rent. I was blessed to have such a financially-solvent and generous father, but now I wanted to stand on my own two feet.

"Helping out is what families do. Where would my Saul be if I didn't work? He couldn't survive on his Disability."

I smiled. Margo and Saul Rabinowitz were the cutest couple I knew. They'd been married for 42 years and were still, quite obviously, very much in love. Their faces lit up whenever they saw each other, and they were always so affectionate, a kiss on the cheek here, a tender caress of the shoulder there. They gave me hope for couples everywhere.

"He's lucky to have you."

"No, I'm the lucky one," she insisted. "Oh, look at the time! If I don't get home by six to get the brisket out of the oven, Saul will forget and leave it in. Then, our dinner will taste like old shoe leather." She pulled a big straw handbag out of her bottom desk drawer.

I rose to my feet. "I should get going, too. I've got a date tonight."

"Good for you!" Margo squeezed my arm on her way to the door. "A pretty girl like you shouldn't be sitting at home by herself every night."

I didn't know whether to be flattered that she'd referred to me, a woman pushing 30, as a "girl," or offended that she thought my social life was so pathetic. It wasn't like I was some unpopular recluse who stayed in every night eating a tub of Rocky Road while I carried on meaningful conversations with my cats. I didn't even have any cats. What I did have was lots of friends and a big family who kept me busy when I wasn't at work. Maybe I had been going through a bit of a dry spell with men, but it wasn't like I wasn't open to going out or developing a relationship with someone special.

"You'll have to give me all of the juicy details tomorrow. Have fun, doll!" Margo disappeared out into the corridor, leaving a trail of White Shoulders perfume in her wake.

I went back to my office, grabbed my purse, and turned off all the lights and office equipment. The last thing I needed was another $298 bill from Florida P&L. If I hadn't been sitting when I'd opened my last statement from that price-gouging utilities company, I would have keeled over from the shock. Damn air-conditioning! In South Florida's sultry climate, you couldn't live without it, but living with it would almost bankrupt you.

Shutting the outer office door behind me, I reached into the maw of my Louis Vuitton handbag and began to rummage around in search of my keys. The expensive leather purse, which had been embellished with a whimsical cherry print, was something I never would have bought for myself, but I'd had no compunction about accepting it as a hand-me-down from my older sister, Ana, the lawyer's wife, who'd carried it as a status symbol for one season. Whether the bag was out-of-style or not didn't matter to me, I only cared that it was big and sturdy since I had a habit of using my purse to haul around things as disparate in size and weight as my old psych textbooks and cartons of Chinese.

After locking my office door, I stood back for a moment and gazed at the name plate that adorned it: *Pilar Alvarez, Psy.D.* Seeing those four letters after my name never ceased to thrill me. They had been hard-earned. Years of school, supervision by my mentor, Dr. Fields, for countless hours while I gathered experience, the EPPP examination, the state laws and rules test, and finally, my license to practice psychology in Florida. It had been heady stuff when I'd first held that all-important piece of paper in my hands. There was so much power in it, power to help people, to shape their lives, to make a difference in the world. And being called "Doctor" wasn't a bad bonus.

I scampered down the stairs that took me to the lobby of the almost 80-year-old Mediterranean Revival-style building where my office was housed. It was a beautiful building, fully restored with stone floors, stucco walls, and a clay barrel tile roof. There were three offices on the ground floor (a CPA, travel agency, and graphic designer) and three on the second level (a wedding planner, me, and an empty suite that had been vacated by an architect the previous month - he had run off with one of the wedding planner's brides-to-be two days before she was supposed to walk down the aisle. It had been quite a scandal.)

I had gotten to work early that morning, so I'd scored an excellent parking space directly across from my office building on 11th Street. I jaywalked over to my car, which probably wasn't the smartest move since the City of Miami Beach Police Station was less than a block down on the left, but I was too lazy to hoof it up to the next crosswalk at Jefferson. My silver Miata was right where I'd left it; its metallic paint glistening in the late afternoon sun. I took down the black vinyl convertible top so that I could enjoy the nice weather on my ride home, then climbed into the driver's seat.

Removing the tortoise shell clip that I had my hair twisted up with, I ran my fingers through the long, wavy tresses. I have nice hair; it's thick and healthy, and I can wear it curly or straight (of course, that would require a ton of product, an hour of blowdrying, and a non-humid day, which was something of a rarity in what I affectionately called "the sweatbox.") The color of my hair is unremarkable - medium brown, I guess you'd call it, but I have pretty caramel highlights (courtesy of the sun) that most women have to go to a salon and pay good money to get.

I strapped myself in, put on my Ray-Bans, and started the Miata's engine. My car was almost 5 years old, but it didn't have a lot of mileage and it ran like a dream. Cruising up the Macarthur Causeway on my way home from work was the most enjoyable part of my day. Katy Perry on the CD player, the wind in my hair, the Biscayne Bay on either side of me, who could complain? Although I lived only 10 miles from my office, it took a good 30 minutes to cover that territory during rush hour because of the slow-and-go traffic on I-95. Bitching and moaning about our clogged freeways was a favorite pastime of many South Floridians, and the frustrated expressions I saw on the faces of my fellow commuters every day made me very glad that I didn't have to trek back and forth from Fort Lauderdale or Boca.

At five past six, I pulled into the concrete ribbon driveway outside my house. *House* might be a slight exaggeration. It's really a bungalow, an adorable yellow bungalow with palm trees in the front yard and avocado trees in the back. With the help of my father, who'd given me the $30,000 down payment, I'd bought the property two years ago and had loved every minute of living within its cozy confines.

As per my daily routine, I removed the mail from the black metal box attached to the wall next to my front door, then let myself in.

"I'm home!" I shouted over the sound of the screen door crashing closed behind me.

No response. It wasn't like my house was so big that you could be out of earshot in any part of it. She was ignoring me.

"Izzy!"

Izzy was my younger sister, Isidora, and my sort-of roommate. *Sort-of* because the term "roommate" implied that the person paid rent, and Izzy never had. She'd moved into my place "temporarily" after graduating college the year before because she couldn't stand living with my parents, who were "too controlling," and had never left.

The relationship between my parents and their youngest child was a complicated one. Izzy had been their "Ooops!" baby. Ana had been born ten months after my parents' marriage (both grandmothers had actually brought calendars to the hospital and counted back from her day of birth to confirm that she'd been conceived in holy wedlock.) I'd arrived the following year, and my parents had thought that they were through with procreating. Then, six years later, "Ooops!" *Mamá* became pregnant with Izzy. My parents loved Izzy just as much as their other daughters, but she'd always been a trial for them. It was almost as if she'd sensed in the womb that she was an accident and so, she'd come into the world with a "Here I am, deal with it!" attitude.

"Hey." Izzy padded into the living room on bare feet. She wore her standard uniform of short shorts that sat obscenely low on her lean hips and a midriff-baring halter top that exposed her pierced belly button. I couldn't look at it without feeling queasy.

"How was your day?" I asked conversationally as I sorted through the mail. *Phone bill. Visa statement. Victoria's Secret catalog.* "Any luck with your job search?" She'd been fired from or "quit" so many jobs in the last year that I'd lost count.

"Not really." She picked up a half-eaten Snickers bar that she'd left sitting on the coffee table and took a bite of it.

"Did you go on any interviews today? Look at the job

listings online?"

"I checked Simply Hired and Monster. There wasn't anything new."

She was probably lying, but I let it slide. "Any phone calls for me?"

"Yeah." She plopped down on the couch, tucking her long, tanned legs underneath her. "The psycho called."

"You're going to have to be more specific than that. I meet a lot of psychos in my line of work," I said with a playful smirk, then handed her a piece of junk mail that had her name on it.

"I'm not talking about one of your patients. I'm talking about your psycho ex, Victor."

I made a face. I hadn't heard from Victor in almost a week, and I'd been hoping that he'd finally gotten tired of pursuing me. I'd given him his walking papers a month ago, but he didn't seem to understand the concept of breaking up. "What did he say?"

"He said he missed you and wanted to know what you were up to. I told him that you'd moved to a remote island in the South Pacific so that you could provide psychological treatment to a tribe of cannibals there."

I chortled. "I don't suppose he believed you?"

"'fraid not." Izzy balled up her candy bar wrapper and tossed it in the general direction of the coffee table. The wrapper missed by a few inches and fell to the ivory throw rug beneath it. "He said that no matter where you went, or what you did, he wasn't giving up on you. Your love was destined to be . . . or some crap like that."

I rolled my eyes. Funny that Victor had never said anything about his undying love for me when we were together. Like most men, he just wanted what he could no longer have.

"You should take this seriously, Pilar," my sister warned.

"I think that Victor's *loco*. He'll probably come here in the middle of the night and murder us in our sleep."

"You watch too many movies about serial killers. In my professional opinion, he's harmless. Annoying, but harmless."

"If you say so . . . I'm hungry!" She abruptly changed the subject and jumped up from the couch. "I'm going to heat up some beans and rice. Want some?"

I followed her into the kitchen. "No thanks. I'm going out to dinner with Sara. Our double date, remember? She's setting me up with a friend of Matt's."

"Who's Matt?" Izzy wondered as she peeled off the lid of some Tupperware she'd taken out of the refrigerator.

"Ugh!" She crinkled up her nose with disgust when she got a whiff of its rotted contents. "This is nasty. I don't even know what kind of meat it was." She threw the open container into the sink, where it would most likely stay until I scrubbed it out.

"Matt's the PR guy Sara's been seeing for the past month. He's cute. Hopefully, his friend will be, too."

"A double date *and* a blind date? That sounds like a fun evening . . . *not*." Izzy popped another piece of Tupperware, this one full of leftover black beans and rice, into the microwave.

"Well, it's not like I'm meeting anyone on my own, so I can't turn down an opportunity. I'm sure it'll be fine. Sara knows my taste."

"*You* don't even know your taste." Izzy opened the silverware drawer and pulled out a fork.

Good point. I really wasn't sure what I was looking for in a man. I only knew that I'd recognize that indefinable something when I came into contact with it.

"I'd better get ready. I have no idea what I'm going to wear. Clean up after yourself, please." I waved at the mess she was making on the kitchen counter.

Izzy used her hand to scrape up a forkful of beans and rice that she'd just dropped. "Wear your coral top!" she yelled after me. "Guys love a bare back."

CHAPTER 2

"This top is fabulous!" Sara enthused as she circled me, looking at the item of clothing from every conceivable angle.

"It fits you perfectly. The color complements your skin tone. And the way it dips down and sort of pools at the small of your back . . . very sexy. Is this 100% silk?" She rubbed the thick strap that sat on the slope of my right shoulder before I could answer her. "Oh, yeah, this is good stuff." A fashion designer by trade, Sara was quite passionate about things like the quality of fabric.

"I'm glad you approve," I said with an amused smile. The line that we were standing in, waiting to gain entry into SoBe's newest, hippest pan-Asian restaurant, began to move. "You can borrow the top if you want."

Sara guffawed and made a dismissive hand gesture. "Please! You know I don't have the boobs to fill it out."

Maybe she didn't have the boobs, but Sara had everything else. She was tall (at 5'10, she stood three inches above me) and slender with long, coltish legs, straight, silky, blonde hair (currently cut in a stylish bob), a flawless complexion, and eyes the color of the Caribbean Sea. She had always been beautiful, but didn't seem to care, which was one of the qualities that had endeared her to me when we'd met in our freshman year at the University of Miami.

A large, dark-suited man ushered us through the front door of Wasabi where we encountered another huge crowd of people, most of whom were standing around chatting even though it was almost impossible to hear yourself think, much less talk, over the din. Sara and I pushed our way up to the hostess stand and informed one of the blank-eyed, black-clad girls there that we had a reservation. She didn't look impressed.

"We'll call you when your table is ready," she told us in a

so-bored monotone.

We moved off to the side and staked claim to a small unoccupied bit of space up against a wall. I leaned into Sara and almost-shouted, "How are preparations coming along for the show?"

The "show" was the Miami Summer Fashion Extravaganza, which was an annual event held at the Fontainebleau Hotel. Sara would be debuting her new line of bathing suits there and since hundreds of buyers from all over the world, as well as important members of the fashion press would be in attendance, it was a huge opportunity for her.

"I'm totally stressed out. I've got less than three months until the show, and everything's falling apart. The ruby chips I wanted for my jeweled bikini are too expensive, so I'm going to have to go with something cheaper like amethysts or aquamarines, which means changing the color of the suit. It's just a nightmare! I may end up throwing myself into the Atlantic before this is all over," she proclaimed. Like all creative geniuses, Sara had a flair for the dramatic.

"You'll deal with it," I assured her. "When you were with Versace, you always had to make changes to your designs at the last minute."

"True, but it's my name on the label now. So, every setback just seems more catastrophic. By the way, I've changed the name of my line."

"What was wrong with Sara Reade Swimwear?" I wondered.

"It was boring and unmemorable. I need a name that's catchy, something that no one will forget. How does Serafina Swimwear grab you?"

"Serafina?" I let the name roll off my tongue as I considered it. "I like it! It's colorful, exotic, alluring."

"Just like my suits! See, it's perfect. Oh, there are the guys." She waved at Matt and his friend, who'd just walked into the restaurant.

"Hey, baby," Matt greeted his girlfriend with a quick smooch. "Pilar, this is my buddy, Ben."

Matt and Ben? I was tempted to make a *Good Will Hunting* joke, but it was just too easy.

"Hi." I extended my hand for Ben to shake, but he was so busy giving my body the once-over that he didn't notice. Matt had to give him an elbow in the side.

Ben grunted. "Huh? Oh, yeah, hi. Nice to meet you." His hand was cold and clammy. *ICK*

"Looks like our table is ready." Sara saw the hostess signaling us.

We trooped into the restaurant's dining room and were seated at a center table. Sara and I took chairs next to each other, while our dates faced us. We'd barely had time to place our napkins in our laps when our waiter appeared to ask if we wanted something to drink?

"I'll have a Chocolate Banana Martini." Sara was a self-admitted chocoholic who had to have it in some form or another at every meal (yes, even breakfast.) I'd actually seen the woman melt Hershey's Kisses in with her scrambled eggs.

I ordered one of the most popular cocktails in South Beach, "A Watermelon Mojito."

The guys opted for beer, and our server was off to get our beverages.

"So, Pilar, tell me about yourself." Suddenly, there were three pairs of eyes on me. I hated the getting-to-know-you part of first dates. I felt like I had to sell myself as an interesting person in 25 words or less.

"Well, as you probably know already, I'm a psychologist."

"Oh, yeah," Ben tried not to look bored and failed as he pulled a slightly crumpled pack of non-filtered Camels from the inside pocket of his suit jacket and set them down on the table in front of him, "that must be a drag, listening to people bitch and moan about their problems day in and day out."

He was a smoker *and* he disdained my profession? Two strikes and we hadn't even opened our menus.

"Actually, no, I enjoy helping people."

"Yeah, that's what Matt and I do, help people. Right, buddy?" He gave his friend a hearty slap on the back.

Grimacing, Matt replied, "In a manner of speaking, but our PR firm helps corporations, not individuals."

"We work for the biggest PR firm in Miami, JKR Communications. You've heard of it, right?"

I started to say "no," but Ben plowed ahead before I could get the word out.

"Our clients are HUGE! The Miami Heat, Univision, Sony . . . Matt and I were just put in charge of this new cruise line account that we're going to make a mint on. We'll probably get bonuses in the $75K range this year and that's on top of our salaries, which means we'll take home close to a quarter mil' in 2012."

Men who bragged about the size of their bank accounts were usually overcompensating for a lack of size elsewhere. Strike three. I wanted to go home.

Ben removed a cigarette from the pack he'd been unconsciously caressing ever since he'd placed it on the table and shoved the cancer stick between his lips. A waitress, who was bustling by with a tray full of food, screeched to a halt and said, "I'm sorry, sir, but there's no smoking in this restaurant."

"Do you see any smoke, sweetheart?" he queried irritably. "As long as this cigarette's not lit, I'm not breaking any of the Health Department's Fascist, anti-smoking laws, so stop hassling me and go back to filling up ketchup bottles."

The waitress retreated, looking chastened and embarrassed.

Men who abused wait staff were petty and tyrannical in nature. Strike fo--, oh wait, I was out of strikes. I'd have to start issuing demerits.

"Nicotine withdrawal is making somebody cranky," Sara observed. "Matt, why don't you give Ben some of your Nicorette?"

"You'd think I'd pulled out an Uzi, instead of a cigarette," Ben groused. "Smokers get no respect; we're treated like second-class citizens everywhere we go. If we want to light up, we're forced to leave whatever restaurant, club, or store we're patronizing and stand outside like social pariahs."

"Smoking's too much trouble now; I'm glad I quit," Matt remarked as he searched his pockets for his nicotine gum.

"I'm glad I never started."

My date gaped at me. "You've *never* smoked?"

I shrugged. "It's just something that's never appealed to me."

"Oh, man, I've been smoking a pack a day since I was 15. You have no idea what you're missing."

Heart disease? Lung cancer? Emphysema? I was pretty sure I could do without all of those things and I was just about to tell Ben that and give him the name of a hypnotherapist, who specialized in the treatment of people with addictions, when our drinks arrived.

I took a big swig of my Mojito, then another one.

"Uh, Pilar . . ." I thought Sara was going to tell me to slow down or suffer the consequences. Instead, she muttered, "Take a look at the bar. 3:00."

I turned ever-so-subtly to my right and saw an all-too-familiar face. Just when I thought the night couldn't get any worse . . .

"Would you excuse me for a minute?" I politely asked my date as I rose from my seat. "I have to take care of something."

Sara stared up at me. "Do you want me to come with you?"

"No, I can handle this." I took a few steps away from the table, then stopped and went back for my Mojito. I had a feeling I was going to need it.

"Hello, Victor," I acknowledged the dark-haired man in the cream-colored designer suit who was conspicuously perched on the corner stool at the bar.

He swiveled around to face me. "*Buenas noches, mi amada.*" Victor was not bilingual, but he liked to pepper his conversation with Spanish words and phrases as though he was. It enhanced his Latin lover image, or at least he thought it did. "This is a surprise."

"I doubt that. You followed me here, and now you're spying on me and my date. Remember that discussion we had about boundaries? You're not respecting mine."

"But I am!" he insisted with a hurt expression. "I didn't come to your table. I was just admiring your beauty from afar."

"I don't want you admiring me *period*. We broke up, remember?" I kept using that word as if he suffered from amnesia. Selective memory was more like it. Most of what I said to Victor seemed to go in one ear and out the other.

"I don't accept that." Before I could stop him, he dropped down on one knee and took my free hand in his, clutching it to his heart. "I love you, Pilar. No other man will ever love you like I do. I eat, breathe, and sleep you. You are in my thoughts every minute of every day!" It was quite an impassioned speech, but then Victor had always been one for the big romantic gesture.

"You are developing an unhealthy fixation on me, Victor. Please, get up." I tugged on his arm, and with a plaintive sigh, he rose to his feet.

"You have no romance in your soul, *mi querida*," he

chastised. "Most women would be thrilled to have a man fall at their feet and pledge his eternal devotion."

"So, why don't you go find one of them and leave me in peace?" I suggested.

"Pilar, Pilar . . ." He gazed at me with rueful brown eyes. "It doesn't work like that. You are the only one for me. Another woman will never do."

"As I recall, plenty of other women did just fine when we were dating. Let's see, there was that jailbait cashier at Pollo Tropical, your brother's girlfriend, the one who liked to sunbathe by your parents' pool topless - I think her name was Stacey, the lingerie model who was built like Pamela Anderson . . . shall I go on?"

He threw up his hands in exasperation. "So, this is why you won't take me back? Because I committed a few," he saw my raised eyebrow and corrected himself, "alright, *several*, indiscretions during our relationship. If I had known that my extracurricular activities were going to upset you so much, I never would have . . ."

"Please," I stopped him, "let's not rewrite history. It would be an exercise in futility. We can't change the past and we both need to move forward."

"Together?"

"No!" I was starting to get really frustrated with him. I gulped down the rest of my Mojito in an effort to calm my nerves, then set the empty glass on the bar.

"I need to get back to my date before he thinks that I've deserted him, and you need to leave."

"You're not planning to sleep with him," Victor glanced over at Ben and curled his lip derisively, "tonight, are you?"

"Did I sleep with you on the first date?"

"I think it was the twenty-first."

"Then, rest assured, that my virtue is safe. Pay your bill and go back to your own bar," I instructed.

In Need of Therapy

Victor owned a *tapas* restaurant and bar a few blocks over on Collins Avenue, and that's where our ill-fated first meeting had taken place. I'd gone to Liscano's (named after Victor's family since his parents had given him the seed money for the business) with a group of girlfriends to celebrate the opening of my new office, and he'd sent us a round of drinks on the house. Later, he'd come over to our table and introduced himself. At the time, I'd been impressed. Victor was handsome (he had a young Andy Garcia thing going on), successful, and charming. And most importantly, he knew just how to flatter a woman and make her feel special.

When he'd asked me to join him for a trip around the bay on his sailboat the following day, I'd consented without hesitation. And we'd been happy for a while. Picnics on the beach, regattas at the Miami Yacht Club, salsa dancing, hot air balloon rides, Dolphins games, impromptu getaways to the Keys, life with Victor Liscano had been a non-stop thrill ride, but eventually, I'd gotten nauseous and wanted to get off. My discovery of his cheating had given me the excuse I needed to end our relationship.

The truth was that Victor and I had never been *simpático*. He was Mr. Party-All-The-Time, while I was more serious and work-oriented. Not that I didn't like to have fun, but the main focus in my life was my career. I wanted to make a name for myself as a psychologist in South Florida and building a thriving practice required commitment and hard work. Victor's idea of working hard was dropping in at Liscano's for an hour or two every night so that he could flirt with the female customers. He pretty much left the actual running of his restaurant to the manager.

"Fine. I'll go." Victor pulled out his wallet and slapped a $20 bill down on the bar. "But I'm not discouraged. Our time will come again, Pilar. I am certain of that. Until then,

24

I can be patient."

I was beginning to think that he should *be* a patient. Maybe I should refer him to Dr. Fields?

He leaned over and gave me a kiss on the cheek. He was wearing so much cologne that the scent tickled my nose, and I almost sneezed.

"*Adiós, mi corazón.* I'll call you later."

"Don't--," I made a half-hearted attempt to protest, but didn't even bother to finish my sentence. Victor was going to do what he wanted to no matter what I said. It was a hopeless cause.

I turned around and smacked my hand on the bar. "Bartender," I called.

"Another Watermelon Mojito." I slid my empty glass towards the young stud who responded to my summons. "No, wait. Give me a Sunburn. Those are strong, right?"

"They're made with two kinds of rum."

"Perfect." I hoped the alcohol would give me enough of a pleasant buzz to get through the rest of my date with the obnoxious Ben, then block out my memory of the night completely.

CHAPTER 3

I was rooting through my desk drawers for a bottle of aspirin when my phone intercom buzzed loudly. I protested the noise by moaning miserably and covering my ears. Hangovers sucked. I hadn't had many of them in my life, but thanks to my splitting headache and queasy stomach, I was having sensory-induced flashbacks to a few out-of-control keggers at UM. I vowed never to drink two cocktails in one evening again.

Taking a sip of room-temperature water, I responded to my receptionist's call. "Yes, Margo."

"Your 9:00 is here," she informed me in a voice that sounded a lot more nasal and grating than usual.

Great. My new patient. I was going to make a wonderful first impression.

"Thank you. I'll be right out."

"You can do this. You're a professional," I told myself, but the pep talk didn't work. I still felt like I was going to throw up.

Using the corner of my desk for support, I rose to my feet shakily and tried to ignore the nauseating way the room was spinning. My *abuelos*, Hernando and Luis, who, for two decades, had shared a bottle of Havana Club's best aged rum every Friday afternoon when they'd gotten together to play dominoes, were probably in heaven shaking their heads with disappointment at their pitiful, liquor-intolerant granddaughter. Drawing strength from my memory of those tough old men, I muttered, "Mind over matter, Pilar," and purposefully headed for the door.

Fortunately, I'd had the foresight to wear my Kate Spade pumps with the sensible 2-inch kitten heels, so I didn't have any balancing issues. I took deep breaths in and out as I traversed my office, and by the time I reached the door, I almost felt human again. I tucked some stray pieces of hair behind my ears and self-consciously fiddled with the belt on my brown sleeveless dress before venturing into the waiting area.

My new patient was sitting in a chair on the opposite wall with his face buried in the latest issue of *Sports Illustrated*. He had long legs, encased in raggedy-looking jeans with holes in the knees and frayed hems, and he wore flip-flops. Nice, name-brand flip-flops, not the cheap, rubber ones that tourists bought at beach-front drugstores because they'd forgotten to pack them, but they were still flips-flops, which was a pretty odd choice of footwear for a doctor's visit.

"Mr. Buchannon," I addressed him.

He set the magazine down in the empty chair next to him and stood up.

Woah! My eyes almost popped out of my head. I'd seen plenty of good-looking men in my life, but this one put all the others to shame. He was tall, definitely over six feet, with tousled, sun-streaked hair that looked like it hadn't been cut in a few months, bronzed skin, pale green eyes, and a couple days' worth of stubble that was a few shades darker than his hair and drew attention to his full, sexy mouth.

"Call me 'Mitch'," he requested with a charmingly roguish grin that made the dimples in his cheeks deepen.

It took me a few seconds to recover from the stupefying effect of those dimples, but I finally found my voice. "Alright, Mitch, if that makes you more comfortable. I'm Dr. Alvarez."

I offered my hand to him, and he shook it, his eyes never leaving mine. His hand was large and warm, and it felt a little calloused like he'd been working (or playing?) outdoors. I wondered if he was a surfer? He certainly had the upper body of a surfer - broad, well-built shoulders, muscular arms and chest, flat stomach. His tight, washed-out orange polo didn't leave much to the imagination.

"Why don't we go into my office?" I suggested, gently disengaging our hands, which was something he didn't seem to be in any hurry to do.

"Sure thing." He moved in that direction, which afforded me a very nice view of his backside, and I wasn't the only one admiring it. Margo started to fan herself with her phone message pad after Mitch had strolled past her desk.

"A hot flash?" I teased her in a whisper as I passed by.

"I may be old, honey, but I'm not dead," she replied. "And even if I was, one smile from that man would probably revive me."

I chuckled softly. I didn't know if Mitch Buchannon could resuscitate a corpse, but he did appear to be the cure for the common hangover. I hadn't thought about feeling sick since I'd first laid eyes on him.

"Hold my calls until 10," I told Margo, then stepped into my office and closed the door behind me.

Mitch was standing uncertainly by the couch. "Am I supposed to lay down here?" He pointed to the furniture.

"That's up to you. Most of my patients prefer to sit." And that's what he did.

I took my usual seat in the chair I'd positioned next to the top of the couch. Crossing my legs, I picked up a pen and pad of paper from the table in front of me. While many therapists liked to tape their sessions, I was more old-school. I knew shorthand, so I could make notes quickly while listening to patients, and those on-the-spot insights and impressions were invaluable to me when reviewing cases and mapping out strategies for future sessions.

"Why don't you tell me a little about yourself, Mitch?" My therapeutic M.O. was to ease my patients into revealing what their problems were. Asking for confidences upfront usually put people on guard and made it more difficult to develop a rapport.

Mitch relaxed back into the soft wheat-colored cushions of my sofa. "Okay, I'm 31 and I was born and raised here in Florida. I lived in Tampa until I was 20 and decided to move down here."

I was surprised to hear that he'd spent his entire life in the Sunshine State. I thought I detected a little bit of a drawl when he spoke. Maybe he had a parent who hailed from Alabama or one of the Carolinas?

"And what do you do here in Miami?"

"As little as possible," Mitch said, then laughed with naughty amusement at himself.

"So, you don't have steady employment?"

"Oh, I work. It's just that my job's so easy, it's almost like not doing anything. I'm a lifeguard."

Aha, that explained the perfect tan, the swimmer's physique, and the beach bum apparel.

"Family?" I prompted him.

He rubbed his palms up and down his denim-covered thighs a couple of times. A nervous tic? Or maybe he was just a tactile person? "Both parents are dead. No siblings."

"How about a spouse or children?"

"None that I know of." He reached out a hand and knocked on the wooden arm of my chair.

"Do you have a significant other? Someone who's special in your life?"

Mitch shook his head and frowned unhappily. "That's why I'm here actually. I think there might be something wrong with me."

"In regard to relationships?"

"Yeah." He scratched the whiskers on his chin thoughtfully. Definitely tactile, which meant that he relied heavily on his sense of touch in order to comfort and ground himself as well as to form impressions about people and his environment. That's why he'd held on to my hand so long out in the waiting area. He was trying to get a sense of me via skin-to-skin contact. Interesting. Men were usually more visual than tactile, although there were exceptions to that rule. Creative men, such as artists and chefs, were very tactile.

"I was seeing this girl, Keri, and she accused me of being sexually compulsive."

"Because you cheated on her?"

"I guess, which is stupid, because technically I wasn't even cheating on her. You can't 'cheat' on someone when you never made any kind of commitment to them or talked about being monogamous, right?"

"Either way, Keri obviously felt betrayed. The question is: Do you think you're sexually compulsive?"

Mitch shrugged. "I like sex and I'm good at it."

Clearly, he did not suffer from a lack of self-confidence.

"Do you have trouble controlling your sexual impulses?"

He leveled an earnest gaze at me. "Doc, I've got a job where I meet young, beautiful, half-naked women every day, and a lot of them come on to me. If I didn't respond, I'd have to be gay or have some kind of medical problem."

My diagnosis: Mitch Buchannon did not suffer from sexual compulsion or addiction; he was a man whore. I knew the breed well, having encountered many of its kind in the course of my dating career. As a rule, they were physically attractive, extremely self-assured, and had very little emotional depth.

"Mr. Buchannon--"

"Mitch," he reminded me.

"Mitch," I corrected myself, "you seem to be okay with your lifestyle choices, so why come to me?"

"Because I started to think that maybe Keri was on to something with the whole sexual compulsion thing. I mean,

I'm over 30 and I've never had a serious relationship with a woman."

My left eyebrow shot up. "Never?"

"Nope, I've always been a serial dater, going from one woman to the next, not staying with anyone long enough to get attached. I've never lived with a woman; I've never told one that I loved her. Meanwhile, most of the guys I know are settling down, getting married, having kids."

"And you feel like you're missing out on something?"

"Maybe. I'm not saying I'm ready to walk down the aisle or anything, but it might be nice to wake up with the same person every morning."

Self-awareness and a desire for change and emotional growth? There might be hope for this man whore yet.

"Then, we need to get to the root of your intimacy issues and work on resolving them."

"I'm game. Where do we start?"

Where do psychologists always start? "With your childhood."

Our parents and their relationships with both us and themselves are the cause of so many of our adult problems . . .

* * *

Using the spare key my parents had given me when they'd moved into their condo on the 15th floor of the ritzy Bayshore Heights, I let myself in.

"*Mamá*," I shouted from the foyer.

Like a perfectly coiffed hurricane, my mother blew in from the living room; the unbuttoned red silk shirt that she wore over a matching camisole billowing out behind her, and the heels of her gold slingbacks clickety-clacking on the tile floor. "Oh, *mija*, thank *Dios*, you're here!" she declared, then threw herself into my arms and squeezed me tightly.

Pulling back, she surveyed me with a critical eye, paying special attention to my midsection. "Have you put on weight?" she wondered. "You know you'll never get a man if you're too hippy."

"I haven't gained a pound."

"Are you sure? Maybe you should weigh yourself? I have a scale in the bathroom." Of course, she did. She also had tons of expensive makeup, lotions that did everything from erase fine lines to remove cellulite, a walk-in closet full of designer clothes, and two full-length mirrors to look at herself in. Not to put too fine a point on it, but my mother's vain. And since her daughters are a reflection of her, she's always been overly concerned with our appearances as well.

"*Mamá*," my tone was exasperated, bordering on irritable, "I rushed over here because you said there was an emergency." She'd caught me on my cell phone when I was halfway home from work. The connection had been bad, and I'd lost the call right after she'd told me in a hysteria-tinged voice that I needed to come to the condo immediately. I'd raced over, imagining all sorts of terrible things like my father having a heart attack or one of my nephews drowning in a swimming pool accident.

"It's your sister!" My mother blinked back tears and placed a hand tipped with red acrylic nails over her heart.

"Ana?" I started to panic.

"No, Isidora."

My stomach sank. With my younger sister's penchant for calamity, anything was possible. She could have wrapped her car around a tree or run off with some Mambo instructor who'd knocked her up. "What happened?"

Mamá's lips quivered with barely restrained emotion, and I wrapped a supportive arm around her shoulders. "She hung up on me!"

I dropped my arm and gave her an incredulous look. "That's it! You called me over here and scared me half to death because Izzy hung up on you?" *Ladies and gentlemen, my mother, the drama queen.*

"It was terrible! Before she hung up on me, she called me an 'interfering witch' and told me to stay out of her life."

"She was probably just having a bad day. Maybe she was PMSing or something?" I tried to ease the sting of my sister's rejection.

"PMS? Bah! That's no excuse for being disrespectful to your mother. The way that girl talks to me is shameful."

She walked back into the living room, and I followed, taking a seat on her plush white sofa while she fixed herself a cocktail at the small bar that my father kept well-stocked for company. "Do you want something?" She held up a bottle of white wine.

"God, no." I rubbed my stomach, which still hadn't recovered from my mini-drinking binge at Wasabi's the night before.

"I just don't understand why your sister hates me so much," *Mamá* lamented as she joined me on the couch, perching daintily on its edge with her glass of Chardonnay in hand.

It was time once again for me to play my designated role in the Alvarez family. Ana was the bossy one, Izzy was the brat, and I was the mediator who had to step into the middle of everyone's fights, soothe away all of the hurt feelings, and try to make both parties see things from the other person's point of view. With training like that, it was no wonder I'd become a psychologist.

"Izzy doesn't hate you. She's just incredibly strong-willed and she doesn't like to be told what to do." *Kind of like someone else I knew.* Izzy had inherited her hotheadedness and stubborn streak from one of our parents, and it certainly hadn't been my sweet teddy bear of a father.

"I never tell her what to do!" my mother was affronted. "I might make a suggestion once in a while . . ."

"You should stop. Don't offer Izzy any advice unless she asks for it."

"She could benefit from my years of experience if she'd only listen to me."

"But she won't, so you have to let her go her own way. And if she makes mistakes, that's okay. It's all part of growing up."

"Isidora is already grown up. She's 23 years old for heaven's sake! Look at how much I'd already accomplished at that age."

Uh oh, here we go, I groaned inwardly. My mother never missed an opportunity to talk about her glory days as a beauty queen. The tiaras, the parades held in her honor, the offers to model and do commercial work, and how she gave it all up to be a wife and mother. I'd heard it all a thousand times before.

"I was Miss Miami at 20 and first runner-up in the Miss Florida pageant at 21. I married your father that same year and had Ana when I was 22." She smoothed back her salon-styled black hair as if to say, 'See, it's just as silky, thick, and gorgeous as it was the day I was crowned.'

"You were an early bloomer, probably because you were an only child and had to assume adult responsibilities at a young age. Izzy is the baby in our family, and youngest children tend to develop more slowly because they're coddled by their parents and older siblings. I have a really interesting book on birth order you should read."

"Bah! I don't need to read a book. I already know what's wrong with your sister. She's lazy. She has no goals and no ambition. I don't know why your father paid all that money for her to get a college education. What has she done with it?"

Izzy had spent her four years at the University of Florida partying like it was 1999. She'd changed majors three times, and her grades had been so sub-par that she'd barely managed to graduate with her degree in General Arts Studies. I wasn't even sure what General Arts Studies were. The course requirements had probably included a few museum visits and a fingerpainting final.

"She just needs time to find herself and figure out what she wants to do with her life."

"Find herself?" my mother scoffed. "What she needs to find is a husband. If Isidora had a good man to take care of her, your father and I wouldn't have to worry about her so much."

"23 is too young for Izzy, or any woman, to be contemplating marriage." *Oh, crap, had I just said that out loud?* Stupid, stupid Pilar. Don't ever discuss your views on marriage with your mother.

"Of course, you would say that, Miss Independent, Miss I'm A Doctor, So I Don't Need A Man. You don't care about having a nice house and a husband and children to love."

"I have a nice house," I reminded her. "And I never said that I didn't care about having a husband and children. I plan to have a family one day." Dear God, when had this conversation taken such a harrowing turn on to Me Street? I was much better at defending my sister's actions than I was my own.

My mother eyed me skeptically. "You're almost 30, Pilar. How many *days* do you think you have left?"

"I'm not ready to collect Social Security just yet. I still have time to wait for the right man."

"You already broke up with the right man," she said indignantly. "Victor was perfect! So charming, so handsome, such good manners. He has his own business, and his family has *mucho dinero*. When his father dies, Victor will probably inherit the yacht brokerage. Do you know how much that business is worth? Millions! You could have been married to a millionaire, Pilar. You could have lived in a mansion, driven a Mercedes, been a member of the country club--"

"*Mamá* . . .," I attempted to interrupt her, but she ignored me and kept right on delivering her long-winded speech on 'The Many Virtues of Victor Liscano, and the 5-Star Life You Could Have Had With Him.'

". . . and he doted on you. But no, that wasn't good enough for you. You're too picky. You think that rich, attractive men just grow on trees . . ."

"*Mamá!*" I shouted this time, which startled her into silence. "Victor and I only dated for a few months. Our relationship was never that serious; he certainly wasn't going to propose to me. And we were *not* compatible. So, you've got to let . . . it . . . go."

She sniffled and looked wounded. "Is it wrong for me to want the best for my girls? You're so smart and pretty . . .," squinting, she leaned towards me, ". . . are you plucking your own brows? You really should get them waxed; you get a much better shape that way. I'll give you Shelley's number. Nobody else in Miami can arch a brow like she does."

I groaned and leaned back against the sofa cushions, clutching my head.

"What is it?" *Mamá* asked worriedly.

"I've got a headache. I should go home." At that point, faking an illness was the only way I could think of to get away from my mother.

"You probably haven't eaten all day, and that's why your head hurts. I'm cooking *Picadillo Estilo Cubano* for your father tonight. He'll be home from the office soon. Why don't you stay?"

I could smell the seasoned meat simmering in the kitchen, and the aroma was delectable. My stomach grumbled, reminding me that I'd only had a few bites of salad for lunch, and it needed filling. I took a minute to mull over my options: stay at my parents' for a delicious, home-cooked meal and listen to *Mamá* complain about Izzy, or worse, tell me how to run my life, or go home, pop a Healthy Choice in the microwave, and watch the Dr. Phil special on TV.

Standing up, I said, "Thanks, but I really have to go," then made a beeline for the door before she could stop me.

"Are you sure?" She chased me into the foyer. "Your father will be upset he missed you."

"Give him my love and tell him I'll see him soon." I kissed her once on each tanned cheek and slipped out the front door.

Sticking her head out into the hallway, she shouted after me, "Remind your sister that my birthday is coming up, so she can't stay mad at me forever. I expect to see her at my party. The whole family will be here. If she doesn't come, I'll be disgraced. Ask Isidora if she wants her mother to be disgraced on her 50th birthday." This would be the third year in a row we'd celebrated my mother's 50th birthday.

"Yes, *Mamá*," I dutifully replied as I stepped onto the elevator with my temples throbbing. At least, I hadn't lied about the headache.

CHAPTER 4

Patient's name: Meghan Faber
Age: 16
Occupation: High school student
Diagnosis based on initial evaluation: Met with patient's parents, Craig and Belinda, first. They are concerned about daughter's "obsession" with getting plastic surgery (last year, she wanted a nose job, now it's a breast augmentation.) Parents' refusal to accede to these requests has led to an emotional rift with their daughter. She has become surly, uncommunicative, and disobedient. Diagnosis pending first session with patient, but sounds like typical teen angst caused by body image issues. Peer pressure may be involved.
Goal of therapy: Help patient to achieve more confidence and a healthy body image. Reopen lines of communication between parents and child.

"I hate my mother!" declared the sullen girl who sat in a slumped position on the couch opposite me with her arms crossed defensively across her chest. I considered it something of a breakthrough since up to that point in our session, Meghan had done nothing but stare off into space with a petulant expression on her freckled face while I had a rather uninteresting conversation with myself.

"Why?" I asked calmly in contrast to her violent outburst.

"For starters, she never listens to me. And she doesn't care what I think or how I feel."

"She wants you to be happy."

"That's a crock," Meghan said, twirling a fuchsia-streaked strand of her long, dark hair around her index finger. If my mother wanted me to be happy, she'd let me get a boob job. But no, she'd rather I be flat-chested and miserable."

"Why is having large breasts so important to you?" I

queried.

"Well, duh," Meghan looked at me as though I was a drooling idiot, "being flat-chested sucks! I can't fill out a bikini top, guys never notice me, I'm embarrassed to get undressed in front of other girls because they're all so much bigger than me, and they don't make pretty bras in an A-cup."

That was a compelling list of reasons.

"It's not like I'm asking my parents for double-Ds or anything. I just want to go up to a C cup so that I can look normal."

"Women's bodies come in all shapes and sizes, Meghan, and they're all considered to be *normal*. You're actually quite lucky to be an Ectomorph."

"A what?"

"An Ectomorph. That means that your body is long and lean, you have small bones, and very little body fat," I explained. "You don't ever have to diet, right?"

"No, just the opposite. I'm always trying to gain weight. I drink protein shakes and eat tons of carbs, nothing ever works. I guess I have a fast metabolism."

"I would love to have a fast metabolism. Everything I eat goes straight to my butt." I wasn't exaggerating. Like most Latinas, I was curvy, and while my rear end had yet to reach the epic proportions of JLo's, it might if I wasn't careful.

"Yeah, my friend Amy is the same way. She's always complaining about her 'fat ass' and 'thunder thighs.'"

"So, see, being an Ectomorph has its plusses. You don't have to worry about your clothes suddenly being too tight or getting any unsightly cellulite."

She shrugged. "I still wish I had boobs. A girl can't be sexy without 'em."

"I disagree. Look at all the beautiful actresses who are built like you. Michelle Pfeiffer for instance"

"Who?"

Go younger, I told myself. *Think Generation Y.* "Keira Knightley."

"She's cool," Meghan decreed as she played with the silver bangles on her right arm. "My friend Ryan likes her. Who else?"

"Um, Kate Hudson. Natalie Portman. Kate Bosworth. The girl who's in those *Twilight* movies."

"Kristen Stewart."

"Right. They're all small-busted women and they're considered to be hot."

"I guess." She wouldn't admit that I'd made a good point, complete with examples she could relate to, but I could tell she was thinking it.

I looked down at my watch and saw that it was 3:47. Since I'd done all of the talking up until the last five minutes, I didn't feel like this had been a particularly productive session. But, at least, I'd finally gotten Meghan to engage in some sort of meaningful dialogue, and I hoped we could continue with more of the same the next time we met.

"I'm afraid that our time is almost up."

Acting like a prisoner who'd just been granted parole, Meghan sprung up from the couch, grabbed her backpack, and headed for the door.

"Not so fast." I stopped the teenager, getting up from my chair and walking towards her. "I want you to think about something and come back with an answer for me next week."

"Oh, God, are you giving me a homework assignment?"

"It won't take much time, I promise. Just make a list of three things you like about your body."

Meghan rolled her large brown eyes. "That is *so* lame."

"No, it's not. You spend a lot of time thinking about the things you don't like about your body, don't you?"

"Yeah," she admitted sheepishly.

"Then, you should give equal time to focusing on the

positive."

Sighing like she was the most put-upon girl on the planet, Meghan grumbled, "Fine. Whatever."

I opened the door, and she darted out into the waiting area intent on getting out of my office as quickly as she could.

"See you next week," I called after her.

"Can't wait," the sarcasm in her tone was unmistakable.

"That girl's got a real attitude problem," Margo stated the obvious after Meghan had disappeared into the hallway.

"She's at a difficult age. She'll grow out of it," was my prognosis. "That was my last appointment for the day, wasn't it?"

"Uh-huh. Why don't you call it a day? I can close up the office."

Leave early? What a novel concept! Izzy had said that she had plans for the evening, which meant that I would have the house all to myself. I pondered the delicious possibilities . . . I could watch the local news, make some pasta, dance around in my underwear . . . well, probably not that last one, but I might put on a CD, pull out my yoga mat, which was collecting dust somewhere (maybe under the bed?), and do some stretches. It would be heaven to have some alone time to relax and unwind.

"I think I'll take you up on that, Margo. Thanks!"

I went back into my office to tidy up and collect my purse.

"Enjoy your evening, hon," my receptionist bid me farewell as I slipped out the front door with a smile on my face.

Humming the tune to some Nicki Minaj song I didn't know the name of, I headed down the stairs. Just as I reached the landing that divided the steps before they veered to the left, I heard the muffled sound of my cell phone ringing. I stopped and unzipped my purse. Extracting the phone, I checked the Caller ID. Victor. *UGH!* There went my good mood. I could have just let the call go to voice mail, but I was annoyed that my ex was once again intruding on my life and I suddenly felt confrontational. So, I answered it.

"What do you want?" was my curt greeting.

"To take you out for a romantic dinner at Tantra, *mi amor*." Tantra was a Miami Beach hot spot that was known for its sensual environment. Its exotic smells, decor, and cuisine were all designed to enhance and arouse the senses, and there were, in fact, several aphrodisiacs on the menu. When a man took a date to Tantra, it was with one goal in mind.

"That's not going to happen. *Ever*," I said firmly.

"But you love Tantra! Don't you remember we went there for our one-month anniversary? I hand fed you lobster dipped in bleeding heart truffle vinaigrette and grilled quail with fresh figs." *Mmmmmmm, he was making my mouth water.* "Then, we went back to my place and spent hours experimenting with Kama Su--"

"Victor!" I interrupted him before his walk down memory lane became X-rated.

"Okay, you don't like Tantra anymore. I'll take you to B.E.D." Where patrons ate their meals while sitting on large mattresses. A theme seemed to be developing with Victor's restaurant choices.

"I don't want to go to B.E.D. with you." It sounded like I was turning down a proposition much more salacious than dinner.

"Alright, you'd rather not commit to sharing a meal with me. I understand. We can just take a walk on the beach and talk."

"We are *not* a couple anymore, Victor." In my agitated state, I began to pace back and forth on the landing. Three steps towards the wall, pivot, then three steps back to the top of the stairs. "We broke up. And people who are broken up do not spend time with each other."

"But you said we could still be friends, and friends spend time with each other."

"Friends give each other space when they ask for it."

"I've given you plenty of space."

"Then, why do I feel so claustrophobic?" I questioned irritably. "You've got to back off."

"If I do that, you'll find somebody new, and I can't bear the thought of you with another man."

In that moment, I actually felt a pang of sympathy for my former lover. Maybe his campaign to win me back wasn't all about his over-inflated ego? Maybe he did have real feelings for me?

Softening towards him, I said, "Don't worry, Victor. It's not like I'm going to walk out the door tomorrow and run into my soul ma--" I bumped face-first into a hard, flat surface, let out a startled yelp, and staggered back against the wall. My cell phone clattered to the stone floor and I watched dazedly as a leafy green plant toppled off a large cardboard box being carried by a tall man with a square jaw and thick brown hair that was attractively disheveled.

"Damn," he cursed and dropped the box down on the pile of potting soil that now covered the landing. It hit the ground with a loud thump. "Sorry. The plant blocked my view and I didn't see you. I shouldn't have tried to carry so much in one trip. Are you okay?"

He had a brusque way of speaking that immediately outed him as a New Yorker. There were plenty of retirees in South Florida who hailed from that part of the country, so I knew the accent well.

I blinked hard a few times, trying to reorient myself. "I-I think so."

"What about your head? Did you bang it when you hit the

wall?" There was concern in his eyes, eyes that were the most brilliant shade of blue I'd ever seen. Gazing into them was almost like staring directly into the sun; I felt dazed, woozy, like the back of my head was going to split open and my brain would fall out . . . okay, so it wasn't the color of this man's irises that was having such a strange effect on me, I'd obviously suffered a serious cranial injury.

When I didn't answer him, he moved towards me. "Here, let me take a look."

"Thanks, but that's really not necessary." I pulled away from the wall and felt a sharp jolt of pain shoot through the back of my skull. "Ow!" I placed my hand over the spot that was throbbing, hoping the pressure would make it stop.

"Do you have a lump?" He reached out for me, and I instinctively backed away. Subdural hematoma or not, I wasn't in the habit of letting strange men touch me.

"It's okay. I'm a doctor," he assured me, taking my face gently in his hands and tilting my head back so that he could look into my eyes. I noticed he had some silver strands of hair mixed in with the brown and wondered how old he was? Late thirties, maybe?

"Your pupils aren't dilated, so you don't have a concussion." Threading his fingers through my hair, he began to cautiously inspect my scalp with his fingertips.

"I'm a doctor, too," I told him for no particular reason as I stared up at him. Even though I was wearing heels, he had several inches on me. "Not a medical doctor, a psychologist."

"Oh, yeah?" He gingerly touched the area below the crown of my head. "How does this feel?"

I winced. "Pretty tender."

"Well, there's no swelling, so I think you're just badly bruised. An ice pack and a couple of aspirin should alleviate any discomfort." He let his hands fall to his sides. "A psychologist, huh? You must be my new neighbor, Dr. Alvarez."

"Neighbor?" I repeated dumbly, still trying to process the fact that I didn't need to rush to the nearest medical facility for a CAT scan.

"Yeah, upstairs." He pointed up the flight of steps I'd just come down. "I'm moving into Suite 2-C."

"Oh, I didn't realize that that space had been rented." A handsome male doctor was moving into the office across the hall from me? I couldn't believe my luck. It looked like all those candles I'd lit at St. Andrew's over the years had finally paid off.

"I'm Jonathan Fordham." He held out his hand, and I gave him mine.

"Nice to meet you, Dr. Fordham."

"Call me 'Ford'," he requested after he'd released my hand. "Everyone does."

Ford, huh? I liked that. Its simplicity suited him.

"If you'll call me 'Pilar'," I countered.

"Okay, *Pilar*, it looks like your cell phone is busted." He gestured at the ground where it lay in several pieces.

"Your plant's not in very good shape either." The poor thing looked as though it'd been trampled. Ford had obviously stepped on it when he'd come to my aid.

"Yeah, we've made a pretty big mess." He bent down and picked up his box. "Why don't you bring your phone upstairs, and I'll see if I can put it back together for you?"

I gathered up the broken phone pieces, as well as another item that was half-buried in the dirt, and followed him.

"Looking for these?" I jangled his keys when I found him standing in front of his office door, patting his jeans' pockets.

"I was wondering what had happened to those. Thanks." Ford shifted the box so that its weight rested more firmly on his hip and he could support it with just one arm, then he used his free hand to take the keys from me and unlock the door.

"After you." He waved me in. We passed through the outer waiting area and entered his office, which was a lot bigger than mine.

"Nice," I commented as I glanced around. He already had his furniture in place, a large cherry wood desk, matching book shelves and filing cabinets, a green and taupe striped couch, brown leather chairs. It was all very masculine, as opposed to my office, which was light, airy, and neutral-colored.

"Are you a therapist, too?" God, I hoped not. I really didn't need the competition, especially not from someone older and more experienced.

"A psychiatrist." He sat down on the edge of his desk. "I was on staff at Mount Sinai for 7 years. I decided to shift gears and go into private practice when we moved here."

Mount Sinai? That was impressive. Only the best and the brightest worked at that hospital. Its reputation was unparalleled in the medical community. Wait a minute! Had he just said, "when *we* moved here?" Oh, crap. My eyes went to the ring finger of his left hand, and sure enough, I saw a gold wedding band there. Why was I surprised? Weren't all successful, good-looking men over the age of 30 married? Ford probably had a litter of adorable, dark-headed ankle-biters with high IQs at home, too.

"From New York to Miami, huh? You must be experiencing some major culture shock." I set the assorted pieces of my cell phone down in a pile next to him.

"It's definitely different here," he conceded as he picked up a part that looked like a small circuit board and inserted it in an empty slot on the back of the phone. "For one thing, I'm not used to all of this sunshine. 85 degrees in April is just unnatural."

"We only have one season in Miami . . . summer. So, stock up on shorts and t-shirts and get used to wearing sunblock with a high SPF."

Ford slid the cell phone's battery back into its designated compartment. "Does it ever rain here?"

"Oh sure, we get tons of rain in September when all of the tropical storms and hurricanes come through," I said with a smirk.

"Great. At least, I won't have to shovel snow in January." He positioned the back cover of the phone over its exposed guts and popped it into place.

"Okay, that should do it. Let's see if this puppy still works." He turned on the repaired phone and was rewarded with a beep. "Looks like you've got service and a whole bunch of messages. Eight, to be exact. You're very popular."

"I'm sure they're not important." I took the phone away from Ford and turned it off. "Thanks for fixing it."

He smiled; it was a nice smile, one that made the person receiving it feel all warm and fuzzy inside. "It was the least I could do seeing as how I caused you bodily harm."

I smiled back at him. "Well, since it was unintentional, I won't hold it against you."

"Glad to hear it." His blue eyes twinkled.

The sound of someone banging on my office door ruined the moment. "Pilar! Pilar!"

I pretended not to hear Victor calling me.

"So, when will you be open for business?" I questioned Ford conversationally.

He furrowed his brow. "Is that one of your patients? Maybe it's an emergency?"

"Pilar! Answer me, Pilar!" Victor was becoming more insistent.

I let out a beleaguered sigh. "It's not an emergency."

Backing up a few steps, I yelled out to the hallway, "In

here, Victor!"

He came rushing in with a panicked expression on his swarthy face. "*Mi querida*, thank goodness you're okay!"

Before I could respond, Victor embraced me with bone-crushing fervor and proclaimed, "I was so worried! You screamed, and then the line went dead. I tried calling you back, but there was no answer. I could only assume the worst."

"I'm fine," I mumbled into his silk-covered chest.

He pulled back, his hands still gripping my shoulders. "Are you sure? What happened?"

"Dr. Fordham," I gestured over at the man who was still perched on his desk, looking bemused by the proceedings, "and I just had a little accident on the stairs."

"An accident?" Victor's voice rose with alarm. "Were you hurt? You look pale, *mi amor*. I should take you to the emergency room."

"I just bumped my head against the wall when Dr. Fordham and I ran into each other. It was no big deal."

Victor turned to Ford. "You should pay more attention to where you're going. You could have seriously injured my *fiancée*."

"Your *what*?" Had Victor lost his damn mind? Not even 15 minutes ago, I'd refused to have dinner with him, and now he was referring to me as his bride-to-be?

Victor held up his hand to silence me. "There's no need to speak. You've obviously been through quite an ordeal. You should eat and get some rest. I'm going to take you home and stay with you all night to make sure you don't have a concussion."

"I've already checked her out, and she doesn't have a concussion," Ford interjected.

"What do you know?" Victor dismissed him.

"I told you he was a doctor."

"It doesn't matter. Only I know what is best for you, *mi amada*."

What a controlling, chauvinistic jackass . . . if there hadn't been a third party present, I would have happily told my ex-boyfriend where to shove his imperious tone. But I didn't want to play out any more of this drama in front of Ford.

"Let's just go," I said wearily.

"*Bueno*." Victor smiled smugly, thinking he'd gotten his way. Of course, I planned to set him straight as soon as we were alone.

"Thanks again for your help with my phone, Ford," I threw back over my shoulder as Victor hustled me out into the waiting area.

"Why are you calling him 'Ford?'" Victor chastised me. "You shouldn't be acting so familiar with a man you just met. You'll give him ideas. I didn't like the way he was looking at you . . .

CHAPTER 5

"Are you sure you don't want to go out with Ben again?" Sara queried as she sprinkled some chocolate chips on a piece of pepperoni and mushroom pizza she was eating. *YUCK* "He really liked you."

"The feeling was *not* mutual," I said, nibbling on the crust of my own slice.

"He is a bit of a blowhard," she conceded.

"In more ways than one, since he's got that nicotine problem." I paused to take a sip of my diet soda before adding, "I swear, he looked more lustfully at that pack of Camels than he did at me."

Sara sighed. "I'm sorry. I shouldn't have pushed you into going on that date. I just assumed that any friend of Matt's would be as laid-back and nice as he is."

"It's not your fault. I've come to the unhappy conclusion that my luck with men just stinks."

I opened up the still-warm box from Andiamo's and extracted another cheesy piece of the large pie. It was my third. I was pretty sure that once all of the saturated fat and carbs got into my bloodstream, I'd fall into some sort of pizza-induced coma.

"That's not true," my best friend mumbled with her mouth full.

"Oh, no? Let's review. In the past week, I've gone on one horrible blind date that was interrupted by my recently dumped boyfriend, who's turned stalking me into a full-time job, and I met two very attractive men, both of whom are completely off-limits to me."

"Off-limits? Why?" Sara wondered.

"One of them is a patient, and the other is a married colleague."

"Mmmmm, the married thing is no good. Stay away from

Tracie Banister

him."

"That might be difficult since he just moved into the office across the hall from me."

"Uh oh."

"It'll be fine. My crush on Ford was short-lived." Wedding rings had a habit of dampening a woman's ardor. "So, there won't be any weirdness there. I'm actually kind of excited about having a psychiatrist as a neighbor. Ford has amazing credentials, and he seems like a really intelligent guy. It'll be nice to have someone around to ask for advice if I run into a problem with a patient. I don't really have many people to talk shop with."

"What about the patient? What's his story?"

I wiped my tomato sauce-covered mouth with a napkin and pushed my plate away. "Mitch is gorgeous enough to be a movie star, and he knows it. He emits this rascally, 'You know you wanna do me,' vibe, and he oozes pheromones out of every pore; he even had Margo swooning when he came into the office the other day. You probably met a bunch of guys like him when you were modeling in Europe."

"Oh yeah, I met and slept with more dim-witted, cleft-chinned pretty boys than I care to remember." Giving up on the pizza, Sara scooped a handful of chocolate chips out of the bag and began popping them into her mouth.

"Mitch isn't dim-witted. In fact, he strikes me as being rather clever."

"Looks and smarts? Sounds like the perfect package."

"He's not perfect, far from it. The man's got issues. That's why he's seeing me."

"So, you'll find the cure for whatever ails him, then you can cut him loose as a patient and start examining his body instead of his mind." She gave me a saucy wink.

I frowned. "That wouldn't be very ethical."

"Ethics don't buy a girl jewelry, or give her multiple Os."

51

She had a point, but I still didn't like the thought of crossing that line. Not with Mitch and not with the sexy new doc on the block. I planned to maintain a polite, professional distance from both of them.

* * *

"Knock, knock." I peeked my head in the open door of my neighbor's office. Ford was standing on the far side of the room, brushing the dust off a large leather-bound medical tome that he was about to place on one of his bookshelves.

"Pilar, hey. Come in and save me from the torture of unpacking."

"I brought you something," I announced as I entered the office carrying a small flowering plant.

He eyed my gift with interest. "I've never seen anything like that before. What is it?"

"A bromeliad. I thought that it would add a tropical touch to your new office, and it's easy to care for. Just put it in an area that gets indirect light and don't overwater it."

"That won't be a problem since I can never remember to water my plants," Ford said with a self-deprecating grin. He took the exotic plant from me and set it on the corner of his desk. "This was really thoughtful of you. Thanks."

"Well, I was sort of responsible for the untimely death of your last plant, so I felt like I owed you one."

I noticed a framed photo sitting next to the bromeliad. "Is this your son?" I asked as I picked it up to take a closer look. The little boy in the picture was precious. He had a thatch of thick brown hair, large, wide-set eyes that were almost as dark, and a very serious expression on his cherubic face.

Ford beamed with fatherly pride. "Yep, that's my little Einstein. His name's Nate. He's not even 6 yet and he's already smarter than I am."

I smiled, seeing a man's love for his child was a beautiful thing. "He looks just like you."

"You think?" Ford took the photo out of my hands and stared down at it intently, searching for signs of himself. "I've always thought he looked like his mother. He has her soulful eyes."

This was the first time he'd mentioned his wife. I was incredibly curious about Mrs. Dr. Ford. What kind of woman was she? Was she a stay-at-home mom who baked cookies and carpooled? Or a highly-educated, career-oriented type like her spouse? A tall, slinky brunette? Or maybe a petite, wholesome-looking blonde? I was just about to ask Ford to fill me in on his better half when he set the framed photo back on his desk and changed the subject.

"Are you hungry?"

"I could eat."

"Good, because I'm starved and I have no idea where to find a decent burger around here."

"I can definitely hook you up."

Fifteen minutes later, we were sitting at one of Big Pink's outside tables. Big Pink was a hip, close-to-the-beach diner that attracted both locals and tourists in droves. It offered giant-sized portions of comfort foods like mac and cheese and meatloaf. And no one in South Beach made a better burger. Its triple-decker Pink Daddy Mack was a culinary work of art.

"Wait until you've tasted the polenta fries," I told Ford after we'd placed our orders. "You can die happy after you've eaten one."

"I don't know. They'll have to be pretty phenomenal to beat the seasoned cheese fries at Duke's."

"Where's Duke's?" I inquired.

"In Brooklyn, where I grew up. My family's been there for five generations. My brothers still live in the old neighborhood."

"And your parents?"

"They're retired. Mom was a schoolteacher for 40 years, and Pop worked for the Postal Service."

So, he came from a working class background? I wondered how he'd gotten from a Brooklyn stoop to Mount Sinai.

"Thanks," I said to the waiter who'd just brought our beverages. "Where'd you go to school?"

"NYU. On an academic scholarship. And you?" Ford took the straw out of his lemonade and drank directly from the clear, plastic glass.

"I went to the University of Miami. On my father's dime," I added with a smirk.

"Oh yeah, what does he do?"

"He's a senior partner in one of the most successful, Latino-owned law firms in Miami, Davila, Guererra & Alvarez."

"What type of law does he practice?"

"Estate law, wills, trusts, that kind of thing. With all of the elderly, rich people here in South Florida, his line of work is very lucrative."

"I can imagine. You never thought about going into the family business?"

"God, no. I find the law to be incredibly dull." I leaned across the table and said in an exaggerated whisper, "Don't ever tell my father I said that."

Ford chuckled. "My lips are sealed."

"So, why does everyone call you 'Ford?'" I queried, then removed the cap from my bottled water and took a swig. The scorching noonday sun was beating down on our heads, and I was starting to get warm.

"It all started in the first grade. Parents in Brooklyn aren't very creative when it comes to naming their children, so there were 6 Jonathans in my class at P.S. 321. My teacher, Mrs. Lindstrom, who was old and a little batty, had to find some way to differentiate all of the Jonathans so that she wouldn't confuse herself . . . or us. She was going to refer to me as 'Jonathan F.,' but that was a mouthful. One of the other kids suggested 'Ford,' and it stuck."

"How many brothers do you have?"

"Two, Danny and Chris. I'm the oldest."

"I come from a family of three, too. All girls. I'm the middle child."

"Have you read Ken Simmons' book on birth order?"

"Oh my God, yes!" I bounced on the edge of my seat excitedly. "That book was fascinating. I thought his theory on . . ." I was interrupted by the ringing of my cell phone. Sometimes I really hated those things.

"Excuse me," I said as I reached down for my Louis Vuitton bag. I pulled the phone out and checked the caller ID before answering.

Without realizing it, I must have made some kind of disgusted face because Ford gave me an amused look and asked, "Your *fiancé*?"

I turned the phone off and shoved it back into my purse a bit more forcefully than was necessary. "Victor is *not* my *fiancé*. He purposely misled you the other day. I'm sorry that he was so rude to you."

Ford shrugged his broad shoulders. "I'm not easily offended. I come from New York, remember?"

"Still, he behaved badly. He has no right to act territorial with me. Our relationship ended over a month ago."

"He obviously hasn't accepted that."

"Victor is a very hard-headed man. I've told him repeatedly that we're through, but he continues to pursue me. He actually showed up at the restaurant where I was having dinner with a date last week."

"Maybe Victor keeps coming back because your rejections lack conviction? Maybe there's some part of you that enjoys all of the attention?" Ford posited.

I arched an eyebrow. "Are you psychoanalyzing me, Dr. Fordham?"

"Just some food for thought, Dr. Alvarez."

"And here's some food for our stomachs," I said as the waiter approached our table with two burger and fries-filled plates. His timing couldn't have been more perfect. While I enjoyed shrinking other people's heads, it made me nervous when the same was done to mine.

CHAPTER 6

Patient's name: Kyle Kotowski
Age: 34
Occupation: Computer systems analyst
Diagnosis based on initial evaluation: Patient was referred by his internist, Dr. Scott Meyer. Dr. Meyer feels that patient's continual complaints about his health have no basis in reality. An extensive array of medical tests has been run on Mr. Kotowski, and no evidence of illness was found. Rather than alleviating patient's concern, this clean bill of health has made him even more anxious. He has now taken to diagnosing himself and thinks that he has a different terminal illness every week.

Patient was born prematurely and was sickly as a child, so his current fears about his health relate back to that period of time in his life. As he was frequently isolated in those early years, he developed an overactive imagination, which is now manifesting itself in hypochondria.

Goal of therapy: Help patient break out of his shell and find something to focus on other than himself. Teach him coping mechanisms so that he can handle his fears without letting them control his life.

"I've definitely got Arachnoiditis," said the twitchy man sitting opposite me.

"Arachnoiditis? Does that have something to do with spiders?" I hoped he didn't think he was turning into one.

"No. It's a pain disorder caused by inflammation of the arachnoid, which is a membrane that surrounds and protects the nerves of the spinal cord." Kyle sounded like he was reciting a description out of a medical dictionary. No doubt he'd been on the internet looking up rare diseases again.

"One of the symptoms of Arachnoiditis is the feeling that

insects are crawling on your skin." He made a strange yelping noise and started to scratch his leg like fire ants were swarming up it.

"Kyle," I reached forward and placed my hand over his in an effort to stop his frantic movements, "there's a simple explanation for the itching sensation. Either your skin is dry or the fabric of your pants is causing an irritation." *Or it was all in his head.* My money was on the third option.

"Dry skin?" He mulled the possibility over for a few seconds. "That could be a sign of eczema or something more serious like psoriasis, right? Can't a person be born with a genetic predisposition towards psoriasis? My great-aunt Connie suffered from the condition for years. She had these disgusting, rough red patches of skin all over her body. It was horrible! When she had a bad flare-up, she looked like some sort of scabby monster. Oh my God, what if that happens to me? I won't be able to leave my house! I'll have to go on Disability and . . ."

"Kyle," I cut off my health-obsessed patient with a calm, but firm voice, knowing that if I let him continue in this vein, he'd soon have himself banished to the modern-day equivalent of a leper colony, "you do *not* have psoriasis. There is nothing wrong with you that a little body lotion with Vitamin E or Aloe won't cure."

"Vitamin E or Aloe? Let me write that down." He pulled a small memo pad and a pencil from the breast pocket of his nerdy-looking checked shirt. "Can you recommend a particular brand?"

"Anything for sensitive skin should be fine."

"Okay, good, maybe if I start religiously applying the lotion now, while the psoriasis is in the early stages, I can avoid . . ." His watch beeped several times. "It must be 11:45. I have to take my immune boosters at the same time every day. I hope you don't mind."

"Not at all." If the herbal supplements would give him peace of mind and make him feel stronger mentally, as well as physically, then I was all for them. I'd recently told Dr. Meyer to start prescribing placebos for Kyle's faux illnesses. My hope was that receiving treatment (even if it was in the form of sugar pills) would free Kyle from some of his anxiety about the state of his health.

Kyle removed six green caplets that smelled like freshly mowed grass from a plastic baggie, which had also been stuffed into his shirt pocket. He methodically put each pill in his mouth, then swallowed it with two sips of water from the liter of Evian he'd brought with him. This process seemed to take an eternity and by the time it was done, our session was officially over.

I walked Kyle out to the waiting area and had Margo confirm his appointment for the following week. "I'll be coming in a few hours later than usual because I'm having an MRI done that morning," he explained.

Frowning, I inquired, "Didn't you just have an MRI done two weeks ago?"

"Yeah, but I'm pretty sure that the machine at that outpatient facility was broken. It made this weird noise like *eeeeeeeeeeeee*," Kyle affected a high-pitched whine. "And that's not right. An MRI is supposed to make a low hum and a knocking sound." He should know since he'd gotten the same test done several times before.

"Hopefully, the test at the hospital will be done correctly so that I can find out what's causing all of my lower back pain. I think it's kidney failure. What if I have to go on dialysis?" He turned terrified eyes on me.

"You will *not* have to go on dialysis. Now, go back to work," I gave him a gentle shove towards my office's exit, "and stop worrying."

Kyle opened the door to leave just as Sara walked up. He

stood back so that she could enter.

"Thanks, handsome." She bestowed one of her dazzling cover girl smiles on him.

His ears turned bright pink, and he scooted out into the hallway. Sara didn't appear fazed, probably because she was used to getting that reaction from men.

"What brings you by?" I questioned my friend.

"I was struck by inspiration at 3:00 this morning, so I got out of bed and started sketching. I'm really excited about my new ideas and I'm thinking about using a few of them in the show, but I wanted to get your opinion first. Do you have a minute to take a look?"

"Sure. Margo, why don't you go ahead and take your lunch now?"

"Do you want me to bring you back something?" my receptionist wondered.

"Where are you going?"

"Where else? Jerry's."

A deli sandwich did sound good . . . "Get me a turkey on wheat. No onion. Sara?"

"Nothing for me, thanks. You know that I lose my appetite when I'm in the creative zone." She walked into my office, carrying a large sketch pad under her arm, and I followed her.

"So, let me see what you've got." I held out my hands towards my friend.

Sara flipped the front cover of the pad over, exposing her first sketch. "Prepare to be blown away," she told me.

No one could ever accuse Sara of being unsure of herself or her talent. With an indulgent smile, I took the book of designs from her.

"A gold bikini? Wow!" I exclaimed when I saw the first of her new suits. "This will definitely be an eye-catcher on the beach."

"The gold *lamé* is cool, isn't it? I've also got a suit with silver spangles like a disco ball. They're part of this whole retro line I want to do. See," she came to stand beside me and started to turn the pages of the sketch pad, "these others have paisley and tie-dye prints. And I'm going to do some more bikinis with what looks like bumper stickers on the back of the bottoms that say things like 'Make Love Not War' and 'Have a Nice Day.'"

"You've really outdone yourself. These are all fantastic. I'm sure you'll get a lot of attention at the Summer Extravaganza with this line."

"I need to do everything I can to stand out from the crowd of swimwear designers. You know what they say about only having one chance to make a good first impression. Oh, I also came up with some ideas for cover-ups. Check out these cabana pants, pareos, and sarongs."

I was ooooing and awwwwing over a plum-colored pareo with fringe when I heard a male voice say, "I hate to interrupt . . ."

Looking up from the sketch pad, I saw Ford hovering in the doorway to my office.

"Hey, what's up?" I asked.

"I was wondering if you had a hammer? I could have sworn that I packed one, but I've been through all of my boxes and I can't find it. I really wanted to get my diplomas hung today."

"In case one of your patients wants proof that you're a real doctor?" I teased him, and he smirked. "Sorry, but I'm not the type of girl to have tools lying around. I think my decorator hung all of the pictures in here. There's an Ace Hardware about a mile up on Alton though."

"I'll take a walk up there then. I could use some fresh air."

Sara cleared her throat not-so-subtly.

"Oh, I'm sorry." For a minute, I had actually forgotten

that she was there. It had been rude of me not to introduce her. "Sara Reade, this is my new neighbor and colleague, Dr. Fordham."

"Ah, the infamous Ford," she said, sizing him up as if he were one of her models and she was wondering how he'd look in a pair of tight swim trunks.

"Infamous?" He lifted a dark eyebrow questioningly.

"You mowed my friend down on the stairs, didn't you?"

"Fortunately, yes."

"Fortunately?" I repeated.

"We might not have met otherwise, and then how would I know where to find the best burger in South Beach?"

I chuckled. "I'm sure you would have managed."

Sara removed the sketch pad from my hands. "I'm glad you're here, Dr. Fordham. I could use a straight man's opinion."

"On?"

"My designs, of course. I'm about to debut Serafina Swimwear's 2013 collection at the Miami Summer Fashion Extravaganza."

Ford suddenly looked nervous. I thought I saw a bead of sweat forming on his forehead. "I'm just a guy from Brooklyn. I don't know anything about fashion."

"*Au contraire*, you know what you like to see a woman wearing, don't you? And women buy swimsuits to attract or please men. So, no one's opinion of my work is more valuable than the average man on the street's, and that's what you are. Here, take a look at this." She shoved her open sketch pad into his hands. "What do you think of that bikini?"

"Well, it's sexy. I like the way it ties between the uh, the um . . ."

"Breasts," I supplied the word he was fumbling for.

"I know what they are, Pilar, thank you. Anatomy was

my best subject in medical school."

"Just trying to help," I said with a feigned innocence that was belied by the twitching of my lips.

"Okay, so you like the way the bikini ties between the breasts. What about the bottom half of the suit? Which of these two styles do you prefer?" Sara pointed to his options.

"The one on the right. It shows less skin, but it's somehow more provocative."

"You like the boyshort, huh? Interesting. I thought you'd pick the Brazilian-cut."

"I can if you want me to." Ford was nothing if not flexible.

"No, no, I wanted your honest opinion. Now, let's talk colors." She turned to another page of her design book. "Classic black, lime green, or watermelon?"

"I like the last one."

"The watermelon? Any particular reason?"

"The color's vibrant, and I think it would look good on a woman with any hair or skin color."

"An excellent point."

"Glad that I could help. Now I really need to get that hammer." Ford edged towards the door.

"Just one more thing." Sara grabbed him by the arm before he could escape. "What are your thoughts on this design?" She pulled a piece of folded-up sketch paper out of her purse and offered it to him.

With a beleaguered expression, Ford exchanged her sketch pad for the drawing, opened the paper up, and studied it for a moment. "I'm not crazy about this suit," he determined.

Sara pursed her glossy lips. "Why not?"

"The bows, the lacy ruffles, the polka dots, it's just too cute. I'd expect to see a bikini like this on a little girl, not a grown woman. And the Lolita thing doesn't work for me."

I held my breath, waiting to see how Sara would react to Ford's criticism. Would she curse at him? Throw something? Anything was possible if she went into wounded diva mode.

To my surprise, she burst out laughing. "Oh my God, that was brutal! Thank you! No one else has had the guts to tell me the truth. I knew that that suit was a total disaster, but all of the sycophants who work for me kept insisting that it was 'darling.' UGH," she grunted with disgust. "I should fire all of them."

A look of concern crossed Ford's face. He obviously didn't want to be responsible for anyone ending up on the unemployment line.

"She's kidding," I assured him. "Go get your hammer."

"Okay. Nice meeting you, Sara. Good luck with the show," he said before departing.

"*Ciao.*" She waved at him.

When he had disappeared through the door in my outer office, my best friend murmured, "Yummy. Break me off a piece of that."

"You like him, huh?" Apparently, Ford's appeal wasn't just limited to me.

"What's not to like? He's got those rugged good looks, he's straightforward and smart and . . ."

". . . married," I reminded her.

"Oh yeah." Sara grimaced. "Major buzzkill. You need to find out if he's got a younger brother who's single."

"He has two younger brothers, but they're both in Brooklyn."

"Then, you should relocate."

I laughed, although I think she might have been serious.

CHAPTER 7

I was standing barefoot in my kitchen, making Cajun Guacamole with the avocados I'd just picked from the trees in my backyard, when the honk of a horn blasted through the open window behind me. The noise was so startling that my hand jerked, and I nicked my finger with the knife I was using to slice the green onion. I yelped in pain and muttered a few expletives *en español* (I've always thought that Spanish swear words were more expressive and violent-sounding than their English counterparts), then turned on the water in the sink and held my bleeding finger under the stream of cold liquid.

Hearing that obnoxious horn blare once again, I wrapped my finger tightly in a paper towel and stomped angrily over to the window to see who was disrupting my quiet evening at home. The perpetrator of this crime against my senses was the driver of a rusted old Harley that sat curbside in front of my little bungalow. He wore dark sunglasses, had long, stringy brown hair, and sported a variety of colorful tattoos that covered his arms from wrist to shoulder. Another one of my sister's charming boyfriends.

"Isidora!" I screamed her name, but my voice was almost drowned out by the sound of the motorcycle's engine being revved.

"What?" She strutted into the kitchen dressed in a silk babydoll dress that belonged to me. It was a little too short on her, but, of course, that's the way she liked to wear all of her clothes.

"Your date is here." I pointed out the window. "I don't remember you asking to borrow that dress."

"We're sisters." She picked up a chunk of avocado and popped it into her mouth. "What's yours is mine and vice versa."

Since Izzy had nothing of value, that seemed like a pretty rotten deal to me.

"Where are you going, and who's the rebel without a car?"

"His name's Marco. We met at the beach the other day," she said as she headed towards the front door and I trailed behind her. "He seems cool. He's taking me to this new club down on Ocean. His friend, Bruiser, bounces there, so we can get in for free."

Bruiser? The company my sister kept really did leave something to be desired.

Izzy reached out her hand for the door knob, but I stepped in front of her before she could make contact with it. "I don't want you riding on that motorcycle without a helmet. It's against the law and it's dangerous."

"What are you - my mother?"

"No, but speaking of mothers, have you called ours yet?"

"Why should I?" she asked petulantly.

"Because you owe her an apology for hanging up on her last week. You really hurt her feelings."

"I don't care. She deserved it. She's always so hateful to me. I can't do anything right in her eyes."

"We're always hardest on the ones we love the most."

"Spare me the psychobabble," Izzy sneered.

The horn sounded for a third time. If crotchety Mr. Miller across the street hadn't already called the police to report a public disturbance, I was sure that his hand was now poised over the telephone.

"I've got to go," my sister insisted irritably.

I didn't budge. "Please, just give *Mamá* a call and keep the peace."

"That's your job. Mine is to stir the family pot and as long as one of our parents is threatening to disown me, then I've done my duty. Now if you'll excuse me, my date is waiting." She reached around me for the door handle, and I resignedly moved out of her way.

"Don't get anything on that dress," I warned.

"Don't worry. I'll bring it back good as new. I'll even wash it for you," she promised as she stepped outside, letting the screen door slam shut in my face.

"That dress is not washable silk! You'll have to take it to the dry cleaners!" I yelled through the mesh at her retreating back.

Without acknowledging what I'd said, she hopped on the back of Marco's bike, and they took off . . . without putting on helmets.

Sighing, I went back to my guacamole in the kitchen and finished chopping up all of the ingredients. I had just started to mash the avocados when my phone rang. "Am I ever going to get to eat?" I grumbled as I grabbed the cordless.

"Hello."

"Pilar, it's *Mamá*." Of course, it was. She always knew when people were talking about her. All I had to do was say her name out loud and her ears began to burn no matter how many miles separated us. I was surprised that she had waited until five minutes after my argument with Izzy had ended to call.

"*Buenas tardes, Mamá*. How are you?"

"As well as can be expected under the circumstances."

"What circumstances?" I asked while I squeezed a lemon into a measuring cup.

"You know how my birthday depresses me every year. I hate getting older."

"Age is just a number. What's important is how you look and feel, and you look beautiful."

"You think so?" she fished for more compliments.

"Of course, I do. You attract attention everywhere you go. People are always saying that you look like Salma Hayek, aren't they?"

"I don't know why," she scoffed. "I'm much taller than she is." *Not to mention a good 10 years older.*

I folded some diced red bell peppers and quartered cherry tomatoes into the avocados. "It's still nice to be compared to an international sex symbol, isn't it?"

"I suppose," she acceded, "but I don't want to talk about me anymore."

Since when? My mother's favorite subject had always been herself.

"I called because I have some exciting news for you."

Sprinkling an assortment of seasonings into the mixing bowl, I murmured, "Oh, yeah, what is it?"

"I ran into an old friend of mine at a dinner party last night, and we started chatting about our lives and families . . ."

"Uh huh." I stuck my finger into the guacamole and did a taste test. Not spicy enough, I decided and reached for the cayenne pepper.

" . . . and it turns out that Marisol has a son who's just about your age. And he's single!"

Oh, crap. I knew exactly where this was going.

"*Mamá*, you know how I feel about fix-ups."

"Don't be difficult," she chastised. "This man is a good prospect for you, *mija*. He's Cuban and he's never been married, so there are no ex-wives or children to worry about. He's, also, a successful businessman."

"What type of business?" I found myself slightly intrigued.

"He owns a couple of health clubs up in Fort Lauderdale."

"Does he live there, too?"

"Yes, he has a nice condo a few blocks from the water. 3 bedrooms, 2 1/2 baths, underground parking, a terrace with an incredible view. He bought it last year at a really low interest rate." Leave it to my mother to get all of the pertinent details.

"I don't know. Dating someone outside of Miami is such a hassle. With the demands of my job, I just don't have the time to commute back and forth."

"It's a 40 minute drive for heaven's sake! You're never going to get a man if you don't put some effort into it, Pilar."

I took a bag of tortilla chips out of the pantry. "Do you know what he looks like?"

"Marisol showed me a picture. He's very handsome," she enthused. "Dark hair, olive skin, well-built, good teeth."

"You're sure that it was a recent picture?" I dipped a chip in the guacamole, then shoved it into my mouth.

"Pilar!"

"I'm just asking," I said with my mouth full. "You probably carry around a photo of me that was taken in college."

"I wouldn't have to if you'd give me something more current."

"Why don't I get some head shots taken? Then, you can pass them out to every eligible bachelor in South Florida. Of course, you'll want to list my vital statistics on the back of each photo . . . Age: 29, Hair: Brown, Eyes: Hazel, Measurements: 36-25-36, Likes: Stargazer lilies, rainy weekends, Bossa Nova, movies that make her cry . . ."

"You're making a joke, but this isn't funny. Do you want to be the first woman in our family who's unmarried when she turns 30? Even your cousin Sancha managed to find a man by the time she was your age, and she's got that lazy eye and a laugh that makes her sound like a donkey! Your father and I will be totally disgraced if you don't . . ."

"Alright, alright," I interrupted my mother's harangue, "I'll go out with . . . what did you say his name was?"

"Tony Escarda," she replied. "You're going to meet him for dinner Friday night at eight."

"Did you already pick out the restaurant and make a reservation?"

"No, I thought I'd let the two of you work that out when Tony calls to confirm. I gave his mother your home, office, and cell numbers."

I groaned with exasperation. "*Mamá*! You shouldn't have given out my phone numbers without getting my permission first."

"Bah! You'd never get a call from a man if I didn't give out your phone number. I went to a lot of trouble to get you this date, Pilar, so don't make a mess of it."

"I know how to conduct myself on a date." I crunched down on another guacamole-covered chip.

"Apparently not, or you wouldn't be alone," she managed to work a dig in before she began reeling off her rules for ensnaring a man.

"Be friendly, but not too friendly. You don't want him to think that you're a *puta*. Men don't marry girls who are easy. Don't pick at your dinner. Latin men like to see a woman enjoy her food. But don't stuff your face, or he'll think that you don't have any self-control. Laugh at all of his jokes. Let him do most of the talking, and try not to act too smart. You scare men off when you start babbling about all of your degrees and use strange words like *superego* and *Jungian*."

"Right, I wouldn't want a potential mate to know that I have a functioning brain," I quipped.

"Be sure to mention that you love babies," she continued, completely ignoring my sarcasm. "It never hurts to let a man know that you have a strong maternal instinct."

Or I could just offer to bear his children right after we'd introduced ourselves. That seemed like the more straightforward approach. "Thanks for the advice, *Mamá*. I'll be sure to keep it in mind. Now, I've really got to go. I haven't eaten dinner and I've got some case files to make notes in."

"You work too hard, *mija*. You need more balance in your life. If you had a family, you'd have something other than your crazy patients to focus on. Wouldn't it be wonderful if you and Tony hit it off? You could have a short engagement and get married at Christmastime. I just love holiday weddings! Dark green bridesmaids' dresses would be so pretty on your sisters, and we could do red . . ."

"Let's see how the first date goes before you plan out the next fifty years of my life with this guy, okay?"

"I guess I was getting a little bit ahead of myself. It's just that I want grandchildren so badly."

"You already have grandchildren," I reminded her about the trio of holy terrors Ana had given birth to.

"Bah! They're boys. What am I going to do with boys? I can't buy them anything pink, or braid their hair, or paint their little fingernails. Boys are so loud and dirty, and Ana just lets hers run wild. That's why they're always getting into trouble.

Did I tell you that George has been setting things on fire? First, it was paper, then it was piles of leaves and twigs in the backyard. Yesterday, he almost burned down the neighbors' garage. Their cat barely escaped with its life. What's next? Pouring lighter fluid on one of his brothers and striking a match? My grandson's an arsonist; he'll probably end up in prison and we'll all be disgraced."

"George is not an arsonist. It's perfectly normal for boys his age to experiment with fire. But if it will make you feel better, I'll have a talk with him and rule out any pyromaniacal tendencies."

"Pyro-what-ical? Oh, never mind," she said wearily, "just promise me that you won't use that word, or any others that have more than two syllables, when you go out with Tony. A man shouldn't have to bring a dictionary with him on a date."

"Good night, *Mamá*."

"Before you go, do you have any idea what you're going to wear on Friday? I think your yellow sundress would be perfect. Yellow's such a nice color on you; it brings out the gold in your eyes. Of course, you can't wear that dress without a tan and you looked a little pasty when I saw you last week. Have you been out in the sun at all since then? If not, maybe you could make an appointment at one of those tanning salons?"

"I don't have time--"

"Oh, your father just got home! He must be starving. I need to go and fix him a plate. I'll call first thing Saturday, and you can tell me all about your date with Tony, okay? Love you!"

I heard a kissing sound, then a click when she hung up the phone. I put my cordless back in the cradle and laid my head down on the kitchen counter. Conversations with my mother were always so exhausting.

CHAPTER 8

"You'll be proud of me, Doc."

I looked up from my notepad where I'd been scribbling some thoughts about my last session with Mitch. "Oh, really? Why's that?"

"Well, I had plenty of offers from beautiful women for hot, sweaty, no-strings-attached sex this past week and I turned them all down." Leaning back against the sofa cushions, Mitch locked his fingers behind his head and gave me one of his it's-good-to-be-me grins.

"You showed remarkable self-restraint then."

"No shit. There aren't too many men who could say 'no' to twins. Gorgeous 18-year-old twins with a fetish for licking warm honey off of--"

"Yes, well, it sounds like you did an admirable job of resisting temptation." It was suddenly very warm in my office. I pushed the sleeves of my cream-colored linen blouse up to my elbows and considered unfastening the button at the neckline.

"I think I was being tested by God, or the universe, or something."

"If that was the case, then you passed the 'test' with flying colors. How did that make you feel?"

Mitch ran his fingers through his damp hair while he pondered my question. I wondered if he'd come to my office fresh from the shower or if he'd been at the beach. Maybe he was one of those guys who liked to get up early and go for a swim in the ocean? He had to do some kind of strenuous exercise to maintain that physique of his.

"Pretty good, I guess. More mature, more responsible."

"That's excellent. By refraining from casual, impulse-driven sex, you're showing more respect for yourself, as well as the women you encounter. The next step is for you to start viewing women as something other than sex objects."

Mitch looked confused. "What else are they?"

Somewhere on the planet, Gloria Steinem let loose a primal scream.

"Women can be many things: colleagues, friends, mothers, partners, teachers. If you open yourself up to the possibilities, you can learn a lot from women and they can enrich your life on many levels, not just the physical. One of the reasons why you've never been able to achieve true intimacy and a lasting relationship with a woman is because you've never looked beyond the external."

"You mean appearance?"

"Right. Tell me, what's the first thing you think about when you meet a woman, any woman?"

"Uh . . . well . . . I don't . . .," he struggled with his reply.

"What's the first thing you thought about when you met *me*?" I reworded my query, making it more specific.

"Do you want the complete, uncensored truth?"

"Of course."

"You're not going to like it."

"No matter what you say, I'm not going to judge you."

Mitch eyed me skeptically for a moment.

"Alright," he finally relented. "When I first met you, I thought, 'Man, this chick is smokin'! She's got a great rack and an ass to match. I bet she's a wildcat in bed. Those intellectual types always are, once you get their clothes o--'"

"Yes, thank you," I interrupted him before I started blushing. "You just proved my point. You only see women on a superficial level."

"And how am I supposed to change that?"

"Start thinking about women as people, not just potential conquests. Engage them in conversation. Ask them questions about themselves and listen, really listen, to their answers."

"Okay." Mitch slid forward to the edge of the couch and fixed an interested gaze on me. "Why did you become a psychologist?"

I chuckled nervously. "I didn't say that you had to practice this approach on me."

"Why not? You're a woman, and I've objectified you in the past. If I'm going to turn over a new leaf, then I might as well start with you. So?"

It was a strange twist on role-playing, but thinking that it might benefit my patient I decided to answer, "I became a psychologist because I'm interested in people and why they behave the way they do."

"And how many years of school did that take?"

"I went to four years of college, then I moved on to graduate school for five years where I earned my Psy.D, which is a Doctor of Psychology degree."

"Nine years of school?" Through pursed lips, he emitted a low-pitched whistle of amazement. "I only made it through three months of junior college. You must be really smart."

"I like to think so," I said with a smirk.

"Are there any other doctors in the Alvarez family?"

"That's very good," I commended him. "You asked about my work, my education, and my family. And you complimented me on my achievements and intelligence rather than a physical attribute. See, it's not that difficult."

"Yeah, well, you make it easy, Doc. You're more than a pretty face and a hot body; you're actually interesting. The same can't be said for most of the beach bimbos I meet."

"Then, you need to expand your horizons and look for women outside your work environment."

He frowned. "I've never really looked for women. They've always just come to me."

"Therein lies your problem. You're not being selective; you're just taking whatever is offered to you. If you want to find a woman of quality, then you're going to have to put some effort into it."

"Effort, huh?" It was obviously a foreign concept to him. "Alright, yeah, I can do that. Where do I start looking for these women of quality?"

"They're everywhere. You just have to keep your eyes open, although I would advise against looking in bars and clubs. It's hard to make a real connection with anyone in those places."

"No bars and no clubs. Got it. You know, Doc, the stuff you say makes a lot of sense. I think that these sessions are really helping me."

"I'm glad to hear it."

"Maybe I should start seeing you twice a week?"

I actually heard the sound of a cash register ka-chinging in my head. I did some quick mental calculations and concluded that if Mitch doubled up on his sessions, I'd make $300 a week on him. $1200 a month! But how would a lifeguard get that kind of money? $1200 was probably a whole month's salary for him and as much as I could have used the extra revenue, I didn't want to break the poor man's bank.

"I appreciate your enthusiasm, Mitch. I really do. But I don't think your problems warrant two sessions a week."

"But if I came in twice a week, I could resolve my issues twice as fast."

"It doesn't necessarily work that way."

"I'd still like to do it. That is, if you have room for me on your schedule."

Oh, I had room. I had plenty of room. And seeing Mitch Buchannon's scruffily handsome face twice a week certainly wouldn't be a hardship. He was sort of a diamond in the rough and the more time I spent polishing him (I meant that figuratively, of course), the better chance I had of helping him realize his full potential not only as a man, but as a human being.

* * *

"Hey, neighbor."

As fate would have it, Ford and I were both leaving our offices at precisely 5:47PM that day.

"Pilar," he greeted me with a lopsided grin.

"You saw patients today?" I could tell because for the first time since I'd met him, Ford was wearing a suit rather than jeans. Sara would have been able to name the designer of his perfectly tailored black suit at ten paces, but I didn't know my Armani from my Savile Row. Ford's blue-and-white striped dress shirt was a little funky and he didn't wear a tie, so his overall appearance was professional, but not intimidating.

Sitting his briefcase down, he stuck his hands in his pants pockets. "Yep, I'm officially a practicing psychiatrist in the state of Florida."

Obviously not finding what he was looking for in his pants pockets, he started to pat the pockets in his coat. "Damn it, where are my keys? I must have left them on my desk."

He opened the door that led into his outer office and strode back in. I wasn't sure if I should follow him or just wait. I opted for the latter. Several minutes passed during which time I could hear desk drawers being slammed shut and papers rustling.

"Find them?" I called out and received a frustrated grumble in return.

Men always made the simplest tasks so difficult.

"Where did you last see them?" I inquired as I entered his turned-upside-down office.

"I had them in my hand when the temp agency called me about a receptionist."

Good, I thought, *he needed one.* Doctors tended to get scatterbrained when they had to handle administrative duties, as well as see patients. Before I'd hired Margo, my office had been a disaster and I hadn't known whether I was coming or going half the time.

"Okay and you've checked the surface of your desk and the floor around it?"

He nodded.

"What about those bookshelves behind you? Or maybe you dumped them in your briefcase?"

"Nope."

I scanned the room quickly. "You filed some patient folders after your phone call, didn't you?"

"How did you . . .," he glanced over at his file cabinets and saw that his keys were lying atop the middle one. "I'm an idiot."

"Once you get some help in here, you'll feel less rattled."

"I probably shouldn't have scheduled so many patients on my first day," he conceded as we walked back out to the corridor.

He'd had an overwhelming number of patients on his first day? I'd only seen two people in the entire first week that my practice's doors had been open. I was probably going to hate myself for asking, but I had to know.

"How many patients did you see today?"

He locked his office door and turned towards me. "Let's see, there were two manic depressives, a schizophrenic, an exhibitionist, an obsessive-compulsive, and a patient with Intermittent Explosive Disorder. So, that's six in all."

"Wow, you had a busy day." I was jealous.

"I'm getting a lot of referrals, which is nice. Shall we?" He motioned in the direction of the stairs.

"I hope traffic won't be bad. I promised Nate I'd be home by 6:30 so that we could grill out hot dogs. I used to be able to get away with being a few minutes late, but now that he can tell time . . ."

He took my arm when we reached the steps, which I thought was a very gentlemanly thing to do. I wondered if he helped ladies out of cars and stood up every time they left the table, too?

"It sounds like your son is very bright."

"Precocious is probably a better word. He could read and spell and do addition and subtraction by the time he entered kindergarten. He makes his teachers nervous. They want him to skip first grade and go straight to second next year."

"And you're not keen on that idea?"

"I don't know. He is more advanced academically than most of the kids his age, and I don't want him to be bored in school. But . . ."

"You're worried about how he'll fit in with the older kids?"

Ford stopped just before we reached the front door in our building's lobby. "Kids can be brutal, and it's not easy being labeled 'gifted.'"

"Is that the voice of experience I hear?"

He smiled at my perceptiveness. "Busted. I skipped the 6th grade and spent the next two years getting into scuffles with kids who thought that being smart made me a wimp. My own brothers were the worst. I got this scar here," he pointed to a jagged white line across the knuckles of his right hand, "when I punched Danny in the kisser because he called me 'Brainiac.' He was wearing braces at the time."

"Ow!" I said, shaking my hand as if I could feel the pain of metal cutting into flesh.

"14 stitches, but it was worth it," Ford assured me with a wink as he held open the door that led out to the street.

"Things got better for me in high school," he continued when we were outside. "I started to run track when I was a sophomore and the cool factor that came with being Jefferson High's star sprinter offset the geekiness of my 4.0 grade average."

"Did your son inherit your athletic ability, as well as your intellect?" I questioned while pulling my sunglasses out of my purse.

"Nate does love baseball. He's absolutely obsessed with the Yankees. Derek Jeter is his idol. When he grows up, he wants to be a Shortstop . . . or a Herpetologist."

I laughed. "Your 5-year-old knows what a Herpetologist is?" I wasn't even sure that I knew.

"His mother got him a turtle for his 4th birthday. He asked for a reptile encyclopedia last Christmas, and the rest is history. Where'd you park?"

"Hmmmm?" I was still filing away the fact that a Herpetologist was someone who studied reptiles. I planned to impress my nephews with that information the next time I saw them.

"Where's your car?" he repeated.

"Oh, over there." I gestured at my Miata.

"Damn, how'd you score such a great spot? I'm two blocks up, and it took me forever to find that space this morning."

"The secret is to get here early. I usually come in around 6:30, then I beat the other business people and tourists."

With a frown, Ford said, "I have to drop Nate at school at 7:00, so I guess I'm screwed."

He glanced up and down 11th Street. "Looks like we have a break in traffic. Do you wanna make a run for it?"

He jaywalked? Ford just kept getting more perfect every minute.

I nodded, and he grabbed me by the hand, pulling me

across the busy road. We were almost clipped by an El Dorado whose driver honked at us angrily and yelled a Spanish epithet out his window. I stopped in the middle of the thoroughfare, raised a fist in the air, and yelled something equally derogatory at the hunk-of-junk's bumper, which was just barely holding on with the help of some silver duct tape.

By the time I reached the curb, Ford was already there, laughing so hard that he was having trouble catching his breath. "Did you just insult that man's mother?" he queried in between gasps.

I shrugged, feeling a little embarrassed. "Latinas and their fiery tempers. It's *cliché*, but true."

"And I thought the girls in Brooklyn were tough. *Damn.*"

"You're going to be late for your cookout with your son if you don't get going," I reminded him.

Ford looked at his watch. "Oh, shoot, you're right. I only have half an hour now."

He started to back away from me. "Lunch? Later this week?" he shouted.

Chuckling, I made the "Call me" sign.

CHAPTER 9

I was leaving my office to go home and get ready for my dinner date with the man my mother had pinned all her hopes for my future on when the phone rang. Without considering the ramifications, I picked up. *Big mistake.* The caller was Kyle, who was bordering on hysteria because a mosquito had bitten him on the arm and he was absolutely sure that he'd contracted the West Nile Virus. The poor man was having a full-blown anxiety attack, complete with heart palpitations and shortness of breath, so I had to talk him down. When we finally hung up forty-five minutes later, he'd downgraded his imaginary disease to malaria, which I told him could be treated with medication and would not lead to his horrifically painful death by encephalitis.

Running short on time and not having a change of clothes with me, I was forced to work with what I had. I refreshed my makeup in my office's small bathroom, then released my hair from the clip I'd pulled it back with and did my best to finger-fluff the wavy tresses into some sort of a soft, tousled style. Sadly, I could only do so much with what I was wearing. In an effort to make my outfit look less business-like, I removed the jacket that matched my black cotton pique skirt. The turquoise silk stretch top I had on underneath was curve-hugging and bared some skin, so exposing it made me feel a bit more feminine and date-ready. I glanced down at my feet and groaned. My shoes were all wrong for a night out on the town; there was just nothing sexy about functional black pumps. I promised myself that if Tony and I made it to date number two, I'd wow him with some flirty, pedicure-flaunting footwear then.

As I raced up I-95, I tried to call Tony on my cell to let him know I was running behind. When I realized that the damn thing was dead because I'd forgotten to recharge its battery, I was so frustrated that I hurled the phone at the dashboard, taking a chunk out of the vinyl right above the speedometer. My crappy luck continued as I was forced to maneuver my way around not one, but two, accidents on the freeway. Fortunately, they were both confined to a single lane, so traffic wasn't backed up; it just moved slowly for a few miles due to everyone gawking at the police cars and tow trucks.

It was a quarter past seven when I reached the seafood place on Las Olas Boulevard where I'd arranged to meet Tony, which not only made me late, but guaranteed me getting an earful from my mother.

'You've disgraced the family with your tardiness! I'll never be able to look Marisol in the eye again, not when you've treated her son so shamefully. What's wrong with you? I set you up with el hombre perfecto, and you let a silly, unimportant thing like your job interfere. Ay, I give up! Die alone! See if I care!'

I valet parked because it would have taken me another hour to find an empty spot in that trendy part of town on a Friday night. Although it was still early, the street was already bustling with cars and people, who were there to eat, drink, and get their party on at the numerous bars, clubs, and restaurants.

Once inside The Reef, I scanned the crowded waiting area, looking for a single man with an irritated expression. I saw one who fit the bill, standing by a large potted palm near the hostess station. Remembering my mother's words, I plastered a 'friendly, but not too friendly' smile on my face and made my way over to him.

"Tony?" I queried when I was close enough for him to hear me.

"That's me. You must be Pilar."

"Yes. I'm so sorry I'm late. I got held up with a patient. I tried to call, but my cell wasn't working."

"Not a problem. I'm just glad you made it."

He seemed nice, although he wasn't really my type physically. I'd always been attracted to men who were tall, and Tony was on the short side. However, what he lacked in height, he more than made up for in width. His body was incredibly bulky. Like Dwayne "The Rock" Johnson bulky. The muscles of his upper torso were straining so hard against the fabric of his fitted shirt that it looked as though it might burst open at the seams. And when he held out his hand to shake mine, the veins on the inside of his arm looked as though they were pulsating.

The hostess sat us at a cozy table for two on the far side of the main dining room, which was decorated in soothing shades of blue. There were candles and fresh flowers on the table, and the music being piped in above our heads was something jazzy and subdued.

"This is lovely," I complimented Tony on his choice of restaurants. "Have you been here before?"

He rubbed the dark stubble on his head. Did I mention that Tony's head was shaved? He probably hadn't taken a razor to it in a few days, so there was a little bit of regrowth sprouting up. I found myself remembering the Chia Pet I'd used for a science experiment in the third grade. I'd called him 'Ramon,' and he'd gotten me an A-, which I'd been very proud of.

"Yeah, a couple of times. They've got a good menu here. Lots of healthy food. Most of your fancier restaurants only serve entrees that are high in trans fat. They cook their meat in hydrogenated oil, then smother it in cholesterol-rich sauces and gravies. They even load their vegetables down with grease." Ramon, I mean *Tony*, made a disgusted face.

"I guess that you really have to watch your diet since you work out so much?"

"I work out a minimum of four hours a day, mostly doing weight training and cardio, which requires mega-energy, so I'm on a 3500 calorie diet. How many calories do you consume daily?"

What a strange first date conversation! Was his next question going to be, 'How much do you weigh?' If so, I was leaving.

"I have no idea."

"Guess," he persisted.

"Um, 1800?" I just threw out a number that sounded good.

"And what's your exercise regimen like?"

"Well, I don't really have a regimen. I do yoga when I can, and I walk a lot."

Tony shook his head. "That's just sad. I wouldn't even call that exercise."

"I suppose I could do more, but I work such long hours . . ."

"Excuses, excuses. If you don't take care of your body, how can you expect your body to take care of you?"

"What can I get you to drink?" An extremely perky waitress suddenly appeared at our table.

"We're ready to place our dinner order," Tony replied.

We were? I hadn't even looked at my menu yet.

"Ma'am?" the young server looked at me.

"Why don't you let me order for both of us?" my date suggested.

I smiled my acquiescence, although I feared that I was going to end up with some boring, low-carb, no-fat, doesn't-have-any-taste-or-flavor meal.

"We'll have the portabello mushrooms with low-fat vinaigrette for our appetizer, and for our entree, the red snapper without the caper sauce. Please, tell the chef not to use any butter in the cooking of the fish. As for the vegetables, bring us some sweet potatoes and steamed broccoli."

Broccoli? Yuck. I hated broccoli.

"And to drink?"

"Bottled water. No bubbles."

Apparently, carbonation was too wild and crazy for Tony.

"As I was saying, you need to get motivated about exercise," he continued once the waitress was gone. "I suggest getting a personal trainer."

"Is that what you do at your health clubs?"

"That's right. But I mostly train serious bodybuilders. You need to get a trainer who specializes in women. I plan to have several different types of trainers, each with their own area of expertise, at the location I'm opening in Hialeah later this summer."

"You're opening a third club? That's great!" I enthused. "Business must be booming."

"The Ripped gyms here in Lauderdale are extremely profitable. And my business partner has been encouraging me to expand to the south since everyone in Miami is so fitness-conscious."

The name of his gyms was *Ripped*? Nothing subtle about that.

Our waitress returned with a bottle of Panna and a basket of bread, which she sat down in front of me. I reached for a sourdough roll and met with a disapproving stare from Tony.

"White flour is not your friend," he told me.

"I don't know. We've had some really good times together," I joked in return.

Tony didn't even crack a smile. He obviously took the subject of nutrition very seriously.

"Try the whole wheat." He placed a different roll on my bread plate, which seemed rather presumptuous to me.

"The secret to eating carbs without gaining weight is to

eat good carbs. Brown breads and pastas, long grain rice, sweet potatoes . . . you want to avoid anything that's white."

Please, like any self-respecting girl with a drop of Cuban blood in her would give up black beans and white rice? Was he nuts?

Humoring him, I took a bite of my wheat roll. It was dry and could have really benefited from a nice glob of butter, but I didn't want to get another lecture on the evils of fat.

"You should really get your body fat checked."

Great. I was going to get the lecture anyway.

"I'm sure I'm in the normal range."

"Do you even know what the normal range is?"

What was this? A pop quiz? "40%?"

"No, a woman's body fat should be between 25 and 31%. It's lower for men - 18 to 25%. I'm in the best shape of my life right now, and I'm at 18.75%."

"Good for you," I muttered and removed what appeared to be some kind of a corn muffin from the bread basket.

"Too much sugar," Tony warned. "And you know what sugar is . . ."

Sweet? Delicious? Fun?

"Empty calories. Your body gets absolutely no benefits from sugar, which is, big surprise, white. There's nothing good about foods that are white."

Tony was starting to sound like a food racist. I put the corn muffin back, even though I was starving, and wondered if my date would have any objection to me chewing on my napkin? I looked down at the piece of fabric in my lap. It was white, of course.

Tony reached across the table and took my hand. At first, I thought that he was trying to be romantic, but he disabused me of that silly notion when he lifted my arm up and inspected it like a side of beef.

"Your triceps need a lot of work. That's a problem area

for most women. After 30, those muscles start to lose tone. If you don't take some preventative measures now, you're going to have nothing but flabby skin here," he poked the flesh on the underside of my arm, "in another 5 years or so."

"I'm not 30 yet." There was an edge to my voice as I pulled my manhandled limb back.

He shrugged. "Close enough. It's just a matter of time before gravity catches up with you."

If our server hadn't brought out our appetizer just then, I probably would have decked him.

While I tried to enjoy the mushrooms, Tony blathered on about deltoids and triglycerides and circuit training and . . . I was officially bored by the time the fish arrived and mentally checked out of my date, surreptitiously glancing around the room to see if people at other tables were having a better time than I was.

There was a nicely dressed older couple behind Tony, who were toasting each other with champagne. Maybe they were celebrating an anniversary? They looked so happy and in love . . . like there was no place else on Earth they'd rather be. Due to my circumstances, I had a hard time relating to that feeling.

Looking past the blissful marrieds, I saw a table populated with five women. They were laughing and sharing a plate of fried calamari drenched in marinara sauce, which beat the hell out of plain grilled fish. I was tempted to get up and join them.

At the table to the ladies' right sat two men, both wearing rimless glasses and suits, who were deeply engrossed in conversation. I wondered what they were talking about. *Business? Politics? Their golf games? Which superhero had the hottest girlfriend?*

A hostess was leading a man with dark, thinning hair and a bleached blonde in an obscenely tight red dress to a table in the opposite corner of the dining room. He had his hand draped possessively over her shoulders, and she was whispering in his ear (naughty nothings, no doubt.) I wasn't particularly interested in middle-aged men and their plastic surgery-enhanced bimbettes, but there was something about him that struck me as familiar. So, I watched as they took their seats. From my vantage point, I could only see the mystery man's profile. He was quite handsy with his companion, stroking her bare forearm, touching her cheek, and finally, squeezing her too-tan thigh, which was almost entirely exposed by her short skirt. She reciprocated by nibbling on his neck. He adjusted his position in order to give her better access to the area behind his ear, and that's when I finally got a good look at his face . . . with a gasp, I dropped my fork.

"I know. It's shocking, isn't it?" Tony obviously thought that I was reacting to something he'd just said.

I nodded my head uncertainly.

"With that high a percentage of this country's population being overweight or obese, America is the fattest country in the world, and it's just going to get worse if people don't start learning discipline. Discipline in their diets, and discipline in sticking to an exercise plan."

"Uh huh," I half-heartedly agreed before turning my attention back to the PDA-crazy pair across the room.

I knew the man because he was a patient of mine. Actually, he and his wife, who was a demure, sweet-faced brunette, not a platinum-haired hoochie mama, were patients of mine. They'd been coming to me for marital counseling for about three months. Annette had been concerned that after 16 years of marriage, her husband had lost interest in her. Joe had assured her repeatedly over the course of our sessions that that wasn't true, that he'd just been preoccupied with work, that he still loved and appreciated her even if he didn't tell her or show her often enough. *Bastard*, I fumed. I should have known that he was cheating on his poor trusting wife.

"Pilar?" Tony interrupted my reverie.

"Hmmmmm?"

"I asked if you wanted me to check your body fat after we're finished eating? I've got some calipers in the car. With a simple pinch test, I can determine what your number is. Then, you'll know how many percentage points you've got to lose when you start with your trainer. It's always helpful to have a goal in exercise."

A pinch test? Was this the equivalent of Tony asking me if I wanted to see his etchings? *UGH* Forget it. I'd had enough of this guy and his fitness-mania.

"Thanks, but I don't think so. If you'll excuse me, I see a business acquaintance and I need to say hello."

"But . . .," Tony started to protest, but I was gone before he could finish.

With fiery indignation, I marched over to Joe's table. He didn't see me approach because he was too busy sucking on his girlfriend's fingers.

"Mr. Scolari, what a surprise!" I greeted him.

He dropped the blonde's hand like it was a ticking bomb and lifted his eyes guiltily to me. "D-d-doctor Alvarez, what are you doing in Fort Lauderdale?"

I could read his thoughts as clearly as if they were tattooed on his forehead. *'I sneak off to another city to be with my mistress so that I don't run the risk of running into anyone I know, and I still get busted?'*

"I'm here on a date. And you?" I couldn't wait to hear what lie he would come up with.

"Um." He looked helplessly at the woman to his left, and she just stared back at him blankly. The two of them were apparently a real braintrust.

Fidgeting with the collar of his dress shirt as though it were suddenly strangling him, Joe said, "Candy, uh, Mrs. Lowenstein, is a client of mine, and she's, uh, given my company a lot of referrals, so I'm, uh, treating her to dinner. It's just my way of saying, 'Thank you.'"

"Buy a lot of pool supplies, do you?" I addressed Candy.

"Oh, sure," she replied in the squeakiest voice my ears had ever had the misfortune of hearing. She sounded like Minnie Mouse on helium. "My husband and I have two pools at our house in South Beach. One inside, and one out. Of course, I'm the only one who uses them because Henry's been stuck in bed since his last heart attack."

So, she was some sick, old guy's trophy wife? *Color me shocked.* "Poor Henry," I sympathized with the cuckolded man.

"What's that?" I pointed to a jewelry box that was sitting in front of the gold digger.

"It's from Joey. Look." She opened the box with hands that were adorned with an assortment of garishly large rings and offered it to me.

"An emerald pendant," I murmured as I surveyed the green stone. I knew very little about jewelry (much to my mother's dismay), but it looked expensive.

"Emerald is my birthstone. Isn't that sweet?" Candy squeezed "Joey's" arm, and he sank down in his chair, looking like he might be sick.

I wondered when he'd last given his dutiful wife a nice piece of jewelry. It certainly hadn't been on her birthday. During a recent therapy session, Annette had burst into tears after telling me that Joe had completely forgotten her 40th. He hadn't even bought her a card. *Bastard.*

"Sweet's probably not the word I'd use," I grumbled and returned the pendant to its undeserving owner. "I should get back to my table. Mr. Scolari, I'll see you Monday at 11."

"Huh?" He glanced up at me with a startled expression.

"Your weekly appointment," I reminded him.

"Oh." He started to play with his silverware, rearranging the order of the forks. "I might not be able to make it. I've got a couple of salespeople out on vacation next week, so I'll have to cover for them."

Smiling complacently, I said, "That's okay. I can have a solo session with Annette. I'm sure that we'll have *plenty* to talk about."

Joe blanched.

"No, no, I'll be there," he promised me. "I'll just rearrange some appointments."

"That's what I like to see in my patients, an unswerving dedication to the therapeutic process. I look forward to our session on Monday, Mr. Scolari." *Bastard.*

CHAPTER 10

"Joe. Annette. Good to see you both," I welcomed the couple sitting in my waiting room, and they rose from their chairs.

"Annette, if you don't mind, I'd like to speak with Joe alone for the first part of our session today."

"Oh." Looking at first surprised, then a bit flustered, she sat back down. "Okay, whatever you think is best, Dr. Alvarez."

"Would you like something to drink while you wait?" I offered.

Annette lowered her soft brown eyes to the floor. "No, no, I don't want to be a bother."

"It's no bother." I made a mental note to work with Annette on asserting herself.

"Margo, would you please get Mrs. Scolari a cup of coffee? Or maybe you'd prefer water?" I gave her a choice.

"Um, coffee would be nice. Decaf, if you have it."

"And here's the new issue of *Travel & Leisure*." I grabbed the magazine, which was lying on the side table, and handed it to her. "Maybe it'll give you some good ideas for your next vacation? Joe," I summoned him in the same stern tone I would have used on a disobedient dog, and he scurried into my office. I followed him and shut the door behind us.

He was standing in the middle of the room, his posture slouched and an uncertain expression on his pudgy, mustached face. I walked towards him and stopped when there was only a foot of space between us. Crossing my arms in front of my chest, I stared directly at Joe and I waited, not saying a word. He did the same. I felt like I was in one of those old spaghetti Westerns that my father loved to watch. Of course, I was flinty, vengeful Clint Eastwood and Joe was the black-hat-wearing villain and no matter who pulled their gun first, he was going to be the one with a smokin' bullet hole between the eyes.

"I've been thinking, Dr. Alvarez," he finally spoke. "You can't say anything to Annette about seeing me with Candy Friday night."

"Oh, really? And why is that?"

"You can't violate doctor-patient confidentiality."

So, he thought he had me beat on a technicality?

"You're right; I can't. But I'm not bound by doctor-patient confidentiality in this case."

Confusion made him frown. "Why not? I'm your patient, and you're my doctor."

"Yes. However, you didn't confess your adulterous behavior to me during a session. I witnessed it when I was off-the-clock. So, you're not protected by doctor-patient confidentiality, and I'm free to do whatever my conscience dictates."

"Oh, crap." Moving over to the couch, he slumped down on to it, looking defeated.

I sat in the chair opposite him and folded my hands in my lap. "Do you love your wife, Mr. Scolari?"

"Of course, I do," he answered without hesitation. "We've been together for 17 years. She's the mother of my children."

"Then, why is there a Candy in your life?"

"A man gets bored. Marriage isn't very exciting."

"Maybe a woman gets bored, too. How would you feel if Annette decided to amuse herself with another man?"

"Annette would never do that," he scoffed as if the idea was completely absurd. Why should his wife stray when she had a prize like him coming home to her every night?

"Probably not, because she loves you and is committed to your marriage. But that doesn't mean that she isn't just as bored and dissatisfied with your relationship as you are. Why do you think she wanted to come to therapy in the first place?"

"Because it's what all her friends do?"

"No." The man was seriously obtuse. "She's trying to figure out what went wrong in your marriage and how to fix it. And if you're not willing to meet her halfway and work on your issues, then you're just wasting my time and I'll have to put a stop to these sessions."

"What? Wait! No!" He held his hands out beseechingly to me. "If you do that, then Annette will want to know why."

"I'm sure she will, and it'll behoove me to be honest with her."

Joe started to perspire . . . heavily. "You can't do that! She'd flip out. She'd take the kids and leave me."

"And I could supply her with the name and number of Steven Myles, the most ruthless divorce lawyer in Miami." Leaning forward, I whispered, "He plays tennis with my father."

"No, no, we can't get a divorce," his voice was becoming higher-pitched as his panic level increased, and the sound of it gratified me. "We don't have a pre-nup. She'd take me for half of everything."

I inspected my manicure, seemingly indifferent to his plight. "Hmmmm, yes, that would probably be unpleasant for you."

"Okay, fine, I'll break things off with Candy." He waved the proverbial white flag.

"That's a step in the right direction, but you're going to have to do more."

"Such as?"

"Such as, making an effort to salvage your marriage. Successful marriages take work, Mr. Scolari. You can't expect to keep the romance alive by working 12-hour days and ignoring your wife."

"I guess I could spend more time at home."

"And?"

"And pay more attention to Annette." He didn't sound too thrilled about the prospect.

"You need to put the fun and spontaneity back into your relationship with your wife," I advised. "Surprise her, make romantic gestures, be affectionate, spend time together away from the kids."

"And if I do all that, you'll keep the Candy thing to yourself?" He wanted to confirm the terms of our bargain.

"As long as you're making a genuine effort, I won't enlighten Annette. Of course, if I have any reason to suspect that your eye is wandering again . . ."

"You won't," he promised. "I know how much I have to lose."

I hoped that he was talking about the love of his wife and not 50% of his assets.

"I'm glad we understand each other. Let's call Annette in, shall we?"

* * *

"I blackmailed a patient today." Ford and I were strolling down the beach, eating a couple of Cuban Big Macs that we'd picked up at David's Café, when I made this pronouncement.

"Well, that's an interesting therapeutic technique," he said before taking a huge bite out of his sandwich, which was a taste bud-pleasing combo of pork, ham, Swiss cheese, pickles, and mustard.

"I couldn't think of any other way to handle it. If I'd told the wife that her husband was cheating on her, she'd have been devastated and their marriage would have been damaged beyond repair. And if I did nothing, he would have gone right on boffing that bleached blonde bimbo of his and neglecting his poor wife."

"How'd you know the husband was cheating?" Ford asked.

"I ran into him and his girlfriend at a restaurant up in Lauderdale over the weekend. I was there on a date."

He raised a dark eyebrow. "With Victor?"

"God, no! It was a blind date arranged by my mother, and big surprise," the sarcasm in my voice was unmistakable, "it was a total disaster. I don't know why I let *Mamá* talk me into these things. The guy looked like he was on steroids, and he spent the whole night yammering on about exercise and how unhealthy every food I wanted to eat was. He actually implied that I had too much body fat if you can believe it."

Ford smirked. "That's the way to a woman's heart."

"I ended the date abruptly because Tony was working my last nerve and I was in a snit after seeing Jo- . . ." *ACK! Don't use real names*, I reminded myself. ". . . Patient X in a compromising position. I tried to explain this to my mother when she called and woke me up at 6:00 the next morning to tell me how ungrateful I am and how it would serve me right if I ended up an old maid, but she didn't want to hear it."

"Relationships with mothers can be tough," he sympathized.

"Especially when your mother is prone to histrionics and won't butt out of your personal life. She and I are no longer on speaking terms, by the way."

"Yikes." He winced. "Sorry."

I waved my hand dismissively. "She'll get over it. She just needs to pout for a few days to make her point. Meanwhile, I get a break from her matchmaking and giving me unsolicited advice on everything from how I should lie about my age and pretend to be an airhead in order to get a man to what brand of toothpaste will make my teeth look whiter."

"Your mother sounds like a character."

"I love her, but she's a lunatic. How's your sandwich?"

"Spicy, salty, a little greasy, just the way I like my food." He smiled playfully, and the corners of his eyes crinkled. *Cute.*

"I'm glad you suggested we come down here to eat. It's such a pretty day."

The sun was shining brightly in a cloudless blue sky, and there was a hint of a breeze wafting off the ocean. With my shoes in hand, I walked to the edge of the water and reveled in the feel of the warm, wet sand squishing between my toes.

Ford followed me to the shoreline, and we stood side-by-side, silently watching the waves crash at our feet. He didn't seem to care that the hems of his trouser legs were getting soaked.

"I would have never been able to do this on my lunch hour when I was in New York," he remarked.

"Miami definitely has its advantages."

He turned to me. "So, what happened with Patient X?"

"I threatened to spill the sordid beans to his wife if he didn't shape up and start participating in his marriage. You're about to drop some mustard on your shirt." I pointed to a big glob of the yellow condiment that was stealthily oozing its way out of the bottom of his Big Mac.

"Damn, these things are messy." He flipped the sandwich over and licked the mustard off the bread.

"I'm afraid that I took this situation with Patient X too much to heart," I lamented. "I got so irate when I saw him with that woman."

"Because you identified too closely with the wife, or because his actions sabotaged all of the work you'd done with the couple in therapy?"

I mulled the question over for a moment before deciding,

"The latter. I took his cheating as a personal affront. I'd thought that I was helping Patient X and his wife. Then, I found out that he'd disregarded every word I'd said in our sessions over the last few months and I was pissed."

"I've been there and so has everyone in our field. When we start out, we all think, 'I'm going to save the world one maladjusted person at a time.' But patients don't always listen to us, and it can be incredibly frustrating."

"Tell me about it," I grumbled.

"You'll learn to disassociate yourself and not take it personally."

I sighed. "Easier said than done. In case you haven't noticed, the female of the species is a very emotional creature."

"Which is what makes them so fascinating." Grinning, he shoved the last of his lunch between his lips.

"Oh! I've got something for you." I unzipped my purse and began to root around inside.

"Dessert?" he queried hopefully.

"If a stick of sugar-free gum counts as dessert, then yes. Otherwise, it's a name and a phone number." I handed him a post-it note with the info written on it.

Ford examined the small pink piece of paper. "Raymond Castaneira. Who's he?"

"My brother-in-law. He's married to my older sister, Ana. I've probably mentioned her before. After our talk about Nate and his obsession with baseball the other day, I remembered that my nephew, Charlie, who's about Nate's age, plays on a Tee-Ball team that his dad coaches."

"Tee-Ball? Nate would love that."

"I thought so, too. Plus, it would be a good way for him to meet kids his own age. I know you were concerned about him not being able to do that if he skips a grade next year. I called Raymond to get the scoop on the Pee Wee League, and he said that practices just started two weeks ago."

"So, it's not too late for Nate to join?"

"No, you just need to contact Raymond, and he can tell you which team is based in the area of town where your family lives and put you in touch with the right coach."

"Wow, this was really thoughtful of you. Nate's going to be thrilled." He reached out for my hand and gave it a grateful squeeze. "Thank you."

I felt ridiculously pleased, knowing that I'd done something to help Ford and make his son happy. Blushing, I murmured, "*De nada.*"

Ford's watch beeped and he dropped my hand to take a look at it. "We'd better hoof it back to the office, or we're going to have a couple of angry two o'clocks."

"I'm ready." I tossed what was left of my sandwich into a nearby trash receptacle and headed for the sidewalk, wondering why my hand was suddenly feeling all warm and tingly. Too much sun probably. I was absolutely 100% positive that it had nothing to do with Ford touching me. He was attractive, yes, but married, and I wasn't the type of woman who got all hot and bothered over a hopeless cause.

CHAPTER 11

"It's hopeless!" Lori threw her hands up in the air. "He hates me!"

"Jiff doesn't hate you. Dogs aren't capable of hating anyone."

Jiff was the mutt Lori had adopted a couple of weeks earlier. After seeing a photo of the straggly-looking thing, I'd suggested that she call him Benji. But she'd opted for an acronym of her last four boyfriends' names (James Isaac Felipe Finn) instead.

"Then, why won't he sleep on the bed with me and why does he try to run away every time I take him to the park?" she asked.

"You haven't had the dog for long. He just needs time to get used to you and his new surroundings."

"I've done everything I can to make him comfortable. I bought out Petsmart so that he'd have his choice of treats and toys. I hand-painted his name on his food and water bowls. I brush his hair a hundred strokes every night before bed and talk to him like he's a person. I even made him a doggie wardrobe with swimtrunks for the summer, a rain-repellent poncho for bad weather, and festive sweaters for the holidays . . . I need to find some patterns for pajamas, too. Wouldn't he look adorable in some of those PJs with the little feet and the flap over the butt?"

Poor Jiff, I thought. He probably would have been better off if he'd stayed at the Humane Society.

"Lori, you know how we've talked about your tendency to overwhelm men with your love?"

"Uh-huh." Distractedly, she pulled on one of her corkscrew curls, which had recently been restored to its original coppery color after the intervention of some of Lori's co-workers at the salon.

"Well, you're doing the same thing with Jiff. Enthusiasm is good, but you need to take it down a couple notches. If you come on too strong, the natural instinct of anyone, be they human or animal, is to retreat."

Lori thought about it for a minute. "So, no PJs?"

"No. And when you're with Jiff, just relax and let him come to you. He will eventually. Dogs are pack animals; they enjoy affection and the feel of a warm body next to them."

"Don't we all?" she remarked wistfully.

I couldn't argue with that. For a second, I toyed with the idea of getting a dog myself, then I remembered that Izzy was allergic. Living with her was like having a pet anyway since she cost me a small fortune and I had to feed and clean up after her all the time.

Out of the corner of my eye, I could see that the clock read nine 'til the hour. "Looks like that's it for today's session," I announced.

"Yeah, I need to get home and walk Jiff," Lori said, standing up. "He hasn't been out since lunchtime. His bladder's probably about to burst."

We both chuckled, and I led her out of my office. When I opened the door to the waiting area, I was met with a colorful surprise. Four crystal vases filled with arrangements of deep purple orchids and lily grass crowded the surface of Margo's desk.

"Oh, my God!" Lori squealed with excitement and rushed over to the flowers. "These are gorgeous!"

"I'll say," I murmured appreciatively. "What's the occasion?"

Margo peeked her overly-teased head around one of the vases. "You tell us." She handed me a small white card.

My jaw dropped. "These are for me?"

"That's your name on the envelope, isn't it?"

I checked. Sure enough, it was addressed to Dr. Pilar Alvarez. I opened the envelope and drew out the card slowly, while Margo and Lori waited with bated breath.

"Read it aloud, Dr. Alvarez," Lori urged.

"'Rare, exotic beauties for the most rare and exotic beauty of all.'"

Lori clutched her heart and looked as though she might swoon. "That is *so* romantic."

"Who are they from?" Margo wondered.

"There's no signature," I told her.

"A secret admirer," Lori rhapsodized. "You are *so* lucky, Dr. Alvarez. Nothing like this ever happens to me."

Secret admirer? Hardly. The ostentatious display and the accompanying poetically-worded sentiment had 'Victor Liscano' written all over them. I had to give him credit; the orchids were stunning. I bent down to smell one of the purple blooms. *Mmmmmm, nice.*

"Would you like to take one of the arrangements home?" I asked Lori.

"Oh no, I couldn't!"

"Please." I picked up one of the heavy vases and shoved it into her arms. "As lovely as they are, I certainly don't need this many orchids. Margo, you take one home, too."

"If they were mine," Lori said dreamily, "I wouldn't want to part with a single flower."

"What can I say? I love to share." I gently pushed my patient towards the door and waved her out.

"They're from Victor, aren't they?" Margo inquired after Lori was gone and I'd turned back to face her.

I nodded.

"The man is persistent."

"Bordering on obsessed. Will you put one of these vases over there?" I pointed to the top of the table where the magazines for the patients were spread out. "And I'll take this one for my office." I hoisted one of the remaining vases up with a groan. It felt like it weighed more than I did.

I spent the next few minutes trying to decide what the perfect spot for my flowers was. Did orchids require sunlight or no? I wasn't sure, so I placed them on a shady corner of my desk. Then, I sat down to admire them. They really were beautiful and they provided a vibrant splash of color in my shades-of-beige office. Although I'd never admit it to him, Victor had done well.

My phone intercom buzzed.

"Which line is he on?" I questioned Margo.

"Two," she replied, and I picked up the phone.

"*Gracias*, Victor. The orchids are beautiful."

"Not as beautiful as you, *mi querida*. I hope the flowers looked fresh; I had them flown in straight from Hawaii this morning."

Damn, that must have been expensive.

"You shouldn't have gone to all that trouble."

"It was worth the trouble if they made you happy. Did you notice how many orchids I sent?"

"Uhhhh . . . a lot?"

"A hundred and four, one for every day I've loved you."

"So, that counts back to . . .?"

"The day we met, of course. I'll never forget looking across my crowded restaurant and seeing your face for the first time. You were so lovely, so luminous, like a star in the night sky. You took my breath away. I stood transfixed, watching you for the better part of an hour, while I worked up the nerve to go over to your table and talk to you."

I chortled with amusement at his memory of our first meeting. "You are such a liar! You weren't paralyzed by my beauty for a minute, much less an hour. You noticed me and my friends as soon as we walked in the door of Liscano's and you sent us a round of Margaritas right after we were seated.

You were on your way over to our table when you got sidetracked by a pair of redheads at the bar who looked like they were underage, and you spent twenty minutes flirting with them before you finally sauntered over to put your patented smooth moves on me."

"I like my version better."

"I'm sure you do."

"Give me another chance, *mi amor*. I've changed, I swear. I am a model of maturity and trustworthiness now. No more partying, no more goofing off."

I found myself wanting to believe him. Did I still have feelings for Victor? Or was the intoxicating aroma of the orchids making me go soft in the head? I moved the flowers to the other side of my desk just in case.

"I hope for your sake that that's true, Victor. Regardless, a romantic relationship would never work for us."

"How can you be so sure?"

"I'm not what you need any more than you're what I need," I told him.

"And what do you think I need?"

"A playmate, someone who'll devote herself to you 24/7, someone who'll stroke your ego and make you feel like you're the center of her universe."

"I was the center of your universe for a while," he pouted.

"No, you weren't, and no man ever could be. I'm too independent, too driven. I need someone who doesn't require my undivided attention, who'll understand and support my devotion to my career, a partner, an equal in all areas."

"I can be that for you."

"Really?" I sounded skeptical.

"I know you think I'm all flash and no substance, Pilar, but there's more to me than meets the eye. I have hidden depths."

"Do tell."

"Well, I'm sensitive for one thing. I have feelings and a heart that was broken when you left me."

"You brought that on yourself, Victor, so don't play the victim. You have to take responsibility for your own actions." I wasn't going to cut him any slack.

"You're right and completely justified in your distrust of me. I just want you to know that I've suffered for my sins and I'm penitent," said like the good Catholic he wasn't.

"You can put away the sackcloth and ashes. What's done is done. Hopefully, you've learned from the mistakes you made with me and you'll be faithful to your next girlfriend."

"I want to be faithful to you, *mi amada*."

"Give it up, Victor."

"Never! I will prove myself to you. I'll show you that I'm worthy of your love."

"Knock yourself out, but it won't change a thing. Now, I have to go. I'm expected somewhere at six."

"Where are you--"

"Thanks again for the orchids," I said, then hung up before he could give me the third degree about my plans for the evening.

* * *

"Feel this," Sara ordered, throwing a bolt of raspberry-colored fabric down on the cluttered table sitting in the corner of the warehouse where she worked.

Tentatively, I rubbed some of the fabric between my thumb and index finger. "It feels a little rough."

"That's because there's polyester in it. POLYESTER! It was supposed to be a high-quality nylon/spandex blend, and they send me this crap." She looked down at the cloth with an expression of revulsion that was usually reserved for the maggot-covered corpses on *CSI* . . . or sugar-free chocolate.

"I'm never using this manufacturer again. Idiots! Do they think that Serafina Swimwear is going to be hanging on the sale rack at Wal-Mart? I'd sooner walk into oncoming traffic than put my name on a bikini made from this cheap, hideous-looking excuse for a fabric."

"It'll be alright. Just sit," I took Sara by the shoulders and pushed her down on to a stool, "and take a deep, cleansing breath."

"I'm too angry to breathe. Why is everyone so incompetent?"

"It's just a little snafu. Don't let it rattle you."

She sighed. "I know. You're right. I've just been having a meltdown over everything today. I looked at a calendar this morning and realized that I've got less than two months to go until the show, and there's still so much work to be done. I don't know how I'm ever going to manage it."

"Aren't you the same girl who wrote two term papers, designed and made all the costumes for the UM Holiday Jamboree, baked twenty sweet potato casseroles for Thanksgiving dinner at the homeless shelter, and threw me an amazing surprise birthday party-slash-luau in just six days?"

"Yeah, that was me, but I took a lot of No-Doze back in college," Sara said with a self-deprecating smirk.

"No-Doze might have kept you awake, but it didn't make you clever, or focused, or talented. You're all those things naturally. And when you put your mind to it, you're capable of accomplishing great things."

"I do thrive under pressure, don't I?"

"Of course, you do." I rubbed her shoulder reassuringly. "Just keep your eye on the prize."

She glanced up at me. "You know what my secret fantasy is?"

"To make wild, hot monkey love to Johnny Depp?" I

teased her.

"No. I mean, I wouldn't mind that, but this is a work-related fantasy, not a personal one."

"Okay, so what's your secret work-related fantasy?"

"I want to wow everyone at the Miami Summer Fashion Extravaganza," she said, staring off into the distance with a faraway look in her eye. "I want to blow their minds with the sexiness and originality of my suits. I want the other designers to hate themselves because they didn't think of my ideas first. I want the fashion press to call me 'a visionary' and I want the buyers to throw fistfuls of cash at my feet and beg me to sign exclusive contracts with their stores."

"If anyone can turn fantasy into reality, it's you," I told her.

She gave me a grateful smile. "Thanks for the vote of confidence and for coaxing me back from the brink of insanity."

"That's what psychologists do."

"No, that's what great friends do." Sara rose to her feet and gave me a hug. When she pulled back, I could see the fatigue in her bleary eyes.

"You look exhausted. Why don't you take a break from all this tonight?"

"Is that an offer?"

"No, sorry, I really need to go home and get some work done. Why don't you call Matt? A quiet, romantic dinner for two is just the distraction you need."

"Matt?" Sara acted as though she didn't know who I was talking about. "Oh yeah." She started to straighten her work table. "I forgot to tell you. We broke up."

"What?!?! Why?"

"He was stifling my creative genius." She dropped several colored pencils into a coffee mug that she'd made the last time we were at Paco's Pottery.

"How'd he do that?"

"Oh, you know, he was making too many demands on my time and he just didn't get me or my work. I need to be free . . . free to create and free to experience life. I can't be tied down with some boring, left-brained guy."

Not for the first time, I wished that I could break up with guys as easily as Sara did. When she was done with a boyfriend that was it, no discussion, no angst, just 'thanks for the memories and don't let the door hit you on the ass on the way out.'

"Well, that's too bad. He seemed nice."

With a dispassionate shrug, she said, "He was, but we were just too different. What they say about opposites attracting is true. I just don't think that they can stay together for the long haul and be happy."

"That's probably why things didn't work out for me and Victor."

"Victor?" Her expression was puzzled. "He's not still bugging you, is he?"

"I'm afraid so. My continued rejections only seem to inflame his desire for me. Apparently, he likes a challenge. I got a delivery of about a zillion purple orchids from him today, along with an equally flowery note in which he praised my 'exotic beauty.'"

"The man has style; I'll give him that."

"He claims he's changed, that he's perfect boyfriend material now."

Sara stopped in the middle of stacking her scattered sketches and fixed me with a penetrating gaze. "You're not buying that, are you?"

"No, not really. But he does have to grow up and start behaving like an adult at some point, right?"

"Hmmmmm," Sara's response was non-committal.

"Do you know something I don't?"

"Well, I wasn't going to mention this, but I saw Victor at Mynt the other night. He was in the VIP room, drinking Cristal out of Leighton Meester's La Perla bra."

"She wasn't in it at the time, was she?"

"No, he won the bra from her in a game of strip limbo."

"Strip limbo?"

"Yeah, it's the new thing at clubs. Everyone in the VIP room at Mynt was playing. Adam Levine was down to his tighty whiteys when I got there." Sara pursed her lips thoughtfully as if she was flashing back to the incident. "His body is amazing, although I could really do without all those tatts. What is it with musicians and body art?"

With a frown, I queried, "Isn't Adam Levine married to Gwyneth Paltrow?"

"No, that's Chris Martin from Coldplay. Adam's one of the judges on *The Voice* and he's the lead singer of . . . oh, never mind, it's not important. What *is* important is that your ex is still a skirt-chasin', alcohol-guzzlin' sleaze with the emotional maturity of a 16-year-old, so don't believe for a second that he's changed. He's just telling you what he thinks you want to hear. He's trying to make you believe that his love for you has had a transforming influence on him."

"The only thing that's going to have a transforming influence on Victor is an STD," I grumbled.

"Exactly, which is why you need to cut this guy off, Pilar. Once and for all. Stop being nice. Stop talking to him. Stop accepting his conciliatory gifts. Stop trying to save him from himself."

Had I been doing that? Yeah, I guess I had. I always wanted to help people and believe that they were sincere. It was my fatal weakness.

"Alright, I will."

She looked doubtful. "Promise?"

"Promise. Next time I see, or hear, from Victor Liscano, I

will tell him that he's a jerk and . . ."

"And?"

"I don't want anything more to do with him."

"Excellent.   You might want to threaten him with a restraining order, too."

"But I would never--"

"It doesn't matter. The threat's enough to show you mean business." Sara threw an arm around my shoulders. "Now, how about you buy a hot fudge sundae for a struggling fashion designer? I haven't had any chocolate all day."

"That's probably why you've been acting so mental. Chocolate's addictive, you know."

"A girl's got to have a vice, doesn't she? Come on!" She grabbed me by the arm and pulled me up.

"But my work . . .," I protested half-heartedly as Sara dragged me out the door.

CHAPTER 12

"I have a date tonight," Mitch confided after we'd spent a half-hour discussing the loveless (by all appearances) marriage of his deceased parents.

"Oh, really? With whom?"

"Her name's Cynthia. I met her at the grocery store. I was keeping my eyes open for nice girls like you told me to and boom, there she was, in the produce section at Publix."

"And what was it about Cynthia that attracted you to her?" I willed him to say something other than "her knockers."

"Uh, well, she was very natural-looking. Hair in a ponytail, no makeup, and she was wearing this pretty dress with little pink flowers on it. I don't know; she just seemed different. I'm used to chicks who let it all hang out, if you know what I mean."

Indeed, I did. The beaches and clubs in Miami were full of women who liked to flaunt their assets in as little clothing as they could without being arrested for public indecency.

"So, how did you approach Cynthia?"

Smirking, he replied, "I handed her a couple of casabas and asked her to squeeze my melons and tell me if they were ripe."

"And that worked?" I was incredulous.

"She laughed and said that it was the cheesiest pick-up line she'd ever heard, but she had to admire my improvisational technique since I'd made good use of the props at hand."

"Sounds like Cynthia has a good sense of humor."

"Yeah, she seems to. And she's smart, too. She's a grad student at UM."

A fellow Hurricane? That was a point in her favor, at least in my eyes. "What's she studying?"

Mitch shrugged. "Beats me."

Baby steps, I told myself. Her name and how she occupied herself while the sun was out was probably more information than Mitch had ever collected on any of the women he'd slept with.

"So, you'll have plenty to talk about on your date tonight. What are you planning to do?"

"I don't know. I figured I'd play it by ear. What?" he questioned the disapproving expression on my face. "That's no good?"

"Some thought should go into a date, especially a first one. You want to impress this woman, don't you?"

"I guess."

"Then, show her you think she's special by taking her some place nice."

"Such as?" he asked.

"Well, you can't go wrong with dinner at a good restaurant. It doesn't have to be anything fancy or expensive; you just want to be sure that the restaurant has the right ambiance. It should be quiet so that the two of you can talk and since you don't know what Cynthia likes or dislikes when it comes to food, go to a place where a variety of *entrées* are offered."

"I don't know much about nice restaurants," Mitch admitted.

"I can suggest a few if you like?"

He nodded his assent, and I scribbled three names down on a blank piece of paper in my notebook, then ripped out the page and handed it to him. Mitch rubbed the stubble on his chin as he studied his options.

"Make a reservation. Wear something appropriate. And . . . you might want to shave."

He stopped rubbing his whiskers and looked up from the paper. "I don't know, Doc. Chicks love the stubble."

"We love it from a distance, but up-close?" I grimaced.

"Alright, I'll get a razor," he grudgingly conceded. "Dating's a lot of work."

"It's worth it when you meet the right person."

He eyed me with curiosity. "Have you?"

"Excuse me?"

"Have you met the right person?"

I averted my gaze and squirmed uncomfortably in my chair. "I don't really think that that's pertinent."

"Come on, Doc, share and share alike. I've told you a bunch of personal stuff about myself. Now, how 'bout it?" he prompted.

"Have I met the right person?" I pondered the question for a moment before replying, "I don't think so, but who knows? The perfect man could be waiting for me just around the corner or he could already be right under my nose . . ."

*   *   *

"Dr. Fordham on Line 1."

"Thanks, Margo."

I put down my pen and picked up the phone. "Ford?"

"Busy?"

"I'm just reviewing some notes. What's up?"

"I was hoping that you could come to my office for a few minutes. There's someone I'd like you to meet."

"Who?" I wondered if it could be Mrs. Dr. Ford. Maybe she'd come to meet her husband for an early dinner, and I was finally going to get a look at her? I was incredibly curious about the woman since I knew next-to-nothing about her other than her name was Sam, which was presumably short for Samantha. And I'd only found that out when I'd seen the address label on some personal mail Ford had left lying out on his desk. For some reason, Ford hardly ever talked about his wife, and I felt like pumping him for more data so early in our friendship wasn't appropriate.

"You'll have to walk the two hundred feet over here to find out."

"Give me five," I said, then hurriedly slammed the phone receiver down and dashed out my office door.

"Be right back," I told Margo as I scurried past her desk and out into the hallway.

Ford's waiting area was empty, so I proceeded to the closed door of his office. I knocked softly and tapped my foot impatiently while I waited for him to answer.

"When you said 'give me five,' I thought you meant minutes, not seconds," he greeted me with a twinkle in his blue eyes. His suit jacket was off and the sleeves of his pale purple shirt were rolled up to just below his elbows.

"You were so mysterious on the phone that I was intrigued." I leaned a little bit to my right, trying to sneak a peek into his office, but Ford's tall, broad-shouldered frame effectively blocked my view.

"Don't let me keep you in suspense then." He stepped back and waved me in.

I entered the room and glanced around, expecting to find Mrs. Dr. Ford sitting on the couch, or in the chair behind his desk, but there was no one in sight.

"So, where's this person you wanted me to meet?"

"Oh, he's here," Ford replied, the corners of his mouth twitching as if he was trying to suppress a smile.

He? Was Sam a man? If that was true, then that meant that Ford was . . . gay! How was that possible? We hadn't known each other for long, but we'd spent quite a bit of time together, sharing lunches, swapping war stories about our work, parents, and siblings. I'd never once suspected he was gay. The thought hadn't even crossed my mind. And I was supposed to be insightful for a living!

I heard the sound of a child giggling, and my eyes

traveled to the floor, where I saw a skinny boy with unruly brown hair shimmy out from underneath Ford's desk. Taking him by the hand, Ford led him over to me.

"Nate, this is the friend I was telling you about, the one who gave me all the info on the Pee Wee League. Her name's Pilar."

Ford's son gazed up at me with big brown eyes that radiated an intelligence and maturity far beyond his years.

"Pee-lar," he tried my name out, putting an unnecessary emphasis on the first syllable. "What kind of name is that?"

"It's Spanish," I told him.

He cocked his head to the side and squinted up at me. "Are you Spanish?"

"Actually, no, I'm Cuban, Chilean, and American. My sisters and I like to call ourselves 'Cubchilicans.'"

"That's funny," Nate said in a deadpan voice. "I've heard of Cuba, but not that other place . . .," He looked to his dad for help with the name of the country.

"It's called Chile."

"Like the food?" Nate wondered.

"It's spelled differently, with an 'e' on the end instead of an 'i,'" Ford explained.

"Where is Chile?" Nate directed this question to me.

"Way down in South America."

"Maybe Pilar could show you on the globe?" Ford suggested, gesturing towards the round, freestanding map of the world that resided in the corner of his office.

Nate dropped his father's hand and took a hold of mine. "Would you?" he inquired politely.

"I'd be happy to."

The three of us walked over to the globe, and Ford spun it around so that South America was facing us.

"Okay, see this long strip of land on the west coast?" I pointed to that area of the continent on the globe, and Nate nodded. "That's Chile. My mother's mother, my *abuela* Rosalinda, came from there."

"What about Cuba? Where's that?"

"Cuba is an island up here." I placed my finger on it.

"It's not far from Florida," Nate observed with interest.

"That's right, and that's why so many Cubans immigrate to Miami. There's an area of Miami not too far from here called 'Little Havana,' where a lot of Cubans live and work, and our native culture's been preserved through the food, music, and architecture."

"Sounds neat! Can we go there some time, Poppa?"

"Sure." Ford tousled his son's hair affectionately. I had a feeling that there wasn't anything he wouldn't agree to do for Nate. "But the only place we're going right now is Tee-Ball practice."

"Is today your first day?" I queried.

"Yes," Nate puffed out his little chest proudly, "I'm going to play for the Diamond Backs."

"How exciting!" I enthused. "I think that that's the same team my nephew Charlie plays for."

"It is," Ford confirmed. "Ray still had an open slot on his roster and we live near the practice field, so it worked out perfectly. Ready to go, sport?"

"First, I want to ask Pee-lar something." Nate tugged on my hand, and I knelt down on the floor so that we were eye-to-eye.

"Yes?"

"You speak Spanish, don't you?"

"I do. Everyone in my family is bilingual, which means that we speak two languages."

"There are some bilingual kids in my class, too. I'd like to learn Spanish. Would you teach me?"

"Oh, Nate," Ford put his hand on his son's shoulder, "it takes years to learn a foreign language, and Pilar's not a teacher; she's a doctor."

"She could still teach me." Nate wouldn't let it go. "I'm a fast learner."

"I'll bet you are. How about this? Whenever we see each other, I'll teach you one word in Spanish."

"Two words," he bargained.

I chuckled. "Okay, two. Your first word for today is *tortuga*. That means 'turtle.'"

"I have a pet turtle."

"I know, your father told me."

"So, Vinny is a *tortuga*?"

"Yes, very good. Your pronunciation was *perfecto*," I praised him.

"And that's your two words in Spanish. Now we need to hit the road or we'll be late for your first day of practice, and you don't want to start off on the wrong foot with Coach Castaneira."

"*Perfecto* doesn't count as a word," Nate protested.

I stood up. "Your dad's right. You should get going. Do you have your *guante de béisbol*?"

Nate's brow furrowed with confusion. "My what?"

"Your *guante de béisbol*. That's your baseball mitt."

"Did you hear that, Poppa? Baseball mitt is *guante de béisbol* in Spanish."

"I heard." Ford picked up his suit jacket and briefcase. "Now, what do you say to Pilar for being so nice?"

"Um," he thought about it for a second, "*gracias*?"

Ford frowned. "How did you know that *gracias* meant 'thank you?'"

"I was watching Univision last night. It was one of those shows where people are either yelling at each other or kissing."

With an amused snicker, I said, "A *telenovela*. My mother loves those."

Ford gave me a 'don't-encourage-him' look before addressing his son. "That's a grown-up show, Nate. I don't want you watching that channel anymore."

"But it's a good way to learn Spanish, Poppa," Nate defended his actions as his father propelled his small body through the waiting area, and I trailed behind them. "Last night, I learned *gracias* and *de nada* and *adiós* and *hazme el amor*. I'm not sure what that last one meant, but the people in the *telenovela* said it a lot."

We were out in the corridor now, and Ford was locking his office door. "'*Hazme el amor?*'" he raised an eyebrow questioningly at me.

I put my hands over Nate's ears and whispered the translation, "Make love to me."

"Oh, geez." Ford looked embarrassed, which I thought was cute. He motioned for me to remove my hands so that his son could hear him. "No more Univision, understand?"

"But . . ."

"No 'buts.' We'll get you a Spanish DVD or a book or something."

"Promise?"

"Yes, I promise. Now, let's go." He reached for his son's hand, then pulled him away.

"See you tomorrow, Pilar. Bye Pee-lar," the Fordham men bid me a hasty farewell before disappearing down the stairs.

CHAPTER 13

I was in the lobby of my office building, pushing some envelopes into the Outgoing Mail slot, when I heard a wolf-whistle coming from behind me. I turned to see Ford standing at the bottom of the stairs with a playful grin on his face. "That dress looks great on you," he complimented me.

"Thanks," I replied, crossing over to him in my espadrilles with the high wedge heel. I was wearing a halter dress the color of lime sherbet that I knew was very flattering to my curves, but it was still nice to have it confirmed by a member of the opposite sex.

"Hot date tonight?"

"Sadly, no, a family dinner. It's my mother's birthday."

"Ah, so, she's speaking to you again?"

"Yes, all is forgiven. *Mamá*'s feeling very benevolent this week. She also called a truce with my sister Izzy. So, we'll be one big, happy family at her birthday bash tonight . . . at least, that's what my mother wants all of our relatives to think."

"She cares a lot about appearances?"

"Hence, the manicure," I held up my hand so that he could see my freshly-painted fingernails, "the 30 minutes I spent in front of the mirror in my office bathroom doing my makeup, and the boutique-bought dress."

"No doubt she'll be suitably impressed."

"Yeah, we'll see. Hey, what time is it?" I wasn't wearing a watch.

Ford glanced at his. "6:23."

"She's late," I grumbled. "I told her 6:15."

"Someone's picking you up?"

"Yeah, Izzy. I loaned her my car for the day. Hers is in the shop, and she had a job interview." I strode over to the glass doors that led from the lobby out to the sidewalk and peered through them. "Damn it, where is she?"

"She probably got stuck in traffic on the causeway."

"Probably." I didn't sound convinced. "If you need to go, don't let me keep you."

"That's okay. We're eating dinner late tonight. I can stay and keep you company for a few minutes."

"How's Nate doing with Tee-Ball?" I wondered.

"The first practice went really well. He had a lot of fun and made some new friends. He really liked you by the way. He said that you were 'an interesting and informative lady,'" Ford mimicked his son's very earnest and precise way of speaking, "which is high praise coming from him."

With a chuckle, I said, "I'm glad I passed muster. 5-year-olds can be tough."

Hearing a car screech up to the curb outside, I winced, knowing that it was Izzy. I'd just put new tires on my Miata, and they hadn't been cheap. I was going to kill her if she'd worn down the tread already.

"There's my sister," I told Ford. "Come on, I'll introduce you."

He held the door open for me, and we stepped out into the stifling early evening heat. Izzy had the top down on my convertible, and the radio was blaring with what sounded like, God help me, rap music. She was so busy singing along to the somewhat questionable lyrics that she didn't even notice Ford and me as we approached the car.

"Izzy!" I screamed in an attempt to be heard over the music.

Turning towards me, she yelled, "What?" in return.

I motioned for her to lower the volume of the stereo, which she did with an annoyed expression.

"Izzy, this is my colleague, Dr. Fordham. Ford, my sister, Isidora."

"Nice to meet you." Ford stretched out his hand.

Izzy eased her Jackie O. sunglasses down her nose and gave him an appraising look over the top of them. "You're the shrink who works across the hall from Pilar?"

"That's me."

"Huh." She shook his hand, then shoved her sunglasses back up. "Are we going or what? You know *Mamá* will have a fit if we're late."

"Maybe I should drive?" There was less chance of us getting a speeding ticket if I was behind the wheel.

She heaved a beleaguered sigh as if dealing with me was such a trial. "Would you just get in already?"

"Fine." I tossed my purse in the back seat, then stood aside so that Ford could open the car door for me. He waited until I'd gotten in and put my seat belt on before closing it.

"Have fun, ladies."

"Not likely," Izzy retorted before shifting the car into gear and peeling away from the curb.

Thirty minutes later, we exited the elevator on the 15th floor of my parents' building, bickering like we were still in grade school.

"I can't believe you didn't buy *Mamá* a birthday present."

"What was I supposed to buy it with? My good looks. Hello? I'm unemployed."

"I would have loaned you the money, or you could have made her something."

"Arts and crafts?" she scoffed. "I don't think so."

We stopped in front of unit #1508, and Izzy knocked on the door.

"*Niñas!* You're finally here!" our mother greeted us with her typical theatrical flourish. "It's so late that I thought you'd decided not to come."

"Jesus, it's only five past seven," groused Izzy as she tromped over the threshold of my parents' condo.

I followed her into the foyer, where we could hear the

sounds of a party, talking, laughing, soft music, clinking glasses, filtering in from the living room, and the smells of a Cuban feast wafting in from the kitchen.

Giving *Mamá* a hug, I said, "*Feliz cumpleaños.*"

"Yeah, happy birthday," Izzy echoed my sentiments unenthusiastically.

"You look beautiful," I enthused.

"I do what I can," she dismissed the praise, but I knew that she secretly relished it.

"Look at what your father gave me." She jiggled her wrist in front of our faces.

"Stop it, you're blinding me," I teased.

Izzy gaped at the diamond bracelet. "Holy shit, that's some serious bling. It must have cost *Papá* a fortune."

"Don't curse, Isidora. It's vulgar," *Mamá* chastised her. "I'm a lucky woman. Your father is very generous."

She looked from my sister's empty hands to mine. "Neither of you has a gift for your *mamá* on her fiftieth birthday?"

"It's not your fif-"

I shot my sister a quelling glance. The last thing any of us needed was for Izzy to remind our mother what her real age was.

"Of course, we do," I said, reaching into my purse and extracting a large envelope with 'Luisa Alvarez' written in gold calligraphy on the front of it.

"Hmmmm." *Mamá* appeared less-than-impressed, but she took the envelope from me and opened it anyway.

"A full day of beauty treatments at Paradise Spa!" Her face lit up with excitement. "Oh, *niñas*, this is the perfect gift. You know how much I love to be pampered."

"We know," Izzy and I responded in unison.

"Maybe I'll try one of those warm stone massages, or a seaweed body wrap?"

"Whatever floats your boat. It's kind of stuffy in here. Is there somewhere I can put this sweater?" my sister asked.

"Just hang it in the closet." *Mamá* motioned towards the door to her left.

"I can't wait to use this gift certificate! My friend Judith is going to be *so* jealous. She's been dying to go to Paradise ever since it opened, but her husband, that old penny-pincher, said, 'No, it's too expensive. Just give yourself a facial at . . .'" my mother suddenly gasped and grabbed her throat like she couldn't breathe.

"What is it? What's wrong?" She hadn't been eating or drinking anything, so I knew she couldn't be choking.

"It's--, it's--," she sputtered and stabbed the air violently with her index finger.

I figured out she was trying to tell me to look over my shoulder, so I did. "Oh, crap," I muttered when I saw what had her so agitated.

Izzy had removed her lightweight sweater, and her back was turned to us while she placed the cover-up on a hanger in the foyer closet. She was wearing a fairly demure sundress that tied around her neck and bared only a few inches of her back. However, enough flesh was exposed so that the upper portion of a large black cross, wreathed in red roses, could clearly be seen on one shoulder blade.

". . . a tattoo!" my mother shrieked in a voice so piercingly high-pitched that I expected to hear the sound of wine glasses shattering in the next room. Instead, most of my immediate family came running into the foyer, practically tripping over each other in their rush to see what all of the fuss was about.

"Don't panic," I told everyone as I hurried over to my younger sibling. "I'm sure it's just one of those temporary tattoos, and it'll wash off in a couple of days." I licked two of my fingers, then used them to rub frantically at the blight on Izzy's back.

"Ew, stop that!" She tried to reach around and smack my hand. "I don't want your spit on my skin."

"Too bad." I continued to rub.

Shoving me away, she announced to the crowd at large, "It's a permanent tattoo. Marco gave it to me. He's a tattoo artist."

"Who's Marco? Another deadbeat boyfriend? I'll bet this one doesn't have a high school diploma either," my sister, Ana, jeered.

"Shut up," Izzy retorted petulantly.

"That's real mature. When are you going to grow up and stop embarrassing everybody?"

I stepped in to referee. "Ana, please, don't antagoni--"

"I'd rather be immature than a judgmental bi--"

"Girls!" My father moved between my contentious siblings. "Is this any way to act on your *mamá*'s birthday? Look how you've upset her."

All three of us glanced over at our mother, who was tearfully clutching a rosary (where had that come from?) and mumbling a prayer for strength in Spanish.

"There, there, Luisa, it's not that bad," my aunt Drina attempted to comfort her.

"'Not that bad!'" my mother wailed.

"*This*," she grabbed Izzy by the arm and spun her around so that her tattooed back could be seen by all and sundry, "is not that bad?"

There was a collective gasp of horror, followed by several of my older relatives making the sign of the cross.

"Coooooool," my eldest nephew, George, moved closer to Izzy so that he could get a better look at the design on her shoulder. "I wanna get a tattoo."

"No!" both of his parents shouted, and Ana pulled him back to the safety of the group.

"It's sacrilegious; that's what this is." My mother pointed

at Izzy's body art. "Can you imagine what Father Ramirez is going to say when he hears about this? The whole family will be excommunicated. We'll be disgraced! We'll have to change our names and leave the country!"

"Now, Luisa, I'm sure it won't come to that," my father sought to mollify her.

"*Mamá*, *Papá*, may I see you in the kitchen please?"

"I don't think this is the time, Pilar."

"It's the perfect time, *Papá*. Please, it'll only take a minute." I was insistent.

The rest of the Alvarez clan eyed the three of us with curiosity as I gently pushed my parents into the kitchen and closed the door behind us.

"*Ay*, Arturo! This is such a nightmare! What did I ever do to deserve this? All I wanted was a nice party for my birthday, and now, it's ruined! *Ruined!*" My mother threw herself into *Papá*'s arms with a loud sob.

"It'll be alright, *mi querida*. This doesn't have to leave the family. We'll find a good plastic surgeon for Isidora, and she can have the tattoo removed."

Mamá pulled back from my father's reassuring embrace. "Removed? Are you *loco*? If she has it removed, then she'll have a scar. I don't want my baby to have some big, ugly scar on her back. No decent man will ever want her if she's disfigured."

"The two of you may not realize this, but you're giving Izzy exactly what she wants."

"Eh?" They both turned towards me with looks of surprise as if they'd forgotten I was in the room.

"Why do you think Izzy pulls these stunts?"

My question was met with blank stares, so I answered it myself. "She wants to get a reaction out of you, even if it's a negative one, because it shows that you care. Izzy has been doing this since the day she was born. When she was little and wanted attention, she would break something valuable, or throw a temper tantrum, and that always served her purpose. *Papá* would be quietly disapproving, while you, *Mamá*, would resort to hysterics."

My mother's back stiffened. "Of course, you would blame Isidora's bad behavior on us. It's always the parents' fault. Isn't that what they teach you at psychologist school? But what about you? You're Isidora's older sister; she lives with you. You're supposed to look out for her and keep her from making stupid mistakes like getting a religious symbol tattooed on her back!"

So, now it was my fault?

"Izzy is an adult, and I can't babysit her 24/7. Even if I'd known that she planned to get a tattoo, I couldn't have stopped her. Just like I couldn't stop her from getting her navel pierced."

"She got her WHAT pierced?" *Mamá* screeched, while *Papá* blanched.

Smooth, Pilar, very smooth, I admonished myself.

"Let's just focus on the problem at hand, okay? We need to go back out to the party and act like Izzy's tattoo is no big deal."

"But it is a--"

I held up a hand to silence my mother. "We are giving Izzy too much power in this family, and she's using it to disrupt and cause turmoil. We need to break this unhealthy cycle of outrageous action/over-the-top reaction. If we want Izzy to change, then we have to take the wind out of her sails, starting now."

"I agree," my father weighed in on the subject.

"You always agree with Pilar," *Mamá* pouted. "Why can't you side with me for once?"

"We are all on the same side," I assured her. "Now, do you think you can keep your emotions in check for the rest of the evening, no matter what Izzy says or does?"

"If I must." She played the martyr complete with stoic expression and quivering lip.

"Good, let's go back out and enjoy the party then."

I went through the kitchen door first. The murmur of whispered conversation stopped, and all of our relatives fixed inquisitive gazes on me. "Dinner's almost ready, everyone. Doesn't it smell delicious?"

"*Mmmmmm.*" "*Yes.*" "*I'm sure you've outdone yourself, Luisa.*" All of our relatives gave their vocal support.

"Ana, Drina, I could use your help in the kitchen," my mother said, and both women moved in that direction.

"Why don't we head out to the terrace?" *Papá* suggested, then ushered our remaining family members out of the foyer.

I pulled Izzy aside.

"There's bound to be a cool breeze out on the terrace, and I'd hate for you to get a chill. So, why don't you wear this?" I grabbed her sweater from the hall closet and shoved it at her. I was hoping that if she covered the damn tattoo up, everyone would just forget about it. Out of sight, out of mind, as the old saying goes.

"It's like 90 degrees outside," Izzy protested.

I took the pale pink cover-up from her and draped it over her shoulders. "Wear it, or I'll throw all your stuff out on the street when we get home tonight," I muttered through clenched teeth.

"You wouldn't--"

"Try me," I dared her and saw a flicker of uncertainty in her dark eyes. Was I serious? Did she want to push her luck with me and run the risk of ending up homeless?

The doorbell rang.

"I'd better get that."

Izzy slipped her arms into the sleeves of her sweater. "See you outside," she said, then scurried off to join the other partygoers on the terrace.

So, I had my bratty sister under control. My mother, the High Priestess of Histrionics, had promised to remain calm for the next few hours, and I was about to sit down to a flavorful five-course meal (I couldn't wait to wrap my taste buds around *Mamá's Flan de Coco y Ron*, that's a Coconut Rum Flan for you non-Cubans.)   Things were definitely looking up.

I opened my parents' front door with a welcoming smile at the ready.   But when I saw who was standing out in the corridor, my face fell.

"You have got to be kidding me," I groaned.

CHAPTER 14

"What are you doing here, Victor?"

He was dressed in one of his nicest suits, a pale gray number that hung just so on his solidly-built frame, with a crisp white shirt that provided a sharp contrast to his dark tan, and he held a box wrapped artfully in gold paper and ribbons, so the answer to my question was obvious. But I still wanted an explanation from him.

"I'm here for Luisa's party, of course. She invited me."

"She's dead," I muttered.

"What was that, *mi amor*?"

"Never mind." I took the box from him. "I'll tell *Mamá* that you dropped this gift off, but you couldn't stay."

"Lying to your mother on her birthday? Tsk, tsk." Victor shook his head in a reproachful manner, then snatched the present out of my hands.

With a groan of frustration, I made another grab for the box, but he stepped back so that it was out of my reach. Not wanting to play keep-away with my ex for the rest of the night, I placed my hands on my hips and scowled at him.

"You can't stay, Victor. It would be completely inappropriate. This is a family gathering, and *you* are not family."

"Ah, but Luisa disagrees and since this is her special day, I think we should respect her wishes."

"Victor!" My meddlesome mother sashayed up to the door, carrying a plate of *Papas Rellenas* (stuffed potato balls.)

"I was wondering when you were going to show up. Why are you standing outside? Pilar, where are your manners? Let my guest in."

Grudgingly, I stood back so that Victor could enter the condo.

He kissed *Mamá* once on each blush-streaked cheek, then said, "This is for you," and presented her with his birthday gift.

She beamed like a teenage girl who'd just been given her first corsage by her date to the junior prom. "Aren't you sweet? Isn't he sweet, Pilar?"

Tiresome, relentless, and purposely dense would have been the words I would have chosen to use when describing Victor, but to each their own.

"Just put your box on the table over there, and I'll open it later. We're about to eat out on the terrace, so follow me."

"Please, let me carry that plate for you, Luisa. It looks heavy, and your hands are so delicate." Victor poured on his own special brand of unctuous charm.

"Such a gentleman!" My mother gave me a meaningful look that said, '*See, what a prize you're missing out on?*' as she handed Victor the appetizers.

I rolled my eyes in return.

We walked out to the terrace, where the rest of the family was waiting for us, and I gave quick hugs and kisses to the relatives I hadn't had a chance to greet earlier.

"Please, everyone, take your seats," the party's hostess instructed. "I've got name cards at each place setting. Victor, you're on my left, and Pilar is next to you."

I would have rather sat between Rique, my weirdo cousin who smelled like the pet store where he worked, and my great-uncle Juan, who had to gum his food because he refused to wear his dentures, but I did as I was told like a good daughter.

The first three courses passed without incident, but things got dicey a few minutes after the *Ropa Vieja con Arroz* was served.

"So, Isidora, have you found a job yet?" Aunt Brigida asked in between bites of the beef. It was an innocent enough question and I don't think she was trying to start trouble, but Izzy immediately got defensive.

"No, but I've been looking."

"You had an interview today, didn't you?" my father inquired.

She shrugged. "Yeah, but it was a total waste of time."

"Theirs, I'm sure," my older sister snarked.

Izzy let her fork drop, and it hit her china plate with a clang so loud that it made me and several other people at the table flinch. "And what's *that* supposed to mean?"

"Well, you're not exactly ideal employee material."

"What would you know about being ideal employee material? You've never worked a day in your entire life. You went straight from *Papá*'s house to your husband's. The only things you know how to do are: get married and get pregnant."

"Being a wife and mother is very hard work," Ana said indignantly.

"Not if you job-share with a housekeeper and a nanny."

Ana had no immediate rebuttal for that, so Solana, the eldest of my father's three sisters, took the opportunity to jump into the conversation. "Izzy, if you'd like to come and work at the bakery with me, there's an opening. The girl who was working the cash register on weekends just quit."

Solana owned a very profitable *panaderia* in the heart of Little Havana. Her Cuban bread was so good (perfectly crispy crust - warm and doughy on the inside) that it was almost legendary. Devoted customers lined up outside her shop at the crack of dawn every day so that they could buy loaves fresh from the oven when she opened at 7AM.

"*Gracias, tia*, but I don't think I'm cut out for--," 'a job that would require me to wear a hair net' probably would have been the rest of that sentence if my mother had let Izzy complete it.

"You shouldn't be so quick to say 'no,'" she advised. "Solana could teach you to bake, then you'd have a trade to fall back on if you don't find a husband. Like Pilar. She's got her psychology practice, which is a good thing because it doesn't look like she's ever going to get married."

I heard my cousin Sancha snicker.

"You might be wrong about that, *Mamá*." Izzy winked at me from across the table. "Pilar's got a new man in her life."

"No, I don't," I mumbled because my mouth was full of plantains.

"Oh, come on, Pilar. You talk about him all the time," she teased me.

Victor turned to me, his face darkening as if a storm cloud was passing over his head. "What's she talking about? Who's this man?"

"I have no idea. Isidora, how many glasses of Sangria have you had?" If this was my sister's way of diverting attention away from herself, I did *not* appreciate it.

"Only one. Don't be shy, Pilar. Tell everyone about Ford. That's what she calls him," she clued my family in, "but his full name is Dr. Jonathan Fordham."

"Oooooo, a doctor," all three of my aunts murmured their approval.

"Is he a real doctor, or just a psychologist like you?" my bitchy cousin Nita wanted to know.

"Ford's a medical doctor - a psychiatrist. But he is NOT my man."

"I should hope not." Victor threw his napkin down on the table with disgust. "That *gringo*'s not worthy of you."

"What do you know about Ford and his worthiness? You only met him once."

"Once was enough!" he declared. "I disliked him instantly."

"Because he was talking to me."

"Because he has no respect for women. He pushed you into a wall and injured your beautiful head. He could have killed you."

My father eyed me with concern. "Is this man abusive, Pilar?"

"No, *Papá*. What happened was an accident that was mostly my fault. If I hadn't been on the phone being harassed by Victor," I paused to make a face at my former boyfriend, "I would have been paying more attention and I would have seen Ford coming up the stairs. He felt really badly about bumping into me."

"He has shifty eyes." Victor lodged another complaint against the man he perceived to be his rival.

"Shifty, as in deceitful and untrustworthy? You must be confusing Ford with yourself," I retorted hotly. "There is nothing shifty about Ford's eyes. They are very expressive and full of honesty and intelligence."

"What color are they?" Sancha wondered.

"They're this really vibrant shade of blue . . . like Daniel Craig's."

"Ooooooo, Daniel Craig," several of the women at the table cooed.

"Pilar likes Ford," Izzy said in a singsong voice.

"Well, of course, I like him. He's a nice person, as well as a friend and a colleague, but that's as far as it goes."

"Why?" *Mamá* asked, leveling dark eyes at me.

"Huh?"

"If this Dr. Fordham is such a wonderful man, why don't you want to be more than friends with him?"

I stabbed some shredded meat with my fork. "Because he's married."

"You're involved with a married man?" Nita made it sound scandalous.

"My relationship with Ford is perfectly innocent and

above board. It is possible for two mature people of the opposite sex to have a platonic relationship based on common interests."

"Not really," Izzy muttered, and I shot her a 'shut up or die' look. "What? I'm just saying that in my experience . . ."

"Which is vast." Ana couldn't resist making a dig.

Izzy ignored her. ". . . in my experience, a man and a woman can't be 'just friends' forever. Sooner or later, an attraction will develop, and then the clothes will start flying."

"I know you're not familiar with the concept, Izzy, but there is a little thing called 'self-control,'" Ana asserted.

"Self-control has its limits."

"She's right." *Dear God, had my mother just agreed with Izzy?* Somebody needed to call the Pope because I was pretty sure that that qualified as a miracle. "You're playing with fire, *mija*."

"You should listen to your mother," my aunt Drina counseled.

"Yeah, you don't want to be a homewrecker," Sancha moved closer to her rat-faced husband and placed her hand over his as if she needed to protect him from me.

"You're all being ridiculous," I grumbled irritably. "I talk to Ford about work, and we go out to lunch once in a while--"

"Who pays?" Nita queried.

My brow furrowed with confusion. "What?"

"Who pays when you go out to lunch with this Ford guy?"

"Well, he does--"

"Aha! Then, it's a date!" my cousin crowed triumphantly.

"A man should always pay for the meal. It's the gentlemanly thing to do," said an old, shaky voice from the other end of the table.

"Yes, thank you, Uncle Juan. Ford's just being polite. And besides, he makes a lot more money than I do, so he can afford to treat."

"Ah, so your business isn't doing well, and you're hurting financially." Nita and her sister, Sancha, shared a sly smile. I knew that it would make their day if I admitted to having trouble with my practice. They had a combined IQ somewhere in the double digits, and it had always galled them that I'd achieved a higher level of education than any other woman in our family and now had a prestigious career.

"On the contrary, business is booming. I just got three new clients this week and I'm totally overwhelmed with referrals." If my nose grew, I had no one to blame but myself.

"Are you sure, *mija*? I'd be happy to give you a loan," my father offered.

"Thank you, but there's really no need."

"You should take the money. Supporting Izzy has got to be a huge financial burden."

"She doesn't support me, you cow!"

"Isidora, don't call your sister a cow," *Mamá* admonished. "She just lost 17 pounds at Jenny Craig and she looks very pretty."

Ana turned crimson, and Nita, who needed to lay off the *merengues* herself, smirked.

"If she'd marry me, Pilar would never have to worry about money again," Victor chimed in.

Solana turned to Drina. "Was that a marriage proposal?"

"Oh, *mija*!" My mother clapped her hands together excitedly.

I was just about to pinch myself in hopes that the self-inflicted pain would rouse me from the nightmare I found myself trapped in when Aunt Brigida crinkled her nose and asked, "Did you leave something in the oven, Luisa?"

"I turned the oven off twenty minutes ago. You're imagining it," my mother said with a dismissive wave of her hand. "Where is Pilar's engagement ring, Victor? If you're going to ask for my daughter's hand in marriage, you're going to need a ring."

"Well, I hadn't really--"

"I smell smoke, too," Rique remarked, which came as a shock since it was the first time he'd spoken all evening.

Everyone started to sniff.

"It doesn't smell like burning food . . ."

"No, you're right," Sancha concurred with her sister. "It's more like burning fabric."

I glanced quickly around the table, silently counting small, dark heads. There were only two. "Where's George?"

Ray lifted the tablecloth and looked underneath it for his son. When he shook his head, Ana rose to her feet and screamed, "George Arthur Castaneira!" at the top of her lungs.

He suddenly appeared at the sliding glass door that led from the terrace to the living room. He had black smudges on his face and he was hiding something behind his back.

"Yes, *Mamá*?"

"What have you been up to?"

"Nothing. I--" The high-pitched beep of a fire alarm interrupted him, and pandemonium ensued as everyone leapt to their feet and stampeded into the living room amidst cries of "*Call 911!*," "*Try not to breathe in the smoke!*," and "*I'm too young to die!*" the latter coming from my mother, of course.

CHAPTER 15

"And I can't replace it. That sofa was custom-made, and the fabric came from Italy. It's not even available anymore."

"Yeah, you mentioned that." In fact, it was the fourth time in the last ten minutes. "So, you can't get the same sofa. I'm sure you'll find another one that's just as beautiful and unique. Didn't *Papá* say you could spend as much as you want?"

"I don't want another sofa. I already had the perfect one, and the whole living room was decorated around it. If I get a different sofa, then I'll have to change everything, the rugs, the artwork, the accessories, even the plants!"

"But you love having a big project to work on. Think of all the fun you'll have shopping and arranging things." If I was lucky, my mother would be so busy redecorating her living room that she wouldn't have the time to make any more of these early-morning calls to my office.

"I can't even go into the living room right now; it's too upsetting. I don't know what was in that fire extinguisher your father used, but there's this grainy yellow powder covering everything. And the room still smells like smoke. We'll probably never be able to get rid of that odor," my mother's voice broke as she was overcome with emotion. "I told Arturo that we should move."

"That's a bit drastic, don't you think?" I took a sip of the *Café con Leche* that I'd bought on the way into work. It had finally cooled off and was the perfect temperature.

"You don't know how I've suffered, what painful memories that living room holds for me now."

"Your grandson set your sofa on fire. It's not the end of the world. At least, no one was hurt."

"I was hurt! My property was damaged, and my party was ruined. But I guess you don't care about any of that.

You don't care about my mental anguish."

"Of course, I care, *Mamá*." I used my index finger to scoop some whipped cream off the top of my caffeinated beverage, then stuck it in my mouth.

"Ana doesn't care. She's not even punishing George."

"Well, it was an accident. George didn't mean to torch your furniture."

"He meant to light that bowl of potpourri on fire, didn't he?"

"Yes, but he thought the fire would be contained--"

"Well, he was wrong, wasn't he?"

It had been a gross miscalculation on the part of my firebug nephew. The bowl of potpourri had been sitting on the coffee table next to Victor's present, and the flames from George's "experiment" had reached high enough to ignite the long, dangly ribbons hanging over the edge of the box. Nothing burns faster than paper, so the gift had quickly turned into a small bonfire. George had done his best to put it out with a pillow from the sofa, but that had caught fire, too. Fortunately, he'd tossed the blazing pillow back onto the couch before it could burn his hands.

"Cut the kid a break. He said he was sorry."

"Bah! He doesn't know the meaning of the word. That little arsonist isn't allowed back in my house until he learns some respect."

Was that supposed to be a punishment?

"I've told Ana again and again that her children are out-of-control, that they need to be disciplined, but does she listen? *No.* She just lets them do whatever they want. Did I tell you that Charlie and David locked their nanny in the laundry room the other day? She was stuck in there for three hours! I'm surprised she didn't quit."

"I'm sure they were just playing--"

"Playing like a couple of juvenile delinquents. Ana needs

to start spanking those boys."

"You never spanked us." Probably because she didn't want to risk breaking a nail.

"And that's where I made my biggest mistake as a parent. Maybe your sister wouldn't have turned out so spoiled and willful if I hadn't spared the rod when she was little."

Were we still talking about Ana or had she just segued into another one of her rants about Izzy?

"*Mamá*, I'd love to debate the merits of corporal punishment with you," a blatant lie and we both knew it, "but my 9:00 is going to be here any minute--"

"And work is more important than your family, I know." She tried to put a guilt trip on me.

"My patients pay me to help them with their problems; my family doesn't," I reminded her.

"If you'd stop being so stubborn and marry Victor, you could quit that silly job of yours and--"

"Goodbye, *Mamá*." I ended the call before we could get into another argument about my party-crashing ex and began to sort through the stack of files on my desk, looking for Leonard Dyson's. He was a patient who'd randomly picked my name out of the yellow pages and had called for a consultation the week before.

Patient's name: Leonard Dyson
Age: 29
Occupation: High school bus driver (resigned from job recently)
Diagnosis based on initial evaluation: Patient is suffering from acute anxiety due to recent financial windfall (he won the Florida Lotto jackpot of $8 million.) As patient was raised in a series of lower middle-class foster homes and has worked hard to make ends meet his entire adult life, he has no idea how to handle money and is overwhelmed by his

newfound wealth and the accompanying responsibilities, which has resulted in identity confusion. All of his issues are symptomatic of Sudden Wealth Syndrome.

Goal of therapy: Help patient adapt to and embrace the changes in his life and bolster his confidence so that he can move forward and make intelligent, well-informed decisions about his finances and the people he comes into contact with.

"How are you doing today, Leonard?" I asked the overweight black man who sat on my couch looking down at his hands, which were neatly folded in his lap. Leonard seldom made eye contact because he didn't like being the focus of anyone's attention. I had traced this shyness back to his childhood when it had behooved him to fade into the woodwork at his various foster homes lest his caretakers think that he was too much trouble and send him back to Child Welfare.

"I'm okay, I guess," he responded in a subdued baritone.

"You don't look okay. Would you like to tell me what's wrong?"

"I haven't been sleepin' very good. I keep havin' these nightmares . . ."

"About?" I prompted.

"Big dollar signs chasing me. They chase me everywhere and I try to get away from them, but they're always too fast."

"What happens when they catch up to you?"

He shrugged. "Different things. Sometimes I trip and fall down, then they all pounce on me, which makes me feel like I'm being smothered. Last night, I dreamed they chased me off a cliff and I just kept fallin' deeper and deeper into this dark, bottomless pit."

"Interesting." I jotted down a few notes on my pad. "The dollar signs are representative of your wealth which your subconscious feels there is no escape from."

"What can I do to make the nightmares stop?"

"We need to continue working on your issues with money. Once you realize that it's not something to be feared, and that you're in control of it and not vice versa, then the nightmares will go away."

Leonard sighed sorrowfully. "I miss my job."

"That's understandable. You worked for the school district for how long?"

"10 years."

"10 years," I mused. "That's a remarkable accomplishment. Not many people stay with the same job for that length of time."

"It was a great job. I woulda stayed with it forever if they hadn't made me quit. When I won the Lotto, they said I should give up my job so that someone who needed it could have it. I wish I'd never bought that stupid lottery ticket. I want things to go back to the way they were."

"Change is always scary, Leonard," I said in a placating tone, "but you won that lottery for a reason, and you have to look at this as an opportunity to do something wonderful with your life."

"Like what?" He picked at a loose thread that was hanging from the sleeve of his tattered green shirt. It was telling that the man had become a millionaire months ago but had yet to buy himself any new clothing.

"Well, you could go back to school and study something that's always interested you like . . . computers or photography or creative writing."

"I was never a good student," he dismissed the idea.

"Alright, then you could travel and meet new people and learn about other cultures. With all of your money, you could go anywhere and do anything. Maybe a tour of the pyramids in Egypt? Or a ski trip to Switzerland? Is there a foreign country you've always wanted to visit?"

He scratched his head thoughtfully for a minute before responding, "No, I'm not very adventurous. I like stayin' at home."

I couldn't fathom why since Leonard was still living in his crummy one-bedroom apartment in Opa-Locka, one of the poorest and most crime-ridden parts of Miami. "If home is where your heart is, then why not buy yourself a nice house? It's a buyers' market right now and purchasing a home could be an investment in your future."

"I don't know," he vacillated. "I'm comfortable where I am."

"You wouldn't like to have more room? Or a swimming pool? Or one of those big-screen hi-def TVs?"

He played absentmindedly with a button on the section of his shirt that covered his large, Buddha-like belly. "Not really."

"Okay, so you don't like to spend money on yourself. Maybe you could find fulfillment and purpose in your life by using your lottery winnings to help other people?"

A big smile spread across Leonard's chubby-cheeked face. "Yeah, that's what I wanna do, help other people, like my brother."

With a frown, I queried, "What brother? I thought that you were an orphan?"

"I am. I'm talkin' 'bout my foster brother, Miguel. We lived in the same house for a coupla years when we were teenagers."

"So, you were close with Miguel when you were kids and you've kept in touch over the years?"

"Well, we were never really close. He was always kinda mean to me. He stole my stuff and made fun of me because I was fat. I hadn't seen or heard from him in almost 13 years, but he called me up outta the blue last week."

I had a sinking feeling I knew where this was going.

"Miguel said that he's been goin' through a rough time and he needed some--"

"Money?"

"Yeah, how'd ya know? He said he needed money so that he could go to drug rehab out in California."

"How much did you give him?"

"$5000 . . . but he's gonna pay me back," Leonard assured me. *Poor, gullible man.*

"Did he tell you when, or leave you a forwarding address?"

He shook his head.

"Miguel took advantage of you, Leonard. He didn't need to go all the way to California to get help with his drug problem; there are plenty of good rehab facilities right here in South Florida. He probably wanted that money for more drugs. And I bet that he'll be back on your doorstep in a month or two, asking for another hand-out."

"Oh, I hope not." Leonard started to bite the cuticle on his right thumbnail nervously. "I have a hard time sayin' 'no' to people."

"I know you do, and that's another thing we need to work on. It's important that you learn how to stand up for yourself so that you can protect your money from people who don't have your best interests at heart. I think we should try a little role-playing . . ."

When my session with Leonard was over, I walked him out to my empty waiting room and sent him on his way with the same encouraging words I offered all my patients, "Don't worry; everything's going to work out."

Once Leonard was gone, I plopped down on the corner of Margo's desk and said, "I wish I had his problems."

I waited for my receptionist to respond with one of her snappy one-liners, but she just stared back at me with an uneasy expression on her face.

"What?" I asked, finding her silence unnerving.

"I just opened today's mail."

"And?"

"I think you'd better take a look at this." She handed me a high-quality ivory envelope, and I looked to see who the sender was. *Corman & Mackelvy Management Co.* The name didn't ring a bell, but the letter looked official, which inexplicably filled me with a sense of dread. Despite that, I removed the letter from the envelope and read it.

"Oh, God," I murmured when I was done.

"I know. It's bad. I'm sorry, honey." She gave my arm a sympathetic squeeze.

Pulling it together, I stood up and announced, "I've got some phone calls to make. I'm free for the rest of the morning, right?"

"Yeah, the Scolaris are on vacation for a few weeks, so they won't be coming in."

With a nod, I walked back into my office and closed the door behind me.

Two hours later, I was slumped over my desk, contemplating the irony of having a patient who had gobs of money he didn't have any use for while I had a desperate need for cash and no way of acquiring it, when I heard the squeak of my door being opened and the sound of carpet-muffled footsteps approaching.

"Pilar?" Ford queried tentatively. "Are you okay?"

"I'm depressed," I mumbled without moving.

"Maybe you need a psychiatrist?" he joked.

"Unless you're offering your services *gratis*, I'm going to have to pass since I'm about to be destitute." I extended my hand, in which the life-destroying letter I'd received earlier was clutched and felt Ford pry it loose from my fingers.

The room was silent for a minute while he perused the notice from the management company that represented the new owners of our office building. "Jesus, I can't believe they're raising your rent $1000 a month. Don't you have a lease where you're locked in for a specific amount?"

"I signed a six-month lease, which is up on the 1st of July, so the new owners can raise the rent as high as they want any time after that," I addressed my reply to the top of my desk as I didn't have the will or the energy to lift my head. "The previous owner was a friend of my father's, and he gave me a deal on this office. I've been paying below fair market value since I moved in."

"Have you talked to this management company? Maybe the owners would be willing to work with you? Surely, they'd rather keep a good, long-term tenant than deal with someone new who might be less stable and not as respectful of their property."

Deciding that I was being rude, I finally gazed up. "I spoke with the head honcho at Corman & Whoever. He contacted the owners on my behalf, and the bottom line is - they don't care. There's no loyalty, no sympathy. They just want a tenant who can pony up $4500 a month. What's with the glasses?" I wondered about the black wire-frame specs with the rectangular lenses that were perched on the bridge of Ford's nose.

"I fell asleep with my contacts in Saturday night and scratched my corneas. So, now I have to wear these damn things," he touched the side of his glasses and grimaced, "until my eyes heal."

Propping my chin up on my hands, I considered his eyewear. "They make you look really . . .," *sexy* was the word I wanted to use - I'd always had a thing for men who wore glasses, dating back to Luke McCabe, my four-eyed first boyfriend. *Mmmmmm, he was a great kisser* - but sexy wasn't a word that should be applied to a platonic, male friend, so I settled for, "smart."

His right eyebrow shot up questioningly. "I didn't look smart before?"

"Sure, but those glasses take it to a whole new level. You look Mensa-smart now, like you might start reciting Einstein's Theory of Relativity any minute."

"Nate said that they make me look like a 'doofus.'"

I chuckled, then remembered that I was supposed to be in mourning for my soon-to-be-defunct practice.

"Oh, why am I laughing?" I groaned and laid my head back down on my desk. "My life is over."

"No, it's not. Come out to lunch with me, and we'll discuss your options."

"What options?" I raised my eyes back to his. "Become a bank robber? Start smuggling Cuban cigars? My cousin Felipe already does that and," I dropped my voice to a whisper, "it's not as profitable as you would think."

Ford sat down in the chair facing my desk. "You could get a business loan from your bank."

"Great. More debt. Just what I *don't* need."

"Why not go to your father? He's helped you out before, hasn't he?"

"He's done enough. I need to make a go of this business on my own now. I don't want to be a *gorróna*. A freeloader," I translated when Ford gave me a quizzical look.

"So, you need to find a way to bring in more revenue."

"Right, but how?" I drummed my fingers while I thought about it. How could I advertise and bring in new patients without spending a lot of money? *Billboards?* That would probably cost a fortune. *Flyers?* Too cheesy. *Mail-outs?* Maybe, but I'd have to buy a list of names and addresses, pay someone to design the artwork for an ad, and incur the expense of postage.

With a sigh of defeat, I said, "I could just admit that I got in over my head with this office. If I scaled back and moved into a smaller space in a less ritzy part of town . . ."

"No, no," my companion shook his dark head, "you don't want to do that."

"I don't?" I leaned forward on my elbows, curious to know why Ford thought me moving was a bad idea. Could it be that he liked having me around?

Sliding back from the edge of his seat, Ford gave me an all-business reply. "Moving to another office wouldn't be smart from a financial standpoint. You'd have the expense of putting down deposits for the new space and to get your phone lines and utilities hooked up. Plus, there'd be the moving truck and labor and--"

I held up my hand to stop him. "Point taken, thank you. I'll just have to stay here and figure something out."

"Maybe if you made a list of your monthly expenditures, both personal and business, you could find a way to cut costs?" he suggested helpfully. "Also, make a list of any monies you have, checking and savings accounts, stocks, CDs, IRAs. You might be able to cash something in without any major penalties."

"I do have some savings I could dip into," I noted. "There's not much in there, but I should be able to cover the difference in rent for a month or two, which will buy me some time to--"

My phone buzzed.

I hit the intercom button. "Yes, Margo?"

"Your sister's on Line 1."

"Which one?"

"Izzy."

Didn't I have enough on my plate already? The last thing I needed was my irresponsible little sister heaping another one of her trivial problems on it.

"Take a message."

I was about to switch the intercom off when Margo said,

"I don't think you can call her back where she is."

Sighing irritably, I inquired, "And where's that?"

"Jail."

CHAPTER 16

My sister had finally gone and done it. She'd gotten herself arrested. And not just on some minor charge like Shoplifting or Driving Without Insurance. Oh no, she'd been accused of committing Grand Theft Auto, Resisting Arrest, and something else that was considered a felony - why couldn't I remember . . . oh, yes, Aiding and Abetting a Fugitive, the "fugitive" being her skeezy boyfriend, Marco. Who knew that he was a wanted man with three outstanding arrest warrants to his name? Not Izzy. She'd sworn on the lives of our nephews that she'd been completely clueless. When Marco had picked her up in a brand-new red Ferrari, she'd believed his assertion that he'd borrowed it from a friend. Why would she doubt him? He'd never lied to her before, and she'd never witnessed him doing anything criminal.

All that had changed an hour later when they'd been cruising up I-95 and two police cars had appeared out of nowhere with lights flashing and sirens wailing. Izzy had told Marco to pull over to the shoulder, but he'd refused, putting the pedal to the metal in an attempt to elude the law. Fortunately, his escape had been thwarted by a pile-up around Exit 16. Marco had been forced to slow down to a standstill, and that's when Miami's finest had moved in to apprehend him, along with my hysterical sister, who'd screamed "police brutality" as the cops tried to shove her into a squad car (in actuality, the only one who'd inflicted any bodily harm at the scene of the arrest was Izzy, and Officer Alex Muñiz had the teeth marks on his hand to prove it.)

So, my wayward sibling had been fingerprinted, and a mug shot had been taken of her tear-streaked face. When I'd arrived at the jail 90 minutes after she'd been thrown into a holding cell, she was still sobbing because being booked had been the "most humiliating and traumatic experience" of her life. As angry as I'd been, I had felt kind of sorry for Izzy - she'd obviously been through quite an ordeal, and I knew that she hadn't willingly committed any of the crimes she'd been accused of. But I'd felt even sorrier for myself when I'd had to empty out my savings account in order to retain the services of a defense attorney, then hand the deed to my house over to a sweaty bail bondsman with ketchup stains on the front of his shirt - all so that I could get Izzy released.

"Doctor Alvarez?"

"Huh?" The sound of Kyle Kotowski's voice came as a bit of a shock to me. I'd been so busy thinking about my own problems that I'd forgotten I was supposed to be listening to his.

Sitting up straight in my chair and focusing on my patient, I said, "I'm sorry. What was your question again?"

"Does my left hand look bigger than my right?" He held them both out for my analysis.

"Well . . ." They looked identical to me, but I decided to humor him since I felt guilty about ignoring him for most of the hour. "Maybe a little bit."

"Not just a little bit! Look!" He placed his hands palm-to-palm. "My left hand is clearly 1/8 of an inch larger than my right. I measured them both, so that figure is accurate. Did you know that an enlarged hand is a sign of Acromegaly?"

So, we were still on diseases that started with the letter A? I despaired that I would have my first gray hair long before we reached the Bs.

"I've never heard of Acromegaly."

"Of course not. There are only 816 cases of Acromegaly reported in the US every year. It's a very rare hormonal disorder that causes excessive growth."

"And you think you have Acromegaly just because one of

your hands is slightly larger than the other one?"

"That's just the most noticeable symptom. I have plenty of others: headaches, excessive sweating, skin tags . . ."

My mind wandered once again to the Izzy situation. I really wanted to call my father and tell him what had happened, but Izzy had begged me not to. She'd said that her lawyer would "fix things," and that there was no reason to upset our parents with the news of her arrest. Respecting her wishes was one thing, but I couldn't shoulder the financial burden of her legal expenses alone, not if I wanted to save my practice. I thought about calling Raymond. He was family and an attorney, which qualified him to offer legal advice, and he'd probably be willing to subsidize the 'Keep Isidora Out of the Slammer' fund if I asked. Of course, there was no way that Raymond would do anything without consulting his wife first (my brother-in-law was a great guy, but he was totally whipped), and Ana was incapable of keeping her mouth shut. No doubt she'd break a land-speed record running to the phone to call our mother and tattle on Izzy.

". . . and I'm pretty sure that my spleen is swollen." Kyle tentatively touched the area under his ribs on the right side.

"Your spleen's located on the left side, and it's higher," I told him.

"Oh." He moved his fingers over to that side of his torso and began to cautiously press down on the flesh there.

"As for your hands, it's perfectly normal for one to be larger than the other. You're left-handed, aren't you?"

"So?"

"So, it makes sense that your left hand would be bigger since you use it more. There's more blood rushing to that hand, and the muscles are getting more exercise, which can make it increase in size. I'm right-handed and see," I placed my hands together palm-to-palm as Kyle had done earlier, "my right hand is larger than my left."

He leaned forward and gazed at my hands with rapt fascination, "Oh, wow, there's a huge difference between your hands. The right one is at least 1/4 of an inch bigger than the left one. You should have that checked out, Doctor Alvarez. You might have Acromegaly, too."

"Neither one of us has Acromegaly, Kyle." The tone of my voice betrayed my growing irritation.

"You don't know--"

"I do. Now, let's change the subject, shall we?" Not waiting for him to answer, I forged ahead, "I want you to find a hobby."

"A hobby?" The word appeared to confuse him.

"Yes, 'an activity or interest pursued outside one's regular occupation and engaged in primarily for pleasure,'" I quoted the dictionary.

"I guess that researching medical conditions is my hobby."

"It's a fixation, not a hobby," I corrected him. "You need to find something you enjoy doing that has nothing to do with your health, or computers." I excluded computers because Kyle worked with them all day.

"Okay, but why?"

"You need to take the focus off yourself and your body. Redirect all of the energy that you expend worrying about your health into something that makes you happy. If you do that, I think you'll see an improvement in your stress levels, as well as your physical well-being, and that is our goal here, right?"

"I suppose." The prospect of getting better made him look glum.

"Excellent. Why don't you give it some thought and bring a list of hobbies that sound interesting to you, preferably ones that will get you out of the house and interacting with other people, to our session next week?"

"Our time isn't up already, is it?" Kyle looked anxiously at his watch.

"I'm afraid so."

Truth be told, I was relieved. My session with Kyle had been the longest 50 minutes of my life. I had a short supply of patience and I couldn't concentrate with the Izzy mess hanging over my head. I had no idea how I was going to get through the rest of the day, feeling as out of sorts as I did.

I managed, but it wasn't easy. I was so exhausted from the stress that I almost nodded off in the middle of my session with Mr. Stearne (a malcontent who hated his shrewish wife, his dead-end job, and his receding hairline and liked to spend our time together every week complaining about all of it.) And I was sorely tempted to smack Lori Bryant, who was in a particularly whiny, woe-is-me mood, when she arrived late for her appointment. So what if she didn't have a boyfriend? At least, she had a steady income and a roof over her head, and none of her family members were looking at 10 to 15 in the State Pen.

I let Margo go right at 5:00 because I knew that she had special plans with Saul (It was the anniversary of the day they'd first said "I love you" to each other - how sweet was that?), then I settled in at my desk to work on the list of assets and expenses that Ford and I had talked about. I was hoping that if I got organized and figured out exactly where I stood financially, I wouldn't feel so overwhelmed. Unfortunately, the list ended up being horribly unbalanced with three times as many entries on the EXPENSES side and very little of worth in the ASSETS column. It was official: I was in dire straits.

A knock on my office door came just as I was toying with the idea of crawling under my desk and curling up into the fetal position. "Yes?" I called out.

The door opened and in walked Ford, holding the hand of his adorable, Yankees baseball hat-wearing son.

"Nate!" I rose from my chair. "What a nice surprise!"

"*Hola*, Pee-lar!" the little boy greeted me.

"I'm glad you're still here," Ford said. "I have a favor to ask."

"Whatever you need, the answer is 'yes.' I owe you big time for yesterday."

Ford really had gone above and beyond the call of duty when I'd gotten Izzy's upsetting call. Not only had he cancelled all of his appointments for the rest of the day and accompanied me to the police station, he'd helped me find a good lawyer, stayed with me through the bail hearing, and even offered to loan me money. He'd been incredibly calm, comforting, and supportive every step of the way. I don't know how I would have gotten through it without him. He'd been a real lifesaver.

"You don't owe me anything. I was happy to help," he assured me.

Smiling, I wondered, "What's the favor?"

"If you've already got plans, I'll understand. I know it's a lot to ask at the last minute . . ."

"Poppa needs you to babysit me," Nate cut to the chase as 5-year-olds had a habit of doing.

"Well, that sounds like fun. For how long?" I looked to Ford.

"An hour or so. I got an emergency call from a patient who's off her meds and having a meltdown. Her husband's bringing her in now and my receptionist's already left for the day, so I don't have anyone to look after Nate while I'm in session."

"We were supposed to be going to Marty's Crab Shack for dinner," Nate groused. He was obviously not happy about the change in plans.

"Hey," Ford tilted his son's chin up so that he could see his eyes, "Boys' Night Out is still on. I just have to help this patient who's not feeling well first."

"In the meantime, maybe you and I could go down to the beach?" I offered up a consolation prize.

"Don't you mean '*la playa*?'" Nate gave me a cheeky grin.

"You've been working on your Spanish." I was impressed.

"Poppa got me this book on Spanish vocabulary." He pulled a small picture book out from under his arm to show me. "I'm not sure about some of the pronunciations though."

"We can work on those together. Let me just grab my purse." I returned to my desk and pulled my handbag out of its bottom drawer.

"Would it be okay if Nate and I got some i-c-e-c-r-e-a-m while we're down at the beach?" I questioned Ford.

"Ice cream!" Nate clapped his hands together and jumped up and down excitedly.

"I warned you that he could spell," Ford muttered as I came to stand beside him.

I winced. "Sorry. I'm used to my less advanced nephews."

"Ice cream, Poppa. Please?" Nate begged.

"It'll spoil your dinner."

"No, it won't. I have a really big appetite."

"Okay," Ford gave in with a sigh, "one small scoop, but no weird flavors. Remember what happened with the Peppermint Bubblegum Surprise."

"Yeah," he scrunched up his face with disgust, "it made me super sick."

"That's right, and I was the one who got the surprise when you projectile vomited on me." Ford shuddered at the memory.

"What's the Spanish word for vomit?" Nate questioned

me.

"Don't answer that," Ford ordered under his breath. "You two should really get going. My patient will be here any minute."

"Why don't you call me on the cell when you're done and I'll let you know where we are, then you can come and pick Nate up?" I suggested as Ford walked us out of my office.

"Perfect. Now, Nate," he took his son by the shoulders when we reached the corridor, "I want you to . . ."

"Don't worry, Poppa." He moved away from Ford and slid his little hand into mine. "I'll take good care of Pee-lar."

Ford chuckled and brushed Nate's cheek affectionately with the back of his hand. "I know you will."

And we were off to the beach. It had rained a few hours earlier, which had cooled things off a bit, so it was an almost-bearable 85 degrees. Nate and I stopped at a tourist-filled ice cream parlor along the way and bought a couple of cones. Having apparently learned his lesson from the Peppermint Bubblegum Surprise, Nate elected to get a scoop of good, old, reliable Strawberry, while I decided to live *la vida loca* and get Mint Chocolate Chip. As we continued our walk to the beach, we fought a losing battle with the ice cream, which melted faster than we could lick it. By the time we reached the shore, our tongues were frozen to the point of numbness, and our hands were covered with sticky goo (green in my case, pink in his), but we were smiling happily. We took off our shoes and spent the next forty-five minutes wading in the warm Atlantic, talking about the things that 5-year-old boys found fascinating: amusement parks, baseball trading cards, Harry Potter books, and sea creatures of all shapes and sizes.

"What's whale again?" Nate asked as we sat down on an empty bench on the boardwalk.

"*Ballena.*"

"*Ballena*," he repeated. "And shark is *tiburón*?"

I nodded.

"Maybe I'll be a marine biologist when I grow up," Nate declared. "A bilingual marine biologist."

"I think you're smart enough to be anything you want to be."

"That's what my momma said. Do you wanna see a picture of her?"

Was he kidding? I was dying to see a picture of Ford's wife. Of course, I didn't want to appear over-eager, so I shrugged and affected nonchalance. "Sure."

He reached into the back pocket of his khaki shorts and extracted a small wallet; it was one of those waterproof billfolds that closed with a strip of Velcro. My nephew, Charlie, had one just like it. Nate opened the wallet and pulled a folded-in-half 3x5 out of the pocket where most people would store their cash. He uncreased the photo and stared at it for a few seconds before handing it to me.

"Poppa took that last year when we went to Coney Island," he explained.

Sure enough, I could see a ferris wheel in the background of the photo, but the focus of the shot was a hot dog-holding Nate whose mom had her arms wrapped lovingly around him. It looked like they were both on the verge of laughing about something. Ford had probably told them to say something silly like "wiener" before snapping the picture.

What can I say about Samantha Fordham? She was undeniably attractive with her heart-shaped face, fair skin, long, honey-colored hair, and dark, wide-set eyes. It was easy to see why Ford, or any man, would fall in love with her. But it wasn't her physical beauty that struck me most when I saw her for the first time; it was the fact that she looked soooooo . . . nice. You could tell by her warm smile and the tender expression in her eyes that she was just a really nice, caring person - the kind of person you'd like to have as a sister or a friend.

"She's very pretty," I told Nate who beamed at my approval of his mother.

"Do you think I look like her?" he gazed up at me questioningly.

I cupped his face in my hands and studied it intently for a moment. "I think you look like the perfect combination of your parents. You've got your mother's kind eyes and your father's nose and lopsided grin."

"Momma said that Poppa's grin was 'hard to resist' when she first met him," Nate related as he tucked his prized photo back into the pocket of his wallet. "They met in the cafeteria at the hospital where they worked. Momma was an O.R. nurse back then. O.R. means Operating Room."

"I didn't realize that your mother was a nurse." Mrs. Dr. Ford just became more interesting all the time. I was about to ask Nate if his mother was still working in her chosen field when my cell phone rang.

"That must be your father." I pulled the phone out of my purse and checked the Caller ID. "Why don't you answer it? Just press that button." I pointed to the one with the blue line on it.

Nate did as I instructed and brought the phone up to his ear. "Poppa? It's me, Nate. Pee-lar and I are having so much fun. We had ice cream and we walked on the beach. I found a really neat shell. It's shaped like a cone, and it has these cool brown markings. I think it might be a Fly-Specked Cerith. Can we check the *Compendium of Seashells* when we get home?

CHAPTER 17

"So, how are things going with Cynthia?"

Mitch gave me a vacant look. "Who?"

"Cynthia, the cute grad student you met in the grocery store last week," I attempted to jog his memory. "You went on a couple of dates, and things seemed to be going well . . ."

"Oh, yeah, Cynthia. That didn't work out. I broke up with her."

Damn, that was quick. I'd gotten lectures from my mother that had lasted longer.

"Are you sure that you gave the relationship a fair chance?"

"I tried, Doc, I really did, but the woman was boring with a capital B. Do you know what she's studying at school? Management Science."

"I'm not familiar with that field."

"It's got something to do with business," he elucidated as best he could. "All I know is that Cynthia spent just about every minute we were together droning on and on about stuff like applied statistics and mathematical modeling. It was a total turn-off."

"I'm sure that that didn't stop you from sleeping with her." The acerbic comment slipped out before I could stop it.

Instead of taking offense, Mitch chuckled. "What can I say? She was hot. Too bad she didn't have the personality to match her looks."

"Yes, too bad," I murmured as I jotted down some thoughts about the demise of his relationship with Cynthia.

"Are you disappointed in me?"

I was actually. I'd thought that I was making some progress with Mitch, but he appeared to be reverting back to his old man whore ways.

"The question is: Are you disappointed in yourself?" I

turned the query back on him, which was the oldest trick in the shrink book.

Mitch chewed his bottom lip thoughtfully for a moment. "I guess I should have taken Cynthia's feelings into consideration. Having sex with her when I knew that there wasn't any future for the relationship, then dumping her the next day wasn't very nice."

"It's good that you realize your mistake, and hopefully you'll think twice before doing it again."

"I'm not making any promises," he said with an impudent grin that made his dimples deepen.

I sighed inwardly and made another note in my pad . . . *Patient still has a long way to go.* On the bright side, that was $300 a week I could depend on for a while, and my bank account needed all the help it could get.

* * *

"Your sister's a pain-in-the-ass," Sara stated bluntly as she circled a model, who was standing in the middle of her showroom wearing an electric blue two-piece that looked like it was made out of suede.

"I know, but I couldn't leave her in jail."

"It might have done her some good. If she had to suffer some consequences for her actions once in a while, she might drop that spoiled wild child act of hers. No, no, this is all *wrong*. Where are your boobs?" Sara gestured at the human hanger's almost-concave chest. "Have you lost weight since I hired you? Because I need curvy bods in my bathing suits, not skeletons."

She walked behind the model and started to pull on her bikini bottom. "You're not filling this suit out at all. It's puckering up everywhere."

"I guess I could eat something," the model suggested

timidly.

"Well, there's a wacky idea," Sara's voice dripped sarcasm. "What do you think, Pilar?"

"I'm always pro-eating."

"I need some fattening food over here NOW!" Sara screamed, then snapped her fingers in the air imperiously.

Almost immediately, two male assistants came running with arms full of packaged snacks. Sara took a green box from one of them and scrutinized it. "Healthy Choice makes cookies! Are you kidding me? I'll bet they taste like cardboard." She tossed the box over her shoulder, and it barely missed my head as it whizzed by.

"I want something with lots of sugar, calories, and fat. Where are the Girl Scouts when you need them? I'd kill for a Thin Mint!"

A flunky tentatively offered her a bag of Double Stuf Oreos.

"Now this is what I'm talking about." Smiling happily, Sara ripped open the cellophane. She crammed two of the chocolate-and-cream sandwich cookies into her mouth before shoving the bag at the model with the protruding hip bones. "Eat those and don't come back until you've gained at least four pounds. Next!"

A voluptuous blonde Amazon emerged from behind a folding screen in a sexy red one-piece.

"Wow! That looks great!" I marveled at the suit.

"If I cinch it in at the waist a little bit, it'll emphasize her hourglass figure even more." Sara took some straight pins out of the small cushion she wore on an elastic band around her wrist.

"So, how are you going to handle this lack of funds problem?" she queried as she pinched up some fabric and started pinning.

"Beats me. It's not like I have a lot of options. I can't go to anyone in the family without ratting out Izzy and I can't get a loan from the bank without collateral."

Sara eyed me sympathetically. "If I had an extra penny to my name, you know I'd give it to you."

"I know and I appreciate that, but you've got your own troubles."

She frowned worriedly. "Thanks for reminding me. If I don't make a serious impression on the buyers at this show and give my investors a return on their money, I'll probably end up in a sweatshop in Mumbai, making fifty cents an hour."

"Things are going to work out."

"For both of us," she assured me.

"Okay, that's it, Nicola. Be careful when you take the suit off. I don't want you to get stuck by any of the pins."

The statuesque woman strutted back to the changing area.

Putting her hands on her hips, Sara pivoted around to face me. "So, your relatives and the bank are out. Who else can you turn to in your time of need?"

"Well, there is one person . . ." Although I didn't say his name, Sara was quick to figure out who I was referring to.

"Oh no, Pilar!" She grabbed me by the arms. "Don't do it. Don't sell your soul to that bed-hoppin', Gucci Pour Homme-wearin' devil. Become an exotic dancer. Sell your O-negative to a blood bank. Anything but that."

"Victor's not as reprehensible as you think. Morally bankrupt, yes, but all that matters to me now is that he's got cold, hard cash, and he'll probably be willing to help me out."

"No doubt, but what's the Latin Lothario going to want in return?" She arched a brow inquisitively.

"It would just be a short-term loan, a business transaction."

"With no strings attached? Yeah, right," she scoffed.

"I can handle Victor."

"He'll probably be the one handling you."

"Have a little confidence in me, please." I pulled my cell phone out of my purse and dialed in Victor's number before I could lose my nerve.

"*Mi amada*, what a wonderful surprise! I was just thinking about you, your soft skin, your beautiful lips, your--"

UGH Was he on the make 24/7?

"Victor, I need to see you."

"At last, you've come to your senses!"

"I need to see you to discuss an important business matter." I wanted to be sure he understood that this get-together had absolutely nothing to do with romance.

"But, of course. I'm here to offer whatever assistance I can."

I was counting on it.

"I'll come by the restaurant in an hour."

"*Hasta luego.*"

I switched the phone off and was met with a disapproving look from my best friend.

"I hope you know what you're doing," she said.

So do I, I thought uneasily. *So do I.*

* * *

"Pilar! Long time, no see," the manager of Liscano's greeted me with a warm hug that probably would have made Victor apoplectic if he'd been witness to it.

"Javier, it's so good to see you. I like the goatee." I playfully chucked his chin where the new facial hair had grown.

"Angel's not so thrilled," he confessed. "She's threatening to divorce me if I don't get rid of it."

I got a mental image of Javier's tiny firecracker of a wife

standing in the middle of their kitchen with a baby on one hip and a toddler clinging to her skirt, while she cursed out her spouse in Spanish and hurled dishes at him like lethal frisbees, and it made me laugh. "I guess you'd better shave then."

"Are you here to see Victor?" Javier wondered.

"Yes, we're meeting to talk about business." I felt compelled to make that perfectly clear. I didn't want Javier or anyone else in the restaurant to think that there was a reconciliation in the works.

"I'll let him know you're here." Javier moved over to the phone at the hostess stand, picked up the receiver, and dialed in the extension to Victor's office.

"Boss, Pilar is . . . okay, I'll tell her." Hanging up, he turned to me. "Victor said to go on back to the office where the two of you can have some privacy."

Privacy? That was the last thing I wanted to have with my handsy ex.

"Tell him that I prefer to meet out here in the restaurant." Where there were lots of people, and I didn't have to worry about him pouncing on me.

Javier picked up the phone again and relayed my counter-offer to Victor. He listened to the other man's response, then covered up the mouthpiece and said, "He insists that you come back."

"Well, I insist that he come out."

Javier hesitated, obviously not keen on transmitting my message, and I could hardly blame him. Victor never reacted well when he didn't get his way. In fact, he was the biggest hissy fit thrower I'd ever known and that included all of the children in my family.

Heaving a beleaguered sigh, I commanded, "Give me the phone," and Javier happily surrendered it.

In a sweet, cajoling voice, I said, "Victor, if you come out here and join me at a table, we can order drinks and have some dinner. I'm starving."

"But I have a surprise for you here in my office, *mi querida.*"

"I don't want a surprise," I muttered through gritted teeth.

"If you don't want my surprise, then I don't want to talk business with you."

He was blackmailing me? That slimy, manipulative son of a--

"Okay, fine, I'll come back to your office." It galled me to capitulate, but what else could I do? I wasn't going to get my money by arguing with Victor on the phone all night.

So, back to his office I went. As I maneuvered my way through the crowded area around the bar, I received appreciative glances from several attractive men who were clearly on the prowl. Normally, I would have ignored them, but knowing that Victor wouldn't like it, I gifted each of them with a flirty smile.

When I reached the door to Victor's office, I took a moment to compose myself, then I knocked. My erstwhile boyfriend answered, looking every inch the suave player he was, his black hair slicked back with at least two bottles of gel (*YUCK* I loathed it when men put product in their hair.), and his pale yellow shirt unbuttoned halfway down so that an enticing (or so he thought) strip of his toned, suntanned chest could be seen. At least, he wasn't wearing any gold chains around his neck, and for that, I was grateful.

"Pilar, *mi amor.*" He kissed my hand and I let him, then he slowly pulled me through the doorway.

Upon entering Victor's office, I immediately saw what my "surprise" was. The room was dark except for the soft glow of light coming from four floating candles that were being used as the centerpiece for a small table. The table was covered with a beautiful red cloth, which had been hijacked from the restaurant, and dishes filled with colorful, delicious-smelling food were spread out on its surface.

"I had the chef prepare all your favorites," Victor said as he led me to the feast. "Artichoke Bruschetta, Coconut Scallops, Chimichurri Beef Tenderloin, Mojo Grilled Chicken Breast, and for dessert--"

"I didn't come here to eat, Victor," I asserted, sliding my hand out of his.

He frowned. "But you said you were 'starving' not two minutes ago."

"I lost my appetite." I couldn't very well tell him that my hunger had just been a ploy to lure him out to the restaurant.

"Well, this is very disappointing." Victor sulked. "I went to a lot of trouble to set this dinner up for you. I thought that you'd enjoy a good meal after a long day at work."

It was a nice gesture and I hated to see a grown man pout, so I yielded. "I suppose I could eat a little bruschetta."

"*Bueno!*" Victor held out a chair for me.

"But I want you to turn on the lights and turn off the music first."

Did I forget to mention the music? Since I'd entered the room, the sultry sounds of Chris Isaak's "Wicked Game" had been emanating from the speakers of Victor's expensive CD player. This was a track off of my ex's "special" disc of romantic tunes, or as I liked to call it, "Songs to Seduce a Gullible Woman By." If memory served me correctly, the next track on his playlist was Marvin Gaye's "Sexual Healing," and there was no damn way I was going to break bread with Victor while listening to that.

"But you look so beautiful by candlelight," he protested, and I gave him my fiercest, 'don't-mess-with-me' look.

I took a seat as he flipped on the lights and killed the make-out music.

"Better?" he queried as he sat down across from me.

"Much."

"Please, help yourself to whatever you like. I have some Chilean Merlot." He reached for a bottle of red wine.

"Nothing alcoholic for me, thanks." I needed to keep my wits about me. Wine and Victor Liscano were too dangerous a combination.

"Bottled water?"

I nodded my assent, and he poured some in my wine glass.

"About my reason for wanting to see you . . ."

"Are you sure you don't want something else to eat?" Victor asked as he gazed disparagingly at my plate. "Some bread with a little dip on it is hardly a proper dinner. Why don't you have some of the scallops?" He pushed the seafood dish towards me.

"I'm fine, thanks." I pushed it back.

"Andreas will be so upset. He made these scallops with extra spicy sauce just for you."

"Can we focus on something other than food for a minute, please? I've got a major problem, problems plural actually, and until they're resolved, eating is not my top priority."

"Then, tell me what these problems are, and I will make them disappear."

I placed my elbows on the table and leaned forward. "What I'm about to say is highly confidential, so I need you to swear that you will not breathe a word of it to anyone, especially my parents."

"Ah, Pilar, I am honored that you want to share your secrets with me, that you are willing to put your trust in me once again." He reached for my hand, but I pulled back before he could capture it.

"This has got nothing to do with our romantic relationship, Victor. I am confiding in you as a friend. Now, can I rely on your discretion or not?"

"May God strike me dead with a bolt of lightning and let vultures make a meal of my charred remains if I ever betray you."

Those terms seemed agreeable to me, so I proceeded.

"Izzy was arrested on Monday."

"*Dios mio!*" He threw his hands up in the air. "Why?"

"It's a long and involved story. Suffice it to say, that the charges are very serious, and she could end up doing jail time if her lawyer can't get them dropped or convince a jury that she's innocent."

"And your family doesn't know about any of this?"

I shook my head. "Izzy didn't want to involve Ana or our parents. I bailed her out of jail and got her a good defense attorney, which pretty much wiped me out. On top of that, I received notice that the rent on my office has been raised $1000 a month effective immediately. I'm just so overwhelmed by it all. I want to do right by my sister, but I can't bear to lose my practice. You know how much it means to me, Victor, how hard I've--"

He held up his hand. "Say no more. What's mine is yours."

"Really?" I hadn't dared to hope that getting a loan from my former lover would be so easy.

With a shrug, he said, "What good is my wealth if I can't use it to help the people I love?"

Victor Liscano, the altruist? This was a side of him I'd never seen before. Maybe if he'd shown it to me sooner, our relationship wouldn't have failed?

He got up from his chair and came over to kneel down in front of me. "Tell me how much money it will take to put a smile back on your beautiful face."

"I hadn't really thought of a specific amount. I just need enough to cover the hike in my rent for a few months while I work on building up my clientele, and then there are Izzy's legal expenses. She's promised to get a job so that she can help out with those, but--"

Victor placed his hands over mine. "Ten thousand? Twenty? Fifty?"

My mind reeled. "How about five?"

"I can go to the bank in the morning and get you cash."

"You don't have to do that."

"Anything for you, *mi cariña*." Victor's brown eyes radiated warmth and sincerity. Wow, I had really underestimated him. He wasn't just a shallow, self-centered taker; he was a decent man who was capable of giving out of the goodness of his heart.

"Thank you so much for this, Victor. You've really come through for me."

On impulse, I hugged him. He wrapped his arms around me, giving me a gentle squeeze in return, and I have to admit it felt good. I was always the pillar of strength, the one my patients, friends, and family leaned on, but there Victor was providing me with support, both financial and emotional, and it felt like such a huge relief. I was happy, grateful, hopeful about the future . . . of course, all of these positive sensations were quickly replaced by irritation when he began to nuzzle the nape of my neck.

Before I could tell him to cut it out, he'd unhooked the back of my bra with one smooth flick of his wrist and was reaching up the front of my blouse to grab . . . well, I'm sure that you can guess which part of my anatomy he was aiming for.

I shoved the furtive groper away with such force that he fell backwards on to his butt.

"What the hell do you think you're doing?" I screeched as I jumped to my feet and struggled to close my bra clasp.

"I was trying to comfort you, *mi amor*."

"By removing my undergarments?" I was incredulous.

He stood and used his hand to brush the lint from the carpet off the seat of his expensive trousers. "I am giving you $5000."

"And you think that that entitles you to sex?"

He pursed his lips thoughtfully. "It is a lot of money."

"Which I had planned to pay you back with interest, you oversexed creep! God!" I started to pace back and forth. "I can't believe how stupid I was! I thought that you were being nice, that you really wanted to help me, but you were just trying to buy your way back into my bed."

I picked my purse up off the table and prepared to leave.

"Pilar." He took a step towards me, looking contrite.

"Save it. You've disappointed me for the last time, Victor."

Turning my back on him, I stormed out of the office and slammed the door shut behind me.

"Men . . . ARGH!" I groaned aloud with frustration and got some frightened looks from a couple of guys sitting at the bar.

CHAPTER 18

"Your sister Ana's on Line 2," Margo told me as I walked into the office carrying my breakfast in a McDonald's bag. "She said that she's been calling your cell phone, but it keeps going straight to voice mail."

"Oh, crap," I mumbled the epithet to myself. I'd obviously forgotten to turn my cell on when I'd gotten into the car. Or maybe it was on and the battery was dead because I'd forgotten to recharge it again? I'd been so distracted lately I was becoming downright ditzy.

"I'll take it in my office," I said, heading in that direction.

"Ana?" I put her on speakerphone so that I could have my hands free.

"Pilar, finally!" I could hear the sound of my nephews fighting with each other in the background. "I've been trying to reach you all morning. First, I called the house and woke up Izzy, who was her usual charming self. Then, I tried to catch you in the car."

"Yeah, I heard." I dropped my briefcase and purse on the floor. "Sorry. My cell phone must be out of juice. What's up?"

"I'm calling about *Mamá*."

Oh, brother. I sat down and removed the lid from my coffee cup, figuring that I was going to need some caffeine to get me through this conversation.

"What about her?" I dumped two creams and a sugar into the dark liquid and used a plastic stirrer to mix it all together.

"She's sick." The high-pitched shriek of a three-year-old almost pierced my eardrums. "Charlie, don't pinch your brother," my sister ordered.

"Really sick, or nobody's-paying-me-any-attention-so-I-need-to-fake-a-crisis sick?" I drank some coffee and winced when it scorched the tip of my tongue. *Great*, now I wasn't going to be able to taste my food.

"Really sick. I got concerned when I realized this morning that I hadn't heard from her in a couple of days. George, where do you think you're going with that butcher knife? Give that to me and go put a DVD in for your brothers. They're giving me a headache."

"Come to think of it, she hasn't called me since Monday either." The absence of hysterical rants and critical commentaries on my life had been quite pleasant actually.

"And that's totally bizarre, right? Unless she's mad about something, *Mamá* usually calls us both every day."

"Well, she was in a snit about the whole burning couch incident, and I wasn't very sympathetic . . ." I reached into the McDonald's bag and pulled out my Egg McMuffin and hash browns.

"She didn't even mention that when I called her this morning, so she must be over it."

Not likely. I was sure that my mother would be telling the tale of her arsonist grandson ruining her fiftieth birthday party at every family gathering until the day we buried her, and then she'd probably have *'Luisa Escobar Alvarez, Loving Wife and Mother, who lost the will to live due to the tragedy that befell her beloved sofa on 6/6/12'* etched on to her headstone.

"What'd she say then?"

"Not much. Just that she has some kind of flu."

"Well, there you go. Nothing to worry about. She'll be fine in a few days." I squirted some ketchup on to the crispy end of my fried potatoes, then bit into them.

"I offered to drop by and bring her some soup this afternoon, but she said 'no.' She thinks she might be contagious and she didn't want me to catch anything and take it home to the kids."

"That was thoughtful . . .," and completely out-of-character for my mother, who loved to be waited on hand and foot when she was ill and didn't generally concern herself with the welfare of her servants.

"It just seemed weird to me. Maybe what's wrong with *Mamá* is more serious than the flu, and she's trying to keep it from us? When I spoke to her, she sounded sort of spacey . . . like she was drugged or something."

"She probably just took one of those over-the-counter flu medications that make you drowsy." I chomped down on my egg sandwich.

"You should call her, Pilar. You're the closest thing we have to a doctor in this family."

"Even if I had a medical degree, I couldn't diagnose her over the phone."

My intercom beeped.

I swallowed the sip of coffee I'd just taken and said, "Hold on," to my sister.

"Yes, Margo?"

"Your 8:00 is here."

My 8:00? Oh right, I had a new patient scheduled for my first appointment.

"Give me two minutes, then send her in."

I stuffed some more hash browns into my mouth before switching back to Ana. "I've got to run. There's a patient waiting," I mumbled.

"But--"

"I'll check in with *Mamá* later. I promise."

A child started to wail on the other end of the line.

"God, I hate parent/teacher conference days! Having all three boys home is just a nightmare. What happened, baby? Oh, my God! Charlie, did you Super Glue your brother's hands together? Why would you do something like that? It's alright, David. *Mamá* will get the sticky glue off."

"Try nail polish remover," I suggested.

There was a knock on my door, which made me jump. "Be right there," I yelled. "Ana, I'll call you tonight."

Disconnecting the speakerphone, I grabbed the trash can underneath my desk and swept my half-eaten breakfast into it. I wiped my greasy hands off on a napkin, then hurried to the door. I opened it to find a tall, sharp-featured brunette in a power pants suit.

"Hello," I greeted her. "I'm Dr. Alvarez. Sorry to keep you waiting. I was on the phone."

"I understand. I run a successful business myself. Ariane Wylie," my new patient introduced herself, extending a well-manicured hand as she did so.

"Nice to meet you," I shook her hand. "Please, come in."

Closing the door behind her, I said, "Have a seat," gesturing towards the couch.

Ariane sat down on one of my plump sofa cushions and rubbed her hand across its textured fabric. "This is nice. It's Kreiss, right?"

I reached for my steno pad and pen. "You know your furnishings. Are you an interior designer?"

"No, I'm in commercial real estate." She pulled a small gold case out of the front compartment of her pricey-looking, leather handbag, flipped it open, and extracted a business card, which she handed to me.

I scanned it quickly and saw that she was the president of Wylie Realty Corp.

"My company handles prime commercial real estate listings and offers investment property services. I founded WRC less than five years ago, and it's already the sixth most profitable, female-operated business in South Florida."

"That's very impressive." She made me feel like a serious underachiever.

"It took a lot of blood, sweat, and tears to reach the level of success I have."

"I can imagine." I jotted down the words '*workaholic, driven, and goal-oriented.*'

Ariane's handbag started to vibrate. I looked at it with a puzzled expression.

"That's my BlackBerry. Excuse me." She pulled the handheld device out of her purse and checked the incoming e-mail message.

"Ha! They call this an offer? Cheap SOBs trying to lowball me." She used her thumbs to type in a fast reply, then shut the phone off and returned it to her purse.

"Sorry for the interruption. Where was I? Oh yes, my work is everything to me, Dr. Alvarez, and that's why I'm here. You see, I've been having some personal problems that are crossing over into my professional life."

"How so?"

"Long story short. I've been married twice. My first husband was twenty years my senior and rich. We divorced after four years because he was a controlling bastard. I got a healthy settlement and used that to start my business. I focused on WRC to the detriment of my social life until last year when I met Julio at a Christmas party that was thrown by one of my clients."

"And Julio was a friend of your client's? A business associate?"

"He was a waiter."

"I see," I murmured with an understanding nod of my head, which is what all psychologists do when they're not sure how to respond to something that a patient's said.

"As you can imagine, Julio and I had absolutely nothing in common. He was 12 years younger than me, he'd just moved here from Colombia, and he could barely speak English, but he was gorgeous and eager to please if you know what I mean. So, I thought, 'Why not? I deserve a fling.' Hot sex turned to love, or, at least, I thought it did, and a month later we were husband and wife."

"That's quite a story." In fact, it was more engrossing than anything I'd read in a while.

Ariane smoothed out a non-existent crease on the leg of her black trousers. "Unfortunately, there was no happy ending. We hadn't been married for long before Julio began to show his true colors. He had no ambition, no desire to better himself . . . he just wanted to lay by my pool all day and get loaded on expensive rum. We had argument after argument about his laziness and his drinking, but he refused to get a job. He said that I was the one with all the money, so I should support him. And when I refused to continue giving him an allowance, he started stealing things around the house - jewelry, objets d'art, electronics - and selling them."

"You must have felt very violated and betrayed."

"I did. It was terrible. I kept threatening to throw Julio out, but he'd always talk me out of it. He'd give me some sob story about growing up dirt-poor in Colombia, blah, blah, and I'd feel sorry for him. That all ended when I came home early from a meeting one afternoon and found Julio in the Jacuzzi with two whores. And by 'whores,' I don't just mean girls with loose morals. I mean, actual straight-from-the-street-corner, get-paid-to-bang-strangers whores. I was so irate that I just lost it. I pulled out the high voltage stun gun I carry for protection, turned it on, and hurled it at the water."

My jaw dropped.

"Oh, don't worry." Ariane waved a hand dismissively. "I didn't electrocute anybody, although I wouldn't have been sorry if I had. That little weasel deserved to have his balls fried. But, sadly, my aim was off, and I overshot the water, which gave Julio and his skanks a chance to jump out of the Jacuzzi. I picked up the stun gun and chased them out to the street. Julio's girly screams of terror every time I came *thisclose*," she indicated an inch with her thumb and forefinger, "to zapping his wet, naked ass are one of my most cherished memories."

"So, where do things stand between the two of you now?"

"I filed for divorce, but Julio is being a greedy bastard. He signed a prenup that entitles him to a cash settlement of $20,000, but of course, that's not enough. He's lodged charges of spousal abuse and he wants my Jaguar, half of everything that's in the house, and alimony for ten years as recompense. So, either I pay up, or he drags my name and reputation through the mud in a court of law.

It's so unfair!" She pounded a fist on her knee indignantly. "We weren't even together for six months, and he thinks I 'owe' him a living? He's nothing but an opportunist, a sleazy, useless, self-serving opportunist. I hate that man with every fiber of my being and I hate myself for ever getting involved with him. I lay awake at night and think about how happy I'd be if Julio got hit by a bus, or someone dropped a piano on his head. I could make it happen, too," Ariane assured me with a cold smile that sent a chill up my spine. "It would actually be cheaper for me to hire a hit man to do away with Julio than it would be to keep on paying my team of divorce lawyers to fight him."

"But, you won't, right?" I prayed her answer would be 'no' because I didn't fancy being called to testify in a Conspiracy to Commit Murder trial.

"No."

I breathed an inward sigh of relief.

"But just knowing that I could makes me feel better."

"It's normal to have negative feelings about an ex. It takes time to work through the anger and disappointment when a relationship ends badly."

"The problem is that I don't have time. My rage towards Julio has turned me against anyone who has a Y chromosome, and that's bad for business since most of my clients and colleagues are men. A competitor bought a property out from under me earlier this week, and instead of taking it in stride like I normally would, I stormed down to his office and reamed him out for being a sneaky, unscrupulous asshole. I actually threw a stapler at him, Dr. Alvarez. It was so unprofessional.

And my assistant of three years quit yesterday because I went ballistic on him for putting Equal in my coffee and saying that it was Sweet n' Low. I accused him of being a serial liar and a lazy ingrate. It was awful. I knew I was acting like a lunatic, but I just couldn't control myself. I see Julio and all his character defects in every man I deal with now."

"At least, you understand why you're behaving the way you are, and that's the first step towards change. Here, in our sessions, you can vent your feelings of hostility and anger in a safe environment, rather than repress those emotions and have them emerge at inappropriate times."

"Alright, I'm game." She leaned back against the sofa cushions, relaxing her rigid posture.

The rest of the session went smoothly, and I felt confident that Ariane had a tighter rein on her homicidal tendencies by the time I led her out to the waiting area. While she was settling her bill with Margo, I asked, "How did you hear about my practice?"

Ariane finished scribbling her signature on a check, then looked over at me. "I was referred to you by that psychiatrist across the hall, Dr. Fordman."

"Fordham?"

"Right, Fordham." She ripped the payment out of her checkbook and gave it to Margo. "I'd gotten his number from a friend of a friend whose ADHD son is a patient of his. So, I called and had a brief phone consultation with him. He said that a psychologist would be better able to provide the type of counseling I needed, then he recommended you."

Ford had sent a patient my way? I was flabbergasted. Every time I turned around, he was doing something nice to try and help me. He really was the kindest, most generous man on the planet.

"Thank you, thank you, thank you, thank you, thank you!" I offered my effusive gratitude to Ford as he and I stood at the 11th Street crosswalk a few hours later.

"You've said that like a hundred times now." He gave me a sideways smirk.

"Well, it bears repeating. And you wouldn't let my buy lunch, so I have to show my appreciation in some other way."

When we'd met in the corridor between our offices at one o'clock, I'd been sorely tempted to throw myself into his arms and hug the breath out of him. But decorum had prevailed, and I'd simply squeezed his hand instead.

"It's no big deal," he downplayed his good deed. "I just thought that Ms. Wylie's problems were more up your alley than mine."

"And you weren't wrong about that." The light turned green, and we stepped into the street with the other pedestrians. "I have plenty of personal experience with sexually carnivorous exes who make you want to tear your hair out."

"Still having Victor problems?" Ford deduced.

"I really don't want to talk about it."

"Looks like you're not going to have a choice."

"Huh?" I raised my sunglass-covered eyes to his, and he pointed up the street, where Victor could be seen leaning back against a white stretch limo that was parked illegally in front of our office building. He was holding a dozen long-stemmed red roses in one hand and a bunch of pink heart-shaped balloons in the other.

"And I was having such a good day," I grumbled.

CHAPTER 19

Catching sight of Ford and me as we approached, Victor moved towards us with outstretched arms. "*Mi corazón!*"

"I'm not talking to you, Victor. Go away!" I tried to elbow my way past him, but he kept blocking me with his body.

"I see you're still upset about last night. I'm sorry I offended you, *mi querida*, but I was so overcome by my love for you--"

"That is no excuse for your behavior."

"I know, I know, but how can a man be expected to control himself when you're in his arms? The sweet smell of you, the feel of your soft body pressed against--"

"I think I'll go upstairs." Ford took a few steps back, looking uncomfortable.

"Yes, leave us!" Victor shooed the other man away with a brushing motion of his hand. "Pilar, doesn't need you."

"You have no idea what I need," I asserted defiantly, then grabbed Ford by the arm and pulled him back to my side.

"And this . . .," he smacked Ford in the center of his chest with the roses, and crimson petals went flying everywhere, "*gringo* does? You told me that he was just a friend, that there was nothing going on between the two of you. Was that a lie? If you tell me it was a lie, then I'll have to kill him!" He raised the flowers in the air as if he was going to strike Ford with them again.

"Stop acting like a jealous maniac and give those to me." I wrestled the roses away from Victor before he could hurt someone with their thorny stems.

"Ah," my ex's wild expression softened, "you accepted my roses, so that means you accept my apology."

"Yes, fine, I forgive you," I said wearily as I scooped a handful of rose petals out of my cleavage - I'd picked the wrong day to wear my lavender silk pullover with the v-neck, "but things can't go on like this, Victor. We need to have a serious discussion about--"

The sound of a small plane overhead drowned out the rest of my sentence.

Victor leaned forward and yelled, "That's why I'm here! To have a serious discussion about our future!" And before I knew what was happening, he foisted the heart-shaped balloons off on Ford and dropped to one knee in front of me.

Taking my hand in his, he shouted, "I love you, Pilar! I want to spend the rest of my life with you!"

Victor was proposing? *To me?* I was so horrified that I lost the ability to speak. I kept opening my mouth, but no words would come out. I probably looked like a feeding guppy to passersby.

"Look up, *mi amada*!" Victor pointed above our heads, and my eyes followed the movement of his hand up to the clear blue sky, where I saw '*Marry me, Pilar!*' written in big, fluffy white letters.

So, the plane that had been making all of that noise was a skywriter? I glanced over at Ford, who was shaking his head in wonderment at my former flame's latest stunt.

"Stand up, Victor," I finally found my voice. It was time for me to put an end to all of this foolishness.

"But I haven't shown you the ring yet." He pulled a small, black velvet jewelry box out of the pocket of his linen jacket and opened it to reveal the largest diamond I'd ever seen. My eyes almost popped out of my head.

"It's 5 Carats," he announced, obviously quite pleased with himself. "I got the emerald-cut stone because it looked more like you than the round or the marquise."

I stared with undisguised admiration at the ring. It really was a gorgeous piece of jewelry. Mammoth in size, yes, but somehow it managed to look elegant instead of gaudy. I loved the platinum band, and the setting of the stone between two tapered baguettes. I knew that Ana and my mother would keel over and die if they ever saw that ring on my . . .

"What to do, what to do," Ford teased.

"She's going to say 'yes.' That's what she's going to do," Victor snapped, reminding me that the ring came with a lifetime commitment to him. That being the case, I was going to have to pass.

"Victor, get up," I ordered.

"Ford, will you take these," I shoved my roses into his arms, "and the balloons up to Margo? I need to speak with Victor privately."

"Are you sure?" he murmured.

"Absolutely. I plan to resolve this situation once and for all." I brushed a rose petal off his shoulder and smiled.

Although he looked dubious, Ford wished me luck and left.

"Finally," Victor muttered none-too-graciously when the other man was out of earshot.

"Why don't we sit down?" I gestured towards the bench a few feet up the street at the bus stop.

"So, when will you marry me?" Victor asked eagerly just as soon as my butt hit the sun-warmed wood.

"The question is *if* I will marry you, not 'when,'" I reminded him, "and I'll answer that after you tell me what compelled you to propose to me today. I mean, you've thrown the idea of marriage out before, but this is the first time you've ever backed it up with a ring."

"I proposed because I realized that I'd made a terrible mistake last night, and I wanted to prove to you that I'm interested in more than just sleeping with you."

"And I appreciate that, but marriage is not something to be entered into lightly. Can you really see the two of us together in ten years? Twenty?"

"Of course!" He took my hands in his. "We'll have such a wonderful life, *mi amor*, a beautiful house, lots of children--"

"And who's going to take care of those children?" I wondered.

"Who else? Their *mamá*. And we can leave them with their grandparents when we travel or have a party to go to."

"What about my work? Am I supposed to give that up in order to stay home and change your babies' diapers?"

With a dismissive shrug, he replied, "You won't need your practice anymore, taking care of our family will be your job."

"Victor, you need to listen to me."

"I always listen to you."

"You may listen, but you don't hear. I've been trying to tell you for months that we aren't well-suited, and what you just said confirms it. You want a stay-at-home wife, someone who exists only to make you happy, someone who can love you to the exclusion of everything else. And I can't be that woman for you. I'd be miserable. I need my career; I need intellectual stimulation. I don't even want a large family. One child, maybe two, somewhere down the road . . ."

"We could make it work. I love you, Pilar--"

"I know you think you do, but it's just not the kind of love that can last a lifetime or sustain a marriage. Think back over the course of our relationship. When we were dating, did you ever envision us getting married? Did you look at me and think, 'I can't imagine ever being without this woman?'"

Victor scratched the one o'clock shadow on his cheek as he thought about his reply. Finally, he admitted, "No, but--"

"You only started to think you couldn't live without me after I broke up with you."

"Because I realized what I'd lost, what a wonderful

woman you are . . ."

I shook my head. "No, I suddenly became more appealing to you because I was something that you could no longer have. You're spoiled, Victor. Your whole life everything has been handed to you on the proverbial silver platter. A good education, your own business, cars, clothes, trips, toys, women, all you had to do was snap your fingers and they were yours. I was the first thing that slipped out of your grasp, which is the reason why you want me back so badly. If we were to reconcile, I guarantee you that the thrill would wear off very quickly and we'd be right back to the place we were three months ago. You'd be too demanding; I'd feel smothered. We'd argue; you'd cheat."

"Can't we try anyway?" he pleaded.

"I think we've already expended enough energy on us. It just wasn't meant to be. You've got to let me go so that we can both move on to healthier, more satisfying relationships."

Fixing him with my most serious, 'Don't-b.s.-me' stare, I queried, "Do we understand each other?"

He nodded glumly.

"So, you'll stop pursuing me and abandon this fantasy that we belong together?"

Victor sighed and looked dejected. "As you wish, but I will consider the loss of your love to be the great tragedy of my life."

"You'll probably forget my name in a few weeks," I said with a soft chuckle as I rose to my feet.

"Never!" he swore, clutching my hand.

"Don't romanticize me, Victor. Lost loves were lost for a reason. You'll see, one day you'll meet a woman who will appreciate all of your unique qualities like I never could."

"Now," I removed my hand from his impassioned grip and patted him on the shoulder. "I've got to go upstairs. My 2:00 is waiting." That was his cue to get in his limo and drive out of my life once and for all.

"I think I'll stay here for a while. I have much to reflect on."

"Suit yourself," I mumbled and left with the fervent hope that we would never set eyes on each other again.

* * *

I didn't remember to call and check on my mother until 5:30 that afternoon, then I felt so guilty for forgetting about her that I decided to drop by and see the patient instead. En route to Bayshore Heights, I stopped at the grocery store and picked up some essential items for the bedridden: chicken noodle soup, saltines, orange juice with and without pulp, the latest issues of *Glamour*, *Elle*, *In Style*, and *Vogue*, some tissues with aloe in them, and four different flavors of throat lozenges. Okay, so maybe I was overcompensating. But it occurred to me that the way I'd been treating my mother lately wasn't going to win me any Daughter of the Year awards. I'd been impatient and short-tempered with her on more than one occasion and even though she was a pain in the posterior, she deserved better from me, especially when she was sick.

I let myself into my parents' still smoky-smelling apartment, which was unnaturally quiet and dark due to all of the blinds being closed. Assuming that *Mamá* was in bed, getting some rest, I tiptoed into the kitchen, poured some of the soup into a bowl, and popped it in the microwave. While it was heating up, I looked around for the white bed trays Ana and Ray had bought my parents for their last anniversary. When I finally located them in the cabinet next to the refrigerator, I pulled one out and began work on making a nice place setting for my mother. I used the good china, silverware, and crystal because I knew how she liked things to be pretty. I, then, filched one of the slightly drooping lilies from à floral arrangement left over from her birthday celebration and laid the flower next to the now-steaming bowl of soup. Slipping the magazines into the slots on either side of the tray, I lifted it with both hands and headed down the hall to the bedroom.

The door was slightly ajar, which allowed a shaft of light to escape through the crack. "*Mamá*," I called out softly as I eased the door open with my shoulder.

I entered the room, expecting to find my mother propped up on a bunch of pillows, wearing one of her silk peignoirs, doing her best Camille impression. But her bed, with its rumpled sheets, was empty.

'*She's probably in the bathroom*,' I told myself. '*I'll just set this tray down*' . . . hearing a door open behind me, I spun around and . . .

"Ahhhhhhhhhhhhhhh!" my mother let loose a high-pitched scream, her hands flying up to cover her bruised and bandaged face.

"Ahhhhhhhhhhhhhhh!" I matched her scream with an equally shrill one of my own and dropped the tray in horror at the sight of her.

"*Dios mio!* You've ruined the carpet."

I gazed down at my feet, which were now covered with a sticky combination of chicken broth, noodles, and orange juice. "Forget the carpet. What happened to your face? Were you in a car accident?"

"No, no, I just had a little surgery."

"*A little?*" I cringed. The area under her eyes was a painful-looking shade of purple, and I could see stitches along the lower lids. I had no idea what was going on underneath all of the white gauze bandages that were wrapped around her head, but it couldn't be good since the part of her face that was visible was all swollen.

Mamá fussed unnecessarily with the sleeve of her green-and-gold caftan. "If you must know, I had a face lift," she replied.

"And?"

"And . . . some work done on my eyes."

Some work? She looked like Raggedy Ann on crack.

"Oh, *Mamá*," I groaned, removing my soiled shoes and grabbing some tissues from the bedside table so that I could clean myself up.

"Don't '*Oh, Mamá*' me. You're still young. You don't know what it's like when things start to sag. The loose folds of skin, the bags under the eyes, the double chin--"

"You didn't have any of that."

"Well, I would have . . . eventually . . . if I hadn't taken preventative measures. What are you doing here anyway? You're supposed to be with Victor."

"Why would I be with Victor?"

"You got engaged today, didn't you? Let me see the ring." She reached for my hand.

"There's no ring." I held my hand up and pointed to my bare finger.

"But Victor called your father this morning to ask for your hand in marriage. He said that he was going to propose today. Haven't you seen him?"

"Yeah, I saw him. We had a nice talk."

"About getting married?"

"About going our separate ways."

"WHAT???????" *Mamá* shrieked and even though I'd braced myself for her reaction, I still flinched.

"You turned down his proposal? You said 'no' to that 5-Carat ring? Are you *estupido*? *Dios mio*, where did I go wrong?" She raised her hands to the heavens. "How could I have raised a daughter who has so little sense, a daughter who spits on the holy sacrament of marriage?"

"I do not spit on the holy sacrament of marriage--"

"Yes, you do. You threw away a perfectly good man who wanted to give you his . . . oh, my face! The pain!" My mother clutched her puffy cheeks. "The doctor said I could burst a blood vessel if I got upset and my blood pressure shot up. See, what you've done to me!"

"You're going to be fine," I said, wrapping an arm around her. "You just need to lie down."

I steered her towards the bed, being careful to avoid the broken crockery on the floor.

"Lying down's not going to help me," she whined. "Knowing I have a wedding to look forward to, and my daughter's not going to die a shriveled up, childless *soltera* is the only thing that's going to help me."

"Do you have any pain medication?" I asked as I got her settled back against the pillows that were stacked up at the head of her bed. Maybe if I drugged her, she'd mellow out and stop calling me a 'spinster'?

"In the bathroom."

I fetched the bottle of white pills that was sitting on the bathroom counter next to *Mamá*'s collection of hand lotions and filled a glass with water.

"The label says that you should take two of these every four hours. When's the last time you took a dose?"

"I don't know, maybe around noon."

"You're way overdue then. That's why you're in so much pain. Here." I put two pills in the palm of her hand and gave her the glass.

She dutifully popped the tablets into her mouth and took a sip of water. "Water from the tap?" she chastised after swallowing. "You couldn't get your *mamá* some Evian?"

"It won't kill you," I assured her, sitting down on the side of the bed so that I could check her bandages.

"There's no blood seeping through, so you didn't burst

anything. The pain's probably got something to do with the nerve endings being cut. I can't believe that you let anyone near your face with a scalpel."

"It may look bad now, but you'll see, once everything heals, I'm going to be beautiful. Dr. Preston said he took 20 years off my face."

"Swell, just what I wanted, a mother who looks the same age as I do," my tone was sarcastic. "Whatever happened to growing old gracefully?"

"Why should anyone grow old in Miami? We have the best plastic surgeons in the country here."

"Plastic surgeons," I pursed my lips with disgust, "they just prey on the insecurities of women and try to make us all look like Barbie dolls."

"My daughter, the *feminista*! You'll change your mind about plastic surgeons in a few years when you need Botox to fill in those laugh lines."

I immediately stopped making any kind of expression with my mouth. "I don't have laugh lines. And even if I did, I wouldn't mind because lines give a person's face character."

My mother shook her head. "Character won't get you a man."

"Well, you already have a man, so what are you worried about?"

"I'm not worried about myself. I'm worried about you. You're the one who's got to look her best so that she can attract a new man. Victor was willing to take you as you are, laugh lines and all, but oh no, that wasn't good enough for--"

"I have one thing to say about Victor, then I don't want to ever hear his name come out of your mouth again."

"I can talk about whoever I want to," she said petulantly.

"Of course, you can, just like I can go home, pick up the phone, and start calling family members to tell them all about your face lift. I think I'll start with Aunt Brigida. She's always asking why you never seem to age."

Since my mother was incapable of moving any facial muscles, she just glared at me. "And your father thinks you're the sweet one."

"I am the sweet one. I'm also the one who's tired of you cheerleading for Victor. I know you liked him and thought that he was God's gift to me, but the fact of the matter is, I didn't love him. Did you really want me to marry a man I didn't love?"

She sighed. "I guess not, but--"

"But nothing, when I get married it will be because I've found a guy who makes me feel the way you do about *Papá*. I'm not settling for anything less. And if I never get married--"

"*Ay!*" *Mamá* put her hand over her heart.

"And if I never get married," I repeated, "the world won't stop spinning on its axis."

"It might."

"It won't."

I noticed that my mother's eyelids were starting to droop, which meant the medication was kicking in. Thank God for small favors!

"Why don't you close your eyes and take a little nap? When you wake up, I'll make another bowl of soup for you."

"I am feeling a little drowsy." Her eyes began to drift closed.

They were at half-mast when she asked, "You won't tell anyone about my surgery, will you?"

"What surgery?" I played innocent. "You have the flu, a terrible, highly contagious flu that will probably take you a few weeks to recover from."

"*Youreagoodgirl*," her words slurred together. "*Iforgiveyoufornotmarrying--*"

"Ah-ah," I waggled my finger in front of her face, "you're

not supposed to say his name."

"*Dontworry.*" She patted my hand. "*Illfindsomeonelseforyou. Myperiodontisthasasonwhos gettingadivorce. Hessortaoverweight,alrighthesobese, but hesapartnerinthepracticeandhedrivesa*--" She nodded off mid-matchmaking.

CHAPTER 20

"I don't remember my mother ever showing me any signs of affection. No hugs, no kisses, not even a pat on the back."

"And were you hurt by that?" My pen was poised above my notepad in preparation for writing down Mitch's answer.

"It bummed me out when I saw how touchy-feely some of the other moms were with their kids," he admitted. "I figured that there was something wrong with me, something that made me unlovable. But when I got a little older, I realized that she was standoffish with everyone, even my dad. She never initiated any sort of physical contact with him and she froze up every time he went near her. My dad was always calling her 'a cold fish.'"

"It sounds like your mother was emotionally repressed, and your father's lack of sensitivity exacerbated her problems."

"I told you they were miserable together," he responded with a wry smirk.

"And with their dysfunctional relationship as your primary example of what a marriage could be, you've spent your entire adult life actively avoiding commitment because, on some subconscious level, you fear that intimacy will lead you to the same unhappy fate your parents suffered."

"Wow." Mitch blinked hard several times as he processed what I'd said. "That's deep."

"Does it ring true?"

"Yeah, yeah, it does. I never thought about why I am the way I am, but I think you've hit the nail on the head, Doc."

"Furthermore," I wasn't through with my brilliant insights just yet, "you find it difficult to trust women and give your heart to them because you felt rejected by your mother, who was the most important female in your life during your formative years. So, you've cultivated this insouciant, love 'em and leave 'em persona in order to protect yourself from any more rejection. You figure that if you don't get too close, or let anyone in, then they can't hurt you like your emotionally distant mother did."

Mitch frowned and looked confused. "What does 'insouciant' mean?"

"Carefree, easygoing, happy-go-lucky."

"That definitely sounds like me."

"But that's not really you, it's just a mask you hide behind to protect your wounded inner child."

"And you're saying that I need to drop the mask and let the real me come out?"

"Exactly. You need to stop playing the macho stud, learn how to open up to women, and show them what's inside. If you do, I think you'll be pleasantly surprised by the response you get."

I glanced down at the watch on my left wrist and was shocked to see that it was 5:00. "Look at that, we've gone ten minutes over."

"Sorry to keep you," Mitch apologized as he stood up. "You're probably anxious to get out of here. TGIF, right?"

"It has been a long week," I conceded with a weary half-smile. "I think that today's session was a productive one though, don't you?"

"Absolutely. You've given me a lot to think about, Doc."

We strolled over to my office door together, and I was just about to reach out for its handle when Mitch said, "Please, let me."

He opened the door, then gallantly stepped aside so that I could enter the waiting area first.

"Thanks." I beamed like a proud parent. My man whore, uh, I mean *my patient*, had made a lot of progress. Slowly, but surely, he was becoming more courteous and treating women (or, at least, me) with the proper respect.

My receptionist popped up with an invoice in hand as soon as she saw us. Her purse was sitting on top of her desk, which signaled that she was ready to go. I felt badly for keeping her late on a Friday.

"Margo will check you out, and I'll see you next Wednesday, okay?"

Mitch nodded, and I heard Margo inquire, "Will you be paying with cash as usual, Mr. Buchannon?" as I turned back towards my office.

I spent a few minutes straightening up and collecting my things, then I was off. It felt good to lock the door of my office on that particular afternoon, knowing that I wouldn't have to return for 62 hours. I hadn't been lying when I'd told Mitch that it had been a long week. So much had happened and most of it hadn't been pleasant. The fact that I hadn't collapsed from the strain of dealing with my financially-challenged business, the demands of my family, and my screwed-up love life was a testament to either my fortitude, or my stupidity. I looked forward to going home and getting some much-needed rest. I fantasized that I would turn off my phones and lock myself in my bedroom for the entire weekend. I'd stay in my PJs (the old, faded-out leopard print ones that Izzy always made fun of), watch *The Notebook* repeatedly (a good cry was always cathartic), and subsist on Cool Ranch Doritos and Snapple.

An hour later, I pulled into my driveway with that game plan in mind. I was hoofing it up the walkway to my little bungalow, noting the ankle-high grass and proliferation of weeds (Why had I hired Cousin José's 'lawn maintenance company" to take care of my yard? I paid him for weekly service, but I was lucky if a teenaged boy with a rusty lawnmower showed up once a month.), when my sister burst through the front door like she'd been shot out of a cannon.

"Hi, Pilar. Bye, Pilar," she said as she zipped past me,

acting as if there was nothing the slightest bit unusual about the way she looked.

"Woah, wait a minute!" I chased after Izzy, grabbing her by the arm when I caught up to her.

"What are you wearing?"

"This?" She ran a hand down her body, which was clad in a skintight black leather halter top and matching hot pants that barely covered her tight, 23-year-old butt cheeks.

"It's my uniform." She reached into the purse she had slung over her shoulder and pulled out two pieces of grape-flavored Bubblicious gum, which she unwrapped, shoved into her mouth, and began to chomp on noisily.

"Uniform?"

"Yeah, for my new job." She blew a purple bubble that grew in size until it almost obscured her face

"What job?" I was at a loss.

Izzy sucked in her breath, making the bubble pop loudly and deflate. Twirling its sticky remnants around her index finger, she mused, "Did I forget to mention that I had a new job? Bruiser hooked me up with the manager at the club where he bounces. The guy took one look at me and said, 'You're hired. Get a uniform and come back tomorrow night at 7:00.'"

"This club isn't one of those S&M places, is it?" Her ensemble did give off a dominatrix vibe.

"No whips and no stilettos," she gestured down at her black go-go boots, "so you do the math."

"And you won't be dancing in a cage?"

"I wish! I'd make a lot more money doing that, but unfortunately, the manager didn't have any openings for a dancer. So, I'm just a lowly cocktail waitress, making minimum wage, for now. Of course, if I can work this getup right," she bent over at the waist and adjusted her halter top so that her breasts looked as though they might spill out of its low-cut front, "there's no telling what kind of tips I might get. According to Bruiser, 'the bigger the boobs, the bigger the bucks' from the male customers."

"Are you sure you want to do this?" The feminist in me hated the idea of my sister making a living by flaunting her nubile, young body.

"We need the money, don't we?" she queried irritably.

"Yes, but--"

"But nothing, I promised you that I would pay you back for my legal expenses, and I don't want to be responsible for you losing this house or your practice."

"I appreciate that, but there are other jobs that would be more respec--," I cut myself off because I didn't want Izzy to think that I was judging her. "Why don't you take Solana up on her offer to work at the *panaderia*?"

"Yeah, right," Izzy scoffed, "can you see me getting up at 4AM to roll out bread dough for $7.25 an hour?"

"At least, you wouldn't have to go to work half-naked." I pointed out one of the benefits of a career in baked goods.

My sister chortled. "You are such a prude. I wear less than this to the beach every day. And I get my butt pinched in clubs every night, so I might as well get paid for it. Now, I've got to hit the road or I'm going to be late." She spun around so fast that the ponytail sitting up high on the crown of her head smacked me in the face.

Sputtering, I brushed Izzy's long, dark hair out of my eyes and mouth, then trailed her to the yellow Beetle parked on the curb.

"Isidora, what am I supposed to tell--"

"Afternoon, Pilar." I froze when I heard a creaky voice call out to me.

"Hi, Mr. Cuthbertson." I waved at the spindly-looking senior citizen in the floral print shirt and Bermuda shorts who was walking his equally decrepit Dachshund towards us.

In an effort to block his view of Izzy, I stepped in front of her while she unlocked her car door, but he must have seen something he deemed offensive because he shook his head disparagingly as he ambled by.

"Oh, great," I grumbled, while Izzy climbed into the driver's seat of her VW. "I'm sure he's off to tell all of his cronies on the board about this outfit of yours, and it'll be the hot topic of conversation at next week's Homeowners' Association meeting."

"Who cares what a bunch of old geezers think?" she retorted, fastening her seatbelt into place.

"I do if they fine me, or raise my dues, because I have a houseguest who violated some sort of neighborhood dress code."

"You worry too much. You need to chill, or you're going to stroke out," my sister blithely advised before putting her key in the ignition and starting her vehicle.

"What about--" Izzy pulled her car door shut before I could finish the question. I had to step back so that I wouldn't get a noseful of exhaust fumes when she took off.

Trudging back to the house, I wondered what I was going to say to my parents and Ana about Izzy's latest career choice. After several minutes of deliberation, I decided that keeping it simple would be the best way to go. Izzy got a job as a waitress, end of story. There was no need to embellish. If they asked, I'd say that she was working in a place near the beach (not a club, let them assume that it was one of those touristy restaurants where families from Iowa came to eat while they were in town on vacation), and I couldn't tell them the name of the place because Izzy hadn't mentioned it. Ha! Yes, perfect. I couldn't tell them something I didn't know. Oh, dear, why hadn't I gotten the name of the club from Izzy? What if she never came home from work? What if she was kidnapped by some slave trader, or murdered by a leather fetishist who looked for his victims in nightclubs? I wouldn't even know where to tell the police to start looking for her . . . *Oh, my God!* Izzy was right. I was turning fretting into a full-time occupation, and the last thing I needed was another one of those.

I pushed open my front door and dropped my purse and briefcase on the tile floor in the entryway. Without checking my mail or phone messages, I headed straight for the bathroom. Once there, I popped a jazz CD into my portable player, lit some votive candles, turned the tub faucets on, and examined my bubble bath options. I had a pack of lavender bath salts that I'd never used and I remembered reading an article about aromatherapy that had said the scent of lavender had a steadying influence on the psyche, so I dumped them into the tub. Shedding my clothes, I submerged myself in the deliciously warm water and sighed contentedly.

I could have happily laid there all night, contemplating a myriad of inconsequential things like "What season am I?" and "Who has the sexier accent: Chris Hemsworth or Michael Fassbender?" but after a half-hour, the water was cool and my fingers were all pruney. So, I wearily dragged myself out of the bath and dried off with a fluffy yellow towel. I searched every drawer of my dresser, but couldn't find my leopard print pajamas, probably because they were in one of the ten piles of laundry I hadn't had a chance to do in the last two weeks. Having no other options, I slipped on a cotton tank and some drawstring shorts that were comfy enough to sleep in, then I rounded up some edible goodies in the kitchen and settled into bed with my junk food feast.

I watched Jeopardy for a while, but got annoyed when Alex Trebek said that one of my questions was wrong. Why did he always have to act so smug? He only knew the question for every answer because someone typed it out on a card for him. He should try playing the game without any help from his staff, and then we'd see how smug he was.

I put *The Notebook* disc in my DVD player and set a box of Kleenex out on the bed because I knew from experience that I was going to need it. I always blubbered like a baby when Noah and Allie died in each other's arms at the end of the movie. I must have fallen asleep some time before that happened because there were only a few soggy tissues strewn across my comforter when I was awakened by the sound of my cell phone ringing. Dazedly, I looked at the clock on my nightstand and saw that it was 10:34PM. I reached for my purse, which I'd brought in from the foyer and dumped on the foot of my bed earlier. In my groggy state, it took me a while to find the noisy cell, but I did eventually think to check the zippered pocket inside the purse. Rubbing my bleary eyes, I looked at the Caller ID.

Hal's Bar? What the--?

"Hello?" I answered, sounding a lot crankier than usual.

"Roctor Alderez?" an inebriated voice queried.

"Who is this?"

"Iz me, Roctor Alderez. Iz Itch. Itch Brewchannon."

"Mitch?"

"That's what I said, Roctor Alderez. *Itch.*"

"What's going on, Mitch? Why are you calling?"

"You gamme this number an' you tole me to call it in case of a 'mergency."

"So, what's the emergency?"

"I'm repressed. Noooooo, that's not right," he admonished himself. "I'm DEpressed. Yeah, that's it. I am very, very DEpressed."

"Well, I'm sorry to hear that, but--"

There was a loud thud on the other end of the line.

"Mitch! Mitch, are you alright?" I sat up straight, now fully alert.

"I'm awright," he mumbled. "I just had to lay my head

down. My head iz soooooooo heavy, Roctor Alderez. I think King Kong might be sittin' on it."

"There are no giant gorillas sitting on your head, Mitch."

"Then, iz probably a melephant." He chortled with drunken amusement. "Melephant's a funny word, izn't it? Melephants look funny, too. They have those big, floppy ears and all that wrinkly sk--"

"Hey, buddy. I said that you could use the phone for a couple of minutes. Time's up," a raspy, masculine voice prompted.

"Lea'me alone. I'm talkin' to Roctor Alderez. She helps me."

"Somebody needs to," the other man snarked.

"Did ya hear that, Roctor Alderez? The people here aren't very nice. I asked for a Scotch, and they wouldn't even gimme one."

"You've already had five," the bartender reminded him.

"And they took away my car keyzzzzz."

Thank heaven for that, he was obviously not in any condition to drive.

"Did you need me to come and pick you up?" I probably should have told him to call a cab, but Mitch was my patient and I felt responsible for him.

"I'd like that, Roctor Alderez. I'd like that very much. There's just one liiiiiiiittle problem." He must have cupped the phone receiver with his hand because his next words were delivered in a strange, amplified whisper. "I don't know where I am."

"Let me talk to the bartender."

"Oh no, Roctor Alderez, ya don't wanna talk to him. He's mean and he's really, really ugly. He's got this big mole right on the tip of his--" I could hear the sounds of a struggle as someone tried to wrest the phone away from Mitch.

"No, that's mine! Give it back!"

"He's down here at Hal's Bar on Washington Avenue," the winner of the tug-of-war informed me. "We're next door to the strip club, Slap n' Tickle. You can't miss the big pink neon sign that says 'GIRLS - GIRLS - GIRLS.'"

Charming.

With a beleaguered sigh, I muttered, "Tell Mitch I'll be there in 30 minutes."

CHAPTER 21

I'd been in a few dives in my time, but Hal's Bar took seediness to a new level. The lighting was dim, the air was thick with the stench of high-octane booze and sweaty flesh, and the floor was sticky, so sticky in fact that every time I lifted my foot to take a step, I could feel this gross, gooey suction effect as if the floor was trying to fight me for my flip-flop. The clientele of this watering hole could best be described as "rough." When I first walked through the door, I could feel a multitude of leering eyes shift towards me. Hugging my purse close to my body, I made a beeline for the bar as I was assaulted from all sides by wolf whistles and anything-but-enticing come-ons, my personal favorite being, "*Hey baby, I've got a seat for you right here . . . on my lap.*" SHUDDER

"Excuse me." I tried to get the attention of the burly man who was standing behind the bar, drying double old-fashioned glasses with a stained rag.

"He's over there." The man didn't bother to glance up from his task; he just jerked a thumb to the right, where I could see a body slumped over a table. "I tried to give him some coffee, but he wouldn't drink it."

"How about a couple of bottled waters?"

"If you want water, it'll come out of the tap," the bartender answered gruffly before raising his seen-it-all eyes to mine.

Yikes! Mitch had been right about the mole on this guy's nose. Not only was it unusually large, it was an unnatural shade of purple. I was tempted to give the man my dermatologist's number. Instead, I smiled and said, "That'll be fine. Thanks."

He filled up two clean (I hoped) glasses in the nearby sink and plopped them down in front of me, sloshing a bit of the liquid on the bar.

I picked up the drinks and carried them over to Mitch's table. When I got closer, I realized that he was facedown in a bowl of peanuts.

"Mitch." I shook his shoulder gently after setting the water down.

He twitched before jolting up with a panicked expression. "Huh? What?"

"It's me, Mitch, Doctor Alvarez."

He turned towards me and I saw that he had some peanut shells stuck to his face, so I reached out a hand and began to scrape them off.

"What are you doin' here, Doctor Alderez?" his words were still slurred, but not as badly as they had been when I'd spoken to him on the phone. Apparently, his little "nap" had sobered him up a bit.

"You called me, and I said that I would come and get you, remember?"

"Oh, yeah." He gingerly massaged his temples as if his head was pounding, and no doubt it was thanks to the bender he'd been on. "I don't feel so good."

"I'm not surprised. Here, have some water." I pushed the glass of clear fluid towards him. "You need to flush out your system."

He gulped down the water so fast that some of it dribbled on to his stubbled chin. I offered him a cocktail napkin, but he took care of the job with the back of his hand.

"Do you want to tell me why you've been drinking so heavily?" I asked.

Frowning, he replied, "I dunno."

"I think you do. Earlier, you said that you were depressed. What about?"

"Everythin'." He sank forward on to the table, using his elbows for support.

"After our session this afternoon, I started thinkin' 'bout

my life and how empty and meaningless it was. *Is*," he corrected his verb tense.

"That's not true." In a comforting gesture, I placed my hands on his forearm. "You have friends and a very important job . . ."

"I've never even saved anyone from drowning," he confessed.

"That doesn't mean that you won't . . . some day."

"I have nothin', no reason to get out of bed ev'ry day. It's hopeless." He sighed plaintively and laid his head down on his folded arms.

"That's just the alcohol talking. Liquor is a mood-altering depressant, so it makes things seem a lot worse than they really are."

Propping his head up on his hand, he said, "I dunno. I was feelin' awfully low 'fore I started drinkin', Roctor Alda--, Alba--, Alma--. Can I just call you by your first name? It'd be soooo much easier."

"Sure."

"Good." He grinned goofily. "What is your first name? No, wait, don't tell me, lemme guess."

If I'd let him do that, we would have been in that foul-smelling bar until daybreak. "It's Pilar."

"P'lar," he repeated. "That's pretty. You're pretty."

Yeah, I was a vision with my makeup-free face, finger-combed hair, holey Levis, and unironed pink tunic. The man was obviously suffering from liquor-induced hallucinations. Next, he'd probably tell me that he saw the Easter Bunny hopping through the room.

"That's very nice." I humored him. "Now, why don't I take you home so that you can get some sleep? I think you'll feel much better once you've sobered up."

"Promise?" He looked dubious.

"Cross my heart," which I did as I stood up.

"'kay, I'll wait right here, and you can bring the car to me."

"I can't bring the car in here. The door," I gestured towards the bar's entrance, "isn't wide enough. You're going to have to walk out to the parking lot with me."

"Oh, no," he shook his head, then stopped because the movement was obviously making him queasy. "I can *not* do that."

"I'll help you, and we'll take it slow. Come on." I grabbed his hands and tugged on them.

"This is a very bad idea," Mitch predicted direfully before rising to his feet.

He teetered unsteadily for a moment, but I positioned myself next to him, wrapping an arm around his waist, and that seemed to stabilize his swaying frame.

"Okay, we're just going to take this one step at a time. You let me know if you get dizzy or feel sick."

It took about ten minutes of us moving at a snail's pace, and my body ached from having to support the weight of a 200-pound (at least, that's how heavy he felt) man, but we reached my Miata without incident. I unlocked the door on the passenger's side and pushed Mitch down into the seat.

"I don't think my legs'll fit," he mumbled as he gazed down at his long limbs.

"Yes, they will. You just have to bend them at the knees."

It seemed to be too complicated of a concept for him to wrap his Scotch-soaked mind around, so I did it for him, then shoved his legs into the car and shut the door before he could topple back out on to the asphalt.

I climbed into the driver's seat and buckled myself in. "Okay, tell me where you live. Mitch?"

His head had fallen forward on to his chest, and he appeared to be sleeping.

"Mitch!" I poked him in the arm, and he stirred.

"Whaddya want?"

"To know where you live so that I can take you there."

"Ummmmmmm." He clearly didn't have a clue.

"Okay." Holding out my hand, I instructed, "Give me your license. I can get your address off of that."

"No, you can't. I moved a coupla months ago, and the 'dress on my license is the old one."

Fantastic.

"But I'm pretty sure I don't live far from here."

"Alright, good. That's a start. Now, think hard. Can you remember the name of your street?"

He scratched his chin while he pondered my question.

"It starts with a U!" he exulted a few minutes later.

A street that started with a U in that area of town? I couldn't think of a single one.

"U, U, U, U, U, U," Mitch kept saying the letter over and over in an attempt to jog his memory, "Euclid! That's it! I live on Euuuuuuclid."

That was just a few blocks over, thank goodness. I shifted the car into gear and steered it in that direction.

When we got to Euclid, I drove up and down the street several times as slowly as I could while Mitch hung his head out the window, looking for a familiar sight. He had me stop at an apartment building in the 1400 block, then decided on closer inspection that it wasn't the right one.

"Are you sure about this?" I queried after parking on the curb in front of a five-story white stucco building surrounded by large palm trees.

"Oh, yeah, definitely, this is the place." He opened the car door and staggered out on to the sidewalk.

I came around and offered Mitch a shoulder to lean on. I got him to the front door of his apartment building without much trouble, but had to struggle to maneuver his tall frame through it.

"This is nice," I remarked conversationally as we passed through the lobby, which was decorated in a style my sister Ana liked to call "Florida Cheap" with lots of white wicker furniture, tacky watercolors on the walls, and indoor-outdoor carpet in a hideous shade of blue.

"No, it's not," he begged to differ. "You're just bein' p'lite." He might have been smashed, but he was still astute.

We'd reached the elevators, so I stopped and hit the button with the UP arrow on it. The doors slid open, and I thrust Mitch inside, forcing him up against the back wall of the small, enclosed space. The minute I removed my hand from his chest, his body began to slide down. I caught him under the arms and with some effort, maneuvered him into the corner, where he had walls on either side to hold him up.

I was now panting from all of the exertion. Hauling inebriated men around town was better exercise than spin class.

"What floor's your apartment on?" I asked in between labored breaths.

"The third. No, the fourth. No, the third. I'm in 3B. B for Brewchannon. Get it?" He seemed to be very pleased with himself for making that association.

"Okay, third floor." I punched the appropriate button on the elevator control panel, and the doors closed.

"Here we are," I said a minute later when we reached our destination, slinging one of Mitch's muscular arms around my neck and dragging him out of the elevator by sheer force of will. Fortunately, apartment #3B was only a few feet away, so I didn't have far to go with my cumbersome load.

"Keys?" I prompted.

"Keys?" He stared at me stupidly.

"To unlock your front door." I pointed at it.

"Oh, yeah," he chuckled as if his own obtuseness amused him, "they're in my pocket."

Tracie Banister

"Well, they're not doing us any good in there. You have to pull them out."

"You can do it."

"I am not sticking my hands in your pants' pocket, Mitch."

"I don't mind."

"Well, I do. Now, give me your keys, or I'm going to leave you here in the hallway," I said in a tone that brooked no insubordination.

"Awright." He shoved his hand into the right front pocket of his snug Levis and rummaged around.

"Wanna Tic Tac?" he asked as he extracted a tiny white breath mint.

"No, I want your keys," I reiterated with growing impatience.

"'kay." He popped the Tic Tac in his mouth and almost immediately started to make horrible, gagging noises. I was about to administer the Heimlich when he spit the mint out on to the carpet.

"Lint," he explained, making a disgusted face.

I sighed wearily. "Try the other pocket."

He found the keys that time and proceeded to waste several minutes trying to insert one of them in his front door's lock.

"This is hard," he complained.

"That's because the alcohol is impairing your motor skills." Nudging him to the side with my hip, I took the keys out of his hand and was able to get the door open on the first attempt.

Mitch stumbled over the threshold and would have ended up kissing the linoleum in the foyer if I hadn't grabbed the back of his shirt. "Be careful," I cautioned him, not wanting to spend the rest of my night in the ER while a doctor bandaged up his broken nose.

I flipped on the light switch in the foyer and got my first

look at the interior of Mitch's apartment. There was a small kitchen with a breakfast bar to the left and beyond that was a decent-sized living area, which was dominated by a huge black entertainment center. Big-screen TV, DVR, DVD player, stereo system, Playstation, Mitch had all of the electronic gadgets that were staples in every bachelor pad I'd ever visited. He was also a slob like most of the single men I knew. There were clothes and shoes strewn all over the furniture and floor, dirty dishes in the sink, and empty food and drink containers pretty much everywhere.

I put my foot down on a bag of potato chips that'd been hiding under a discarded t-shirt and heard a loud crunch.

"Are ya hungry?" Mitch inquired. "I could eat. Mmmmmm, Apple Jacks." He noticed an overturned box of the cereal lying on the breakfast bar.

"That's probably not such a hot idea," I counseled, but that didn't deter him from scooping up a handful of Apple Jacks and stuffing them into his mouth.

He was guaranteed to vomit now.

"You wanna tour of my 'partment?" Mitch mumbled as he chewed.

"Maybe some other time."

"I gotta view," he made a sweeping motion towards the sliding glass doors on the other side of the room, "of the pool. I swim there ev'ry mornin'. Fifty laps."

"That's very impressive."

"Thanks. I also like to-- ohhhhhhh." He dropped the box of cereal and clutched the side of the breakfast bar.

"What's wrong?"

"The room's spinnin'. I feel like I'm on one of those Whirl-a-Tilts. Make it stop."

"You need to lie down. Where's your bedroom? That way?" I indicated the hallway to my left.

"Uh huh." He looked like he was about to toss his

cookies.

"Just lean on me," I said, once again slipping my arm around his waist.

As we made our way down the corridor, past a half-bath and a storage closet that had all kinds of sporting equipment spilling out of it, I murmured encouraging things like, "We're almost there," and, "Just a few more steps." I pushed open the door to his room and saw a California King bed with rumpled black sheets and a black-and-tan comforter with geometric shapes decorating it.

"Okay, sit," I told Mitch, and he lowered himself down cautiously on to the side of the bed, while I held on to his arms.

"Good, now I'm just going to fluff up a couple of these pillows . . ." I heard him fall back on the mattress with a groan.

"Mitch!" I crawled over to him. "Are you okay?"

He gazed up at me through heavy-lidded eyes. "My head hurts . . . a lot."

"Hang in there. I'll be right back." I scooted across the bed, then climbed off the other side and went into what I presumed was his bathroom.

The smell of wet towels told me I was right before I even turned on the lights. "Yuck," I muttered, crinkling my nose with disgust when I saw the used bath towels piled up on the floor. No doubt there was mildew in the shower, too, but I wasn't going to look. Some things were better left unconfirmed.

I opened the narrow linen closet located in the corner of the bathroom, intent on finding a clean washcloth. There were a few of those located on the middle shelf, along with towels and sheets. The entire bottom shelf was stocked with an assortment of what else? *Condoms.* Outside of a drugstore, I'd never seen so many condoms in my life. He had boxes and boxes of them: Latex, Sheepskin, Lubricated, Ribbed, Glow-in-the-Dark, Spearmint Tingle, Twisted Pleasure . . . that was a new one on me. I reached for the box so that I could investigate further . . .

"Hey!" Mitch called from the bedroom, and I started guiltily, knocking several condom boxes to the floor.

"Coming," I shouted back as I scrambled to gather up the fallen prophylactics while chastising myself for snooping and being such a klutz.

After I'd returned the boxes to their designated shelf, I wetted the washcloth in the bathroom sink.   Conveniently, there was a large bottle of generic aspirin sitting out on the counter, so I grabbed it and headed back to my sloshed patient.

"Here, take a couple of these." I placed two white tablets in Mitch's hand. "Do you need some water to wash them down? I didn't see any glasses or cups in the bathroom, but I can go to the kitchen and--"

"Nah, this is fine," he assured me, putting the pills in his mouth.

"This should help your head."   I placed the damp washcloth on his brow.

He closed his eyes and a relieved smile played across his lips. "Mmmmmm, that feels good. I ruv you, P'lar."

Huh?

His eyelids fluttered open again. "I mean, I luv you."

I laughed uncomfortably and began to back away from his prostrate body. "You're drunk, Mitch. You don't know what you're saying."

He snatched my hand and pulled me back towards him. "You're right. I am super duper drunk, drunker than I've been in years, but that doesn't matter. I still know how I feel. I luv you."

"No, you don't." I tried to wrest my hand from his

surprisingly tight grip. "You're confusing gratitude, or maybe admiration, with a stronger emotion. I'm your doctor--"

"And you're a grrrrreat doctor. You give the best a'vice; you really do. You said I should stop sleepin' 'round and look for a high-quality woman. And I looked, P'lar, I really did, but nobody's got more quality than you. You're smart annnnnnnd kind annnnnnnnd bee-yoo-tiful."

"There are plenty of smart and kind women in the world--"

"No," he moved his head from side-to-side, "you're special. You unnerstand me."

"I was trained to understand you, Mitch. It's my job. It's what you pay me for."

"You said that if I opened up to a woman and showed her what was inside, I'd be pleasantly s'prised by the 'sponse I'd get. Well, I've been tooooootally honest with you and you've seen the real me, sooooooo . . ."

Oh, God, how did this happen? How did all of the sound, carefully-worded advice I'd doled out to this man over the last few months come back to bite me on the ass? This was every psychologist's worst nightmare. I needed to reestablish my authority and take back control of the situation pronto.

"I think we should continue this conversation at your session next week."

"But you'll forget that I luv you by then," he protested.

"I promise I'll make a note of what we discussed and place it in your file."

"Mmmmmkay, Roctor Alderez. I am kinda sweepy."

"Can I have my hand back?" I queried as his eyes started to drift shut.

"Sure," he said drowsily and released it. Then, I jumped off the bed and bolted for the door of his apartment as if I was being chased by the hounds of hell.

CHAPTER 22

Ford's receptionist wasn't in yet and the door to his office was ajar, so I dispensed with the formalities and just barged in. "I've got a problem," I announced.

He looked up from the medical journal he was perusing and queried, "Another one?" with an amused smirk.

"Yes, and I hate to bother you with this when you've already been so helpful with Izzy and Victor and my financial woes, but," I started to pace back and forth in front of his desk, "it's a problem with a patient, and I don't know what to do. I stressed out about it all weekend. I'm sure that this is all my fault, that I said, or did, something wrong . . ."

Ford got up and came around to my side of the desk. "Have a seat," he instructed, taking me by the arms and gently pushing me down into a chair.

He, then, perched himself on the edge of his desk and spoke in a soothing tone that invited confidences, "Tell me what happened."

"A patient told me that he loved me," I said without preamble.

I expected Ford to react with surprise, concern, maybe even a little sympathy, but instead, he burst out laughing like I'd just told him the most hilarious joke he'd ever heard. He laughed so hard that he had to remove his glasses to wipe the tears from his eyes.

"This is not funny!" I rose to my feet with righteous indignation.

"It is, actually." Ford returned his wire-frames to their perch on the bridge of his nose. "First, poor besotted Victor and now, this patient. You really put the whammy on men."

"Not intentionally," I claimed in my defense. "Victor was an isolated case. I've never had a man obsess over me the way he did, and in the final analysis, his obsession had nothing to do with me. It was just his ego. He couldn't fathom the concept of a woman not wanting him.

And this patient . . . I have no idea why he's suddenly professing his undying love. I never flirted with him, or encouraged him, in any way. And he knows absolutely nothing about me as a person. How can you love somebody you don't even know?"

Turning serious, Ford said, "It's not uncommon for a patient to fall in love with a therapist of the opposite sex. Surely, you've read about Transference?"

"Well, yeah, but I don't know anyone who's actually experienced it. Have you?"

He shrugged. "There were one or two patients who developed crushes on me during my residency at Sinai. Apparently, white lab coats are a big turn-on for some women."

"So, you've dealt with the amorous attentions of patients before. Great!" I plopped down next to him on the desk. "Tell me how to fix this. Is there something in particular I can say to disabuse this patient of the notion that he has romantic feelings for me? I tried to tell him that he was confusing gratitude with love the other night, but he was so drunk that he wasn't able to follow my reasoning."

Ford frowned. "You saw a patient at *night*, and he came to the session *drunk*?"

"Not exactly. We had a session on Friday afternoon. A session that I thought went very well because we made a breakthrough about the patient's mother. She was very cold and distant, so he grew up not trusting women and being unable to form close bonds with them."

"What about the drunk part?" Ford wondered.

"I'm getting there," I assured him. "So, I went home, fell asleep early, and was woken up by a call on my cell phone around 10:30. It was Mi--, I mean *my patient*. He was at a bar and he was obviously three sheets to the wind. He said that he'd been drinking because his life had no meaning and he was depressed."

"And that's when he confessed his feelings for you?"

"No, that didn't happen until later. First, I went to the bar and picked him up."

Ford's jaw dropped down so far that I could see the fillings in his molars. "You can't be serious."

"The man was incapacitated; he needed a ride home. What else was I supposed to do?"

"Call a cab. Call one of his buddies, or a family member. Let him sleep it off in the alley behind the bar."

"I couldn't do that! He's my patient. I'm responsible for him."

"The only thing you're responsible for is the man's mental health. Take it from someone who's been doing this a lot longer than you. You can't get involved with your patients' lives outside your office. If you do, they'll start taking advantage. You are their doctor, not their friend or their mother."

I sighed unhappily. "Okay, so I screwed up."

"It was a rookie mistake," Ford excused my lapse in good judgment. "You'll know better next time. Finish the story."

"I took Mitch," forgetting that I was supposed to be protecting my patient's identity, I used his name, "back to his apartment. He was feeling woozy, so I helped him into bed. Then, I got him some aspirin and a cool cloth for his forehead."

"Jesus," Ford was incredulous, "no wonder he thinks he's in love with you. You come when he calls, you take care of him when he's sick, you're warm, compassionate, supportive--"

"So, I should stop being all of those things?"

"Of course not. Those are the qualities that make you a

good therapist. But you weren't in a controlled environment with this patient the other night. You were in his bedroom, which is a very intimate setting, and you were treating him with tenderness, so he saw you as a woman rather than just a doctor. Factor in your physical charms and you've got insta-love, or maybe lust. He didn't try to put a move on you, did he?" His brow furrowed with concern.

Physical charms? Ford had just said that I had "physical charms," which implied that he found me attractive, but was that in an abstract way like *'She's got a pretty face and a decent body. Maybe I'll set her up with my brother the next time he's in town?'*or in a *'Wow, she's so gorgeous she could give Eva Mendes a run for her money. If I weren't a married man, I'd whisk her off to some secluded beach where we could sunbathe naked and make love all--'*

"Did he?" Ford repeated the question, startling me out of my reverie.

"Huh? Oh, no, no, Mitch didn't try anything; he was too sloshed. Come to think of it, he was so sloshed that he might not even remember what transpired between us the other night. That happens, right? A man can get so inebriated that he has a complete blackout and forgets everything that took place while he was under the influence?" My voice was hopeful.

Ford grimaced, which didn't bode well. "It can happen, but I wouldn't count on it if I were you."

I deflated. "Damn."

"Just proceed under the assumption that your patient will have total recall, and you'll have to discuss his declaration of love. Explain Transference to him and why he's feeling the way he is. Tell him that the two of you can work through this issue together, or you can refer him to another therapist."

"I hope I don't have to do that. I kind of like Mitch and I thought we were making progr--" I trailed off when I saw the disapproving expression on Ford's face. "Alright, I know that I'm not supposed to have favorites among my patients, but I can't help it. I find Mitch entertaining, even if he is a narcissistic man whore."

Ford shook his head. "You women always like the bad boys."

"We like nice doctors, too," I said, giving him a playful nudge with my shoulder.

He chuckled just as his über-efficient receptionist, Trish, strolled into the office with a mug of steaming hot coffee in one hand, and the morning's mail in the other.

"Good morning, Dr. Fordham, Dr. Alvarez," she greeted us in a polite, professional tone.

"I guess it's 7:45," I remarked, pushing myself off the desk and into a standing position. Trish was so punctual that she was more reliable than a clock.

"On the dot," she replied as she set the mug and mail down next to Ford. "Would you like some coffee, Dr. Alvarez? I made a full pot, so there's plenty. Two creams and one sugar, right?"

The woman had made me coffee once, three weeks ago, and she remembered how I liked it? I was impressed, although I would never have wanted to trade her robotic competence for Margo's warmth and quirky humor.

"Thank you, Trish, but I need to get back to my office. I have a patient at nine, and some paperwork to catch up on before he arrives."

With a nod, the reed-thin brunette quietly returned to the waiting area.

"Your nine o'clock's not the infatuated patient, is it?" Ford asked.

"No, he won't be in until Wednesday, so I have a couple of days to formulate a strategy."

"Don't overthink it. You'll drive yourself--"

"Crazy," I said the word along with him.

"Fortunately, if that happens, I know an excellent psychiatrist," I grinned archly, then turned to leave.

"Let me know how it goes," Ford called after me.

"Will do." I gave him a wave over my shoulder.

"Mornin', Margo." I found my receptionist busily typing away on her keyboard.

"I hope you haven't eaten breakfast yet," she responded.

As a matter of fact, I hadn't. I'd been so keyed up about the Mitch situation that I'd rushed into work without the thought of food so much as crossing my mind. "No, why?"

"Saul woke up with a craving for my sour cream coffee cake early this morning, so I worked my magic in the kitchen and . . ." She reached under her desk, pulled out a Tupperware container, and peeled back its lid, revealing a large piece of the confectioners' sugar-dusted breakfast delicacy. YUM!

"Oh, Margo!" I breathed in the sweet, spicy scent of cinnamon and smiled with pleasure. "You are too good to me. Thank you!"

Walking behind her desk, I deposited an appreciative kiss on her powdered cheek, then made a grab for the coffee cake.

"Mrs. Scolari cancelled her appointment this morning. She wants you to call her so that she can explain why." Margo handed me a pink message slip with the Scolaris' phone number on it.

"Okay, thanks." Taking the piece of paper and the Tupperware, I headed for my office.

By the time I reached my desk, I'd already devoured half the walnuts on top of the cake. I knew that I had a fork somewhere in one of my desk drawers, but I didn't feel like wasting valuable eating time while I looked for it. So, I just used my fingers, which were soon sticky and covered with crumbs, making it next-to-impossible to call Mrs. Scolari without creating a big mess. I worked around this problem by pressing down on the number keys of my phone with the eraser end of a pencil.

"Hello?"

I quickly swallowed the half-chewed piece of coffee cake in my mouth. "Annette, this is Dr. Alvarez. I'm returning your call."

"Dr. Alvarez, thanks for getting back to me so fast. I wanted to let you know that Jo-Jo and I won't be coming in for any more sessions."

Jo-Jo? I'd never heard Annette call her husband by that name before.

"Oh, really?" I licked some powdery sugar off my thumb. "Why not?"

"So much has happened in the last few weeks, Dr. Alvarez."

"You've been on vacation most of that time, right?"

"Yes, Jo-Jo surprised me with a trip to Paris, the city I've dreamed about visiting ever since I was a little girl. It was the most romantic thing," she rhapsodized. "One day, he just came home from work with the plane tickets and said that he was taking me on a second honeymoon. We left the kids with my parents and took off the next day."

"That must have been exciting."

"It was! I really didn't think that Jo-Jo had it in him to be so spontaneous. I can't remember the last time the two of us went anywhere by ourselves. And we had the most wonderful time! We took long walks along the Seine, had candlelit dinners with lots of wine and delicious food, went dancing, and the best part was that we talked, really talked, about our relationship and what we needed from each other."

"Wow, sounds like quite an eventful trip." Hard to believe that this was the same couple who never communicated and had been miserable for years.

"I'm so happy, Dr. Alvarez, and so is Jo-Jo. We feel like our marriage is finally back on track. And we have you to thank for that."

"You do?" I mumbled, coffee cake crumbs spilling out of my partially opened mouth.

"Of course! I don't know what you said to my husband when you spoke to him alone at our last session, but it obviously had a huge effect on him. He's been like a different man ever since."

Behold the power of threats and coercion!

"I'm just glad that things have worked out for the two of you."

"We're really grateful for everything you've done for us, Dr. Alvarez. You're a terrific therapist, and I'll definitely recommend you to my friends."

"I'd appreciate that." I needed all the help I could get putting butts on my couch. "And remember, I'm here if you need me."

"Thank you so much."

"Good luck, Annette." I punched the speakerphone button, disconnecting the call.

Well, I'd saved a marriage, but lost some vitally important income. At least, I still had my sour cream coffee cake. With a sigh, I stuffed another piece in my mouth.

CHAPTER 23

After much anticipatory anxiety, the day of my dreaded appointment with Mitch Buchannon finally arrived. Part of me had hoped that he'd call to cancel because he was just too embarrassed to face me, but I was clearly projecting. When Mitch strode into my office with his customary swagger at two minutes past nine, the only one who exhibited any discomfort or embarrassment was me. Fortunately, Mitch seemed to be oblivious to my flushed cheeks and inability to make eye contact. With loose-limbed ease, he flopped down on my sofa and stretched his long arms out along its back.

I followed suit, taking a seat in the chair facing him. However, my posture was much less relaxed. In fact, I'd never felt so uptight in my life. I knew it was my job to say something, anything, but words, which had always been my greatest allies, failed me.

"Well, this is awkward." Mitch broke the ice with a good-humored grin.

"Yes, yes, it is."

He leaned forward, placing his elbows on his knees. "About the other night, Doc--"

"We don't have to talk about it if you don't want to." I was way too quick to let him off the hook and I knew it, but I was a coward and I just wanted to forget that Mitch had ever confessed to loving me and write it off as nothing more than a drunken delusion on his part.

"You did a nice thing coming to pick me up at Hal's, and I want you to know I appreciate it."

Appreciation was fine; appreciation I could handle.

"I'm glad I could help, but it was a one-time occurrence. Our doctor/patient relationship has boundaries, and I don't want you to get into the habit of relying on me--"

"Don't sweat it," Mitch casually dismissed my concerns.

"I understand. No more late-night phone calls. No more dumping my problems on you outside of our sessions."

"I think that that would be best. I don't want you to get confused about my role in your life."

"I'm not confused."

I was relieved to hear it. Obviously, I'd gotten myself all worked up over nothing. In the sober light of day, Mitch was perfectly reasonable and had a firm grasp on reality. He just happened to be one of those mushy drunks who told everyone he loved them. It didn't mean anything, so there was no need for further analysis of his feelings. We could just move on and--

"You're the woman I love."

"No, I'm not," I balked.

"Yes, you are. I've been giving it a lot of thought over the last few days . . ."

Damn it, why did I have to encourage him to be more introspective?

". . . and I guess I've loved you for a while; I just didn't have the guts to admit it. The booze gave me the courage I needed to be honest with myself, and with you."

Lord, help me, he seemed sincere.

"Okay." I took a deep breath in an effort to stanch the feeling of panic that was rising in my chest (or maybe that was acid reflux?) *Great, I was giving myself an ulcer.* "Let's backtrack for a minute here. In our first session, you said that you'd never been in love before, right?"

"Right."

"So, it's possible you don't know what love is and are misinterpreting your feelings." I reached for my trusty pad of paper and a pen.

"Why don't you tell me your symptoms?" I asked as if love was some kind of disease.

"Let's see." Mitch raked his fingers through his long,

sun-lightened hair while he contemplated my query. "I think about you all the time."

"Uh huh." I made some notations on my pad.

"I look forward to seeing you and feel like our time together is always too short."

"Okay." More scribbling.

"Your opinion of me matters more than anyone else's. I compare every woman I meet to you. I fantasize about--"

"Alright, I think I have a clear picture of your feelings now, thank you." Although I was a trained psychologist, I did not feel equal to the task of discussing Mitch's fantasies about me.

"So, it's love, right? It has to be. I've never felt this way about anyone before." His luminescent green eyes were fixed intently on mine.

"Well," I paused to clear my throat self-consciously, "there are varying degrees of love, starting with infatuation and progressing all the way up to a deep and abiding emotion that can bond two people for life."

"It's more than an infatuation." He seemed very sure of that. "I think we should go out on a date and see where it takes us."

"What?!?! No," I shook my head vehemently from side to side, "that's insa--, I mean *completely inappropriate*. I don't date my patients. It would be a breach of ethics."

"Fine." He shrugged his broad shoulders. "I came to you for help with my intimacy and commitment issues and you've cured me, so there's no further need for therapy. Consider this our last session."

"You are far from cured. This crush you have on me is what I would consider to be a *major* setback."

"It's more like an evolution. I'm growing as a person, opening myself up to new feelings and experiences, just like you told me to."

Wonderful, I'd created a self-actualized, love-spewing monster.

"You know what we should do tonight?" Mitch asked. "We should go dancing. I know this great club--"

I groaned and buried my face in my hands.

"I know what you're thinking - it's one of those sleazy pick-up joints I used to hang out in, but you're wrong. My taste in clubs has improved, along with my taste in women."

"Mitch," I looked up at him, "I cannot go out with you. Not today, not tomorrow, not ever."

"What's the problem? You find me attractive, don't you?"

Before I could respond, he answered for me, "Of course, you do. Every woman does. I'm pretty much irresistible." He flashed me his pearly whites and dimples.

"Your attractiveness and irresistibility are beside the point. I," I placed my hand on my chest and spoke very slowly as if English was not his first language, "am your doctor. You," I pointed to him, "are my patient. Nothing's going to change that. So, we need to make the most of the professional relationship we have, which means getting to the bottom of these feelings you have for me."

Yes, good, Pilar, bring it back around to psychology.

"Are you familiar with the term 'Transference?'"

"Nope," he replied with a frown.

"It's the process whereby emotions are passed on or displaced from one person to another," I explained.

"So, you think I'm transferring my love for someone else on to you?"

"More or less. Because you had unmet emotional needs as a child, you're transferring the love you had for your mother to a woman who seems to be nurturing and kind - me."

Mitch scratched the back of his neck before saying, "That doesn't sound right. I'm pretty sure I never had the hots for my mother."

"The sexual component of your attraction to me is not about your mother; it's about you being turned on by the feminine ideal I represent as your therapist. I'm a good listener, I'm sympathetic, supportive, reassuring . . ."

Mitch was looking really confused, and I didn't blame him.

"It's complicated and hard-to-comprehend, I know. That's why I printed up some informative articles about Transference reactions for you."

Getting up from my chair, I walked over to my desk to retrieve the pages that I'd organized and put into a manila folder.

"I could have sworn I put it on top of this pile," I muttered as I leaned across my desk, sifting through the largest stack of files sitting on it.

"Ah, yes, here it is." With the folder in hand, I whirled around and bumped right into Mitch who'd trailed me across the office.

I grunted with surprise.

"Sorry, I didn't realize . . . here's the material I mentioned." I pushed the folder up against his chest, expecting him to take it from me and back off.

He didn't. Instead, he leaned in to me and sniffed my neck. "You smell good enough to eat," he murmured in a low, sexy tone.

Lovelorn romantic one minute, Casanova-on-the-make the next. This guy had more personalities than Sybil.

"You are invading my personal space, Mitch."

He chuckled throatily. "Yeah, I guess I am. What can I say? When you love someone, you just want to be near them. You know, Doc," he placed his hands on my desk, one on either side of my body, "I've had some really steamy fantasies about you and me and this desk."

I wasn't sure if Mitch was trying to shock or seduce me, but he was definitely testing me and it behooved me to keep a cool head and remain professionally detached. I wondered what Freud would have to say about a patient fantasizing that he was having sex with his therapist on the therapist's desk? The desk was obviously a symbol of the psychologist's power and by placing the psychologist in a position of subjugation on that desk, the patient was, in essence, stripping away that power and reclaiming it for-- no, no, no, that was all too highbrow. I was attempting to communicate with a patient, not write a paper for one of my graduate studies classes. I needed to break it down to the basics and put everything in terms Mitch could understand.

"Fantasies are one thing, and reality is another. We are in the latter at the moment, so I would appreciate it if you would comport yourself accordingly."

"I can comport myself any way you want me to, Doc. I'm *very* flexible." Mitch smiled salaciously as he moved his body closer to mine.

"You may not realize this," I said, bending back towards the surface of my desk in order to avoid full-frontal contact with him, "but you are reverting back to your old, self-defeating patterns of behavior."

"Am I?" His lips were now poised right above mine. I could feel his warm breath fanning my mouth when he spoke.

Suddenly, I had a horrifying vision of Margo, or God forbid, another patient, walking into my office and catching me in what appeared to be an extremely compromising position with Mitch. I'd be mortified and my credibility as a psychologist would be shot all because this big lug had decided that I was his dream girl.

Shoving Mitch's bulky frame away, I scrambled out from underneath him.

"This session is over," I announced in the most authoritative tone I could muster while tucking my silk blouse, which had somehow managed to work itself loose from the waistband of my skirt, back in.

"But I have thirty-two minutes left," he protested.

"You can use that time to read this file." I smacked him in the chest with the manila folder that was still in my possession. "Pay special attention to the subsection on Sexual Attraction. We'll discuss it in detail at your session on Friday."

"Sexual attraction's not something I really need to read up on. But if it'll make you happy . . ." He took a few steps back and gave me a flirty wink before exiting to the waiting room.

I spent the rest of the day kicking myself for not having been more firm with Mitch. I knew I should have told him that making a pass at me was inappropriate and threatened to refer him to another doctor if he did it again. But I'd let myself get flustered, and he'd left thinking I was just playing hard-to-get. So, now this was all some big game to him, a game he was confident he'd win because he was so "irresistible." *UGH*

* * *

I was standing over the sink, eating some cold, two-day old Pasta Carbonara out of a Tupperware container without utensils, when my phone rang. I sucked up some noodles and answered with my mouth full.

"Hey-row."

"*¡Hola, Pee-lar! ¿Cómo estás?*" a young boy inquired.

"Nate?"

Childish laughter echoed in my ear. "Yep, it's me! Poppa said it would be okay if I called you. I hope you don't mind."

"Of course not." I ripped a paper towel off the holder hanging underneath the kitchen cabinet to my right and used it to wipe the cream sauce off my fingers. "What's up?"

"I played in my first Tee-Ball game today."

"That's terrific! Did your team win?"

"Nobody wins in Tee-Ball," he informed me. "We don't keep score. We're supposed to be learning the fundamentals and having fun. Of course, I already know the fundamentals, but not all kids watch as much baseball as I do."

"So, how did you do today?"

"I hit the ball twice, so I got on base. And the second time, I got to slide into home."

"Wow, sounds like you have the makings of a great baseball player."

"Coach Castaneira said I was a 'natural,' and he let me play Shortstop for a couple of innings. Derek Jeter plays Shortstop, you know. That's the best position on the field. You can catch ground balls and fly balls there. We've got another game next week. We're playing the Red Sox. Will you come, Pee-lar? Please," he begged. "If you come, we can go to my house afterwards and have dinner. I could ask Poppa to grill out some hamburgers, and you could meet Vinny, *mi tortuga*."

"That would be nice, Nate, but I think that you should check with your parents first to see if it's okay." I didn't want to intrude on any family time.

"Poppa's always saying that we should invite you over. He likes you a lot."

I hadn't gotten any formal invitations yet, so maybe Mrs. Dr. Ford wasn't so keen on the idea? "What about your mother?"

"I don't think she'd care, but I can't really--"

"Nate," I heard Ford call his son's name, "it's time to get ready for bed."

"But, Poppa, I'm on the phone with Pee-lar," he protested.

"And you've talked long enough. You've got summer camp tomorrow, and I don't want to have to drag you out of bed in the morning because you went to bed late. Now, give me the phone and go put your pajamas on."

"Pee-lar hasn't given me my two Spanish words yet," the child stubbornly refused to relinquish the phone.

"*Dulces sueños*, Nate," I interjected.

"What does that mean?"

"Sweet dreams."

"Oh. *Dulces sueños* to you, too, Pee-lar."

"Great, you got your two words. Now, go brush those teeth," Ford ordered. "And don't think that just getting your toothbrush wet is going to fool me. I'm going to check to see if your breath is minty fresh or not."

With a sigh of exasperation, Ford brought the phone receiver up to his ear. "Sorry about that. Bedtime is always a battle of wills around here. I probably shouldn't have let him call you this close to eight, but he was so excited about the game and he was dying to tell you about it."

"I enjoyed his recap."

"I know I've said it before, but I really appreciate you being so good to Nate. This last year . . . this move has been tough on him, and you've been so helpful with the Tee-Ball and the Spanish. He likes you a lot."

Funny that Nate had just said the same thing about Ford.

"The feeling is mutual."

"I was thinking about you today."

For some inexplicable reason, that knowledge made me feel giddy as a schoolgirl.

"Oh, really?" I feigned nonchalance.

"Yeah, I was wondering how your appointment with that lovesick patient went. I would have stopped by your office at lunchtime, but I had an emergency at the hospital that tied me up for several hours. Then, I went straight from there to the game. So?"

"The session was a disaster."

"Elaborate," he prompted.

"I tried discussing, arguing, analyzing, intellectualizing, explaining, reasoning, I even had printed materials on Transference in all its forms, but nothing would dissuade this man from thinking that he loves me. He went so far as to ask me out on a date, and when I said, 'no,' he made advances."

The line went strangely quiet. I couldn't hear breathing, or background noise; there was just dead air.

"Ford?" I queried tentatively, thinking that we'd been disconnected.

"*Sexual* advances?"

"What other kind of advances, are there?"

"I just wanted to clarify," he said, sounding uncharacteristically irritable.

"It wasn't like he pounced on me or anything. He just made some double entendres, said that I smelled good enough to eat, and tried to maneuver me into a horizontal position on top of my desk."

"Drop this patient, drop him *now*," Ford advised.

"That wouldn't be right. I made a commitment to help this man. He's got problems--"

"His main one being an overactive libido. You need to refer him to another therapist, Pilar. You're in over your head. I don't know what this man's motivation is, but it goes way beyond Transference. He's manipulating you and he's manipulating the situation."

"And you've come to this conclusion based on the small tidbits I've shared with you from my sessions with him?" A smart man would have taken note of the edge in my voice. Alas, despite Ford's many degrees and elevated IQ, he was just as obtuse as the other members of his sex when it came to reading signals from women.

"You've told me more than enough. It's clear that--"

"I've spent hours delving into this man's psyche and you've never laid eyes on him, but you think that you've got a better handle on what makes him tick than I do?" I was incredulous, bordering on offended.

"You're too close to the case; you've lost your objectivity and you're leaving yourself open for--"

"I don't remember asking for a performance evaluation," I said waspishly.

"I'm just trying to give you the benefit of my experience--"

"No, you're being judgmental and supercilious and . . . and . . .," I struggled to find another adjective that would be appropriately disparaging, ". . . bossy."

"And you're being hypersensitive, which tells me that deep down you know I'm right about this whole Mitch thing; you just don't want to admit it."

"Stop analyzing me!"

"Stop being so stubborn and cut this patient loose!"

"Poppa!"

Ford groaned with frustration that was probably caused by me, not his five-year-old.

"Coming, Nate!" he yelled.

"I've got to go and tuck him in."

"Fine," was my snippy reply.

"Are you mad at me?"

"Yes." I affected the same wounded tone my mother used whenever she wanted to make someone feel guilty.

And it was effective because Ford was instantly contrite. "I'm sorry if I sounded like I was being critical. You know that I think you're a wonderful therapist."

"What was that? I didn't hear you."

Ford chuckled. "Yes, you did. You're a wonderful

therapist and you know it, but--"

"Ah-ah! If you're going to give me a compliment, don't qualify it."

"Okay, I won't. Will you concede that I might have a valid point about this Mitch character and proceed with caution?"

"I will keep your concerns in mind when I see the patient again on Friday."

"And if that session is more of the same with him hitting on you and not respecting your authority . . ."

". . . I will refer him to another psychologist."

"A *male* psychologist?"

"Naturally."

"Good. I'm glad that that's settled."

Oh, it was settled alright. If Ford thought that I was some lightweight who couldn't handle a frisky patient, then he was about to be proved wrong.

CHAPTER 24

"So, how does wearing it make you feel?" I questioned the teenager who was sprawled out on my couch.

She looked down at her chest, which had doubled in size since the last time I'd seen her, thanks to a gel-filled push-up bra.

"I dunno." She obviously didn't want to talk about it.

"I think you do."

I'd been working with Meghan Faber for almost three months, trying to improve her self-image and boost her confidence, but no matter what progress we seemed to make, she steadfastly refused to abandon her dream of getting a breast augmentation. I'd finally decided that the only way to convince Meghan a boob job was a bad idea was to show her, and to that end, I'd suggested that her parents buy her a bra with enhancements.

"Alright," she caved in grudgingly, "it makes me feel weird."

"And?" I pushed.

"And jiggly. I never realized how much boobs bounced. How are you supposed to run or jump with these things?"

I tried not to smile. "Women who are well-endowed generally wear a lot of support, especially when exercising, sometimes even when they sleep."

"Wearing a bra to bed wouldn't be very comfortable," Meghan muttered. "I guess you can't sleep on your stomach when you have big boobs either."

"That's one of the drawbacks of being more voluptuous."

"I could get used to sleeping on my back if I had to . . ." She wasn't willing to admit defeat just yet.

"How have your friends and classmates reacted to your new look?"

"I'm getting a lot more attention from guys now," she

reported. That should have made her happy, but Meghan's glum expression indicated otherwise.

"But it isn't the kind of attention you wanted?" I surmised.

"I wanted guys to notice me and ask me out. But since I started wearing this bra, all they do is whistle, make boob-squishing hand gestures, and call me names like 'Meghan Melon Tits.' I don't know why guys have to be so crude."

"Unfortunately, it's their nature when they're your age. Your friend Ryan hasn't been teasing you, has he?" From what Meghan had told me about him, Ryan was a nice young man who had a good head on his shoulders. I, also, had a sneaking suspicion that he liked Meghan in a not-platonic way. Of course, she'd been too caught up in her insecurities about her appearance to pick up on that.

"No." She blushed, then ducked her head to hide the involuntary display of emotion.

Okay, maybe she did realize that Ryan was crushing on her, and she shared his feelings?

"He said this bra was 'dumb,' and that I looked better before."

"Maybe he's right? Has having a larger bust improved your life at all?"

"Well . . .," she paused to think about it for a minute, ". . . not really."

"And have you learned anything from this experience?"

"You mean, like a lesson?"

I nodded.

"Oh, man," Meghan heaved a persecuted sigh, "isn't being humiliated and bummed out enough? Why do I have to learn a lesson from this?"

"Humor me."

She rolled her heavily-lined eyes as she was wont to do. "Alright, I learned that . . . men are pigs."

"Not all of them," I corrected her.

"Okay, not Ryan. He's pretty cool."

"What else?"

"I learned that . . . you shouldn't try to be something you're not."

Eureka! She'd finally found the psychological nugget of gold I'd had her panning for since we'd started these sessions.

"Why not?"

"Because you only end up making yourself and everyone around you miserable."

"That's a wonderful insight! Well done, Meghan. Well done!" I clapped my hands together excitedly and beamed with pride.

"Don't even think about hugging me," she grumbled.

* * *

"I'm home!" I yelled as I walked through the front door of my house with a Little Tony's pizza box in my hand.

Izzy danced out from her bedroom, holding an iPod in her hand. One earbud was in while the other dangled down her chest.

"Have you got dinner?" she asked.

I raised the box up. "One Veggie Deluxe, light sauce, no olives."

"Excellent. The DVDs came in the mail this afternoon." She did the barefoot boogie over to the coffee table where I could see two red-and-white Netflix envelopes sitting.

I dropped my purse and briefcase on the tile floor. "What's on our viewing agenda tonight?"

"You have a choice: *Cross Her Heart*, which is a thriller about a serial killer who stalks and stabs redheads, then removes their hearts and carves the symbol of the cross in--"

"No way." I shook my head.

"Are you sure? The detective who's pursuing the serial

killer is played by Dean Cain, and I know you like him. The movie's rated R, so there'll probably be some steamy sex scenes between him and Angie Everhart, or Kari Wuhrer, or both," she sought to entice me.

"Pass. What else did you get?"

"*Bayou Beast*." She pulled the DVD sleeve out of the envelope so that she could read the synopsis on it. "Legend has it that a creature, once a man, now a deformed, ravenous monster, lurks beneath the murky surface of Blackwater Swamp. Environmentalist Michael Hornsby doesn't believe the gruesome folklore until one dark night, Nora, his research partner and *fiancée*, is savagely ripped from his arms and dragged into the swamp. Now, he must find and--"

"Okay, okay, we'll watch that one." Although it sounded like made-for-Syfy crap, *Bayou Beast* was the lesser of two evils. At least, swamp monsters could be dismissed as completely fictional, and therefore, nothing to be frightened off. Serial killers were the stuff of nightmares for single women like me.

"Let's get some drinks and plates," I said, and Izzy followed me into the kitchen.

She got out the dishes and napkins, while I poured a couple of diet sodas into glasses. We returned to the living room, where Izzy insisted on turning out all the lights to set the mood, and made ourselves comfortable on the couch. It occurred to me that she and I hadn't spent any quality time together like this in weeks. We'd been on opposite schedules for so long, me working all day, her slinging cocktails at the club all night, and when we did have a face-to-face it was usually to deal with a crisis of some sort. I missed just hanging out and having fun with my sister.

Izzy put a slice of pizza on each of our plates, while I popped the DVD into the player.

"Damn, we forgot the parmesan."

"I'll get it," I offered since I was already up. "You can go ahead and start the movie."

Ominous-sounding music emanated from the TV as I headed back to the kitchen. It took me a while to find the canned parmesan because someone had put it in the pantry even though I'd told her a dozen times that once you open parmesan, it has to go in the refrigerator or it won't stay fresh. While I was digging around in the pantry, I came across some bread that had gone moldy. I threw it away, then started to wonder when I'd last cleaned out and organized the pantry. I heard a bloodcurdling scream just as I picked up a can of Campbell's New England Clam Chowder. I cringed when I saw that it had expired four months ago.

"Pilar! You just missed the Bayou Beast's first attack. This guy who's playing the environmentalist is HOT!"

"Coming!" My messy pantry would have to wait. I hated eating cold pizza.

"So, where's this hot environmentalist?" I wondered as I handed the cheese to Izzy and sat down. All I saw on screen was a paunchy, middle-aged cop positioned at the water's edge, while a couple of men in a small boat dragged the swamp with what looked like a big fish net.

"Umph." Izzy had to swallow the bite of pizza that was in her mouth before she could answer. "He's in the hospital. He was so traumatized by what happened to his girlfriend that he's semi-catatonic."

"Well, that's no fun."

"Oh, I'm sure he'll snap out of it. Meanwhile, there's a chance we'll get to see him in one of those butt-baring hospital gowns."

Five minutes passed and there was no sign of the hunky tree-hugger, but the Bayou Beast claimed another victim - this one a frat boy so blockheaded (his drunken, Phi Beta

Theta brothers dared him to wade into the swamp at night, and he actually did it) that he deserved to die as far as I was concerned.

"Michael Hornsby's responsive. We need to get over to Memorial and talk to him," the portly cop told his partner after getting a call from the hospital.

I perked up in anticipation of finally seeing the man who'd earned a thumbs up from Izzy.

"There he is." My sister pointed at the TV screen.

There was his back anyway. Michael Hornsby was standing in front of a window, staring outside, when the policemen entered his hospital room. And no, there were no butt cheeks hanging out the back of his hospital gown, just white boxer briefs. The actor did have a great body; he was tall and nicely proportioned with muscles in all the right places. There was something familiar about the set of his shoulders - they were held high and proudly, but with such effortless ease . . .

"Mr. Hornsby, I'm Lieutenant Fields, and this is Detective Lamont. We're investigating the disappearance of your *fiancée*."

The actor he was addressing slowly turned to face the camera.

My mouth dropped open, and the pizza I'd just stuffed into it fell out on to my plate. "Oh, my God!"

"I told you! He's sexy, isn't he? I just wanna run my fingers through that shaggy, blond hair. Rowwwwwr," my sister growled.

"Oh. My. God." I was in such a state of shock that I repeated myself.

The mushrooms on my pizza were obviously having a hallucinogenic effect. What other explanation could there be for me seeing Mitch Buchannon in a B-movie? He wasn't an actor. Maybe this guy in *Bayou Beast* was just a look-alike?

CHAPTER 25

I didn't know who to be more angry with: Mitch Buchannon, *argh*, Derek Reynolds (What kind of dumb, metrosexual-sounding name was that anyway?), for deceiving me, or myself, for being such a gullible twit. I frittered away the majority of the next day going back and forth on the issue, and the more I thought about it, the more incensed I became. How dare he dupe me! Was nothing sacred? A psychologist's office was supposed to be like a confessional - lies were never to be told there. And it's not like Mitch, *ack*, Derek, had just lied about his name and occupation. Oh no, he'd lied about everything from his place of birth (some rural town in North Georgia - *Why hadn't I questioned that telltale drawl he'd let slip several times?* - not Tampa) to his lack of family (He had four siblings and parents that were not only alive, but still married after 39 years of presumably wedded bliss.) In all the hours we'd spent together discussing his thoughts, feelings, hopes, and fears, I don't think that one honest word had come out of that man's mouth.

And the worst part of it was that I didn't know why. Why had he lied? What had he hoped to gain by presenting me with such a colorful patchwork of falsehoods? It just didn't make any sense. But I would find out the truth, so help me, Freud. When Mitch, *dammit!*, Derek showed up for his appointment at 4:00, I planned to confront him and demand an explanation. I deserved that much. Actually, I deserved an apology and I wouldn't be satisfied until I got one.

I didn't have a patient at 3:00, so I had an hour to kill before Mi--, *the big, fat phony*, arrived. I'd let Margo leave early and I couldn't concentrate on work, which left me with no source of entertainment or distraction. I decided to call Sara and see how preparations were going for the fashion show.

"T-minus 21 hours and counting," my best friend said when she answered her cell.

"Are you excited? Nervous?"

"Both. Plus, anxiety-ridden, nauseous, and borderline suicidal. Michelle! *What* are you doing? You're supposed to be slinking down the runway like a sleek, sexy panther, but you're stomping around like a constipated elephant! Jesus!"

"Where are you?" I wondered.

"At the Fontainebleau. We're doing a dress rehearsal. Beautiful, Nicola, beautiful. But I want you to wear your hair down with that suit. It'll draw more attention to the bustline."

"I can't wait to see the show tomorrow."

"I'll need all the handholding and alcoholic beverages you can provide. You'll be here at 11:00, right?"

"Right, and I thought I'd bring Izzy."

"The more, the merrier. Just don't let her drive you here in a stolen car," Sara teased.

"Ha, ha."

"No, no, STOP! Lighting people!" she screamed. "This is where I wanted you to switch from pink to amber. Not yellow, AMBER! Honestly, it's like amateur hour here. That yellow light was way too harsh. It was making my models look like drag queens."

"You're obviously busy, so I'll just let you--"

"I can critique the show and talk to you at the same time. Hold on a minute . . . Where's the freakin' music? Alfonso, find out what's going on with the music. There's no point in having the girls come down the runway without it. They need to time their steps to a beat for Christ's sake. Okay, I'm back. Tell me what's wrong."

"I didn't say that anything was wrong."

commit,'" I imitated Derek in a whiny, high-pitched voice that sounded nothing like him. "You've been married THREE times, so obviously commitment's never really been a problem for you."

"Well, technically, I've only been married twice," he corrected me. "I had that thing with Tara Reid annulled after I sobered up. The rum down in Martinique has a real kick to it. I don't even remember--"

Derek's talk of being hammered made me flash back to the night I'd dragged him home from that sleazy bar down on Washington.

"Oh, my God," I groaned. "You weren't really drunk when you called me from Hal's, were you?"

He smirked. "Pretty good act, huh? I played Grissom's alcoholic nephew on an episode of *CSI* a couple of years ago. The secret to playing a convincing drunk is not to oversell it. A slight slurring of your speech, a little disorientation and clumsiness . . ."

If he wanted me to compliment him on his performance, he was going to have a long wait.

"Why? Why would you pull me out of bed in the middle of the night and have me come to a dangerous part of town when there was nothing wrong with you?"

"I had to play drunk so that I could confess my 'love,'" he actually made air quotes with his fingers when he said the word, "for you. I'd tried flirting with you during our sessions, but that wasn't getting me anywhere. So, I figured you were one of those chicks who only slept with guys you thought you had some sort of emotional connection to."

"And that was the purpose of this whole charade? You wanted to get me into bed?" I gaped in disbelief.

"*Mitch* wanted to get you into bed. He's the one who was lusting after you."

"But you ARE Mitch!" I screeched, losing my

professional cool.

Derek shook his head. "Mitch is a character, a role that I immersed myself in. He's got nothing to do with me. No offense, Doc, but you're not even my type. I like blondes."

"I'm so confused," I lamented.

"The reason I came to see you in the first place was because I got this part in a Lifetime movie that starts filming here in Miami next month. My character is this troubled guy who finds himself attracted to his beautiful, female psychologist. She's drawn to him, too, so they start having this hot love affair. When she ends up dead . . . well, I don't want to spoil the movie for you, but there's a great twist at the end."

I only cared about the plot of his lame cable movie insofar as it involved me. "So, you pretended to need psychological help because--"

"I needed to understand the complicated dynamic between patient and therapist in order to do justice to this horny, emotionally stunted character."

"You could have just asked me," I snapped peevishly. "This whole Mitch ruse was totally unnecessary."

"Interviewing you wouldn't have done me any good. I'm a Method actor. I needed to experience the patient/therapist relationship firsthand."

"And to that end, you manipulated me."

He shrugged. "It was research."

"It was a head game and the fact that you don't see the difference--"

"I really don't know why you're getting so het up about this, Doc. I've created characters and used them as research tools before. It's no big deal."

"It is to *me*." I thumped myself on the chest dramatically. "I care about my patients, I care about helping them. So, when I discover that one of them has lied to me and used me to further his own interests, naturally, I feel betrayed," my voice quivered, and I struggled not to let my emotions get the best of me.

"It's not like you didn't get anything out of our sessions."

"What's that supposed to mean?" I placed my hands on my hips and narrowed my eyes at him.

"Mitch came to you a shallow, self-involved player, and you jumped at the chance to make him over. He was your pet project, a man you could refine and improve, then send back out into the world a better person."

That had pretty much been my strategy with Mitch. But when he put it like that, it made me sound like Professor Henry Higgins gone wild.

"There's nothing wrong with trying to help people improve themselves," I said huffily. "It's my job to counsel and guide--"

"You're a control freak," he diagnosed.

"What??????? I am n-n-n-not!" I was so outraged that I started to stutter.

"Oh, no?" Derek shoved his hands into the deep pockets of his shorts and rocked back on his heels. "Look at how you reacted when Mitch told you he loved you. You freaked out."

"I-I-I was t-t-taken aback." *Still with the stuttering.* Had the stress of this encounter caused a permanent speech impediment?

"You couldn't deal because you lost control of the situation - of Mitch. The next time we saw each other, you were so desperate to get me back in line it was comical. The look on your face when I asked you out on a date!" The memory made him guffaw.

I wanted to say something cutting in return, but I was too busy fighting back tears. This jerk had committed the worst kind of treachery (in my eyes anyway), and now he was laughing at me and impugning my abilities as a therapist?

"You need to leave," a calm, but nonetheless steely, voice instructed.

I glanced over my shoulder and saw Ford standing behind me with a clenched jaw and a fierce look in his blue eyes. I imagined that it was the same expression he'd had on his face all those years ago when his brother had called him "Brainiac." If Derek got force-fed one of Ford's knuckle sandwiches, he had nobody to blame but himself.

"Look, pal," Derek stepped towards him, "I don't know who you are, but you're interrupting a private conversation between me and the doc here."

"Yeah, I heard most of it," Ford admitted to eavesdropping.

When I frowned at him, he explained, "I happened to be passing by, the door was ajar, and I heard shouting."

A likely story. He'd probably been lurking in the hallway ever since Derek had gotten there.

"You," he pointed at my patient, "should get out of here before I advise my colleague to sue you for Fraud."

The color drained out of Derek's tanned face. "She can't do that!"

He was right; I couldn't since he'd only cheated me out of my pride and self-esteem, not anything that had monetary value. But it was a good bluff, and the sadist in me enjoyed seeing Derek sweat.

"Just leave," I said a few seconds later when I grew weary of tormenting him.

"Fine, but if I win an Emmy for my performance in *Loving You Can't Be Wrong*, don't expect me to thank you in my acceptance speech. And you won't be getting any kind of Technical Advisor credit either."

Having delivered what he probably thought was a great exit line, Derek strode out of my office with his vanity intact.

Since I wasn't about to let that two-bit actor have the last word, I scurried after him and yelled out into the hallway, "Oh, yeah. Well, I'm billing you for a full hour even though you only used fifteen minutes!"

And with that, I slammed the door shut and spun back around towards Ford.

"I am the worst psychologist EVER!" I wailed, then burst into tears, which completely mortified me. I wasn't the Alvarez who lost control of her emotions and had messy, public breakdowns. That was my mother or Isidora. I was the one who always held it together, the one who never screwed up, or made a fool out of herself. What had happened to me? In an effort to hide my shame, I buried my face in my hands.

The next thing I knew, Ford's arms were wrapped around me, and I was sobbing pathetically up against his chest.

"You are not a bad psychologist," he said in the quiet, soothing tone that shrinks usually reserved for their most overwrought patients, the ones who were balanced precariously on 12th Floor ledges threatening to end it all.

"Yes . . . yes, I am." I pulled myself together long enough to speak, although I did so haltingly. "I never . . . even questioned . . . I believed everything that Mitch, ohhhhh--," realizing I'd just messed up that deceitful bastard's name for the umpteenth time, I took off on another crying jag.

Ford rubbed my back comfortingly. "You had no way of knowing what he was up to. You had no reason to suspect that he was being untruthful."

"But I did!" I insisted in a tear-choked voice. "There were so many signs . . . they were all there, right in front of me, but I just ignored them."

Most men would have seized the opportunity to say, 'I told you so,' or, 'You really should have listened to me,' but Ford took the high road.

"You're just trusting by nature."

"No." I shook my head from side-to-side, leaving streaks of wet mascara across the front of his royal blue dress shirt. "I'm stupid and obtuse and I have no business being a psychologist."

"Hey!" Ford cupped my face in his hands and forced me to look up at him. I must have been a charming sight with my red, watery eyes and leaky nose. I really needed a tissue.

"Don't get down on yourself just because things went wrong with one patient."

"It's just so awful being lied to and feeling like I have only myself to blame because I wasn't smart or observant enough . . ." Fresh tears spilled from my eyes and streamed down my cheeks.

Ford gently wiped them away with the pads of his thumbs. "You are smart. You just let that compassionate heart of yours override your brain sometimes."

I gazed up into Ford's kind eyes and was reminded of our first encounter on the staircase outside. I'd crashed into him and made him drop his plant, but instead of being irritated, he'd worried about me hitting my head and once he'd determined that I didn't have a concussion, he'd fixed my broken cell phone. It seemed like Ford had been fixing things for me (or, at least, trying to) since the day we'd met.

"Why are you always so nice to me?" I wondered.

A smile tugged at the corners of his mouth. "Because you're easy to be nice to," was his simple reply.

Then, his eyes softened and dropped slowly to my lips. He lifted my chin up, and I knew he was going to kiss me. I could have said "no," I could have shoved him away, but I didn't. When his lips met mine, I kissed him back without hesitation, without a thought for anyone but myself. In my defense . . . *oh, why bother?* There is no defense. I acted selfishly and impetuously. I kissed Ford because I wanted to, because it felt good and, somehow, natural, like his mouth was meant for mine. And it was a great kiss, an amazing kiss, a kiss that should have had a poem written about it, a kiss that started out sweet and tender, then quickly morphed into something so hot and passionate that it was almost primal. Izzy's prediction about our clothes flying off probably would have come to pass if an image of Nate's adorable little face hadn't popped unbidden into my head just as my fingers were fumbling with the buttons on Ford's shirt.

'Oh, God, you're a horrible person,' I rebuked myself. *'You're one of those women everyone at church whispers about, a woman with loose morals who doesn't respect other people's marriages, a no-good, homewrecking hussy!'*

Appalled by this epiphany, I pushed myself away from a very disheveled and confused-looking Ford and backed up several steps.

"I-I-I shouldn't have . . . That was a mistake." I pressed a trembling hand up against my lips, which were now throbbing. "You have a wife, a child--"

"We didn't do anything wrong. Pilar--" He reached out for me, and I panicked, knowing that if he touched me again, I was done for.

So, I bolted. I didn't even get my purse or worry about locking up my office for the weekend. I just threw open the door that led out to the hallway and I ran.

CHAPTER 26

"You look like shit."

My sister wasn't telling me anything I didn't already know, but it still wasn't what I wanted to hear.

"Shut up," I grumbled as we wove our way through the Fontainebleau's Grand Ballroom, which was already filling up with reporters and photographers who were trying to stake out the best spots at the foot of the runway.

"I'm just saying you could have at least put on some makeup. Your skin's so pale; it's just making those dark circles under your eyes stand out more."

I turned to my left and glared at Izzy. Why was it that she looked all glowy and fresh-faced when she'd stayed up until 4AM three nights in a row, and I looked like something that belonged on a slab in the morgue after one fitful night of tossing and turning? I silently cursed her youth.

"Hi. We should be on the list," I told the burly security guard posted in front of the large blue curtain that allowed backstage access.

"Are you a model?" he queried.

Izzy snickered. "Hardly."

I was tempted to jab her in the ribs with my elbow, but I refrained.

"No, we're guests of one of the designers, Pilar and Isidora Alvarez."

The guard scanned the sheet of paper on his clipboard. "Alright," he said when he located our names, "but I'm gonna need to see some picture ID before you can go back."

Izzy and I pulled out our driver's licenses and handed them to the uniformed man. He gave my sister's a quick once-over, then returned it to her. I expected to receive the same cursory treatment, but instead he gazed down at my photo, raised his eyes to mine, furrowed his brow, and repeated the cycle twice.

"Are you sure this is you?" he asked, pointing to the laminated card. "Because this woman looks hot, and you--"

"--look like shit. I'm aware of that. Thank you." I ripped the license out of his hand and stuffed it back into my purse.

"Not that it's any of your business," I leaned forward to read his name tag, "*Phil*, but I had a rough night. Actually, I've had a rough month. Things haven't been going well at work, my sister got arrested for a crime she didn't commit, I'm broke, and to top things off, yesterday, I kissed someone I shouldn't have. So, you'll have to forgive me if I didn't feel like washing my hair and putting on lipstick this morning. The truth is I don't even want to be here. I'd rather be home eating Frosted Flakes out of the box and feeling sorry for myself. But I promised a friend I'd come and support her on what could possibly be the most important day in her life, and I'm not going to disappoint her. Now, are you going to let us through, or do I have to get ugly?"

"Don't you mean *uglier*?" Izzy snarked.

I smacked her in the arm with my purse and scowled threateningly at the rent-a-cop.

"Well?"

"Go on." He lifted the curtain aside and waved us back.

I'd never been behind-the-scenes at a fashion show before. It was like stepping into a whole other world, where the air crackled with frenetic energy. Everyone was bustling to and fro and if you didn't stay alert, there was a good chance you'd be mowed down by a moving rack of swimwear. Designers were shouting orders at impossibly thin models who wore silk kimonos and had makeup artists and hair stylists buzzing around them, trying to put the finishing touches on their faces and 'dos.

"So, who's this guy you kissed yesterday?" Izzy grilled me as we shoved our way through the crowd.

"I don't want to talk about it."

"Was it that actor from *Bayou Beast*, the one who's your patient? I'll bet it was. That guy is totally do-able. I can't believe you waited this long to jump him."

"I did *not* kiss Derek."

I raised myself up on my tiptoes so that I could see over all of the Amazons' heads.

"Well, who then?" Like a dog with a mailman's leg in its mouth, my sister wasn't going to let it go.

"Do you see Sara anywhere?" I deflected her question by asking one of my own.

"That might be her over--"

A small, incredibly hirsute man with a comb in one hand, and a can of styling spray in the other, stopped dead in front of Izzy. "Your hair!" he screamed with rapturous delight as if he'd just laid eyes on a great work of art.

"Yeah, what about it?" She gazed down at the excitable creature.

"The color! The texture! The glossy sheen!" the little man gushed. "I've never seen anything like it. It's all natural, right? No dye? No extensions?"

"Nope."

"What product do you use on it?"

"You got me. Pilar, what's that shampoo I'm always stealing out of your shower?"

"Kiehl's."

"Kiehl's," she told him.

"Can I touch it?" He extended a hand tentatively.

"Be my--"

"Fred!" Sara came barreling up with a lit cigarette dangling out of the side of her mouth. "Get your pervy paws off my friend's virgin hair and go finish brushing out Simone. Don't I have enough problems without having to chase you down?"

He let his hand fall. "Sorry, Sara. I'm on it," he assured her, then cast one last, wistful look at Izzy's shiny black tresses and scurried off.

"I swear, if this day gets any more stressful, I'm going to have an aneurysm!" Sara exclaimed before taking a long drag off of her cigarette.

"Since when do you smoke?" I wondered.

"Since about an hour ago when two of my models called in sick with the 'stomach flu,' aka a nasty hangover, and I realized that my career as a swimwear designer was over before it had even begun."

"Oh, no! What are you going to do?"

"I don't know." Her eyes filled with tears, and her lower lip started to tremble. "I've worked so hard, and now it's all falling apart at the last minute. I'm so screwed. There's no way I can show my full line with just three models. They'll never be able to make the changes fast enough."

"Why don't you model?" I suggested. "I know it's been a while since you've done any runway work, but--"

"God, no! I can't do that!" Sara blanched at the thought. "Designers never model their own creations. That would be gauche in the extreme. I'd be laughed out of fashion."

"Okay, well . . ." I racked my brain for another feasible solution.

"I could do it," Izzy offered.

Sara's jaw dropped as did some ash off the end of her burning cigarette. Distractedly, she brushed it off the leg of her body-hugging designer jeans. "Are you serious? You'd model for me?"

My sister shrugged. "Why not? It's a paying gig, right?"

"Izzy!" I admonished her. Couldn't she do something nice once in her life without expecting a reward in return?

"No, no, that's alright. If she works, she should be compensated. How does $400 sound?"

"$500 has a better ring to it."

Sara crossed her arms and looked Izzy up and down. "You do have an incredible body."

"You don't have to tell me."

"Do you have any modeling experience?"

"No, but how tough can it be? I'm sexy and I know how to move."

"Fine, you're hired." Sara let her cigarette fall to the cement floor, where she ground it out with the pointy toe of one of her copper-colored Jimmy Choos. "You're about the same size as Ricki, so you should be able to fit into her suits."

"Great! Problem solved." I was so relieved for Sara.

"Not quite. I still need another model, preferably someone a little voluptuous . . ." She stared pointedly at me.

"I hope you kept your bikini wax appointment this week," my sister said with a smirk.

"Why? What does that have to do with-- Oh, no. No way!" I shouted, backing away from Sara while I looked around desperately for the nearest exit.

She thwarted my escape by grabbing my hands and begging, "Pretty please with shirtless Channing Tatum on top. I wouldn't ask unless it was a matter of life and death."

"The death will be mine if I have to parade around half-naked in front of a bunch of strangers."

"You don't have anything to be embarrassed about. You have the perfect bathing suit figure. Long legs, a nice rack--"

"She does have a nice rack," Izzy concurred. "We all do. It's the one good trait we inherited from our mother."

"I, also, have a big butt," I reminded them of what I considered to be my worst flaw.

Sara threw her arm over my shoulders and gave me an encouraging squeeze. "That's okay. Shapely booties are in. You can thank JLo and Beyoncé for that. And most of my suits are cut for women with curves."

"No," I said adamantly, shaking my head from side-to-side. "I'm sorry, Sara. You know I love you like a sister, and I'd help if I could. But I just can't. I'm not as uninhibited as Izzy."

"Oh, I don't know about that," my sibling felt the need to chime in. "You did say that you kissed a guy you weren't supposed to yesterday and you couldn't have done that without shedding some inhibitions."

"Oooooooo," Sara's aquamarine eyes lit up, "this sounds juicy. What guy?"

"She won't say."

Sara frowned. "Why not?

"I don't know. I guess it's some big secret. I thought it was that patient of hers, you know, the actor who lied about his real identity? Did Pilar tell you how smokin' hot that guy is? We are talking Grade A beefcake."

"What's his name?" A model, who was sitting in a nearby makeup chair having false eyelashes applied, decided to horn in on our conversation.

"Derek Reynolds," Izzy answered her.

"Hmmmm, that name sounds familiar," she pursed her collagen-injected lips thoughtfully for a minute. "Is he about 6'3 with longish blond hair, perma-stubble, and a killer tan?"

"Yeah, and really sexy dimples."

"I think I slept with him."

"Lucky you!" Izzy enthused.

The other woman made a face. "Not really. It wasn't very good. He's one of those 'Wham-Bam-Is that it?-Damn!' types."

Derek Reynolds, the man who swaggered around like he was the studliest stud who ever studded, was a dud in bed? "Ha!" I guffawed so loudly that Sara and Izzy exchanged worried glances as though they feared for my sanity.

"Thank you." I patted the blonde model on her bony shoulder. "You just made my day."

"So, if you didn't kiss Derek, who did you smooch?" Sara raised a golden eyebrow.

"Yeah, who?"

Nothing like being ganged up on.

"Don't you ladies have a fashion show to get ready for?"

Sara checked her watch. "We've still got an hour. That leaves us plenty of time to harass you about your love life."

"But I don't have a love li--"

"Maybe it was Victor?" my sister postulated. "Kissing that looney tunes would certainly qualify as a mistake."

"I haven't laid a lip on Victor since we broke up."

"Well, thank God for that. So, who else does Pilar know that she shouldn't be kissing?" Sara drummed her French manicured fingertips against her chin.

"A patient? Another doctor? Someone's who's married?" Izzy ran through their options.

"Combine those last two together and who do you get?"

"Alright, alright." I held up my hands as a sign of surrender before either of them could say Ford's name. "If the two of you promise to drop this and never bring it up again, I will model in the fashion show."

"Yes!" Sara pumped her fist in the air triumphantly.

"But no thongs!" I warned her.

"No thongs." She crossed her heart.

"I've got some one-pieces and bikinis that are going to look amazing on you. But first, I need to get you into hair and makeup. Giuseppe can do wonders with concealer and bronzer. And hopefully, Fred will be able to do something with this." She lifted my limp ponytail and eyed it disparagingly.

"Izzy, you can come with me and try on some suits. I might have to pin some of them to get the best fit."

Sara led me over to a makeup chair and ordered Nicola to get out of it.

"But she's-a not done!" a man with a thick Italian accent protested.

"Too bad. We've got an emergency here."

Giuseppe took my face in his hands and leaned down to examine it. "She's-a sallow, dehydrated, and looks-a like she hasn't slept in a week. I'm gonna need at least-a thirty minutes to make her presentable," he determined.

"You've got fifteen, then hand her off to Fred. He's going to have his work cut out for him."

"Hey!" I took offense.

"Don't worry, sweetie. You'll be a knockout by the time the boys are through with you. Let's go, Izzy." Sara walked off, expecting my sister to follow her.

"Can I borrow your cell phone?" Izzy inquired while Giuseppe swabbed my face with some minty-smelling toner and muttered something under his breath about the size of my pores. "I didn't have time charge my battery this morning and I need to call Stephanie to see if she wants me to cover her shift at the club tonight."

"Sure. It should be in my purse."

Izzy dug the phone out and turned it on. "Oh," she said when the cell beeped. "You've got 5 messages."

They were probably all from Ford, and the realization made me feel queasy. "I'm sure they're nothing important."

"Izzy!" We both flinched when we heard Sara's impatient scream.

"Go," I told her.

"I'll bring the phone back later," she vowed.

She could have flushed it down the toilet for all I cared. I'd have had a lot more peace of mind if I'd known that there was no way for Ford to contact me. Since we'd kissed approximately 19 1/2 hours earlier, I'd done everything in my power to avoid the man. I had no idea how long he'd waited in my office after I'd fled the scene of the adulterous crime, but I'd stayed away for almost three hours. Without a phone, money, or my car keys, I'd been hard pressed to kill that much time. I'd managed by going to a little Cuban café four blocks over that was owned by a sweet, old woman named Carmelita. When she'd seen my dazed, tear-streaked face, she'd graciously given me a cup of *Café con Leche* and some *Flan de Chocolate* on the house. Unfortunately, I'd been too upset to do anything more than pick at the dessert, and after what had seemed like an eternity of soul-searching and self-flagellation, I'd snuck back to my office like a thief in the night.

Ford had turned off the computers and all the lights, but the one on Margo's desk. I'd found a post-it note covered in his chicken scratch stuck to the receiver of her phone.

'*We need to talk,*' it'd said, and the word *need* had been underlined several times for emphasis. '*I'll call you.*'

The last thing I'd wanted to do was "talk" with Ford, so his parting line had struck terror in my heart. On the drive home, I'd practiced saying things like, "*I'm sorry if I misled you with that kiss, but I'm really not that kind of girl,*" and, "*We crossed the line, so I think it would be best if we never saw or spoke to each other again,*" but it all came out sounding ridiculously melodramatic.

Even though I'd been afraid to check my answering machine when I'd gotten to the bungalow, I hadn't been able to resist the lure of that flashing red light. There'd been three messages from Ford, each sounding increasingly agitated. He was "worried" about me since it had been such an "emotional" day, and I'd had a lot "to process." What was I? One of his patients? Stupid shrink-speak! He just wanted to "talk" to me so that we could "straighten things out." What was there to straighten out? I'd been overwrought and vulnerable; he'd attempted to console me . . . with his lips. We'd gotten caught up in the heat of the moment, and now, I was confused and consumed with guilt. I was pretty clear on all those points.

I'd erased all of Ford's messages and hadn't answered the phone the rest of the night without checking Caller ID first. In the clear light of day, I could admit to myself that maybe I hadn't been handling the Ford situation in the most mature or responsible fashion, which was kind of sad considering I gave people advice on how to confront their problems and work through them for a living. But we all have off-days and beating myself up over my cowardly behavior wasn't going to help matters. I had to move on and use the weekend to my advantage, taking the time necessary to regroup and compose my thoughts before the inevitable face-to-face with Ford on Monday. Meanwhile, I planned to focus on the task at hand - surviving Sara's fashion show with my dignity intact.

After Giuseppe and Fred were done with me, I took a look in the mirror and was shocked by my own reflection. Could that woman with the sultry eyes and sexily tousled "babe hair" really be me, I wondered.

Leaning her head over my shoulder, Izzy deadpanned, "It's a miracle."

"Very funny. Love the Cher hair." I tugged on a strand of her parted-down-the-middle, super straight 'do.

"Thanks, Sara thought this look would complement the retro line. She's waiting for you back in the dressing room. 15 minutes 'til show time."

"Terrific," I groaned as I got up from the makeup chair. "What are you wearing?"

Izzy opened her robe and flashed me her jungle-print one-piece, which appeared to have less material than most bikinis.

"Wow! Look at all those cutouts."

"Don't you just love this one over the navel?" she pointed to her belly. "It really shows off my piercing."

I trailed Izzy to the small room that had been reserved for Serafina Swimwear. When Sara saw me, she shooed everyone else out, including my sister, so that we could have some privacy. With haste, I tried on eight of her designs with a variety of heels and rehearsed walking around in them while Sara gave me a quick tutorial on the art of modeling. To my surprise, the majority of the suits were quite flattering to my figure, and I felt comfortable in them, not happy-to-flaunt-my-goodies comfortable, but comfortable nonetheless. After Sara had decided which ones worked and which didn't, she pinned numbers to each ensemble in order to avoid confusion during the quick changes that would be made in the wings while the show was in progress. Finally, she put me in a push-up leopard print tankini with a black string bottom, then tied a short, fringed sarong around my hips.

"Beautiful!" she exclaimed. "How do you feel?"

"Like I'm going to throw up."

"You'll be fine," she assured me. "Just watch the other models and emulate them."

There was a warning knock at the door two seconds before a frizzy-haired girl peeked her head in and announced, "It's started."

Sara gathered up all of the swimwear while I donned a kimono and contemplated suicide by strangulation with its sash. I might have actually preferred that to what lay ahead of me. As we made our way to the side of the stage, the thumping beat of rock music resounding in my ears, I reminded myself of all of the anxiety-neutralizing techniques I'd taught my patients over the years. Breathe slowly through the nose. Repeat the mantra, '*I am calm. I can handle this. Nothing bad is going to happen to me.*' Imagine a safe, peaceful place: a garden, the beach, a mountaintop-- What a bunch of crap! Instead of feeling more relaxed, I was becoming more uptight and apprehensive with every step. By the time we reached the other models in Sara's group, I was so frightened that I was having an out-of-body experience. Nothing seemed real, and I felt detached from my surroundings as if I was in a dream.

"Earth to Pilar." My sister snapped her fingers in front of my face, and the noise brought me back to my senses.

"Huh?"

"You were zoning out. Serafina's up next, so you need to ditch the robe. And here," she handed me a couple of tissues. "Blot your face. You're breaking out in a sweat."

The cold sweat of terror. *God, how did I get myself into this?* I asked myself for the tenth time. Pilar Alvarez, college graduate, psychologist, staunch feminist, lover of bad carbs. I wasn't swimsuit model material. The idea was absurd.

"Thanks again for doing this." Sara gave me a warm hug and smiled gratefully. "You really are a lifesaver."

Okay, my best friend needed me, and I was going to come through for her. It was just a few minutes of my life, right? The whole thing would be over and done with before I knew it.

I watched Izzy go out on stage, strutting like she was born to walk the runway.

"Just remember everything I told you," Sara whispered in my ear as we moved forward. I was just one model away from making my fashion show debut now.

"When you get to the end of the runway, remove the sarong, pause for a moment so that the photographers can get their shots, then pivot--"

"Wait! What?" I turned to her in a panic. "You didn't say anything about taking off the sarong. If I do that, then the audience will have an unobstructed view of my butt as I walk back up the runway, and that is *not* a good angle for me."

"Just do it," Sara hissed and shoved me out on to the stage.

CHAPTER 27

Bright lights, deafeningly loud music, thunderous applause . . . the assault to my senses was overwhelming. Thankfully, I had a minute to acclimate myself to all of the craziness while everyone's eyes were on the bodacious Nicola who was prowling back up the runway in an orange shell-covered one-piece. She made it look so effortless, so easy, like prancing around in stilettos and a few strategically-placed strips of fabric was a perfectly natural thing to do. If only I could channel some of her confidence and style . . .

Okay, deep breath, I told myself. Remember Sara's modeling tips. Shoulders back. Chest out, not too far out, you don't want to topple over. Suck in stomach and . . . GO! Strut. Strut. Slow it down. You don't want to trip. Just take long, sexy strides and keep your eyes trained on the end of the runway. Strut. Strut. Swing those hips. Smile. NO! Don't smile. Look haughty and disdainful. Strut. Strut. Almost there. Just a few more steps. Yes! Stop and pose for the photographers. Good grief, those camera flashes are blinding. I'm seeing stars. Okay, enough with the posing. Now, untie the sarong. Damn it, this knot is tight! What was Sara think-- Got it! Alright, remove sarong. Lift arms up. Circle around and . . . did someone just whistle at me? Hey, maybe I look better from the back than I thought I did? Score one for girls with junk in the trunk. Strut. Strut. You know, this modeling thing is actually kind of fun. Not that I'd want to make a habit out of it or anything, but . . .

Once I was safely in the wings, Sara embraced me with bone-crushing zeal. "You did great!" she enthused.

"Yeah, not bad," Izzy agreed as she shimmied into a pair of tie-dye cabana pants. "I thought for sure you were going to upchuck all over the stage, but you came through in the clinch."

"Which means you owe me $20," Simone reminded my sister as she brushed past us in one of Sara's bumper sticker bikinis.

"You bet that I was going to publicly humiliate myself?" I was hurt.

But Izzy was too busy smoothing down her hair to notice. "It seemed like easy money," she blew off her disloyalty.

"A good sister would want me to *succeed*, not fail."

"Don't start lecturing me on being a good sister," Izzy got her back up. "I am a great sister. Well, maybe not to Ana, but I'm pretty sure there was a mix-up at the hospital, and we aren't even biologically related. As for you, I do nice things for you all the time. In fact, I just--"

"Girls!" Sara interjected. "Squabble later; save my career now. Izzy, you're on next, so get into position. Pilar, you've got forty-five seconds to put this suit on." She thrust a hot pink halter-style two-piece into my arms and shoved me behind a folding screen.

The rest of the fashion show went swimmingly (pun intended) and when Sara joined us models on stage after the big finale, she was greeted with an enthusiastically-delivered standing ovation. It's not often in life that you get to bear witness to someone's dream becoming a reality, but I did that day and I couldn't have been more delighted to share my friend's triumph with her. I, also, couldn't wait to get backstage so that I could change out of the brown crocheted string bikini I was squeezed into. It was the skimpiest suit I'd ever worn, and since donning it I'd lived in fear of turning the wrong way too fast and having a body part pop out.

"Have you seen my robe?" I asked Izzy when I couldn't find the garment in the spot on the floor where I was sure I'd dropped it earlier.

"Sara put them on that makeup chair over there." My sister jerked a thumb to the left where I could see a pile of silk.

When I went to retrieve it, I bumped into Nicola.

"Hey, good work," she was gracious enough to give me kudos. "You really looked like a pro out there."

"Thanks, but I don't think I'll be giving up my day job anytime soo--"

"Poppa, why isn't Pee-lar wearing any clothes?"

Was that Nate's voice? *Please, God, just let it be in my head*, I prayed.

"I think she's been doing some modeling, sport."

Now, I was hearing Ford, too. I assured myself that there was no need to panic. I was just having a schizophrenic episode induced by stress. A few antipsychotic drugs, and I'd be right as--

"Pilar's best friend, Sara, designs swimsuits and--"

Whirling around to face the disembodied voice, I found that it was, in fact, real and coming from Ford, who was standing less than a foot away from me, holding his inquisitive little boy by the hand.

I looked down at my nearly naked body, gasped with horror, then grabbed a kimono from the chair and shoved an arm into one of its sleeves in a desperate bid to cover myself. Unfortunately, when I attempted to repeat the maneuver with my other arm, I couldn't locate the hole because the garment was all twisted around my back.

"Need some help with that?" Ford asked, trying not to look amused by my predicament and failing miserably.

"No," I said as I continued to struggle, contorting my body like I was a human pretzel.

"What are you two doing here?" I wondered irritably.

"Aren't you happy to see us?"

"Of course, I'm always happy to see you, Nate." I finally got the robe on, but I was panting from the exertion like I'd just run a marathon without hydrating first. "I'm, uh, just a little surprised that you and your father were, uh, able to track me down."

"Well, you weren't answering my calls, so you didn't leave me much choice." Ford sounded recriminatory.

Izzy strolled up with a Tootsie Pop in her mouth. "Hey, Doc. I see you found the place."

"What? You told him where I was?" If looks could kill, Izzy would have combusted into flame.

"Uh huh," she removed the sucker from her mouth and licked her lips with her purple tongue, "he called while I had your cell phone."

"I told her that I needed to speak with you in person."

"And it couldn't wait until Monday?"

"Obviously not," he replied.

"You're relentless."

"With good reason. It's important not to let things fester. Unresolved issues can be damaging to . . ."

". . . a person's emotional health. Yes, I know."

"Wow, it's like being back in Psych 101. Now, I remember why I dropped that class." Izzy chomped down on the chewy center of her Tootsie Pop. "I'll just leave the two of you to overanalyze yourselves into a stupor."

"No, wait, Izzy." I grabbed her by the arm before she could take off.

"Nate, would you mind hanging out with my sister for a few minutes while I speak with your *papá*?"

"You're putting me on babysitting duty?" Izzy was miffed.

I smiled apologetically at the Fordham men, then turned my back on them and forced my sister to do the same.

"It's the least you can do," I whispered in her ear so that we wouldn't be overheard, "since you're the one who got me into this mess by not keeping your big mouth shut."

"Nice try, but you can't blame this on me," she hissed in

return. "You're the one who macked on a marr--"

"Ten minutes, that's all I'm asking. It's not like I don't do plenty for you."

"Oh, alright," she acquiesced begrudgingly, "but make it quick. You know how children annoy me."

Yes, I did. Izzy had always disliked anything that was cuter or more needful of attention than she was.

"Come on, kid." She extended her hand towards Nate.

Eying it warily, he queried, "*¿Habla usted español?*"

"*Margarita, Piña Colada, Mojito, Havana Loco,*" Izzy ticked off a list of cocktails.

Nate scrunched up his brow in confusion. "What are those?"

"They're what hunky *cabaña* boys fetch for hot girls like me down by the pool. Now, let's go before all the lounge chairs are taken." She wiggled her fingers at him.

"Go on, son." Ford ruffled Nate's thick hair encouragingly, and the child took Izzy's hand.

"Don't let him wander off, and no alcohol while you're watching him," I muttered as my sister brushed past me, and she grumbled, "Party pooper," in response.

I turned back to face Ford, and there was an awkward silence while each of us waited for the other to speak.

"Pilar, I just want--"

"Scusa, scusa," Giuseppe frantically waved us out of the way as he bustled up with a dark-haired model in tow, "we've-a got a self-a-tanner crisis here."

Clearly, the model had forgotten to apply any to the top half of her body because her arms looked quite pasty in contrast to her sun-kissed legs.

"Take-a these . . ." the makeup artist picked up the Serafina kimonos and tossed them at me. I didn't react quickly enough, so the silky garments slid down my body and fell into a heap on the floor. ". . . and-a clear the area so that I can-a work."

"Come on." I motioned to Ford, then led him down a nearby passageway in search of a room that wasn't being used.

When I tripped over some garment bags and wire hangers that had been left behind to litter the corridor, Ford caught me by the arm. "Why don't you take those shoes off before you hurt yourself?" he suggested.

Taking his advice, I leaned back against the wall and removed the four-inch heels I'd been teetering around on.

Ford walked on ahead, pushing open a door that was slightly ajar. "This one looks empty," he said as I rubbed the cramping arch of my left foot.

I hobbled over while he stepped inside and turned on the lights. He was standing in the center of the small, bare room when I got there. Once I was across its threshold, I closed the door for privacy's sake, but didn't move any farther forward because I liked the idea of being within arm's reach of an exit.

"About what happened at your office yester--," Ford began.

"Please," I held up my hand to stop him, which wasn't very polite, but I was more interested in verbalizing the jumbled mix of thoughts and feelings that had been swirling around in my head for the last 24 hours than I was in being courteous, "let me say something first."

When he didn't object, I forged ahead.

"I've been giving this a lot of thought and I think that we've been spending too much time together." I directed my words to Ford's right shoulder because I knew that if I looked at his face, I'd get sucked into the hypnotizing blue vortex of his eyes and any chance I had of expressing myself in an intelligible manner would be lost. "The lunches, the walks, the chats between appointments, the phone calls at home. It all seemed innocent at first, we had so much in common, we enjoyed each other's company, we were just colleagues, friends, but over time we achieved a certain level of intimacy and I started to depend on you, confide in you. My mother told me I was playing with fire and I really should have listened to her, but I was naive. I honestly thought that our relationship could remain platonic and above reproach, that I was safe from any sort of emotional entanglement with you because of your marital status."

"Pilar--," Ford made an attempt to interrupt my monologue.

"I'm not done," I admonished him for daring to speak. "Now, I don't know if you and your wife are having problems, or what's going on at home, but I don't want to get in the middle of it. There's an attraction between us; I won't deny it. But to act on it . . . well, we already acted on it when we kissed so that ship has sailed, but to go any further would be wrong, very, very wrong. And I have too much respect for myself and for the holy sacrament of marr--"

"But my wife--," Ford tried again.

"Nothing justifies cheating as far as I'm concerned, so please don't tell me that your wife is frigid, or that she doesn't understand you." I'd heard those excuses from too many married men with wandering eyes.

"I'd never say that," he assured me. "My wife *did* understand me, better than anyone."

I narrowed my eyes at him. "*Did*, as in past tense? What happened? You grew apart? You stopped communicating?" Despite my assertion that I didn't want to know about the inner workings of Ford's marriage, the psychologist in me was curious.

"She died."

Talk about dropping a bombshell. This one rivaled Hiroshima. I was too stunned to do anything but gape at

Ford for several seconds afterwards.

"What?" I finally croaked.

"My . . . wife . . . is . . . dead," he reiterated very slowly.

"But that can't be right! You're wearing a ring." I pointed to the gold band on his left hand as if that was some kind of proof that he had a living, breathing spouse somewhere.

He touched the ring and a wistful expression took possession of his face. "I know I should take it off. She's been gone almost a year and it's silly to have an emotional attachment to an object, even one with sentimental value, but . . ."

"You're not making this up, are you?" I hated to ask, but I'd been lied to by so many men recently that I wasn't sure what, or who, to believe anymore.

With a sigh, he said, "You can check the obits in the *New York Times* if you want confirmation. My wife, Samantha Montgomery Fordham, was hit by a drunk driver on her way home from work on July 26th of last year. She was just a few blocks from Mt. Sinai, where she was employed as an OR nurse, when it happened. I got the call while I was making rounds. I rushed down to the ER, but . . . she was already gone by the time the paramedics brought her in."

Although Ford related the story of his wife's tragic fate in a steady tone of voice that betrayed no emotion, I could see the anguish in his eyes and knew that the telling of it was very painful for him.

"That must have been awful for you and Nate." I was sympathetic, but resisted the urge to offer him any physical comfort.

"It was. It *is*," he admitted.

"Why didn't you tell me all this before?"

Ford scratched his cheek, which he hadn't shaved that morning.

"I don't like talking about it."

"That's ironic, considering your profession."

"I suppose so," he conceded, "but wallowing in grief wasn't going to help me and it certainly wasn't going to help my son. I left New York and moved here so that Nate and I could get a fresh start, away from all the memories. When I met you--"

"You let me assume that the wedding ring meant you were taken."

"Yeah, I did, and in hindsight, I can see what a huge mistake that was. But, at the time, I had no way of knowing that you'd ever be anything more to me than the psychologist who had an office across the hall from mine. So, why spill my guts to a stranger? As our relationship progressed and we became friends, I found myself really enjoying our time together. Being with you was fun and easy, and it felt good to make a connection with someone."

"A connection based on a misconception," I reminded him, and he looked shamed, which made me feel a twinge of guilt. So, I softened the blow by adding, "I guess I can understand why you chose not to go the full disclosure route when we first met. You were going through a period of transition and adjustment; you were trying to get your bearings after a terrible loss. But we've known each other for months now, Ford. *Months!* And you've had plenty of opportunities to set the record straight, but you never even tried."

"I just wasn't ready to out myself as being single," he explained. "I liked you, but the thought of taking it to the next level, admitting to myself that I had feelings for you, asking you out . . . I just couldn't do it. And, as long as I had my wedding ring on, I felt safe, protected. You'd think that I was unavailable, so there'd be no expectations on your part, and no pressure on mine. I could just take things slow and see what happened."

And that had worked out great for him, but what about me?

"Meanwhile, I didn't know what the hell was going on. Why had you taken such an interest in me? Was I imagining that there was a sexual undercurrent to our relationship, that you found me attractive? How could I be developing feelings for a man who was happily married and had a wife and child at home?"

"Well, it was no picnic for me either," Ford defended himself. "Since you thought of me as just a friend, I had to hear all about your rotten blind dates and stand by while that idiot, Victor, proposed marriage via skywriter. Then, there was that patient who was putting the moves on you. Why do you think I was so adamant about you referring him to another doctor? It wasn't because I'm Super Shrink and could see through his nefarious scheme to seduce you in the name of character research. I was jealous."

"And I thought that you were the better therapist, that you were so much smarter and more perceptive than me!" With a derisive snort, I began to pace back in forth in front of him, becoming angrier with each step. To think that I had listened to Ford, valued his opinion, and questioned my own competence when I hadn't shared it. All the while, he was just trying to eliminate Derek as his rival for my affections.

"I'm not going to apologize for warning you against that creep. I was right about there being more to him than met the eye, about him having ulterior motives."

I stopped right in front of him and placed my hands on my hips. "Yeah, well, I guess it takes a fraud to know one."

He winced. "That's not fair."

"You're right. There's nothing fair about any of this. Since the beginning of our relationship, you've had an agenda that I wasn't privy to. Now, everything you've ever said and done is suspect. The career advice, introducing me to your

son, giving me a shoulder to lean on when Izzy got arrested .
. ."

"I did all of that because I care about you, because I wanted to be involved in your life."

"I wish I could believe that. I wish you were the kind, decent, straightforward guy I thought you were, but the truth is I don't know you at all." That realization filled me with sadness.

"Yes, you do." Ford reached for my hand, but I shook my head and backed away.

"No, I don't, not really. By not telling me about your wife and your life prior to coming here, you held a really big part of yourself back from me."

"Is my past really all that important?" he wondered. "You know the man I am today. That's what should matter. You have to trust yourself, trust your impression of me."

I could feel tears welling up in my eyes. "But I don't," I said in a quavering voice. "I've always thought that I was a good judge of character, of people, but apparently not. Everywhere I've turned these last few months, there's been some form of deception. Lovers, patients, friends . . ." I waved a hand at him.

"I'm not Victor, or Derek."

"I can't make that distinction anymore." I wiped away a rogue tear that had fallen down on to my cheek. "I've been let down and taken advantage of by too many people lately. My instincts have failed me over and over again."

Ford looked me straight in the eye. "You weren't wrong about me, Pilar. If you'll give me a chance, I can prove it to you."

I sniffled. Why did I never have a tissue when I needed one?

"I appreciate you wanting to try, but I'm all out of chances. Rather than letting myself get caught up in another complicated and confusing relationship, I think I just need to focus on myself for a while. I've got to find a way to make rent on my office next week, keep Izzy out of jail, and work on seeing people for what they are instead of what I want them to be."

Ford's disappointment was palpable, but he didn't argue. He just said, "Tell me what I can do to help."

"I need time. Time for all of this to sink in, time to get my self-confidence back, time to figure out what I want."

"I'm not going anywhere," he assured me.

"I'm not asking you to wait."

"You don't have to. You may be unsure about me, understandably so, but I don't have any doubts about you, Pilar, not anymore."

He reached out a hand to stroke my damp cheek. "I had almost three months to make up my mind about you, so I owe you at least that much time. Take every minute of it."

I nodded, too overcome with emotion to speak, and with a rueful smile, Ford turned away from me and walked out the door, leaving me all alone to indulge myself in a good, cathartic cry.

CHAPTER 28

"*Mamá*!" I called out as I entered my parents' condo, lugging several heavy grocery bags.

"In here, *mija*."

I followed her voice into the living room, where she was standing amidst plastic-covered furniture and paint-splattered drop cloths. "You're late," she admonished without even turning towards me. "I expected you an hour ago."

"I'm sorry. I got held up at the fashion show, then I had to go to two different stores to find your cook--"

"What do you think of this color?" she interrupted me, obviously not that interested in my excuse.

"Uh, well." I looked over at the freshly painted wall my mother was staring at. "It's green."

"Yes, but it's not the warm, mossy green I wanted. This," she gestured disparagingly at the wall, "looks olive. I might as well be living in an Army barracks. That decorator your father hired is *inepto*! I told her I needed a color that wouldn't look too dark when the terrace blinds were closed, but did she listen? *No!* So, now, I have to go to the paint store myself and pick out green swatches that don't have this hideous brown undertone. But I can't do that until my face is better, which means a delay of at least a week!"

"Your face doesn't look too bad now." From my position behind her, I could only see a little bit of *Mamá*'s profile, but the purple marks around her eyes and along her jawline appeared to have faded to a less-frightening shade of blue. "If you wore sunglasses and put some foundation and powder on over the bruises . . ."

"Are you *loca*?" she tossed off the question as she stalked past me in her silk lounging pajamas, which were the same tangerine color as the polish on her acrylic nails. "I can't leave this condo until my face is completely healed. The minute I step out that door, I'll run into somebody I know, and they'll see all this swelling and discoloration and jump to the conclusion that I've had work done."

Which she had, but I guess that that was beside the point.

From the doorway of the kitchen she ordered, "Bring those bags in here before my raspberry sorbet melts. I hope you remembered to get the fat-free kind."

"Of course," I replied as I trailed her into the other room. "I got everything on your list: Pirouette cookies, skim milk, pink grapefruit, the latest issue of *Architectural Digest*, Tide with Downy, French roast coffee beans, paper towels, eggs, a loaf of pumpernickel, spicy mustard, and . . .," I paused to set the bags on the granite countertop, "a bottle of your favorite Chardonnay from the liquor store. You know, you shouldn't be drinking alcohol if you're still taking prescription medi--"

"Why are you wearing so much makeup?" *Mamá* wondered, evidently just having noticed my professionally painted face, which I hadn't had an opportunity to wash clean. "And why," she took my chin in her hand and forced me to look at her, "are your eyes all red and puffy like you've been crying?"

"This is stage makeup," I replied, then ducked my head and began to unpack the perishable items that belonged in the refrigerator. "Two of Sara's models didn't show up, so I had to help out. Izzy did, too."

"You modeled swimsuits?"

"Shocking, I know," I handed her the carton of eggs, "but it was actually kind of liberating."

She eyed me skeptically. "So liberating that you cried about it?"

"The crying came later, after the show. I had a discussion with someone that got a little emotional." I opened the cabinet to my left and placed the bag of coffee beans on its bottom shelf.

Rather than put the eggs in the fridge like she was supposed to, *Mamá* set them back down on the counter. "And who is this mysterious 'someone' who brought my Pilar to tears?"

"I'd rather not talk about it."

"Fine!" She threw her hands up in the air. "I try to be a good mother. I try to give you support. And what thanks do I get? You shut me out. You won't confide in me, you won't share, you just--"

"Alright, alright." I surrendered because I just couldn't deal with one of her pout parties after the day I'd had. "I'll tell you, but you're not going to like it."

She leaned in closer; her dark eyes glittering with anticipation. "Tell me anyway."

"I think I'm going to need one of these first." I ripped open the plastic lid of the Pirouette canister and pulled out one of the Chocolate Hazelnut-flavored wafer sticks.

I ate half of it before admitting, "I think I'm in love with Ford."

My mother frowned as best she could with her face being stretched to its limits. "You're in love with a car?"

"No! Dr. Jonathan Fordham, the psychiatrist who works in my building."

"The *married* psychiatrist? *Ay!*" She brought her hands up to her unnaturally tight cheeks. "I knew this would happen! You waited too long to find a husband. All of the good men are gone, and now, instead of being a wife, you have to settle for being a mistress."

"*Mamá*--"

"Poor Pilar." She gave me a condescending pat on the shoulder. "You must have been so desperate, so lonely . . . who would have thought that your life would come to this? I had such high hopes for you, such dreams, such plans!"

She sighed regretfully before continuing, "But don't

worry, I understand and I forgive, just promise me that you won't have any children out of wedlock. There's never been a *bastardo* in our family. It would be a terrible scandal. We'd all be disgraced, and your father would die of shame."

"Are you through?" I raised a brow inquiringly.

"Eh, I suppose."

"Good because Ford isn't married."

"But you said--"

"I know and I was wrong. All this time, I thought he was married because he wore a wedding ring and had a young son, but I found out this afternoon that he's a widower."

My mother perked up. "So, he's available?"

"Yes." I took another cookie out of the tin and started to nibble on it.

"And he's interested?"

"Seems to be."

"Oh, *mija!*" *Mamá* hugged me so tightly that the Pirouette I was holding got crushed between us. "*¡Felicidades!*"

"No! No *¡Felicidades!*" I pushed myself away from her.

"Why not?"

"Because," I glanced down at my hand, which was now filled with crumbled up cookie and creme-filling, "ewwww."

I grabbed the new roll of Bounty off the counter and worked on ripping off its plastic wrap with one hand.

"Give that to me." *Mamá* grabbed the paper towels impatiently. "And explain to me why you're not happy about this doctor, who you think you might be in love with, being single."

Now it was my turn to sigh. "It's complicated."

"Make it simple." She handed me a towel.

That was easier said than done.

"Okay . . . on the one hand, Ford not being married is a good thing," I said as I wiped the cookie debris from my palm and fingers. "I don't have to suppress my feelings for him anymore and I don't have to be racked with guilt because of them. But now that I know the truth, there's a whole new set of issues. I mean, he's been lying to me for months. Alright, technically, he didn't lie, but he never disabused me of the notion that he was married. So, that still counts as dishonesty as far as I'm concerned. And even though I sort of understand why he did what he did, I'm still left with all of these icky feelings."

"Such as?"

I grimaced. "I don't know. It's hard to label all of the emotions. I guess I feel stupid, manipulated, embarrassed--"

"Why embarrassed?"

"Because I told him everything about myself, private, personal things I've never told anyone else. Stuff about our family, my relationships with other men, my interactions with patients, my finances."

"And you wouldn't have shared all of that with him if he'd been your boyfriend?" *Mamá* asked.

"Eventually, when I was sure that all of the craziness in my life wouldn't scare him off."

"It looks like this Ford doesn't scare off so easy. He knows you, along with all of your problems and flaws, and he still wants to be with you."

"God knows why." I really couldn't fathom it. All of my stories about my high-maintenance mother and long-suffering father should have sent him running for the hills long ago.

"Maybe he found your honesty refreshing? Maybe he liked that you trusted him with your secrets?"

"If he liked it so much, he should have reciprocated. I've been letting it all hang out since the day we met, and he's given me nothing in return."

"He listened, didn't he? And he tried to help when he could? Actions speak louder than words with some men, *mija.*"

"Ford has done a lot for me," I conceded. "That's a big part of the reason why I developed feelings for him. I thought that he was this wonderful, selfless guy who was always there for me because it was his nature to be a Good Samaritan."

"But now you question his motives?"

"Of course, I do! Ford's already admitted that he tried to influence how I treated a patient because he was jealous of the man."

"There's nothing wrong with a man showing a little jealousy," my mother informed me. "You can't have passion without the green-eyed monster rearing its ugly head once in a while."

"Victor was jealous 24/7, and all it showed was that he had a guilty conscience and a flair for the dramatic. At least, he was upfront about being possessive. Ford was sneaky."

"Why are you even comparing the two men?" *Mamá* queried. "You said you never loved Victor."

"I didn't, but Victor seems to be the place where I went off track with men. So, I keep coming back to him. Why do men lie to me? And why do I fall for it every time? Am I too willing to accept people at face value? Am I empathetic to the point of being self-destructive? Or am I just hopelessly dense? And why, for the love of God, don't I ever learn from my mistakes? How many times can I be blindsided by a man before I do the smart thing and just give up on them altogether?"

"And do what? Join a nunnery?"

I shrugged. "Maybe. You've said yourself that black and white are good colors on me."

My mother lifted her eyes upward and spoke to the ceiling, "*Ay, Dios*, don't listen to her. She's overwrought. She doesn't know what she's saying."

"You shouldn't joke about things like that," she reprimanded me. "God might take you seriously. I'll tell you what your problem is. You think too much. You always have. I don't know how I ever ended up with a daughter who has such a big brain."

She was right. I did analyze things to death. Maybe if I'd spent less time pondering the big questions in life and more time just living it, I'd be . . . my sister, Isidora, who, despite being experienced in the ways of the world and quite cynical as a result, had still been taken for a ride, in a hotwired Ferrari no less, by a duplicitous male. So, maybe being foolish about men was a family curse? A curse that Ana seemed to have escaped since her husband, Ray, was the very model of masculine perfection: hard-working, intelligent, loyal, caring. He wasn't great-looking, but what did that matter? Quite a bit, apparently, since all the men I'd been attracted to lately were gorgeous. Victor with his dark, smoldering looks, Derek with his shaggy, blond hair and ripped body, Ford with his heart-melting smile and dreamy blue eyes.

"I need to find myself a good, solid, homely guy who'll never run around on me or be dishonest."

Mamá snorted. "Don't kid yourself. Ugly men can be just as faithless and unreliable as the handsome ones. Did I tell you that your cousin Sancha's husband is cheating on her?"

I gasped with surprise. "No!"

"*Sí*," my mother nodded knowingly, "with her sister."

"Which one?" It had to be Raphaela. She'd always been a tramp. Sophomore year, at our high school Valentine's Day party, she'd actually pulled my boyfriend, Tommy, out of my arms in the middle of a slow dance and French-kissed him. I still hadn't forgiven her for that. Him either.

"Nita. Sancha caught them in the act when she came home from her electrolysis appointment early yesterday. It was quite a scene; the wailing and cursing could be heard from three blocks away. There's talk of a divorce," *Mamá* whispered the word as if it was dirty.

"Damn, they haven't even been married a year." I actually felt sorry for my cousin. She might have been smug, hateful, and dumb as a post, but no one deserved that kind of betrayal. "I guess all men are worthless, even rat-faced Diego."

"Is your father worthless?"

"No," I grudgingly admitted.

"What about Raymond?"

"He's a saint."

"He has to be to put up with your sister and those little *diablos* of theirs."

"So, that's two decent men on the entire planet."

"Maybe not. Maybe you've found another one in this psychiatrist? You'll never know unless you give him a chance."

"I can't believe you're encouraging me to pursue a relationship with Ford." Where was the laundry list of objections she usually raised when I was interested in a man she hadn't hand-picked for me?

"A widower with a little boy is better than no man at all. You need to look at the big picture, *mija*. So, Ford misled you. I'm sure he feels badly about it. The important thing is he's a doctor, and we could use one of those in the family. A psychiatrist can prescribe drugs, can't he? I hope so because Ana's boys could really use some of that Ritalin."

"He may be a doctor, but he's not Latino. Don't you want me to be with a man who has the same cultural background?"

She waved a hand dismissively.

"Your *abuelo* Alvarez fell in love with a *gringa* and look how well that turned out: Thirty-seven years of marriage, four healthy babies, a dozen grandchildren, and two plots side-by-side at Our Lady of Perpetual Faith Cemetery. May they rest in peace." She made the sign of the cross.

"Ford's 9 years older than me."

"Your father's 12 years older than me. And you've always said that women are more emotionally mature than men, so an age difference should be conducive to compatibility."

Since when did my mother use words like "conducive" and "compatibility?" She went to bat for Ford, and suddenly, she was Merriam-Webster's.

"He's not Catholic. I don't even know what his religious affiliation is. He's never mentioned going to church. He may be an atheist."

"Then, you can convert him."

I groaned. It was hopeless. Jonathan Fordham, MD was a big catch in the eyes of the Great Latina Husband Hunter and now that she had him in her crosshairs, she wasn't going to let him get away no matter what I said to dissuade her.

"You're getting way ahead of yourself. Ford and I might not even have a future together. We haven't even gone out on a date yet."

"So, what are you waiting for? Time is precious, Pilar. You're turning 30 in less than--"

"Five months. Yes, I know, *Mamá*. I have a calendar, thank you. And even if I'm still single when November 24th rolls around, rest assured that I won't be magically transported to Spinster Island, where others of my kind have been banished to live out the rest of their days in shame and isolation."

"You could live on Happily Married Couples Island if you'd stop being so difficult and . . .," my mother picked up her cordless phone and shoved it into my hand, "call Ford before he decides you're too much trouble and starts looking for someone else."

"I'm not calling him," I stubbornly refused, putting the

phone down and reaching for another cookie. "We agreed to spend some time apart so that I could think things over."

"And where has thinking gotten you so far?"

"It's gotten me a lot further than following my heart ever has."

"You're afraid," my mother realized.

"With good reason. I've made a lot of mistakes lately. I keep misjudging people and I don't want to be hurt or disappointed anymore."

"Ah, *mija*, there are no guarantees in life. Sometimes, you just have to take the risk and hope for the best." And with that sage advice, she took the wafer stick out of my hand.

"Hey!" I objected.

"Ah-ah-ah," she put the cookie back in the tin canister and sealed it shut, "you can eat as many sweets as you want when you have a devoted husband at home who's willing to love you no matter how wide your hips are. Until then, show a little self-control."

CHAPTER 29

While staring fixedly at the phone on my desk, I crunched down on my fourth Pirouette of the morning. It wasn't exactly a nutritious breakfast, but the cookies were the perfect complement to my *Café con Leche*. And if I got fat from eating too many of them, I figured I could just blame the extra pounds on my mother since she was the one who'd introduced me to the damn things in the first place. Those cookies really were like chocolate-drizzled crack. The more I ate, the more I wanted. I knew I was binging because of stress. I always turned to food when I was feeling anxious, or scared, or depressed or . . . clearly, I had an oral fixation, which could also be blamed on my mother because she hadn't breast-fed me.

Why didn't the phone ring?

God, it had been so hard for me to make that call. I'd agonized about it for a full twenty-four hours before picking up the phone and when I finally had, my palms had been slick with sweat, and my heart had thudded so sickeningly in my chest that I'd thought I might throw up. Having to leave a message had just prolonged my suffering. Now, I had no choice but to sit, and wait, and fret . . . it was like being subjected to some exceedingly slow, painful form of torture. He might have been behind closed doors when I'd called, but I could have asked his secretary to interrupt. *Why hadn't I asked his secretary to interrupt?* If I had, this dreaded conversation would have been done and over with and I wouldn't be at risk of developing an ulcer or going into sugar shock before he returned my call. My phone intercom buzzed and I not only jumped out of my chair, but shrieked with fright and knocked my coffee cup over.

"Yes, Margo," I answered while trying to mop up the mess on my desk. *Please be him. Please be him. Please be him.*

"Sara's on the line."

I sighed disconsolately. "Thanks."

"Hello," I greeted my friend after picking up the phone receiver and bringing it to my ear.

"Guess where I am?" she shouted into her cell.

I could hear a lot of background noise, but it was too muffled to make out any sound in particular.

"No clue."

"The airport! I'm wheeling my luggage through the terminal on the way to Gate D-12 as we speak."

"Where are you going, and why do you sound so perky about it?" Sara was a notoriously whiny traveler. She usually started complaining the minute she got her suitcase out of the closet and didn't stop until she'd been back home for a week and had fully recovered from the jet lag, which always afflicted her whether she changed time zones or not.

"I'm going to New York, Manhattan to be precise, and I'm perky because I've got an appointment later today to meet with the HEAD BUYER at Bloomingdale's corporate offices."

"Wow!" I stopped cleaning and sat down. "How did that happen?"

"One of the Head Buyer's minions was at the Fashion Extravaganza on Saturday, and she loved my line so much that she called New York and set up this meeting with all the bigwigs. They're talking about putting Serafina Swimwear in Bloomies nationwide, Pilar, NATIONWIDE!" She could barely contain her excitement.

"What an amazing opportunity! All of your hard work and sacrifice has finally paid off. I am so happy for you!"

"Well, it's not a *fait accompli* yet. I still have to do my presentation, and everyone at Corporate has to agree that I'm fabulous and that my suits will appeal to their clientele."

"Those muckety-mucks in New York aren't going to know what hit them. You've got the whole package: talent, beauty, and personality. You're a fashion star about to go supernova."

Sara chuckled. "I'm electing you president of my soon-to-be-formed fan club."

"I only speak the truth."

"Hold on. I'm making a pit stop at Cinnabon. A cinnamon roll and a Mochalatta Chill please," she placed her breakfast order.

A cinnamon roll? Yum, that sounded good. I eyed the Pirouette canister. What would a fifth cookie hurt? I looked at the nutritional label on the back of the tin. *Holy #&$@!* How could there be that many calories in one skinny, little cookie? I did some quick mental calculations and came to the sad conclusion that even if I spent my entire lunch hour speed-walking all the way to the beach and back, I wouldn't be able to burn off the four Pirouettes I'd already inhaled.

"Pilar, are you there?"

"Yeah, sorry." I tossed the cookie canister in the trash.

"So, we've established that my future's so bright I'm going to have to start wearing SPF 100 or run the risk of getting third-degree burns, but what about you? Come to any decisions about Ford?"

"No, I've backburnered that drama while I stress out over how to pay my rent tomorrow."

"Mmmmm." It sounded like she was swallowing something, probably a delicious, gooey bite of that cinnamon roll. "That's right, tomorrow's the first. How much are you short?"

"$1000."

"The whole amount of the increase? Yikes!"

"It's been a bad month. I lost a couple of patients, and there were all those legal expenses for Izzy. That thousand will just cover my rent. I, also, have to worry about paying Margo and the phone bill next week."

"So, what are you going to do?"

"I've got a call in to my father. I'm going to have to bite the bullet and ask him for a loan, a loan that I'll probably never be able to pay back."

"You know he won't mind," Sara assured me. I heard slurping noises as she sucked her Mochalatta Chill through a straw.

"But I do. I feel like such a failure! I've worked so hard to build this practice and make it a success . . ."

"You need more time."

"I've had six months," I reminded her.

"I just read a report in the *South Florida Business Journal* that said it takes two years on average to get a new business off the ground."

"Are you making that up?"

"The article might have been in *Cosmo*," she admitted, "but same difference. There's no way that anyone could make a business profitable in just six months."

"Maybe I just don't have what it takes to be a good businesswoman? I'd probably be better off working in a clinic, or joining an established practice."

"Where somebody else would be the boss and you wouldn't have control over anything? Nu-uh, bad idea."

"At least, I wouldn't have to worry about keeping books, paying bills, and advertising for new clients. I could just focus on my patients and leave all of those administrative headaches to someone else."

"Okay, you're really starting to depress me with this defeatist attitude of yours. It's not like you to give up without a fight."

"I've been fighting for six months. I can never seem to get ahead. It's like the Fates are conspiring against me."

"That's a bunch of crap, and you know it." Sara refused to let me blame my professional misfortunes on a trio of mythological hags. "You're in charge of your own destiny, just like I was in charge of mine. Look at what I've managed to accomplish with nothing more than a dream and a sketch pad."

"You're a bona fide success story."

"And as such, I'm going to give you a little advice. No, scratch that. What I'm about to offer you isn't just advice; it's a carefully constructed, three-step plan that's guaranteed to make your life a lot easier and happier.

Step one, take your father's money for a few months and don't feel guilty about it.

Step two, out Izzy as the law-breaking screw-up she is and let your parents deal with the legal mess she's gotten herself into, as well as the financial fallout."

"But, I can't--"

"Yes, you can," Sara's tone was firm and unyielding. "You're enabling her and you're hurting yourself in the process, which is counterproductive, self-destructive, masochistic, and to be frank, kind of boneheaded."

I didn't even bother to register a protest because I knew she was right. I had been covering up for Izzy to my own detriment for way too long.

"Step three, find the very tasty Dr. Fordham, tell him that he's an idiot, but so are most men and it wouldn't be fair for you to hold one of the innate deficiencies of his gender against him, so you'll forgive him. Then, throw him down on the floor or up against a wall, lady's choice, and have hot, mind-blowing sex with him."

"You and my mother," I grumbled.

"She wants you to have sex with Ford, too?"

"She wants me to marry him in a big white wedding, move to an expensive beachfront property, and start giving her granddaughters."

"Smart woman."

I groaned with feeling. "This is all wrong. You're not supposed to be pro-Ford. You're supposed to be outraged on my behalf. You're supposed to rant and rave about what untrustworthy bastards men are, then tell me to kick Ford in the 'nads and never speak to him again."

"Well, if it were anyone else I would, but I can't encourage damaging Ford's reproductive organs."

"Why not?" I asked. "What makes him so special?"

"He's the one, Pilar. You may not see it now because you're confused and hurt, but take it from me, I've been your friend a long time, I know what you need, I know what'll make you happy, and Ford is *it*. He's perfect for you in every way imaginable. You're like two peas in a pod, brilliant and kind-hearted, caring and family-oriented, funny and giving. Ford's wife was the only thing standing between the two of you all this time, and it turns out she's not even an issue."

"On the contrary, her specter continues to loom large over our relationship. If Ford had been honest with me about Samantha from the beginning, I wouldn't be feeling all of these doubts and reservations now."

"He messed up. Cut the guy some slack."

"Counsels the woman whose credo regarding men has always been, 'One strike, and you're in my rearview,'" was my acerbic rejoinder.

"I've never met a guy who was worthy of a second chance before. Ford is."

"Since you're so keen on him, why don't I set the two of you up? I hear he's single," I snarked.

"Ha, ha, very funny. I said Ford was perfect for *you*, not me. Like I'd want a guy who'd sit around analyzing my artistic quirks all day," she scoffed. "He'd probably commit me. Hold on, they're making an announcement about my flight."

I could hear an amplified voice saying something about first-class ticket holders.

"Okay, they're boarding my section. I've got to run."

"You're flying first-class?"

"That's right. I'm traveling in style, all expenses paid by Bloomies, baby. I wonder if they still serve champagne in first-class?"

"If so, drink an extra glass for me and good luck!"

"Same to you, with your father anyway. You won't need any luck with Ford. It was meant to be!"

I heard a click, then the line went dead. Hanging up, I rested my chin in my hands and thought about what Sara had said. Why was everyone so sure about Ford except me? My mother, my best friend, even my kid sister were all supporters of the perfect-on-paper shrink. I envied their clarity. Of course, it was easy to have clarity when it wasn't your heart at risk. I was so terrified of taking another wrong turn in my love life; I'd already been down so many dead end roads, and the last thing I wanted was to get permanently lost in disappointment. What I needed was a sign that my faith in Ford hadn't been misplaced, some kind of confirmation that he was a good man who could be trusted with my love.

My intercom buzzed.

"Yes, Margo," I spoke into it.

"Ms. Bryant is here."

Swell. The teary-eyed, desperation-oozing poster child for relationships-gone-awry. Seeing her was just the downer I didn't need.

"Send her in," I instructed, then rose to my feet and headed for the door.

The minute I opened it, Lori threw herself into my arms and gave me the most enthusiastic hug I'd ever received.

"Oh, Dr. Alvarez," she pulled back and addressed me

breathlessly, her face glowing, her eyes bright with happiness, "thank you SO much for seeing me early today."

"No problem." Her animated behavior and appearance were rather disconcerting. Could this be the same Lori Bryant who usually showed up for our sessions hysterical and ready to slit her wrists because some guy had done her wrong yet again? "You know I don't mind working around your schedule."

"And I really appreciate that. It's so good to see you!" She embraced me again, this time a little less zealously, then smiled beatifically before moving over to the couch.

I followed, feeling like I was in some alternate reality where up was down, white was black, and my emotionally overwrought patient was not only calm, but radiating positive energy.

"So," I said as I sat down in my chair and reached for my pad and pen, "how have you been?" Lori had cancelled her appointment the previous Tuesday because she'd gone out of town on a spur-of-the-moment trip, so we hadn't seen each other in a couple of weeks.

"Fantastic!" she enthused. "I've never been more blissed out."

"And why is that?"

Leaning forward with her elbows on her knees, she confessed in a near-whisper, "I met someone, the most wonderful, amazing, special someone."

"Tell me more."

She shook her head, making her tight red curls bounce like springs. "I can't."

I crinkled my brow with confusion. "Why not?"

"I'm afraid I'll jinx it."

"Fair enough." If Lori didn't want to share the intimate details of her relationship with Mr. Wonderful, Amazing, and Special, I wasn't going to push it.

"I will tell you that he treats me like a queen. He takes me to the most romantic places, we just got back from the Bahamas . . . have you ever been to the Bahamas?"

"I'm afraid not."

"Oh, you have to go!" she insisted rather vehemently. "The beaches there are soooo beautiful. We stayed at this resort that had the most incredible spa and restaurants. It was heaven!"

She stared off into space dreamily for a few seconds as she relived her vacation in paradise.

"You know what the best thing about my guy is?"

"He's got a good travel agent?" I responded with a smirk.

"No. The best thing about my guy is that he wants to spend every minute of every day with me, not like all those other creeps I've dated. He doesn't need 'time' or 'space'; he just wants to be with me."

So, Lori had finally found a man as needy and starved for attention as she was? Proof that the old adage, "There's someone for everyone," was true.

"That's great, but what about your job?" I wondered.

She shrugged with indifference. "I quit the salon last week. This relationship is my career now, and I need to devote myself to it fully."

I was appalled.

"But cutting hair was your livelihood! How will you support yourself?"

"Oh, I don't have to worry about that anymore. My boyfriend is rich. He'll take care of me."

"You're moving in together then?"

"It's still a little early in our relationship for that. After all, we just met 12 days ago."

"12 days?!?!?!?!" My voice went all high-pitched and squeaky with disbelief. "You gave up your job for a man you haven't even known two weeks?"

"But it feels like we've known each other a lifetime! This man is the one I've been waiting for, my perfect match, my true love, I feel it down deep in my soul. Please, don't try and talk me out of this, Dr. Alvarez," she begged. "I am *so* happy and I want you to be happy for me."

As her therapist, it behooved me to issue some words of caution about this new, mutually co-dependent relationship of hers, but I didn't have it in me to extinguish the light in her eyes. Who knew? Maybe things would work out for Lori and her mystery man? They obviously had a lot in common, an inability to function on their own, a tendency towards possessiveness and fixations, unrealistic expectations of romantic partners . . .

I took Lori's hands in mine and gave them an encouraging squeeze. "I *am* happy for you. Delighted, in fact. I wish you only the best in this relationship and I hope that it's everything you want and need it to be."

"Really?" My endorsement of her latest hook-up seemed to surprise her. "You don't think I'm rushing into this or letting my emotions carry me away without regard for the consequences?"

"Not at all. I admire you for throwing caution to the wind and taking a chance on love." *I only wished that I was brave enough to do the same . . .*

* * *

"Take care. See you next week!" I waved good-bye to Lori after she'd settled her bill with Margo and scheduled her appointment for the following Tuesday.

"Here." My receptionist handed me an overnight envelope once we were alone. "FedEx delivered this a little while ago."

I looked at the airbill stuck to the envelope and got a pain in my head when I saw that it was from Corman & Mackelvy Management Co. *What did they want?* I wasn't late with my rent yet. Did they think I was going to forget about the increase?

"I hate these guys," I muttered irritably as I ripped the envelope open. I extracted the letter and packet of papers that were inside and quickly perused the former.

"Oh, my gosh! I love these guys!" I exulted.

"Why? What did they say?"

"*Dear Dr. Alvarez,*" I read aloud, not only for Margo's benefit, but for my own, because I needed to confirm that I hadn't somehow misconstrued the contents of the letter.

"*After much consideration and a second review of your file, the owner of the building at 2390 11th Street, in which you currently lease office space, has authorized us, as their agents, to waive the $1000 increase in your monthly rent for an additional six months. Enclosed please find a new lease, which locks in the rate of $3500 thru December of this year. We ask that you sign and date this document and return it to us with your payment for July by the close of business this Friday.*

Thank you for being a valued tenant.

Sincerely,

Roger P. Corman"

"And people say there isn't a God," I murmured reverently.

Margo took the letter out of my hand and gave it the once-over herself. "There is definitely a higher power at work here, and whoever, or whatever, it is saved your toochis just in the nick of time."

I was definitely going to have to go to church, light a few candles, and offer up a prayer of thanks on bended knee, but I had another stop to make first.

CHAPTER 30

"Welcome to Corman & Mackelvy. May I help you?" inquired the attractive blonde who was sitting at the reception desk, wearing a headset.

"Yes, thank you. I don't have an appointment, but I'd like to see Mr. Corman if possible."

"And you are?" She raised an overplucked-to-the-point-of-being-almost-nonexistent eyebrow.

"Dr. Pilar Alvarez. I rent an office in South Beach at 2390 11th Street. It's one of the properties this company manages."

"I see." The young woman rose to her feet. "Please, have a seat over there," she gestured at a grouping of empty chairs and a coffee table covered with books that looked like they were for show, not for reading, "while I pull your file and see if Mr. Corman is available."

She waited until I was settled in a chair before disappearing down a long corridor to her right. The phone rang several times while she was gone and I wondered if the calls were going straight to voice mail, or if the receptionist was able to answer them remotely with that headset of hers. I amused myself by trying to picture Margo with one of those things perched atop her heavily shellacked, teased-up 'do. With her hair being so gravity-defying, she'd probably be able to pick up radio signals and transmissions from outer space in addition to incoming phone calls.

I don't know how long I sat in that waiting area; it might have been a matter of minutes, but it seemed like forever and I got antsy. I was so desperate for some form of entertainment that I was about to crack open a dusty tome entitled "Indigenous Water Fowl of South Florida" when the blonde finally returned.

"Mr. Corman has a few minutes to spare, and he'd be

happy to see you," she proclaimed. "Follow me, please."
Which I did, back to a huge office with a nice view of the
Biscayne Bay out its 21st Floor window. The office was
inhabited by a rotund, ruddy-faced man in a wrinkled white
suit that was a size too small and a blue bow tie. He looked
like a character in a Tennessee Williams play, and this image
was only enhanced by the heavy Southern accent he greeted
me with.

"Well, come on in, pretty lady," he beckoned as he
waddled out from behind his massive desk with a manila file
folder tucked under his arm.

"I appreciate you seeing me without an appointment, Mr.
Corman." I shook the meaty paw he offered me. "And I
won't take up much of your time. I just wanted to thank you
in person for working with me on the raise in my rent.
Having a six-month grace period is such a--"

"Grace period?" His brow furrowed, and he looked over
my shoulder at the receptionist who was lurking behind me.
"Didn't the owner ask us to raise the rent effective
immediately on all the short-term tenants in that building?"

"Yes, but there were special circumstances in Dr.
Alvarez's case. It's all in her file." She pointed to the folder
in his possession.

"Special circumstances? Hrumph," he cleared his throat,
which sounded disgustingly phlegmy, and pulled a pair of
drugstore reading glasses out of his coat pocket. After
placing them on the tip of his bulbous red nose, he opened
the file and slowly flipped through its pages.

"Ah, yes. It's all here. *Special circumstances*," he
muttered the phrase once more, this time with understanding,
then closed the file quickly as if he was afraid something
might jump out of it, and gave me an obsequious smile.

"It's our pleasure to accommodate a responsible, hard-
workin' businesswoman such as yourself, Dr., uh," he peeked

into the folder again in search of my name, "Alvarez."

I was getting a very strange vibe off of this man. Like there was something in that file I should know about, but didn't. What were these "special circumstances" everyone was talking about? And what made me different from all of the other tenants in my building? I'd only rented space there for half a year and since the ownership of 2390 11th Street had changed hands, I didn't have any connections or influence. Should I ask Mr. Corman to explain, or should I just leave well enough alone? I wasn't sure. If I annoyed him by looking a gift horse in the mouth and being too inquisitive, he could rescind his offer of the grace period and then where would I be? Out on the street, with no office, and no place to see patients or ply my trade.

"I'm very grateful," I said, deciding not to press my luck, "and as a show of good faith, I brought my rent payment for July." Reaching into my purse, I extracted a check for $3500.

"Well, that's just fine. Why don't you give the money to Vicky," he handed my file to his assistant, "and she'll give you a receipt."

"I'll do that. Thank you, sir." And that concluded my business with the corpulent Mr. Corman.

Vicky led me back out to the reception area, where she entered the particulars of my payment into her database and was about to print up a copy of the revised invoice for my records, when Mr. Corman buzzed her in a tizzy because he was having trouble opening an e-mail attachment.

"I'm sorry," she apologized. "It'll only take a minute. Would you mind?"

I shook my head 'no,' and she hurried away, leaving me completely and temptingly alone with . . . my file. It sat on her desk, just a few inches from my fingertips. I tried to ignore it, I averted my eyes, I started humming to myself, I even pulled out my cell phone to see if I had any messages, but the paper-filled manila folder that held all of my account information called to me just the same.

'*I have a secret,*' the file sought to entice me. '*Don't you want to know what it is? Come on, you know you're dying to open me. Stop being such a goody two-shoes, and just DO IT!*'

It was my file after all. My name was the one that'd been typed neatly on its label. Ergo, I should be allowed to read its contents, right? What harm could there be in me taking a little peek? Before my conscience could kick in and talk me out of the possibly criminal act I was about to engage in, I grabbed the folder and peeled back its cover.

The first item I saw inside was a copy of a cashier's check from a local bank for $1000 dated the day before. I hadn't given Corman & Macklevy a cashier's check, so who the hell had? The check provided no clues as it had been signed by a representative of the bank, with no mention of the person who'd fronted the money for it. Examining the bank-issued form more closely, I noticed a short description in the memo section: 'Partial payment for Dr. Alvarez's July rent.' Aha! So, the owner of my office building hadn't had a change of heart and postponed raising my rent until next year. Someone had paid the difference for me. But who?

Raymond? Ana? Sara? I ran down a list of my nearest and dearest. *Papá!* Of course, it had to have been him. He must have found out about my financial woes (Maybe Izzy had broken down and told him?) and in order to spare me the humiliation of having to ask for the money, he'd made a deal with Corman & Macklevy on the sly. Yes, that sounded just like something my father would do, the dear, sweet man. I got misty-eyed when I thought about all the trouble he'd gone to on my behalf. How would I ever repay him for his kindness and generosity?

With a sigh, I flipped to the next page in my folder. It was a $3500 invoice for July's rent with my name and address on the top. I'd already seen the invoice when it had been sent to me via FedEx along with the letter from Mr. Corman, so that was nothing new. However, there was a yellow post-it stuck to the invoice with some scribbled instructions that looked interesting. I removed the note and brought it up closer to my face in an effort to get a better look at the almost illegible handwriting.

'Continue to bill Dr. Alvarez $3500/month and send a second invoice for $1000 to . . .' I turned the post-it over, *'. . . Jonathan Fordham, MD at . . .'*

"What?!?!?!?!?!" I shrieked with surprise, then clapped my hand over my mouth and held my breath, wondering fearfully if anyone had heard my outburst.

The sound of footsteps scurrying back up the hallway a few seconds later was my answer. In a panic, I closed my file, threw it down on the receptionist's desk, and hightailed it out of the office.

OHMYGOD. OHMYGOD. OH . . . MY . . . GOD!

My hands were trembling so hard that it took me several tries to push the DOWN button on the elevator. My father hadn't bailed me out, nor had my well-to-do brother-in-law or almost-famous best friend. It had been Ford. FORD! The man I'd mistrusted. The man I'd accused of being self-serving. The man I'd more or less kicked to the curb three days before. I couldn't believe it.

I was still stunned when I arrived home several hours later. Leaving my keys in the front door, I stood motionless in the foyer with the mail in one hand and my briefcase in the other, trying to process everything that had happened.

"What's up with you?" my sister wondered as she came bustling into the living room in a state of half-dress, fiddling with an earring that she was having trouble getting in.

"I have had the most incredible day," I told her.

"You may have cured some bored housewife of her addiction to bonbons and *Judge Judy*, but your day has got nothing on mine."

"Why's that?"

"Well, for starters, I got this amazing job off-- Damn it!" Izzy cursed when she jabbed her finger with the pointy back of the earring, and it slipped out of her hand.

"One that doesn't involve letting drunk men stick fives in your cleavage?" I asked as she bent down to retrieve the jewelry. "Hey! Isn't that mine?"

"Yeah, it matches this top perfectly, don't you think?" She glanced down at her body-hugging halter while she stuck the dangly turquoise earring in her right lobe. "These are too funky for you anyway. You should just give them to me."

"I am not giving them to you. You've already appropriated half my wardrobe and most of my good jewelry."

My sister pursed her lips at me irritably. "You never were good at sharing. Do you want to hear about my job offer or not?"

"Tell me."

"I'm going to do a bathing suit calendar," she announced, reaching behind her back to zip up her short, denim skirt.

"You mean, model? Professionally?"

"Yep. I got this call from a photographer who's doing a shoot down in St. Croix this weekend. He saw me at the fashion show on Saturday and thought I had the right sultry look, so he called to see if I was interested. What do you think? Down or up?" Izzy piled her hair up on top of her head to show me the second option.

"Up, but with a few pieces hanging down around your face," I mumbled distractedly. "Are you sure that this photographer is the real deal? He's not just some sleazy guy who's making you a bunch of false promises so that you'll sleep with him?"

"Please," my sister scoffed, then turned on her barefoot heel and sashayed towards the bathroom with me in close pursuit. "Simon's not even into girls, and I checked him out with Sara. She said that he's like the Francesco Scavullo of swimwear photography. He even shot the cover of *Sports Illustrated*'s last swimsuit issue."

"Wow!" I was impressed. "That's big time."

"It's big money, too. I'll make $5000 for three days' work." Staring at her reflection in the bathroom mirror, Izzy twisted her dark, silky tresses up and secured them in place with a few bobby pins.

"I leave for the islands on Friday," she informed me while pulling down some strands of hair in the front as I'd suggested.

"But how can you do that?" I balked. "You're not allowed to leave the country when you're out on bail with a trial pending. If you do, I'll lose everything, my money, the house . . ."

"No, you won't. You're going to get all that stuff back as soon as my lawyer takes care of the paperwork."

Izzy scooted past me out into the hallway and headed for her bedroom.

"What? How? Why?" I queried as I scurried after her.

"That's the second part of my incredible day," she explained once we were inside her filthy mess of a room.

"Mr. Sullivan called a little while ago to tell me that the private detective he hired found an eyewitness to the theft of that Ferrari." Izzy dropped to her hands and knees and raised her bed skirt, searching behind it for who knows what. "This lady saw Marco, and Marco alone, break into the car, disengage its alarm system, then drive off by himself." Dragging a spiky-heeled boot out from underneath the box spring, she gave it a disgusted look and tossed it in the direction of her closet. "So, I'm off the hook for Grand Theft Auto and Aiding and Abetting a Fugitive."

"Oh, thank God!" I sat down on her unmade, magazine and clothes-cluttered bed and buried my face in my hands. For the first time in weeks, I felt a sense of peace. I didn't have to worry about my little sister going to jail or some sweaty bail bondsman getting his hands on my beloved bungalow. No more anxiety, no more sleepless nights. It was like a hundred pound barbell had been lifted off my shoulders. I was so relieved I wanted to cry.

"Don't start bawling," Izzy ordered as if she sensed the imminent outpouring of emotion.

"I won't," I sniffled.

"Good, then get down here and help me find my black stilettos. I wore them the other night, so they've got to be around here somewhere."

I joined her on the floor and began sifting through the piles of detritus that had accumulated there. "Why are we looking for your black stilettos?" I questioned.

"They're my sexiest shoes. No man can resist me when I wear them."

"Who are you trying to make yourself irresistible for?" I hoped that it wasn't another shady character like Marco.

"Alex Muñiz," she replied matter-of-factly.

"Alex Muñiz," I repeated. "Why does that name sound familiar?"

"He was one of the police officers who arrested me. Remember, I bit him on the hand? Aha! There you are. Come to Momma, my little beauties." She pulled the missing stilettos out of the small trash can on the other side of the room.

"I'm confused," I said, using the bed as a counterbalance to push myself into an upright position. "Why would you want to have anything to do with the police officer who arrested you?"

Izzy hopped around on one foot while attempting to squeeze the other into her fashionably narrow pump. "I've still got that Resisting Arrest charge hanging over my head. To make it go away, I need the officer I assaulted to recant and say that it was all a big misunderstanding."

"Won't the permanent teeth marks on his hand prove otherwise?"

"I didn't bite him *that* hard," she dismissed the man's injury as she slipped on her second stiletto.

"You broke the skin. He had to get a tetanus shot."

"That was just a precaution. I'm sure he's all healed up by now."

"Just don't expect him to forgive and forget," I cautioned. "There might be hard feelings on his side."

My sister smirked. "One look at this," she ran her hand down her tanned, curvaceous body, which was alluringly displayed in her tight clothes, "and the only hard feelings Officer Muñiz is going to have will be below the belt. I am showing enough boob, right?" Izzy gazed down at her cleavage with concern.

"Any more boob and he'll mistake you for a hooker," I retorted.

"Perfect! Guys love slutty. Now, where's my purse?" Her eyes darted around the room frantically, but she didn't spot it.

"ARGH!" she groaned with frustration. "I need to get the hell out of here. His shift starts at 7:00, and I have to catch him before he goes out on patrol."

"Try the living room," I suggested, and we tromped back out there together.

"Yes!" Izzy exulted when she found her faux crocodile clutch tucked into a corner of the couch. She pulled some shimmery pink lip gloss from the bag and hastily applied it to her full mouth.

"How are my teeth?" she inquired, baring them at me.

"Nothing stuck in between them."

"Good." She squirted some spearmint Binaca in her mouth. "Later."

"Hey!" I protested, following her to the foyer. "I never got to tell you about my day."

She opened the screen door and with a bored expression, turned back towards me. "How exciting could it have been? Did you kiss and make up with Ford?"

"No."

"Did you see him?"

"No."

"Talk to him?"

"No."

"Pull your head out of your ass and realize that he's a good guy, you love him, and you need to stop being a chicken shit and tell him?"

"No," was my meek response.

"Get back to me when you do." She stepped outside and let the screen door slam shut in my face.

CHAPTER 31

It was July in Miami, which meant that the beach was the place to be. Not even the sweltering humidity and 94-degree heat could keep the sun-worshippers away. A motley assortment of sandcastle-building children, dreadlocked surfers, and muumuu-clad senior citizens occupied every inch of sand on my favorite strip of South Beach. I stood at the shoreline, letting the ocean lick at my bare feet, but the water was so warm that it afforded little relief. There was no breeze to stir the skirt of my yellow wrap dress, and the mid-day sun beat down mercilessly on my exposed arms. I could feel the skin on my nose burning and I imagined how horrified my mother would be if I freckled.

A hand touched my shoulder gently. "You're getting pink."

"I've been out here a while," I admitted before turning towards him.

Whoa! Had Ford gotten more handsome since the last time I'd seen him? Maybe it was the black aviator sunglasses that seemed to emphasize the strong bone structure of his face? Or the way his light gray dress shirt was casually unbuttoned at the collar, giving me a tantalizing glimpse of his tanned chest? I certainly didn't remember him being so tall. I'd never had to lean my head back when I'd gazed up at him before. Of course, that might have had something to do with the fact that I wasn't wearing any shoes.

Dropping my eyes to my feet, I said, "Thanks for coming."

"I was surprised to get your message. You said you needed time, and it's only been three days."

Three of the longest, most miserable days of my life. It was ridiculous how much I'd missed Ford, how much I'd gotten used to having him around.

"I didn't think it would be fair to either one of us to drag this out any longer."

"I see." With a pained grimace, he shoved his hands into his pockets and looked as though he was preparing himself for the worst.

"No, I'm the one who sees, Ford. I see because I know what you did."

"I don't follow."

"I know you paid the difference in my rent this month, and you made a deal under the table with Corman & Macklevy to keep paying the extra thousand for the rest of the year."

"Oh, crap," he grumbled, removing his sunglasses and rubbing his eyes wearily. "You weren't supposed to find out about that. I swear, I didn't do it to try and ingratiate myself to you. I just hated the thought of you losing your practice when you'd put so much effort and heart into it. And I wanted to give you the chance to make it work, but I knew you'd never take a loan from me and--"

"It's okay. I'm not mad."

His brows knit together in confusion. "You're not?"

"Not at all. You did a nice thing for me, and I believe your motives were pure and unselfish. More than anyone, I think you understand what my practice means to me, and how important it is for me to use my knowledge and skills to help people."

"I do. You remind me a lot of myself when I was starting out in this business. You're passionate and idealistic about what you do, and you care so much about your patients. It's inspiring."

"Really?"

"Really," he assured me. "I think you have what it takes to be an exceptional psychologist."

"Thanks." His praise made me blush. "And thanks for

saving my fledgling career. I owe you."

"No." He shook his dark head vehemently. "I don't want that. I don't want your gratitude and I don't want you to feel like you owe me."

"But I do, and I intend to pay you back in kind." I meant that I would reward his faith in me by making a success of my practice, but he misinterpreted.

"Don't get involved with me because you feel beholden," he commanded gruffly. "There are no strings attached to that money. It's not a romantic inducement, and I'm not trying to buy   your   affection."

"So, now you're trying to talk me out of taking this relationship," I waggled a finger back and forth between us, "to the next level?"

"Hell no. I just don't want you to feel obligated to be with me. If we're going to move forward with this relationship, then we have to be on the same page regarding our reasons for doing so."

"Okay," I agreed, "what page are you on?"

"I'm on the page where the male protagonist takes the heroine by the shoulders, stares deeply into her big, beautiful," he squinted down at me, "brownish, goldish--"

"Hazel," I helped him out.

"Thanks," he said with a sheepish grin. "He looks into her big, beautiful, *hazel* eyes and tells her that he hopes she can forgive him for being an emotional coward and not telling her the truth about his late wife sooner because he's crazy about her, and he can't imagine going another day without hearing one of her amusing anecdotes about her family, or seeing her eyes light up with excitement over a plate of polenta fries or the way her face softens and becomes even more gorgeous whenever she speaks to his son."

"Hmmmm," I murmured, trying not to smile even though I felt happy enough to burst open like a *piñata* filled with too much candy. "That's a good page, one of my favorites in fact, but I think I'm a little further along in the book. I'm at the part where the heroine has already gotten over the male protagonist letting her think he was married when he wasn't because she understands that he was grieving and afraid to open up his heart again. She realizes that he wasn't being manipulative and didn't intend to hurt or deceive her; he was just trying to protect himself."

"This heroine is very insightful." He gently brushed back a strand of hair that had escaped my French twist and fallen into my face. I noticed that his wedding band was no longer on his ring finger. A symbolic gesture that he was ready to move on.

Finally allowing myself to smile, I said, "She comes from a long line of insightful women. It was actually her mother who advised her not to rush to judgment on the male protagonist and to take his kind treatment of her into consideration."

Taking my hand in his, he said, "Remind me to send your mother some flowers."

"I think she'd be happier with a year's supply of Valium."

"Whatever it takes to keep me on her good side. I've got plenty of samples." He winked at me, and I chortled with amusement.

"So," Ford stepped closer and wrapped his arms around my waist, "where do we go from here?"

"I'm glad you asked," I replied, slipping out of his embrace and bending down so that I could scribble something in the wet sand that had been left behind when the tide had ebbed.

"What do you think?" I asked, standing up.

"Date. Me. Ford," he slowly read the words I'd written.

"Sorry, but I'm on a budget and couldn't afford a skywriter," I jokingly referred to Victor's over-the-top gesture, which I'd essentially ripped off.

"I like this much better. The heart at the end is a nice, artistic touch."

"If you say 'yes,' which I hope you will, then we can have our first official date right now. I brought food and everything." I motioned up the beach where I'd spread out a blanket earlier.

Holding out his hand to me, Ford said, "Let's go."

I led him to the blue plaid blanket that I'd pulled out of the back of my hallway closet that morning, along with the picnic basket I'd bought on sale at Pier 1 a year before and had never used. Kneeling down on the sand-covered material, I reached for the basket and began to extract its contents.

"Since we're being completely honest with each other about everything now, I must confess that I didn't make any of this." I handed him an orange soda, which I knew he liked, and a bag of plantain chips.

"That's okay. It wasn't your culinary talent that attracted me to you anyway." He popped open the drink and took a swig.

"Oh, really? What was it that attracted you then?"

"Well, let's see." He stretched out on his side, propping his head up on his hand. "There was your warmth, your intelligence, your sense of humor, your unswerving devotion to your work and family, and, last, but by no means least, your body."

"My body?" I stopped in the middle of unloading the picnic basket.

"I've been secretly admiring it since the day we met, but I don't think I fully appreciated the heart attack-inducing power of your curves until I saw you spilling out of that little brown bikini at Sara's fashion show the other day."

I grinned. "You liked that bikini, huh?"

"*Liked* doesn't begin to describe my feelings about that bikini. I want to dedicate love songs to it. I want to build it a shrine. I want to take it to meet my parents. I don't suppose you're hiding it under that dress?" Leaning forward, he slid the strap of the silk and rayon garment towards the edge of my shoulder to see what lay beneath.

I smacked his hand away before he could expose my not-very-exciting beige bra strap. "Eat," I instructed, pushing a paper-wrapped sandwich at him.

"What is this?" he wondered.

"*Pan con Bistec.*"

He frowned, so I explained, "It's a Cuban steak sandwich."

"Sounds good." He removed the paper from the sandwich and was about to take a bite when he made a face and pulled back. Opening the bread, he looked at what was inside. "Garlic *and* onions?"

"Uh-huh, that's how *Pan con Bistec* is prepared, with lime juice, garlic, and onions."

"If I eat this, I'm going to have such bad breath that an entire tin of Altoids won't help."

"Why do you care about your breath? Were you planning on kissing someone later?" I teased.

"No, I was planning on kissing someone . . . now!" He tossed his sandwich into the open picnic basket and lunged at me. Giggling, I fell back against the blanket with him, and we spent the rest of our lunch hour *not* eating.

* * *

Returning to our office building arm-in-arm, Ford and I were sweaty, sunburned, and had grains of sand in a lot of uncomfortable places, but neither of us cared.

"That was the best lunch ever!" I proclaimed as I snuggled

up against him.

Gazing down at me tenderly, he said, "No arguments from me. We should make that a noontime habit."

"What? The kissing or the skipping a meal?"

"Both. Think how thin we'll be."

"Beats the heck out of exercising."

Stopping in front of Suite #2-B, I looked at my office door and sighed forlornly.

"I guess we have to go back to work now."

"Or . . .," Ford bent down to whisper seductively in my ear, "we could reschedule all of our afternoon appointments and play hooky for the rest of the day."

I gasped and brought a hand to my throat. "How capricious! How irresponsible! Dr. Fordham, you shock me!"

Maneuvering me back against the door, he murmured, "I think our patients can survive without us for a few hours," then began to plant a series of soft, warm kisses down my throat.

I chuckled and twined my arms around his neck. "I can see that you are going to be a very bad influence."

"What can I say?" He nibbled on my ear lobe. "You bring out my inner nonconformist."

"I have a 2:00," I protested feebly, but my words were muffled by Ford's mouth, which descended on mine with passionate intent.

We kissed like a couple of overly hormonal teenagers, so hungry for each other that we were completely oblivious to our surroundings. The sound of someone opening my office door from the inside didn't even register in either of our fevered brains.

With a surprised squeak, I tumbled backwards into my office and probably would have ended up spread eagle on the floor if Ford hadn't somehow managed to keep his balance and hold on to me.

"Dr. Alvarez! I thought that was you I heard out in the hallway," an unaccountably perky voice greeted me.

From my dipped position, I looked over Ford's shoulder and saw Lori Bryant, standing next to the door.

"Lori, uh . . ." I tapped Ford on the chest, and he straightened up with me in his arms.

"I wasn't expecting to see you today. What brings you by?" I queried breathlessly as I adjusted my dress, which had gotten completely twisted around during my clinch with Ford.

"I've got the most wonderful news and I just couldn't wait until next week to share it with you!" She was so excited she was practically vibrating.

"That's great. What is it?"

"I'm engaged!" she squealed, clapping her hands together and jumping up and down like a four-year-old who'd just been given a Premium Pass to the Magic Kingdom.

"Uh, wow!" I glanced over at Margo, who was sitting at her desk munching on a corned beef sandwich.

"You could have knocked me over with a feather," she remarked in her wry way. "Show her the ring, doll."

"Isn't it gorgeous?" Lori stuck a huge diamond in my face.

I gaped at it, too stunned to speak. The setting, the stone, the platinum band . . .

Ford looked down at the glittery rock and frowned. "Isn't that the same ring that--"

I elbowed him in the ribs.

"Ow!" he objected, rubbing his side.

"It's a beautiful ring, Lori."

"Victor said it's one-of-a-kind. No other woman on the planet has one like it."

"No other woman wanted it," Ford muttered, and I shot

him a dirty look.

"You never did tell me how you met your *fiancé*," I prompted my patient.

"If you can believe it, we met right here in front of your office building. It was a couple Thursdays ago, and I had the afternoon off because Jiff had an appointment at the doggie day spa over on 16th. When I picked him up, I thought, *My guy looks SO adorable in his bandanna with the Stars and Stripes pattern,* which I got because--"

"Independence Day was coming up," I connected the dots.

"Right! So, I decided to walk Jiff over to your office and introduce the two of you since I talk about you to each other all the time. And there he was, the most beautiful man I'd ever seen, sitting on a bus stop bench, looking so lonely and miserable. I just had to stop and ask if he was okay. He invited me to join him, so I did, and we started talking about why he was so sad."

"Do tell," I encouraged.

Lori sighed dramatically. "It's a tragic story, full of love, sacrifice, and crushing disappointment. You see, Victor was involved with this awful woman. I'm sure you know the type, Dr. Alvarez. Cold, bitchy, career-driven."

"I hate women like that," Ford interjected, then smirked at me, obviously finding a lot more humor in the situation than I was.

"There are always two sides to the story when a couple breaks up," I told Lori.

"Oh no, not in this case. Victor was definitely the injured party. He did everything to make this woman happy, he offered her the world, and she just stomped all over his poor sensitive heart. She didn't appreciate him at all."

"I guess it's a good thing he found you then."

I never would have thought to put the two of them together, but Lori was such a bottomless pit of need and

Victor could certainly fill that pit up with all of his demands for love, time, and attention. Their neuroses would probably complement each other perfectly.

"Isn't it funny the way things work out?" Lori mused.

"Hilarious," Ford deadpanned.

"So, when's the wedding?"

"November 10th, so mark your calendar, Dr. Alvarez, because you have GOT to come!"

"That might not be--," I tried to beg off, but Lori wasn't listening.

"And, of course, you have to bring your boyfriend. You are Dr. Alvarez's boyfriend, right?" She directed a curious gaze at Ford. "The one who sent her all those beautiful orchids a few months back?"

"Actually--"

"Yep, that's me." Ford draped a proprietary arm over my shoulders and gave me a squeeze. "I just love to shower my little poblano pepper with ridiculously expensive presents whenever I can."

His little *what*?

"Good-looking *and* romantic! Just like my Victor! Oh, Dr. Alvarez," she embraced me with affection, "aren't we both lucky?"

"So it would seem . . ."

"Oooooooo . . ." Lori's eyes suddenly grew wide, and I could almost see the light bulb switching on over her curly red head. "We should have a double wedding!" she exclaimed.

Ford and I exchanged looks of unadulterated horror.

"No, no, we couldn't do that," I insisted in a panic-stricken voice. "This is going to be *your* special day, Lori. You shouldn't have to share the spotlight with anyone."

"Yeah, I guess you're right. But you will be there, won't you? I can't get married without you, Dr. Alvarez. I just can't!"

"If I have that day free--" I certainly wasn't going to make any promises. The last thing I wanted to do was watch my patient walk down the aisle with my ex. The whole situation was just too weird, and it was probably some sort of professional conflict of interest.

"Please, please, please, please . . ."

Damn it.

EPILOGUE

I watch Lori as she walks down the aisle of St. Bartholomew's in her strapless Monique Lhuillier gown, carrying a bouquet of white lilies and yellow roses. I've never seen a bride look so . . . well, happy doesn't really do her over-bright eyes and flushed, beaming face justice. Giddy would probably be a more appropriate word. She's so high on the delight of finally getting the big church wedding she's always dreamed of, I half-expect her to abandon formality and start doing cartwheels up to the altar. As she passes the pew where I'm sitting, Lori glances over and gives me a little wave accompanied by a girlish giggle.

I'm quite sure that I wouldn't be favored in this fashion if she knew the truth about my history with her future husband. I hate lying to her about it, and even more, I hate being in league with Victor to keep our regrettable relationship a secret. But the alternative would probably send the easily agitated Lori into paroxysms of jealousy, and even though she's no longer my patient, I still feel responsible for the woman's mental health. So, what's a little subterfuge if it keeps her on an even emotional keel? As far as she's concerned, Victor's family is old friends with mine, which accounts for our familiarity with one another and my parents' presence at *the* social event of the season.

Lori reaches the altar and gazes with undisguised adoration at a tuxedo-clad Victor, who smiles suavely and takes her pale hands in his. I hear plaintive sobbing coming from the groom's side of the church, but I don't turn my head to see who the weeper is. My mother never has been one to suffer in silence. Although I suggested more than once that she sit this wedding out and spare herself the torture of what-could-have-been, she opted to attend and play the martyr. Her tears are more for my benefit than the bride and groom's.

320

She wants me to know just how disappointed she is that I'm not the *chica* pledging my troth to one of the most eligible bachelors in Miami.

Normally, I'd be annoyed with her for making a scene, but *Mamá*'s had a rough time of it lately. Two months ago, Ana announced she was pregnant again. My mother, egocentric optimist that she is, immediately jumped to the conclusion that her much-prayed-for granddaughter was finally on her way, and she proceeded to go a little *loca,* buying thousands of dollars worth of pink clothing, bedding, and toys. When Ana's doctor did an ultrasound and we learned that the newest Castaneira would be another boy, a devastated *Mamá* took to her bed for a week.

She'd just recovered from that shock when she was hit with the nerve-shattering news that Izzy's moving in with her boyfriend. To no one's surprise, much hysteria and rosary bead-clutching ensued. Personally, I was thrilled because Izzy bunking somewhere else means I get my privacy back. And besides, I really like Alex. He's had a stabilizing influence on my sister, and the irony of an unapologetic rule-breaker like her hooking up with a cop, especially one she wounded with her incisors, is not lost on me.

Falling in love has matured Izzy considerably; she isn't the same temperamental brat who expected her family to foot the bill for her self-indulgent lifestyle. She's working steadily as a model, doing everything from catalogs to music videos, and she reimbursed me in full for all of her legal expenses. Since she's acting like an adult, I think she deserves to be treated like one. Unfortunately, my parents don't share the sentiment. They're threatening to disown Izzy if she disgraces the family by living in sin with a man, and she's threatening to pose in her birthday suit for *Caliente* magazine if they don't respect her right to do as she pleases. And so, their battle of wills goes.

I seem to be the only Alvarez whose life is drama-free at the moment. Business has picked up thanks to some advertising and more than a dozen referrals from my mentor, Dr. Fields, who decided to retire early and relocate to Fiji. The influx of new patients has really invigorated me. I bounce out of bed every morning, full of enthusiasm for my job, and I've never felt more focused and confident about my therapeutic skills. While some of my original patients (the Scolaris, Meghan, Lori), accomplished all that they could in our sessions and moved on to what I hope will be happier, more satisfying lives, the others are still works-in-progress.

Ariane Wylie was able to get her divorce without having to pay the contemptible Julio a single cent. In a propitious twist of fate, he was deported to Colombia just days before he was scheduled to face off with her in court. It seems there was a problem with his paperwork, which had absolutely nothing to do with Ariane knowing one of the higher-ups at the Bureau of Immigration and Citizenship, or so she assured me with a smug smile. We've still got a long way to go with her rage against men and revenge issues.

Leonard Dyson decided to use the lottery winnings that made him so miserable to open a Youth Center in Opa-Locka, the disadvantaged area where he grew up. He said he wanted to give back to the community and offer children both a safe haven and the opportunity to better their lives. Leonard works at the center every day, organizing activities, overseeing group projects, and lending an ear to the kids who come there. By helping these troubled teens, I think he's righting what went wrong in his own unhappy childhood, and it's had a very positive effect on him. He's less timid and more willing to express his opinions now, which is a small, but important, step towards him becoming a proud, self-assured person.

As per my recommendation, Kyle Kotowski took up

astronomy, a hobby that seemed harmless enough at the time. He bought himself a high-powered telescope, attended shows at the Miami Museum of Science Planetarium, and even joined a local group of stargazers. For a few weeks, he talked more about constellations and the Helix Nebula than he did his imaginary physical ailments which I thought was a good sign. Unfortunately, things went horribly awry when another astronomer wannabe told Kyle about a recently published study on the properties of cosmic debris. Apparently, some of these rocks contain submicroscopic parasitic particles that are unknown to our scientists. In other words, *alien viruses*. Since hearing this, Kyle has been afraid to leave his house without wearing a surgical mask, and I've been forced to up him to two sessions a week.

I don't know if Derek Reynolds ever filmed that movie for Lifetime, but I did catch his latest performance . . . in a Hair Plugs for Men commercial! I laughed so hard the first time I saw it that I fell off my bed. The next time the ad aired on late-night TV, I quickly hit RECORD on my DVR so that I would have the product plug (*Hee!*) on hand for my continuous viewing pleasure. There's nothing better than coming home from a hard day of work and hearing Derek say, "*I'm not just an actor; I'm a satisfied client of Hair Plugs for Men.*" I'll bet he has pectoral implants and a Mystic Tan, too.

I redirect my attention to the ceremony. The priest is doing a Scripture reading, so we're only halfway through. I cast a sideways glance at my date, who looks very *GQ* in a navy suit and periwinkle-and-white striped shirt, both of which he bought especially for the occasion because he knows how much I love seeing him in blue (it really makes his eyes pop!) He's staring at the altar with a stoic, '*I'm so bored I might lapse into a coma at any moment*' expression on his face. With my finger, I trace the outline of his chiseled jaw, and he turns towards me.

I mouth the word, "Sorry."

Inclining his dark head, he whispers, "For what?"

"For torturing you like this."

"I didn't realize Catholic weddings were so long."

"Painfully so."

"And to think, I could have been playing golf."

"You hate golf," I remind him.

"Careful or you'll get me kicked out of the AMA," he retorts with a smirk.

The bride and groom are now saying their vows. Lori tearfully recounts how her heart swelled with joy when she first set eyes on Victor and then quotes some incredibly sappy poem about soul mates. Her intended waxes rhapsodic about their love being as eternal as the ocean tides, as beautiful as the sunrise, as full of color and hope as the rainbow that appears after a violent storm . . .

"We'll be sticking with the traditional wedding vows when we get married," my companion mutters.

No doubt about it, I definitely ended up with the right man.

Even though we've only been together 4 months, 8 days, 3 hours, and oh, about 21 minutes (*Yes, that's right, I've been counting.*), Ford and I are so attuned to each other that it's almost like we share a brain. Not that we always agree, but we do understand each other and that's something I've never experienced before. Now, I have someone I can share everything with, my work, my family, my friends, even my love for spicy food and my penchant for do-gooding. And he's given me so much - his affection, his support, his respect, and most importantly, the opportunity to have a relationship with his son, the most brilliant, perceptive, delightful child in the world, not that I'm prejudiced or anything.

Nate is the only person Ford and I have told about our marriage plans. Before proceeding, we wanted to make sure he was okay with me becoming his stepmother, which, of course, he was. He's so excited about being the best man and he's taking the responsibility very seriously. Yesterday, I found him in Ford's kitchen making toast. When I asked him why since he knows he's not supposed to use electrical appliances without supervision, he told me he was practicing because he'd read that the best man has to "make a toast" at the wedding reception. How adorable is that?

Our engagement isn't official yet, so I'm not wearing a ring. Ford did buy me one a few weeks ago, but he's refusing to show it to me even though I've employed every feminine wile from begging to seduction. He says that he wants me to be surprised when he drops down on one knee and presents the ring to me at my birthday party in two weeks. It was his idea to make a big production out of the proposal on my 30th when all of my friends and family will be gathered at my parents' condo to celebrate. My mother's going to love it. I predict she'll spend the rest of the night boasting to anyone who'll listen that her daughter is going to marry a doctor, which is the best match any Alvarez girl has ever made. When Ana protests that she married a lawyer, *Mamá* will scoff that Raymond was just a lowly law clerk at the time of their "I Do"s. Then, she'll pull an armful of bridal magazines from her reserve in the front closet and insist that I pick out a dress immediately.

The next six months will be spent listening to my mother yammer on and on about floral arrangements and designs for ice sculptures. She'll call me at all hours of the day and night with suggestions for wedding cakes (*'Don't let Solana talk you into one of her Black Magic Cakes. They're too rich; Tio Juan got sick on all that chocolate at Sancha's reception. Remember, he threw up in the conga line? Go with the ½*

Cuban, ½ Chocolate, then you'll have devil's food cake for the people who like chocolate and yellow sponge for everyone else.') and Salsa bands ('*Whatever you do, don't hire your cousin Rique. I know he thinks he's a musician now, but playing the bongos with his elbows doesn't make him Tito Puente.*') She'll drop by the office with invitation samples and guest lists. She'll advise me to go on a diet so that I can fit into a size 6 on my wedding day like she did. She'll send me to her colorist for lowlights and recommend that I wear my hair down on the big day because I have a long neck that makes me look like a gira--

On second thought, Ford and I are going to elope.

* * * THE END * * *

<u>AUTHOR BIO</u>

An avid reader and writer, Tracie Banister has been scribbling stories since she was a child, most of them featuring feisty heroines with complicated love lives like her favorite fictional protagonist Scarlett O'Hara. Her work was first seen on the stage of her elementary school, where her 4th grade class performed an original holiday play that she penned (Like all good divas-in-the-making, she, also, starred in and tried to direct the production.) Her dreams of authorial success were put on the backburner when she reached adulthood and discovered that she needed a "real" job in order to pay her bills. Her career as personal assistant to a local entrepreneur lasted for 12 years. When it ended, Tracie decided to follow her bliss and dedicate herself to writing full-time. Her debut novel, the Hollywood-themed *Blame It on the Fame*, was released in January, 2012. And she's following that up with the Miami-set Romantic Comedy, *In Need of Therapy*.

Made in the USA
Lexington, KY
19 October 2012

SURVIVAL GUIDE
FOR YOUNG WOMEN

LEARNING HOW TO NAVIGATE
TODAY'S WORLD WITH
GRACE AND STRENGTH

HOLLY WAGNER | NICOLE REYES

Regal

From Gospel Light
Ventura, California, U.S.A.

For more information and
special offers from Regal Books,
email us at
subscribe@regalbooks.com

Published by Regal
From Gospel Light
Ventura, California, U.S.A.
www.regalbooks.com
Printed in the U.S.A.

Library of Congress Cataloging-in-Publication Data
Wagner, Holly.
Survival guide for young women : learning how to navigate today's world
with grace and strength / Holly Wagner, Nicole Reyes.
    p. cm.
Includes bibliographical references and index.
ISBN 978-0-8307-6249-1 (trade paper : alk. paper)
1. Christian women—Conduct of life. I. Reyes, Nicole. II. Title.
BJ1610.W33 2012
248.8'43—dc23
2012012411

Rights for publishing this book outside the U.S.A. or in non-English languages are administered by Gospel Light Worldwide, an international not-for-profit ministry. For additional information, please visit www.glww.org, email info@glww.org, or write to Gospel Light Worldwide, 1957 Eastman Avenue, Ventura, CA 93003, U.S.A.

To order copies of this book and other Regal products in bulk quantities, please contact us at 1-800-446-7735.

This book is dedicated to all the young women who want to make a difference in the world. Just know that there are women who believe in you and are cheering you on!

—HOLLY

This book is dedicated to my father . . . your love and support has given me the courage to pursue with passion the purpose for my life! You mean the world to me, and I respect and love you more than words can describe! I also dedicate this book to my pastors, Philip and Holly Wagner. I would not be fulfilling the call of God on my life without your love, example and investment. Your belief in me has made all the difference in my life, and I am eternally thankful!

—NICOLE

We need to humble ourselves so that we can learn.

I have had the privilege of leading quite a few young women in the past few years. (In other words . . . I have been their older woman!) My life is richer because they are in it. One of the young women in my world is Nicole Reyes. I have worked with her for almost 10 years. I have watched her grow, make decisions, learn to "shutteth uppeth," deal with issues in her heart, and be committed to fulfilling God's purpose for her life. I have also watched her extend her heart and life to her younger women . . . being committed to seeing them fulfill God's plan. I have asked her to write this book with me, in the hopes that together our voices would bring even more wisdom.

My desire in writing this book is to share some of the things I have learned over the years. As I was writing, I asked myself, *What do I wish I had known when I was in my twenties and thirties?* That is what you will find on these pages. Some of it is fun, random nonsense. But some of it really can help you on your journey.

I am asking you to open your heart and be willing to learn. Maybe reading about my mistakes can keep you from making the same ones.

XOXO . . . HOLLY

• • • • • • •

It was less than a year ago that Holly and I sat down for lunch at one of our favorite restaurants to chat about ministry, family, guys, and the random other topics one can expect to be discussed by a couple of God Chicks doing life together! This routine had developed organically over the years, and as a younger woman gleaning from the valuable wisdom of such an inspiring older woman, I always looked forward to our time together. At this particular meeting, over a couple of salads and a couple of lattes, we began to dream about writing a book that tackled the real issues young women are facing . . . and to have fun doing it!

A rush of excitement, mixed with a profound sense of responsibility, came over me as we brought up topics like dating and career and health and discovering purpose and overcoming issues of the heart. Then we both laughed after throwing in the equally important issue of finding the perfect pair of jeans to flatter a girl's figure! ☺ We decided no topic would be off limits. We wanted to do whatever it took to truly inspire and equip young women to navigate well the seasons of life that lie ahead.

Early on in the writing process, I had my own "aha" moment. I realized that this book is more a memoir than anything else. The wisdom and experience I contribute to these pages represent what I have learned over the past 10 years, largely because of the remarkable older women and men in my world.

Holly Wagner, perhaps more than anyone, has beautifully played the role of "older woman" in my life. As my pastor, leader and friend, she has encouraged and challenged me to fulfill my God-given purpose and destiny, to never settle for less, and to laugh more along the way!

When I met Holly, I was just 19 years old . . . full of dreams and potential, along with my fair share of hurts, brokenness and just plain old stupidity. Fast forward to today . . . I am a 29-year-old single and fulfilled pastor, teacher and executive team member who oversees different teams and areas of church life. I've been able to overcome the hurts of my past and passionately pursue Jesus and His plan for my life. I'm far from perfect, but I'm committed to living out this God-adventure to the fullest, with eternity in mind!

The things I've learned as the younger woman in the years between 19 and 29 have made all the difference! I learned to forgive and overcome hurts from my childhood. I learned to communicate honor and respect to men. I learned to lead different types of people. I learned that life isn't all about me . . . and that's a good thing! I learned how to date smart. I learned how to eat healthy. I learned how to manage my emotions. I learned how to "shutteth uppeth" around those who are older and wiser than I am. I learned how to bring a younger woman alongside me to give her the encouragement and wisdom she needs. I learned how to roast a turkey (even though I still think it's pretty gross having to butter the inside of a slimy bird . . . yuck!).

I learned how to do all of these things from Holly. Her mark on my life is undeniable, and her investment is one for which I will be eternally grateful!

The truth is, I'm still learning! We all are! But now it's time for me to put on the "older woman hat" and pay it forward—to share with you the wisdom that has been given to me over the years! Navigating life as a young woman can be tricky, but it doesn't need to be confusing or heartbreaking!

With some wisdom, you can navigate these years with dignity and grace, purpose and laughter! The decisions you make now can catapult you straight into your destiny! My prayer is that as you read each chapter, you will make choices that position you for the life you've dreamed of—one that makes heaven proud!

XOXO . . . NICOLE

1

Why Am I Here?

HOW TO DISCOVER YOUR
GOD-GIVEN PURPOSE

*Purpose is the place where your deep
gladness meets the world's needs.*

FREDERICK BUECHNER

3. **When I pray, how is the Holy Spirit confirming direction found in the Bible?** Take time to pray and ask God what you should or shouldn't do. When we pray, we should ask for God's perfect will to be done in our lives . . . and that He would show us what that looks like in our current decision-making. Then, we need to *listen*. Prayer is a process of listening and reflecting as much as it is a time of talking. Through faith in Jesus, we have been given access to the Spirit of God, who speaks to us and gives us guidance in our lives! (Tip for free: The Holy Spirit will never lead us to do something contrary to the direction for our lives found in the Bible. If you believe God is leading you in a specific direction, make sure it's consistent with the guidance found in your Bible.)

4. **Does this choice benefit others and the local church?** Take a minute to consider how your decision will affect the lives of those around you. Is the decision you are about to make going to build the local church and make a positive impact on the lives of other people?

5. **What is the honorable thing to do?** Don't just make the easy and convenient choice. Make the decision that honors Jesus and brings glory to Him. That might mean choosing something that is inconvenient or that requires sacrifice . . . but in the end, it will be worth it! Great lives are built on decisions made with eternity in mind, not just what makes sense in the here and now!

FAST FORWARD, PLEASE!

None of us likes to wait. Is there anything more annoying than sitting in a waiting room??? We even give up on a new television show if the plot isn't developing fast enough. Have you ever switched in and out of lanes just to move two cars ahead of the person in the "slower lane"? Or decided to come back to a store later rather than wait in a line with more than four people in it?? Surely we aren't the only two people who do these things . . .

Our "let's-keep-things-moving" attitude has its perks. We can pack a lot of productive activities into one day. We can check off an impressive number of tasks on a to-do list. Tight deadlines inject a weird adrenaline-rush into our workday. We keep our friends and families on their toes with our ever-evolving interests. ☻

But when it comes to fulfilling purpose and destiny, there are just some things (LIKE CHARACTER) that refuse to be put on the fast track.

If our lives were movies, we would prefer to fast-forward through certain parts—mainly the ones where we feel like we're just waiting for the action to heat up. Can we skip the opening credits, the slow-paced back story, and the monotonous "getting-to-know-the-characters" dialogue, so we can get to the good stuff—like the car chase and the explosions and the showdown between the good guy and the bad guy, ultimately ending with the leading love interests defeating the odds and living happily ever after?

(Yes, I am aware that if there were a movie made of my life, it probably wouldn't include a car chase or an explosion, but you get the idea!)

We all wish we had that real-life fast-forward button. We wish we could fast-forward through college and just get handed that degree already! We wish we could fast-forward through the under-paid, crazy-hours job to get that corner office. We wish we could fast-forward past our singleness and press play on our wedding day. We wish we could fast-forward through the challenges in our marriage or family and get to the good stuff—the stuff famous authors write relationship and parenting books about. We wish we could fast-forward the healing process of our soul and restart at the place where we have overcome the hurts and disappointments of our past.

But then I remember King David from the Bible.

Think about David, exiled from Israel even though he was anointed to be the next king. Out of jealousy and insecurity, King Saul plotted to kill poor David. David was forced out of his home, lived in enemy territory, posed as a mental patient, hid out in caves, and was surrounded by disgruntled men who at one point wanted to stone him. He was misunderstood, persecuted and lied about . . . and he hadn't done anything to deserve it.

Glimmers of a great king shone through during these hard times. David became disciplined. He became wise. He became generous. He became forgiving. He became compassionate. He became strong. There were things being forged inside of David in those caves, in the midst of exile. While King Saul was seeking to kill David, God was seeking to make a king out of David.

And God did just that. He used the caves. He used the exile. He used enemy ground. He used disgruntled men. He used a mad and jealous king. Somehow, God was able to take what was meant to destroy David and use it as a tool to bring about transformation in David's soul.

Weapons of destruction, when placed in God's hands, have a way of becoming weapons of divine purpose.

Perhaps the very things we are in such a hurry to fast-forward through are the very things that make us . . . make us more Christlike, make us more compassionate. Make us stronger. Make us purpose-minded. Make us wiser. Make us more obedient. More willing. More Kingdom-minded.

So the next time we feel the need to try to push the fast-forward button by pleading with God in prayer, or fantasizing about quitting or escaping our responsibilities, or throwing a pity party . . . why not first ask ourselves:

What is God up to in this moment of my life? What is He developing in my character as part of the divine purpose He has for me? How is He *preparing me* for what He has already *prepared for me*?

> For we are God's [own] handiwork (His workmanship), recreated in Christ Jesus, [born anew] that we may do those good works which God predestined (planned beforehand) for us [taking paths which He prepared ahead of time], that we should walk in them [living the good life which He prearranged and made ready for us to live].
>
> EPHESIANS 2:10, AMP

MORE, PLEASE!
(Additional reading)
The Purpose Driven Life by Rick Warren
Warrior Chicks by Holly Wagner
Enjoying Where You Are on the Way to Where You Are Going
by Joyce Meyer
Stop Acting Like a Christian, Just Be One by Christine Caine
Weird by Craig Groeschel

2

One of a Kind

HOW TO CELEBRATE
YOUR UNIQUE STYLE

*Today you are You,
that is truer than true.
There is no one alive
who is Youer than You.*

DR. SEUSS

In all of time, there will never be another you. No one else will ever have your DNA, your fingerprints, your destiny . . . or your style. ☻

Before we get into celebrating our own unique styles, it might be good to reshape our minds and hearts about what is beautiful. In our society, beauty is often misunderstood. Sometimes, when I see *People* magazine's "50 Most Beautiful People," I wonder, *Says who? And how come? Who picks and decides what's beautiful?*

I've read articles about women in other countries wearing shoes that are too small in order to make their feet smaller, or having surgeries that lighten their skin. We live in Southern California, where you can have something augmented on every street corner. There is nothing wrong with fixing something you want fixed . . . but you need to understand that changing something on the outside won't change what is inside.

The truth is, we are all created with intention—intricately woven in our mother's wombs (see Ps. 139)—and Genesis 1 tells us that everything God makes is good. If that's true, then we do not have to yield ourselves to media's standard of beauty. We are simply responsible to be our best selves in every area of our lives.

As women, we can be pretty hard on ourselves—and because we're hard on ourselves, we're also hard on each other. Jealousy and judgment can fuel and color our relationships if we're not careful to love what God has given us and appreciate the differences around us. When we truly love ourselves, we can celebrate all kinds of women in our world rather than waste time judging and competing with them.

Jealousy is a wasted emotion . . . and we all face it and have to deal with it in our own hearts. Honestly, how many times has jealousy actually been beneficial to our lives? Jealousy and unhealthy competition hinder relationships and feed insecurity.

When we see a friend who has a pair of shoes or a purse we can't afford, or a new hairstyle we could never pull off, how do we respond? Do we get excited and celebrate with them, or do we become critical and find it impossible to give a compliment? What about those moments at the gym (or flipping through a magazine) when we wish we had someone else's body parts or hair or lips or whatever else we feel insecure about?

One of the hardest jealousy tests is opportunity. When our friends or people we know have opportunities we don't have, how do we respond? A friend gets a boyfriend . . . Someone else gets the promotion we wanted at work . . . At Christmas, every-one except us gets the clothes and shoes we had on our lists.

The thing is . . . what other people have is not the real problem. We need to commit to cultivating gratitude in our hearts for what we do have.

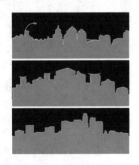

Judgment is another wasted emotion. We all come in different colors, shapes and sizes. We live in different cities, cultures and economic brackets. Because our world conditions us to think a certain way about beauty and style, we make judgments against others without considering the context of their lives.

Have you ever been at school or work or Starbucks . . . and thought to yourself as you looked at someone, *Whoa! Shoulda never left the house like that!* Well, maybe she's a new mom, and because she's breastfeeding every two hours, she hasn't had a shower in two days, much less had time to do her hair (been there!).

Don't we all have a photo (or 2 . . . or 10!) from our pasts that we hope no one ever sees? Some of my (Holly's) outfits from the '80s are scary . . . not to mention the big bangs!

Let's be the kind of women who aren't critics of other women. We don't have to be judgmental—we can give people grace. Let's be the kind of women who aren't overwhelmed with jealousy, but are learning to love and see ourselves the way God loves and sees us.

How we navigate jealousy and judgment determines the way we celebrate. Until we can celebrate what we have and who we are, we can't appreciate our own unique styles . . . or the unique styles of others.

Now, to help you celebrate yourself, here are . . .

TEN THINGS GOD THINKS ABOUT YOU

1. You are one of a kind.

"I will confess and praise You for You are fearful and wonderful and for the awful wonder of my birth! Wonderful are Your works, and that my inner self knows right well" (Ps. 139:14, AMP).

"You are altogether beautiful, my darling, beautiful in every way" (Song of Sol. 4:7, NLT).

2. You are loved completely.

"'Though the mountains be shaken and the hills be removed, yet my unfailing love for you will not be shaken nor my covenant of peace be removed,' says the LORD, who has compassion on you" (Isa. 54:10).

"The LORD appeared to us in the past, saying: 'I have loved you with an everlasting love; I have drawn you with loving-kindness'" (Jer. 31:3).

"Neither height nor depth, nor anything else in all creation, will be able to separate us from the love of God that is in Christ Jesus our Lord" (Rom. 8:39).

3. You are a treasure.

"She is far more precious than jewels and her value is far above rubies or pearls" (Prov. 31:10, AMP).

"The LORD has declared today that you are his people, his own special treasure, just as he promised, and that you must obey all his commands" (Deut. 26:18, NLT).

4. You are purposed.

"'For I know the plans I have for you,' declares the Lord, 'plans to prosper you and not to harm you, plans to give you hope and a future'" (Jer. 29:11).

"The Lord will fulfill his purpose for me; your love, O Lord, endures forever—do not abandon the works of your hands" (Ps. 138:8).

"For we are His workmanship, created in Christ Jesus for good works, which God prepared beforehand that we should walk in them" (Eph. 2:10, NKJV).

5. You are a new creation.

"Therefore, if anyone is in Christ, [she] is a new creation; the old has gone, the new has come!" (2 Cor. 5:17).

"Instead, let the Spirit renew your thoughts and attitudes. Put on your new nature, created to be like God—truly righteous and holy" (Eph. 4:23-24, NLT)

6. You are in right standing with God.

We often hear the word "righteous" in church. Just in case you aren't sure what that means, it simply means that you are in right standing with God through Christ. In other words, God's not mad at you—He loves you, believes in you, and has purposefully placed you on this earth.

"God is all mercy and grace—not quick to anger, is rich in love" (Ps. 145:8, THE MESSAGE).

"If we admit our sins—make a clean breast of them— he won't let us down; he'll be true to himself. He'll forgive our sins and purge us of all wrongdoing" (1 John 1:9-10, THE MESSAGE).

"But I, yes I, am the one who takes care of your sins—that's what I do. I don't keep a list of your sins" (Isa. 43:25, THE MESSAGE).

7. **You have been set free to set others free.**

You have a story to tell. Don't be afraid to share it.

"The Spirit of the Sovereign Lord is upon me, for the Lord has anointed me to bring good news to the poor. He has sent me to comfort the brokenhearted and to proclaim that captives will be released and prisoners will be freed" (Isa. 61:1, NLT).

"God is our refuge and strength, an ever-present help in trouble. Therefore we will not fear, though the earth give way and the mountains fall into the heart of the sea, though its waters roar and foam and the mountains quake with their surging" (Ps. 46:1-3).

"For God has not given us a spirit of fear, but of power and of love and of a sound mind" (2 Tim. 1:7, NKJV).

"There is no fear in love; but perfect love casts out fear, because fear involves torment" (1 John 4:18, NKJV).

"So do not fear, for I am with you; do not be dismayed, for I am your God. I will strengthen you and help you; I will uphold you with my righteous right hand" (Isa. 41:10).

8. You were created for family.

"Even if my father and mother abandon me, the Lord will hold me close" (Ps. 27:10, NLT).

"Father to the fatherless, defender of widows—this is God, whose dwelling is holy. God places the lonely in families; he sets the prisoners free and gives them joy" (Ps. 68:5-6, NLT).

"So you have not received a spirit that makes you fearful slaves. Instead, you received God's Spirit when he adopted you as his own children. Now we call him, 'Abba, Father' [Daddy God]" (Rom. 8:15, NLT).

9. You have a place in the kingdom of God.

"How lovely is your dwelling place, O LORD of
Heaven's Armies.
I long, yes, I faint with longing to enter the courts of
the LORD.
With my whole being, body and soul, I will shout joyfully
to the living God.
Even the sparrow finds a home, and the swallow builds
her nest and raises her young
at a place near your altar, O LORD of Heaven's Armies,
my King and my God!
What joy for those who can live in your house, always
singing your praises.
What joy for those whose strength comes from the
LORD, who have set their minds on a pilgrimage
to Jerusalem.
When they walk through the Valley of Weeping, it will
become a place of refreshing springs. The autumn
rains will clothe it with blessings.
They will continue to grow stronger and each of
them will appear before God in Jerusalem"
(Ps. 84:1-7, NLT).

10. You have a legacy to leave.

"We will not hide these truths from our children;
we will tell the next generation about the glorious

it for a smoky eye, or draw a thinner line above the lash line and on the lower lash line . . . and then apply eye shadow. Eye shadow is an enhancer. In your twenties, you can play around with color a little more—green, purple, gold or other shades applied in a subtle, classy way works for you. After 30, neutrals that vary in depth (light brown to chocolate brown, grey to charcoal, and so forth) are best.

Makeup works best on a clean face. You don't have to buy extremely expensive brands to take care of your skin—there are great products at your local drugstore. Wash your face at night before sleeping and apply a moisturizer or night cream. When you're rising and shining . . . wash your face again. Try a toner and then a moisturizer with sunscreen (very important, no matter your skin color!).

Did you know that your skin is your body's biggest organ? That basically means that whatever you put on your skin . . . you might as well be eating! Try to choose products that are organic or natural—read the labels and try especially to avoid mineral oil and parabens (all those words that end with yl—methyl, propyl, butyl, and so on).

Now, some basic grooming tips:

- **Plucking Eyebrows:** Groomed eyebrows frame the eyes and can help transform our faces. You can pluck at home, if you know what you're doing . . . or leave the fun to a professional! Don't be afraid to remove any other hair (for instance, above the lip or on the chin) to show off your gorgeous face.

- **Shaved, Lotioned Skin:** Listen, I've never met a woman who enjoys shaving her legs. ☻ But, clean-shaven legs conditioned with moisturizer feel and look great. Also, apply lotion to your body after the shower—moisturized skin glows and feels smooth and clean. Remember to read your labels at the store!!

- **Basic Manicure and Pedicure:** Clean nails and cuticles go a long way in helping us look polished and put together. You don't have to get a manicure and pedicure every week—just keep a great top coat and a few colors you like at home to do your own nails. Use a good hand and foot cream to stay moisturized. If you bite your nails or cuticles . . . STOP! Aside from the sanitary reasons, it's just not attractive.

FIND THE PERFECT PAIR OF JEANS

Besides ending world hunger and human trafficking, there are few things more difficult than finding the perfect pair of jeans. Why does it always seem like the jeans we find fit great . . . in one body part only?

The bottom fits, but there's so much space at the waist; the waist and bottom fit, but the calves are so tight they feel like compression socks; they fit perfectly, except they're three inches too short.

booties, pumps (any kind), stilettos (to keep the look modern, but classy, try not to get the platform too high) and even flats look great.

More thoughts on denim:

- **Low-Rise Denim:** Low-rise or even high-waisted denim must be worn with caution. Low-rise jeans especially can result in exposing what you don't want exposed! Generally, if you are blessed with a bottom, choose a jean that is higher in the back to avoid exposure.

- **Rear Pockets:** Décor on the rear pockets is pretty risky and will probably be in style for only a short period of time. We all want our rear ends to look good, but we probably don't need signs that point people to them. For the most flattering look, avoid pockets that are too tiny and those that come below the rear end onto the top of the thigh.

- **Distressed Denim:** Distressed denim detail can be very attractive—the jeans look worn-in and have an interesting look . . . lines that are faded, wiskering, holes, shredding, and so forth. Just make sure the lines are flattering, and the holes are not too revealing.

- **Best Rinse for My Body:** For the most part, medium to dark rinses are best, because they are the most versatile between home, work and social settings. Darker rinses are also the most flattering for every body type.

- **Length of Jeans:** This one can be tricky, especially if you are very tall or short. If you're wearing flats, you want denim that stops just below the top of the flat (or that can be cuffed). If you're wearing heels, the jeans should hang a quarter inch or less from the floor. Ankle-length jeans can also be great—just wear them well!

- **Don't Be Afraid to Tailor:** If you find jeans that fit perfectly, except they're too long or too short or the waist is a little too big, find a great tailor in your city and have those minor adjustments made. Don't be afraid to spend a little more for jeans that you'll wear—it's worth it!

TODAY'S IMPORTANT ACCESSORIES

Now it's time for the next topic to help you celebrate your unique style . . . accessories. We asked a Nordstrom buyer and a few of our friends what accessories they consider essential.

- **Large Pearl Studs:** Pearl studs are classic.

- **Diamond Studs:** Another classic choice.

- **Hoop Earrings:** Hoops work well with T-shirts and tanks, as well as business casual clothes. Hoops also look great with ponytails.

- **Gold Bracelets:** Try wearing a cuff, bangles, or a combination of chunky and skinny bracelets.

- **Silver bracelets:** As with gold, try wearing a cuff, bangles, or a combination of chunky and skinny bracelets.

- **Statement Necklace:** Try a necklace with large stones, or several short strands of pearls, or one necklace that looks like several necklaces in one.

- **Animal or Ethnic Scarf:** Try cheetah or leopard print, or something with a loud, fun color pattern that is flattering to your skin tone.

- **Statement Ring or Cocktail Ring:** This could be a family heirloom, or a ring with a large stone (like turquoise) or a collection of stones.

- **Camel Leather Purse:** This color goes with anything; it translates from day to night, casual to dressy; and it coordinates with outfits for work, home or social outings.

- **Vintage Earrings and Rhinestone Bracelet:** Timeless jewelry that looks great with a little black dress, at a nice dinner or formal event, or on an interview. Beautiful jewelry is also fun with simple V-neck tees and that perfect pair of jeans.

- **Cognac Boots:** Cognac refers to the color of this leather boot. (The name is derived from brandy, a.k.a. cognac, which is amber in color and generally darkens with age.) Like camel, this color goes with everything and translates from day to night and casual to dressy.

- **Skinny Belt:** Skinny belts look great with jeans and a button-up, on a shirtdress, or over the waist of a cardigan and pencil skirt. Try a fun color like red, turquoise or yellow, or a pattern like cheetah.

FIVE VERSATILE MUST-HAVE SHOES

1. **Nude Pumps:** closed-toe pumps, closed-toe platform pumps, peep-toe stilettos . . .

2. **Black Pumps:** closed-toe stiletto, round-toe, thick-heel, pointed-toe . . .

3. **Flat Sandals:** gladiator, gold coach, simple brown . . .

4. **Boots**: riding boots, military-looking boot, cowboy boots ...

5. **Wild Card:** the perfectly you shoe (fun flat, colorful sparkle shoe, turquoise wild shoe ...)

UNDERGARMENTS

- **Really Great Bra:** Yes, we know how awkward it can be to be fitted for a bra . . . and yes, we know they can be expensive . . . but you should have at least one bra that fits you well. A bra that is not fitted can be uncomfortable or squeeze your back too tight. A bra that fits not only feels good, but also looks great under your clothes.

- **Strapless Bra in Black and Nude:** Call us old fashioned, but we believe that straps can ruin an outfit, so strapless dresses, racerback tanks, boatneck shirts and other odd-shaped, cute shirts should be worn over strapless bras. (If you need straps, try a bra with clear straps.)

- **Comfortable Pretty Panties:** Panties that are too tight, or too large, leave underwear lines that can be seen through our workout pants, our work slacks and even our jeans.

- **Undergarments in Nude, Black and Neutral Tones:**
  Undies can be any color you like; however, be sure to
  have some underwear in nude or neutral tones and
  in black, to wear under your nicer clothes, as well as
  your lighter colored pants and skirts (just don't wear
  black under those!!).

EIGHT ESSENTIAL ITEMS (A.K.A. WARDROBE EMERGENCY KIT)[2]

1. **A Full-length Mirror in a Well-lit Area:** Have you
   ever shopped in your favorite department store, stood
   in front of that cheeky little mirror under a sneaky little
   light, and purchased an outfit . . . only to get home and
   discover that the outfit looks nothing like it did in the
   store? Keep a great full-length mirror at home.

2. **A Lint Roller:** This is a necessity, especially if you
   have animals in the house. Synthetic fibers manage to
   catch every piece of hair, dirt and more.

3. **Fashion Tape:** Again, this may seem old fashioned,
   but bra straps can spoil a great dress, shirt or outfit.
   Fashion tape can help keep your button-ups from
   gaping open and your little black dress from revealing too much.

3

Healthy Living

HOW TO LIVE LONG AND LOOK GOOD

He who is loose and slack in his work is brother to him who is a destroyer and he who does not use his endeavors to heal himself is brother to him who commits suicide.

PROVERBS 18:9, AMP

The physical part of you is not some piece of property belonging to the spiritual part of you. God owns the whole works. So let people see God in and through your body.

1 CORINTHIANS 6:19-20, THE MESSAGE

As humans we are three-part beings.

Spirit. Soul. Body.

We often are better at feeding our spirits and nurturing our souls than we are at taking care of our bodies.

Each of us has been given only one body.

God has trusted us with that one amazing body to fulfill the purposes for which He created us.

I want to finish my race strong, so that means I need to do what I can to keep my body strong. I can't control the toxins in the environment, but for the most part, I can manage what I eat and how I treat my body.

Just like the verse in 1 Corinthians says: "God owns the whole works."

Our bodies are His, so let's do the best we can to take care of them!

Seven years ago, I (Holly) was diagnosed with breast cancer . . . and began my healing journey. I started studying and reading a lot about health, and I came to understand that I have an obligation to take care of the one and only body God has given me to fulfill my purpose on planet Earth. There are steps I can take to aid in the prevention of disease.

I really wish someone had told me these things when I was in my twenties or thirties. That might have spared me some of the challenges I faced. So maybe they will help you!

One thing I learned is that even though my doctors were great, I should never just yield my health care to them blindly. While they are certainly knowledgeable, doctors are not infallible . . . and neither is the U.S. Food and Drug Administration (FDA) or the American Medical Association (AMA).

For example, at one point in history, many doctors said that formula was better for the health of babies than breast milk was. They were wrong and have now acknowledged that breast milk is better. The FDA has approved drugs that caused so many problems they were later taken off the market.

These great organizations have made mistakes—they are not perfect. So it is okay for you to ask questions of your doctors. Do your own research.

I am not a doctor, so the things I share here came from my own research and reading. I hope my experience will encourage you to do some reading of your own, and then get busy building a strong and healthy body!!!

FIVE GOOD THINGS I EAT

1. **Organic Vegetables and Fruits.** I choose organic produce whenever possible, because so many pesticides are used in non-organic farming, and our bodies really are not designed to handle the amount of toxins thrown at us daily. I may not be able to do much about the pollutants in the air I breathe, but I can control what goes in my mouth. If you were to do just one thing to improve your health, I would tell you to eat four pieces of fresh fruit and two big raw salads full of vegetables each day.

2. **Whole Food Supplements.** Your body is deficient in vitamins, minerals, enzymes and cofactors. That is

a fact. There is no way you can get all the nutrients you need by eating food, because our soil is depleted of many of the nutrients it once had. There simply is no way you are getting the nutrients you need, unless you are supplementing your intake.

I take quite a few supplements—the whole-food kind (generally not the kind you can get at your corner drug store). You might want to consider taking some as well; however, please remember that vitamin supplements won't compensate for a poor diet. They are meant to help fill nutritional gaps in a good one.

3. **Goat's Milk Kefir or Yogurt.** Yep. Goat's milk. It might take you a minute or two to adjust to the taste, but then you will love it! It contains vitamins, minerals, electrolytes, trace elements, enzymes, protein and fatty acids that are utilized by your body with ease. In fact, your body can digest goat's milk in just 20 minutes. It takes 2 to 3 hours to digest cow's milk.

4. **Omega 3 Fatty Acids.** According to nutrition expert Susan Goodwin, "Omega 3 is good for you because it provides you a wide range of health benefits right from head to toe. They help promote normal body function, even promote good emotional health, weight loss and lower your chances of developing

cardiovascular problems such as heart disease and black arteries. There are also many research studies suggesting that these essential fatty acids help regulate brain function both in children and adults."[1] Some places to get Omega 3 fatty acids: flaxseed oil, salmon, sardines and walnuts.

5. **Black Beans.** According to an article at "Eat This!" black beans "are very high in fiber, folate, protein, and antioxidants, along with numerous other vitamins and minerals. Black beans make a complete protein when paired with brown rice, which is often why they are so commonly included in a vegetarian diet."[2]

A FEW OTHER THINGS I LIKE . . . THAT MIGHT SURPRISE YOU

1. **Coffee.** I have read a few studies lately that document the benefits of coffee! I was so happy to find those!!!

2. **Chocolate.** Dark chocolate not only tastes good . . . but it also has antioxidants in it!!

3. Whole Grain Bread. I really love bread . . . dipped in olive oil . . . or covered with peanut or almond butter . . . or toasted with jam. If the bread is whole grain, that means fiber . . . which is good!!

FIVE THINGS I AVOID

1. Artificial Sweeteners. No matter what color the packet, they are all bad for you. Seriously bad. Use honey, molasses, agave or Stevia instead.

2. The White Stuff . . . Stay away from white flour, white sugar and salt. There are so many healthier alternatives. For flour: lots of whole grain flours. For sweeteners: honey, molasses, agave, Stevia. For salt: natural sea salt or Himalayan salt (which still has some minerals left in it).

3. Fast Food. C'mon . . . you know you shouldn't be eating it!! Most fast foods are high in fat, stupid calories, carbohydrates, and too much artificial stuff!

4. **Processed Food.** If it's boxed, bagged, canned or jarred and has a list of ingredients on the label, it's processed. As scary as it seems, about 90 percent of the money that Americans spend on food is used to buy processed items.[3] Here are just a few reasons you might want to think twice before throwing that box of processed whatever into your shopping cart:

- **Cancer:** Some synthetic chemicals used in the processed foods industry are known to have carcinogenic properties. In fact, a 7-year study, conducted by the University of Hawaii, of almost 200,000 people found that those who ate the most processed meats (hot dogs, bologna, and so on) had a 67 percent higher risk of pancreatic cancer than those who ate few or no processed meat products.

- **Obesity:** Heavily processed foods are usually higher in sugar, fat and salt—and lower in nutrients and fiber—than the raw foods used to create them, leading to unhealthy weight gain and water retention. According to the World Health Organization, processed foods have contributed to the spike in obesity levels and chronic disease around the world.

- **Heart Disease:** Many processed foods contain trans fatty acids (TFA), the dangerous type of fat that you don't want in your diet. TFAs give rise to LDL, the

dangerous cholesterol, and squash HDL, the good cholesterol.[4]

A recently conducted Harvard study found that women who avoid high-carb processed foods cut their heart disease risk by 30 percent.

5. **Bad Fats.** According to Kathleen M. Zelman, director of nutrition for WebMD, "We actually need fats— can't live without them, in fact. Fats are an important part of a healthy diet: They provide essential fatty acids, keep our skin soft, deliver fat-soluble vitamins, and are a great source of energizing fuel."[5]

Dr. Zelman goes on to state that there are two groups of fats: saturated and unsaturated. Unsaturated fats are the "good fats" and include Omega-3s, which are found in fatty fish (salmon, trout, catfish, mackerel), and also flaxseed, walnuts, olives, avocados, hazelnuts, almonds, Brazil nuts, cashews, sesame seeds, pumpkin seeds, and olive, canola and peanut oils.

Saturated fats and trans fats are the "bad fats." Saturated fats are found in animal products like meat, poultry skin, high-fat dairy and eggs. Trans fats are found in frying products, baked goods, cookies, icings, crackers, packaged snack foods, microwave popcorn and some margarine. You should try to avoid both saturated fats and, especially, trans fats.[6]

Okay . . . here is a sixth thing I avoid:

6. **Cigarettes.** This might seem obvious to some of you . . . and yet the number of young women who are smoking surprises me. While walking through an airport recently, I noticed a smoking room. There were so many young people in there. It just makes me sad.

Smoking is not going to send you to hell . . . but you might get to heaven before you want to.

Fifty years ago, we didn't know all the damage that smoking does, but now we do.

It kills you.
Really.
And the death is a slow and painful one.
It also ages you.

Studies have been done, comparing twins—one who smoked and one who didn't. The skin of the one who smoked was far more wrinkled and leathery.[7]

If you smoke, please stop. You have a destiny to fulfill . . . and we need you strong and healthy to do it!!

EIGHT REASONS TO MOVE YOUR TUSH!

The following information, based on studies from the Mayo Clinic, show why it is so important for you to get out there and move your tush! Exercising is a habit I wish I had started when I was in my twenties . . . so please get started now! You won't regret it . . . and you may even thank me later! ☻

1. **Exercise controls weight.** Exercise can help you avoid gaining excess weight and help you accomplish your weight loss goals. Physical activity burns calories—the more intense the activity, the more calories you burn. If you don't have time during your day to do an actual workout, you can get active throughout the day in simple ways—such as taking the stairs instead of the elevator or doing more household chores.

2. **Exercise combats health conditions and diseases.** Keeping active boosts your level of high-density lipoprotein (HDL, or "good" cholesterol) and decreases unhealthy triglycerides. This keeps your blood flowing smoothly and decreases your risk of cardiovascular diseases. Regular physical activity can even help you to prevent or manage a wide range of health problems, including stroke, metabolic syndrome, type 2 diabetes, depression, arthritis and certain types of cancer.

3. **Exercise improves mood.** Physical activity stimulates the production of various chemicals in your brain that may leave you feeling happier and more relaxed. You may also feel better about your appearance when you exercise regularly, which can boost your confidence and improve your self-esteem.

4. **Exercise boosts energy.** Regular physical activity improves muscle strength and increases endurance. When you perform physical activities, oxygen and nutrients are delivered to your tissues, which helps your cardiovascular system work more efficiently. This will give you more energy as you go about your daily life.

5. **Exercise promotes better sleep.** Regular physical activity can help you fall asleep faster and deepen your sleep. However, it is important not to exercise too close to bedtime, as that may make you too energized to fall asleep.

6. **Exercise puts the spark back into your sex life.** As mentioned under items 3 and 4 above, exercise can boost your energy and make you feel better about yourself, which may have a positive effect on your sex life. Regular physical activity can also lead to enhanced arousal for women, and men who exercise regularly are less likely to have problems with erectile dysfunction.

7. **Exercise can be fun.** Engaging in physical activity gives you time to unwind, enjoy the outdoors, or engage in activities that make you happy. Physical activity can also help you connect with family or friends in a fun social setting. Find a physical activity you enjoy, and just do it.[8]

8. **Exercise keeps your brain healthy!** Recent studies have found that aerobic exercise improves brain function among women who are at high risk for Alzheimer's and other forms of cognitive impairment.[9]

DEFLATING THE STRESS BALL

After my cancer diagnosis, I spent a few weeks in a hospital that offered a variety of treatments . . . both conventional and alternative.

One of the tests performed on me was a stress test.

As the doctor hooked me up to a machine, he asked, "Holly, how are you feeling? Do you feel like you are under stress?"

I responded, "Well, I know that I was diagnosed with cancer four months ago, but I think I am handling it well. I don't feel stressed."

He said, "Okay," and began the test.

When he was finished, he told me that in reality, my stress level was as if I were staring a roaring lion in the face. WOW! A roaring lion! That is some stress!! I had been totally unaware of it.

We all deal with stress—and, truthfully, not all stress is bad. Most of us would never get over negative behaviors or change or grow unless we experienced some stress.

Different things cause stress for each of us.

I have a fairly busy travel schedule. I go all around the globe, speaking at churches and conferences. I love that I get to do that. It is not stressful for me. But there are some people in my world who get very stressed by having to deal with packing and airports and the rush of travel. Some people also get stressed with change. Not me.

I tend to feel stress when relationships are under pressure. If I have to navigate a challenge in a friendship or in my marriage, I will feel a bit of stress.

Regardless of the cause, I needed to learn how to recognize when my body was under stress and how to relieve it.

TOP 10 STRESS RELIEVERS

The following information, also based on studies at the Mayo Clinic, give practical tips for handling the stresses that come your way. Incorporating these into your daily routine will give you the upper hand when stress threatens to take over.

1. **Get active.** (I know it seems as if I am harping on this!!) Being active is a great way to relieve stress. Anyone, regardless of their athletic ability or how long it's been since they got off the couch, can incorporate physical activity into their day. Whether you join a gym or just park your car farther across the parking lot from the store and walk, any physical activity can act as a stress reliever. Being physically active increases endorphins that lighten your mood and help you

rise above the irritations of the day. Any increase in activity helps—whether you take a walk, ride a bike, swim, tour a museum or put on some music and clean your house (LOL!). Do anything that increases your activity.

2. **Pray . . . quiet your soul.**
When you pray, you want to focus your attention on the Lord and quiet the noise that may be crowding your mind and causing stress. Prayer allows you to find peace in God's presence and renew a sense of balance that benefits both your emotional well-being and your overall health.

3. **Laugh.** There is nothing like a good laugh!! You may need to begin with intentional efforts to look for humor in your day until you can see through the stress and laugh with genuine abandon. As you laugh, the weight of your mood can begin to lighten and your body will experience positive physical changes. Laughter will increases your heart rate and blood pressure, leaving you with a good, relaxed feeling. Seek out activities and people that will help you laugh—movies, YouTube clips, or an activity that you can share with a goofy friend.

4. **Connect.** Feeling stressed and irritable can make you feel anti-social. You probably don't want to share your bad mood with others or say things in the heat of the moment that you will regret, so you isolate yourself. Spend time with family and friends that can give you support, get you moving or focus your attention on something positive. Good relationships can keep you steady when your circumstances pull you in different directions. You can also find stress relief by serving others and feeling good about doing good. Meet a friend for coffee or a movie, reach out to a relative, serve those who are less fortunate, or get to church.

5. **Assert yourself.** Life is full of busyness—and great opportunities—but you can't do them all and maintain healthy balance in your life. It's okay to say no when your plate is full, or delegate some tasks. It may seem easier to do things yourself in the short run—to keep the peace, avoid conflict or get the job done right—but the long-term effect can be damaging to you and the needs of your family. Having your priorities out of synch can create stress, anger, bitterness and even the desire for revenge—the opposite of the peace you intended to create by doing it yourself.

6. **Sleep.** Stress can wreak havoc on your sleep patterns. All the noise in your life can dominate your thoughts, even when you try to rest and your sleep suffers. Your

body and mind need regular, quality time to sleep so they can recharge and be ready for the next day. Your sleep affects your mood, energy level, your ability to focus and your overall ability to function. Keeping a consistent bedtime routine that allows you time to unwind (music helps here), relax (eliminate distracting "noise") and get enough sleep will help calm trouble you have sleeping.

7. **Journal.** I am not a big journaler (not sure that is a word!), but I have heard from numerous people that putting their thoughts on paper helps them process stressful feelings. It doesn't matter what you write about, just put whatever is on your mind down on paper or on your computer. Sometimes just the process of getting it out helps relieve stress, other times, reflecting on what you write gives you perspective on what you are feeling and helps you address the stress you are experiencing.

8. **Get musical.** Music can be used in many ways to relieve stress. It can take your mind off the stress and help you relax, which lowers stress hormones in your body. It can also energize and entertain you if you turn up the volume and sing or dance along. Different personalities use music in different ways to improve their moods. The point is to help you focus your attention on something that you enjoy rather than all

the things you feel you should be doing that cause you stress. If music doesn't do this for you, any activity or hobby that helps you focus in this way will work—for some it will be gardening, drawing, or being creative by enjoying photography or jewelry making.

9. **Seek counsel.** It's OK to seek professional help when your personal efforts to handle stressors just aren't relieving your stress. This is especially true if stress is derailing your ability to handle daily tasks and responsibilities. If you feel overwhelmed or trapped, or if you worry excessively, a professional counselor or therapist can help you take positive steps in managing your stress.[10]

10. **Breathe.** According to Joseph E. Pizzorno, Jr. and Michael T. Murray in their book *Textbook of Natural Medicine*, deep breathing is a primary way to lower your body's stress responses. Deep breathing starts a cycle where your brain calms down and relaxes and in turn tells your body to do the same. Stress, that affects your body by increasing your heart rate, breathing and blood pressure, decreases as you breathe deeply and relax.[11]

WHAT DOES SLEEP DO FOR US?

Our understanding of the role of sleep in terms of our health has grown tremendously. We know that sleep has a huge impact on our ability to function both physically and mentally. We can't live without it! Studies in animals (rats, to be exact) have shown that sleep deprivation attacks the immune system and leads to death (the rats only lasted 3 to 5 weeks without REM and the other stages of sleep).

Sleep helps our nervous system stay healthy so that we can concentrate, have a strong memory, and perform well at physical and mental tasks. Extended sleep deprivation can result in serious mood swings and even hallucinations—not a good thing!

When we experience deep sleep, our bodies use that time to repair physical damage like what can result from stress and exposure to ultraviolet rays. So literally, deep sleep is "beauty sleep." Deep sleep also impacts our emotional health. The parts of our brains that work so hard during the day to manage our emotions, relationships and decision-making rest and rejuvenate during this time so that we can wake up and tackle the next day's emotional requirements—we need all the help we can get![12]

When we sleep, our bodies release growth hormones that help the growth and repair of damaged tissue. Getting generous amounts of deep sleep allows more growth hormones to be released into the body's bloodstream.[13]

Our bodies follow a 24-hour cycle. During this time, our bodies are on a schedule of automatically cleaning and rebuilding. Having healthy sleep patterns, helps our bodies perform these functions. For example, the liver goes through a cleansing process between 11:00 p.m. and 1:00 a.m. If you are awake during that time, your liver will not cleanse properly. Dr. Joseph Mercola has said that one hour of sleep before midnight is equal to four hours of sleep after midnight.[14]

Dr. Eve Van Cauter, a sleep researcher at the University of Chicago, said, "Americans sleep the least of [anyone in] modern countries. And they also . . . are the most overweight and obese. Perhaps it is worth thinking about the possibility that we don't sleep enough and therefore our appetites are disregulated."[15]

So . . . basically . . . most of us really do need eight hours of sleep a night in order to be firing on all cylinders!!!!!

A LITTLE RANDOM SLEEP NONSENSE . . .

Professor Chris Idzikowski, director of the U.K. Sleep Assessment and Advisory Service, analyzed six common sleeping positions— and found that each is linked to a particular personality type. Here's what your sleeping position says about you . . .

FETUS   LOG   YEARNER   SOLDIER   FREEFALLER   STARFISH

Fetus. Professor Idzikowski describes those who curl up in the fetus position as "tough on the outside but sensitive at heart." If this describes you, you may come off as a bit shy when you first meet someone, but as you become more comfortable you easily relax. This position is the most common—approximately 40 percent of the people studied preferred this position, and two-thirds of those people were women.

Log. Fifteen percent of the people studied prefer the "log" position. If you commonly find yourself lying on your side with both arms down by your side, you are a "log." You tend to be an easy-going, social person. You like being on the inside of any social situation and tend to be trusting of strangers. You also may have the tendency to be gullible.

Yearner. Thirteen percent of the people studied are "yearners." If you like to sleep on your side with your arms out in front of you, you are said to "have an open nature, but can be suspicious, cynical." As a yearner, your cautious nature can make you slow to make up your mind, and once you have, reluctant to change it.

Soldier. Eight percent of the people studied prefer the "soldier" position. If you usually find yourself lying on your back with both arms pinned to your sides, this is you. You are commonly a quiet and reserved person who doesn't like being in the limelight, but you feel it is important for people to live by high personal standards.

Freefall. Seven percent of the people studied are "free-fallers." If this is you, you prefer to lie on your stomach with your hands around your pillow, and your head turned to one side. As a freefaller you are a social person with a humorous bent that at the extreme can be a bit tactless. You can seem confident on the surface, but can be sensitive to criticism, and uncomfortable in extreme situations.

Starfish. Five percent of people are "starfish." If you prefer lying on your back with both arms up around your pillow, this is you. You are great at being a friend because you are generous with others, ready to listen and offer help when needed. You are more comfortable helping others rather than being the center of attention.[16]

TIPS FOR GETTING A GOOD NIGHT'S SLEEP

These tips are adapted from the article "How to Sleep Better" by Melinda Smith, Lawrence Robinson, Joanna Saisan and Robert Segal.

1. **Be consistent about the time you go to bed at night.**

2. **Boost melatonin production at night.** Melatonin helps you sleep and production is triggered by the absence of bright light. If you increase you exposure to light during the day and decrease it at night, you

will have an easier time falling asleep. During the day, get outside and light your workspace. At night, limit your screen time (TV, computers, backlit devices), use low lights when awake and keep your bedroom dark.

3. **Create an environment that invites sleep.** Most of us can't avoid all noise . . . after all, our neighbors have barking dogs!! ☻ But sound machines that produce white noise can be helpful. Temperature also matters—most people sleep better when the room temperature is about 65 degrees (Fahrenheit).

4. **Eat a light, early dinner.** Digesting is work and can keep you awake if you eat close to bedtime. What you eat makes a difference too. Save the spicy foods for lunch.

5. **Cut down on caffeine in the later afternoon.** We often underestimate the effect caffeine has on our sleep patterns—even 10 hours after consumption!

RELAXING BEDTIME RITUALS TO TRY

- Read a book or magazine by a soft light

- Take a warm bath

- Listen to soft music

- Do some easy stretches

- Wind down with a favorite hobby

- Listen to books on tape

- Make simple preparations for the next day[17]

H$_2$O . . . LIQUID GOLD!

Water, water, water!! There is no more important drink for us than water!

Water helps regulate body temperature.
It carries nutrients and oxygen to the cells.
It cushions joints.
It protects organs and tissues.
It removes toxins.
It maintains strength and endurance.
It makes up 92 percent of your blood plasma and 50 percent of everything else in your body.[18]

I have also heard that drinking water keeps our skin hydrated . . . so therefore reduces wrinkles!! Yippeeeee!!!

Dr. Don Colbert in his book *The Seven Pillars of Health* makes the following observations about drinking water:

I saw singer Tina Turner in a television interview, and even though she was well into her sixties, her skin looked fabulous. She said it was because she drank at least two quarts of water every day. . . ; I believe that water is the single best beauty treatment on the planet. It keeps your skin supple, your eyes bright, and your body spry. Consider this: Remove water from plums, and you get prunes. Remove water from your skin, and you get wrinkles.[19]

Drink that water!!!

Most of us know that we are supposed to drink eight glasses a day . . . but do we do that???

Dr. F. Batmanghelidj writes, "Every twenty-four hours the body recycles the equivalent of forty thousand glasses of water to maintain its normal physiological functions." He adds, "If you think you are different and your body does not need [eight to ten glasses] of water [each day], you are making a major mistake."[20]

Purified water without chlorine is best. Since most tap water contains chlorine, it's a good idea to get a filter for your sink. They are not that expensive . . . and they're totally worth it.

I always carry a bottle of water with me and drink from it throughout the day.

Water is a resource often overlooked by those seeking to lose weight. Many times, dieters confuse hunger and thirst. They think they are hungry when actually they are dehydrated. Drinking water will not only hydrate the body, but also put a damper on those hunger pains coming from the pit of the stomach. Jordan Rubin, author of *The Great Physician's Rx for Health and Wellness,* suggests, "If you're trying to lose weight, drink an eight-ounce glass of water the next time you feel hungry. Drinking a glass a half hour before lunch or dinner will act like a governor on an engine, taking the edge off your hunger pangs and preventing you from raiding the fridge or pillaging the pantry."[21]

CATCH SOME RAYS!

I have a chest covered with brown spots (some call them sun spots) that are definitely NOT attractive. I wish I had listened to someone who gave me a little warning about sun baking! As a young woman, I slathered on baby oil and lay out in the hot midday sun for hours. That's what spring break was for! Not a good decision.

But staying totally out of the sun is not a good decision either. The sun, in moderation, is good for us!

Jordan Rubin writes, "While it's true that a small segment of the population experience higher rates of melanoma and other forms of skin cancer, I believe that's more because they lack adequate nutrients in their diets, especially antioxidant-rich fruits, vegetables, and healthy fats. Think about it: before the modern era, people used to spend much more time outside— and they didn't get skin cancer in the rates we see today."

Rubin concludes: "The reason we're having more skin cancer is not because we're getting too much sun. That can't be true because we're getting *far less* sun since so few people work outside these days. Getting sunlight is extremely important for our bodies because of the way the skin synthesizes vitamin D from the ultraviolet rays of sunlight. Exposure to the sun is a significant source of vitamin D."[22]

According to the National Institutes of Health, 10 to 15 minutes of sunlight are sufficient to allow vitamin D synthesis to occur. After that, it is wise to apply a natural sunscreen (SPF 15 or higher) to protect the skin.[23]

Vitamin D is a big deal. It actually isn't a vitamin, but a critical hormone that helps regulate the health of more than 30 different tissues and organs, including the brain. It is a super-powerful disease fighter that plays a role in regulating cell growth, the immune system and blood pressure.

So make sure you are getting a little sun ... just not hours in the middle of the day! Because sunburn is not good! Neither are premature wrinkles and brown spots. Trust me ... you won't like them!

HOW MUCH SHOULD YOU WEIGH?

We are very much aware that this is a sensitive subject. Some of you reading this may be underweight and dealing with an eating disorder. Please, please, please get some help!! You are so loved and valuable, and we need you strong. Some of you may be a few pounds overweight, and others of you may be obese.

Check out this website to get the answer to the question about how much you should weigh: www.howmuchshouldiweigh.org.

Remember, your body is not your own. It is the vessel that God entrusted to you to fulfill His purpose in you. You need to take care of it! Maybe you are just 10 pounds overweight. Well, if you keep gaining just 10 pounds every year, in 10 years you will be 100 pounds overweight ... and losing 100 pounds is a lot harder than losing 10!

Most weight loss begins by changing our thinking.

Once you are on the journey to redirect your thoughts, there are many weight loss plans from which you can choose. Pick one, and just do it!

Twenty years from now, you don't want to be looking back and wishing you had done something sooner to improve your health. Decide today that you are going to do what's best for your one and only body.

You can do it!!

MORE, PLEASE!
(Additional reading)

The Great Physician's Rx for Health and Wellness by Jordan Rubin

The Seven Pillars of Health by Don Colbert, M.D.

Stress Less by Don Colbert, M.D.

None of These Diseases by S.I. McMillen, M.D. and David E. Stern, M.D.

4

What's in
Your Wallet?

HOW TO MANAGE FINANCES

*Too many people spend money they
haven't earned, to buy things they don't
want, to impress people they don't like.*

WILL SMITH

MONEY MATTERS

Money means a lot of different things to a lot of people. Most of us have some and want more. We secretly dream of marrying a very rich (and handsome) man or winning the lottery, so we can finally afford the house with the pool . . . or at the very least, that designer purse we've been drooling over!

Some of us are taking active steps to create a strong financial future for ourselves. Some of us may even be reaping the benefits of years of budgeting and saving! Some of us really do enjoy crunching the numbers and finding new ways to invest in and increase our financial successes!

But for many of us, money is a rather stressful thing. We missed the "How to Balance Your Checkbook" elective in high school. Our parents may have fought a lot about finances, and their conflicts over the matter have left us with residual fears and anxiety when it comes to handling money. Some of us may have avoided the responsibility of managing our finances altogether, and that neglect has landed us in some rather sticky financial situations.

Jesus teaches us that how we view money—and what we do with ours—really does matter. In the Gospel of Luke, Jesus describes the attitude towards finances He wants to develop in us:

> Be generous. Give to the poor. Get yourselves a bank that can't go bankrupt, a bank in heaven far from bankrobbers, safe from embezzlers, a bank you can bank on. It's obvious, isn't it? The place where your treasure is, is the place you will most want to be, and end up being (Luke 12:33-34, THE MESSAGE).

Jesus in essence is saying that what we do with our money (our treasure) matters because it reveals the condition of our hearts . . . how we trust God, how we view ourselves, what we think about others . . .

Someone once told me that if you want to know what a person really values and cares about, you should take a look at his or her schedule and receipts.

We learn a lot about ourselves when we take a step back and examine our spending.

Are we fearful that God won't provide for us?

Do we struggle with a need to be instantly gratified, even if the cost is more than we can afford?

Do we invest in things that make us feel good about ourselves, but lack the ability to satisfy our souls in the long run?

Do we give generously, the way Jesus has given to us?

Or are we afraid that if we give, our own needs won't end up getting met?

When we make the commitment to honor God with our finances, we open our hearts to be transformed by the Holy Spirit! We begin to see where fear or doubt or insecurity or greed has been holding us back from the abundant and blessed life to which God has called us! When we begin to have Jesus' attitude in our hearts about finances, we become more like Him and discover new opportunities to be blessed by God to be a blessing in our world.

So this chapter is dedicated to you and me learning how to be smart with what's in our wallets . . . how to honor God with our finances . . . how to live generously . . . and how to manage wisely the resources with which God has blessed us.

For many of us, this may seem a bit scary—after all, it's the kind of stuff grown-ups do. You may be wondering if you are really ready for this type of responsibility . . .

You are! God wants to bless you and entrust you with finances that will make a huge difference in our world! He has all the wisdom you need to experience financial peace and prosperity. You can do this! Pull out your big-girl panties and get ready to grow into a money-savvy, generous and capable woman!

WHAT'S A TITHE, ANYWAY???

People have a lot of interesting ideas when it comes to what God thinks about money. Some people think that God hates money—that the poorer you are, the "holier" you are. Others think that God wants us to be rolling in the dough—that if you don't have a lot of money, you must not have enough faith. So which is it??? Does being a Christian mean being poor or being rich??? Does God even care about money???

The truth is, God does care about our finances . . .

He doesn't want to see us scraping by, always stressing about whether or not we can pay next month's rent. Neither does He want us greedily acquiring more and more "stuff" for our own selfish enjoyment.

God wants to provide for us financially both to meet our needs and to give us the resources to be a great financial BLESSING to others in our world. In short, God's will for you and me is that we should *be blessed to be a blessing.*

That kind of financial provision from God begins when we honor Him with our finances. When we manage our money in obedience to God's Word . . . when we discover what the Bible says to do with our money and choose to DO those things . . . we position ourselves to experience the incredible ways God can use our resources to make a huge difference in our own lives and the lives of those around us.

The very first way we honor God with our finances is by consistently tithing to our local church.

You may be wondering what in the world "tithing" is? Is that a fancy word for giving?

Tithing is the practice of *giving the first 10 percent of our income to the local church* as a biblical application of honoring God with our finances.

The word "tithe" literally means "10 percent." The Bible discusses tithing in depth in the book of Malachi:

> "Bring the whole *tithe* into the storehouse, that there may be food in my house. Test me in this," says the LORD Almighty, "and see if I will not throw open the floodgates of heaven and pour out so much blessing that you will not have room enough for it. I will prevent pests from devouring your crops, and the vines in your fields will not cast their fruit," says the LORD Almighty. "Then all the nations will call you blessed, for yours will be a delightful land," says the LORD Almighty (Mal. 3:10-12, emphasis added).

Jesus discussed giving multiple times, and His words challenge us to view our finances as a way of cultivating generosity towards our local churches and all those around us:

Give away your life; you'll find life given back, but not merely given back—given back with bonus and blessing. Giving, not getting, is the way. Generosity begets generosity (Luke 6:38, THE MESSAGE).

The Early Church took Jesus' words to heart and gave even more than 10 percent of their income to meet the needs of others:

They devoted themselves to the apostles' teaching and to the fellowship, to the breaking of bread and to prayer. Everyone was filled with awe, and many wonders and miraculous signs were done by the apostles. All the believers were together and had everything in common. Selling their possessions and goods, they gave to anyone [who] had need. Every day they continued to meet together in the temple courts. They broke bread in their homes and ate together with glad and sincere hearts, praising God and enjoying the favor of all the people. And the Lord added to their number daily those who were being saved (Acts 2:42-47).

Tithing is the first step in honoring God with our finances. When we actively tithe to our local churches, we develop a growing trust in God's provision. We begin to see God's blessings in new ways, not only in our finances, but also in every other area of our lives!

We also develop a heart of generosity! We begin to understand that it really is better to give than to receive. We become a part of seeing lives eternally changed by the message of Jesus as we actively tithe to our local churches. As we help finance

God's plans in people's lives, we ourselves are transformed. Our hearts enlarge towards God's plans and people's lives . . .

In short, we become more like Jesus as we tithe.

If you haven't yet made the decision to tithe to your local church, don't put it off! Begin tithing today! You may need to reallocate some of your spending budget. Maybe you will have to cut back on your shoe shopping or eat out fewer times a week. Maybe tithing seems like a big stretch of faith for you right now.

Whatever your financial situation may be, you can confidently trust God! His way is the best way! He is your perfect heavenly Father who loves you as His very own daughter. You are precious to Him. He won't withhold from you anything that you need. As you step out in faith and choose to honor and obey God with your finances, God will take care of you every step of the way! He will provide in every situation exactly what you need! He loves you, and His desire is to bless you!

> If God gives such attention to the appearance of wildflowers—most of which are never even seen— don't you think he'll attend to you, take pride in you, do his best for you? What I'm trying to do here is to get you to relax, to not be so preoccupied with *getting*, so you can respond to God's *giving*. People who don't know God and the way he works fuss over these things, but you know both God and how he works. Steep your life in God-reality, God-initiative, God-provisions. Don't worry about missing out. You'll find all your everyday human concerns will be met (Matt. 6:30-33, THE MESSAGE).

JUST SAY NO TO PLASTIC

I (Nicole) remember the first letter I ever received from Visa. I was 18 years old, and the president of Visa was "personally" writing me to congratulate me on my pre-approval! According to Mr. President, I had a $1,500 credit line waiting to be used! All I had to do was call the 1-800 number to activate my very own credit card.

Wow! Me?! I was surprised to find out that the big shots over at the bank were interested in giving li'l ol' me my very own credit card! I wasn't even out of high school yet, and I was already approved for my own plastic! And $1,500?! (When you're 18 years old and about to go to college, $1,500 sounds like a lot of money!)

Needless to say, I called the bank and talked to a very friendly representative—who assured me that having a credit card was a part of being a grown-up, and that all the cool kids were doing it . . . Okay, maybe he didn't say that, but he did convince me that having a credit card was crucial to living on my own. In his words, it was an "essential step" towards being a financially stable individual in today's world, and without it I would never be able to "establish good credit" for future purchases and investments.

That phone call cost me thousands of dollars over the next few years! The credit card that I told myself would only be used for emergencies became very helpful for the

"Starbucks-run-emergency" and the "I-have-nothing-to-wear-emergency" and the "who-needs-a-budget-anyway-emergency" and . . . well, you get the idea.

All the while, every time I swiped my card at the store, interest charges were stacking up a mile high against me!

Proverbs teaches us that "the rich rules over the poor, and the borrower becomes the lender's slave" (Prov. 22:7, NASB).

I certainly felt like a slave to my credit card bill! Any extra money I earned each month went straight to the credit card company . . . but even so, the total payoff amount never seemed to go down! My debt was hindering my ability to create a real savings account for myself, and I was limited in terms of how I could financially plan and dream for my future!

I wasn't alone.

There are more than 1.3 billion credit cards in circulation in America.

American consumer debt totals more than $2.7 trillion.

Forty-five percent of American credit card holders make only the minimum payments on their consumer debt.

The average balance per credit card-holding household is more than $9,300.[1]

Yikes! I knew I needed some help, stat! If I didn't come up with a game plan, I was never going to get out of debt.

I started to read books on finances. I mapped out a strict budget that would allow more money to go towards paying off my credit card balance. I asked my friends to hold me account-able to that not-so-friendly-to-a-girl's-new-wardrobe budget!

Then the big moment came. I got my big-girl scissors out and made a very big-girl decision to cut that stupid piece of plastic into tiny little bits. It was scary to see my financial security blanket chopped up and lying in pieces at the top of the trash. But it was also liberating.

I paid off my credit card bill later that year. Over the next year and a half, I went on to pay off my student loans and began living debt free!

I am now able to plan for my future in ways I never thought possible. I can give more financially to my church and to nonprofits than ever before! I am able to live generously towards my friends without hesitation!

This kind of financial freedom begins when we say no to the crazy cycle of accumulating more and more debt. Your ability to reach your dollar-sign goals AND live a generous life to the full begins when you pull out the scissors and JUST SAY NO TO PLASTIC!

STEPS TOWARD SAYING GOODBYE TO DEBT!

These steps come from concepts presented in *Dave Ramsey's Financial Peace University*, which is a great program for anyone serious about achieving financial success!

1. **Quit borrowing!** Avoid the temptation to take out a loan to pay off a credit card, or to use a credit card to make your car payment. Cut up those credit cards and repeat after me, "Plastic is not my friend." Now say it again . . . only this time stop trying to figure out how you can tape the card back together for a quick trip to the mall. "Plastic is not my friend." Very good.

2. **Save, save, save!** Be willing to make BIG adjustments to your spending plan. You might have to say no to trips to the mall, eating out, and even your favorite Starbucks Frappucino for a while. In order to rid yourself of debt, you need to make the tough sacrifices now. Remember: No pain, no gain.

3. **Prayer works!** God's desire is to see you debt-free! When you commit to a plan of tithing, budgeting, saving, and paying off debt, you can trust God to bless your hard work in some MIRACULOUS ways. God blesses plans that bless Him!

4. **Sell what you can.** Do you really need that brand new car with the expensive payments? Do you have to have a timeshare in Cancun? Is the furniture in the guest room really essential? Why are those seven bridesmaid's dresses still hanging in the corner of your closet? Be willing to downsize and eliminate items that could help provide for your financial freedom!

5. **Work it!** Pick up an extra shift at your job. Babysit one night a week. Work part-time as a barista. Use

the extra income to pay off your debt. This may be a humbling thing to do, depending on what season of life you are in, but God helps the humble! A little humility is a small price to pay compared to the investment you'll be making towards a stronger financial future!

6. **Apply the "debt snowball."** In Dave Ramsey's words, "The idea of the snowball is simple: pay minimum payments on all of your debts except for the smallest one. Then, attack that one with intensity! Every extra dollar you can get your hands on should be thrown at that smallest debt until it is gone. Then, you attack the second one. Every time you pay a debt off, you add its old minimum payment to your next debt payments. So, as the snowball rolls over, it picks up more snow."[2]

THE BIG B-WORD!

No, no. Not that word. The other B-word . . . BUDGET.

Most of us have love-hate relationships with our budgets. We love that sticking to a monthly budget means we are actively taking steps towards our financial goals. But sticking to that monthly budget also means we may have to say no to those cute boots we saw at Nordstrom! So unfair!

However we feel about the idea of a monthly budget, we have to acknowledge how very essential it is to our financial well-being!

There's no way around it . . . If we want to live financially successful lives, we have to develop *love-love* relationships with our monthly budgets! The monthly budget creates an actual plan for financial success. It acts as the bridge from where we are now to where we want to be in our financial futures!

So take some time this week to sit down with your bank account statement and a list of your monthly expenses, bills and income. Create a plan that you can live by . . . and pray that as you commit to a monthly budget, God will bless you financially! Ask God to show you how to become more responsible with your money . . . because at the end of the day, it all belongs to Him anyway! When we learn to be great stewards of our finances, we become the daughters to whom our heavenly Father can entrust even more!

SAVINGS: THE BIG-GIRL PIGGY BANK

Most of us have been told at some point—probably by our mothers—that we should "always be prepared for a rainy day." We have to admit, living in Southern California means we don't have to be prepared for rain very often. (In fact, only a few days a year. Okay, now we're just bragging about the gorgeous sunny weather we live in.)

Of course, our moms weren't really talking about the weather. They wanted us to be prepared for the challenges (as well as the opportunities) that life would throw at us.

Our finances are one area where preparation is crucial. Over the course of our lives, we will face many unexpected financial costs and opportunities. We should plan NOW to be prepared for these events in the future.

There's the last-minute flight home . . . or the check-engine light that goes on in the car . . . or the visit to the emergency room . . . or the cutbacks at work. Then there's the exciting new business opportunity . . . or the fundraiser we want to contribute to . . . or the kitchen remodeling we've been dreaming about since we first moved into the house.

These are the things in life we need to be financially prepared for . . . and it all begins with establishing a savings plan!

HERE ARE SOME QUICK TIPS AND SIMPLE WAYS TO SAVE

1. **Open your very own savings account with your bank, if you haven't already.** It's so easy that you can do it online or over the phone with most major banks!

2. **Do whatever you can to get $1,000 dollars into your savings account immediately!** Tighten your budget or pick up extra hours at work. This first $1,000 becomes your "emergency fund" for those unexpected events that life throws your way!

3. **Get out of debt ASAP!** Once you have your $1,000 "emergency fund" in the bank, shift your focus to becoming debt-free. The sooner you are out of debt, the faster you can start taking the money you've

been spending to pay off bills and investing it in your savings!

4. **Set a goal of having two to six months' worth of income in savings!** This may take some time, but it will provide you with a new sense of financial security as you navigate different seasons of life!

5. **Each month, try to put at least 10 percent of your income into savings.** The basic rule of thumb is to tithe 10 percent of your income, save 10 percent of your income, and live off the remaining 80 percent of your income (including giving generously as you are able).

FINDING THE DRESS FOR LESS AND OTHER SHOPPING TIPS

Who says you have to break the bank to look cute or enjoy a fun night out with your girlfriends? Below are some easy tips for getting the most bang for your buck!

1. Stop by your local mechanic's shop once a month to get the air pressure in your tires adjusted for free. Fifteen minutes a month can save you hundreds of dollars in new tires down the road!

2. Instead of hitting up the mall, try a consignment shop or second-hand store! You can find some really funky vintage pieces or the perfect pair of gently worn jeans to add to your wardrobe without having to empty your wallet!

3. Did you know that your local library has DVDs you can borrow for free? Enjoy a girls' night in with a classic romantic comedy, courtesy of your public library card!

4. Unplug those appliances that aren't in use. Most people spend much more than they need to on their electric bills, simply because they forget to unplug the hairdryer, coffeemaker, laptop and iPhone charger!

5. See if your favorite restaurant has a "happy hour" and score a great deal on a yummy meal! Even if they don't, you can always split a large entrée with a friend!

6. Say hello to the great outdoors! Instead of spending $25 at the movie theatre, opt for spending the day outside . . . Enjoy a hike, a day at the beach, or a picnic in the park with friends!

7. Clip those coupons! You can also find great deals online through websites like www.Groupon.com to help you save money on your everyday spending!

8. Discuss a simpler style with your hairstylist. Find a cut and color that require less frequent salon visits and fewer dollar signs!

EIGHT TIPS FOR THE WORKING GIRL

It's easy for us to get comfortable in familiar circumstances. If we're not careful, jobs we once were ecstatic about become, over time, jobs that simply pay the bills. We once woke up early, excited to go to work. Now we crawl out of bed after hitting the snooze button three times and wishing we had more caffeine to get us through the day! We once gladly put in extra hours; now we add extra minutes to our lunch breaks!

In short, we get bored.

Or worse, we develop a sense of entitlement. We assume that we will get a promotion or a raise. We expect the corner office or the successful business or the fat paycheck without remembering that all those rewards (and the responsibilities that come with them) require hard work and dedication—or as the Bible puts it . . . FAITHFULNESS.

It doesn't matter if you are a Starbucks barista or an unpaid intern or a substitute teacher or a marketing consultant or a pastor. We have each been given different opportunities and interests. God has placed a specific job in each of our hands . . . but what He has given us matters less than what we choose to do with it. God grants more opportunity to those who prove themselves faithful with what is *currently* in their hands, regardless of how little or big it may seem to others. God can confidently give more to those who understand that they have been entrusted (not entitled), and who do their best to be faithful stewards of what they have been given!

Below are some tips for making the most of the current job God has placed in your hands. Whether or not it is your "dream job," it is a chance for you to grow and to develop the character and skills you may need later on. Perhaps God is using your *present* job to prepare you for the *future* opportunities you dream about!

1. **Early is the new on-time.** Make sure to arrive early to your shift at work or to your meetings. No one likes to hear the "traffic was so bad" or "I overslept" excuses!

2. **Be proactive.** If you feel like you have a job that isn't challenging you, then make it your responsibility to challenge yourself! My (Nicole's) dad is the hardest-working man I have ever met! As a manager, he always taught me that I should never just stand around waiting for someone to give me work to do. He told me that the best employees are the ones who have eyes to see a problem . . . and then proactively fix it! Great employees seek out ways to do *more* for their companies or organizations.

3. **Create solutions, not problems, for your boss.** Be the most uncomplicated employee you can be. By uncomplicated, we mean someone who doesn't take

things personally, isn't easily offended, and consistently has a great attitude! If your supervisor asks you to solve a problem, do everything you can to come up with a solution using the resources available to you. Be the kind of employee that makes your boss's job easier, not harder!

4. **Stay away from water cooler gossip.** Avoid workplace drama. Don't participate in gossip, and keep confidential information confidential! Make sure that you speak highly of your boss and your coworkers when they aren't around.

5. **Be a team player!** Work well with those around you. Be someone who adds to the productivity of the team and cares for the needs of teammates. Don't vie for recognition; instead, find opportunities to help coworkers shine. Don't fight for the spotlight, but rather trust that God will promote you and give you favor at the right time. *He will never ask you to sabotage someone else's success to get to the top.*

6. **Learn to communicate well with different personalities.** Not everyone you work with thinks or communicates like you. That's a good thing! The world would be very boring if everyone thought and spoke the same exact way! But truth be told, these enlivening

differences can also make for some misunderstandings in the workplace. Go out of your way to get to know the people you work with, and make every effort to communicate respect and care to each and every one of them. Read books and listen to presentations that can help you improve your communication skills in the workplace.

7. **Integrity matters.** Don't allow "little white lies" to undermine your potential. Refuse the temptation to cut corners on the expense report, take a few dollars for yourself out of the cash register, call in sick so you can enjoy a "free" day off from work, leave the office a few minutes early without telling anyone, or take credit for something you didn't do. The work you do isn't just for your company or your boss—it's for Jesus . . . and the best way we can honor Jesus at work is in the details, whether or not people notice!

8. **Represent Jesus!** The people you work with have front-row seats to the way you do life. Pray and look for opportunities to talk about Jesus in ways that are welcomed and encouraging. While remembering that no one is perfect, commit to being the best example of a Jesus-follower you can be at your job! Who knows . . . you may be the only representation of Jesus your coworkers will ever see . . . and the one who will lead them to their own authentic relationships with Him!

TEN WAYS TO BE GENEROUS

1. **Treat a friend to lunch.** Bonus points if you are able to pay for the check without them noticing!

2. **Pay for the order of the person behind you at Starbucks.** I love doing this! People are always surprised that a complete stranger would practice random generosity!

3. **Add quarters to someone's parking meter.** Save someone from one more parking ticket!

4. **Sponsor a child.** Help a child in a developing nation receive food, medical attention and education simply by making a monthly donation. When children are given opportunities for transformed lives, they will ultimately transform their communities. For more information, visit www.compassion.com.

5. **Give above and beyond your regular tithe to your local church.** Set a goal to give more in one year than you ever have before, and know that your generosity will make an eternal impact in the life of someone else!

6. **Surprise a family member or friend who is struggling to make ends meet with a gift card to a grocery store or nearby gas station.** Your generosity may be an answer to their prayers!

7. **Treat a girlfriend to a mani-pedi.** No special occasion . . . just because!

8. **Surprise a friend with a piece of costume jewelry or a scarf that totally reminds you of her!**

9. **Pass on your maternity clothes or your baby's newborn clothes to a woman in your world who just found out she's having a baby!**

10. **Buy lunch for a homeless person.** Make sure to let them know that you are praying for them, and that you care! Don't be stingy; treat them to whatever meal they want!

MORE, PLEASE!
(Additional reading)
The Total Money Makeover by Dave Ramsey
Managing God's Money by Randy Alcorn
Rich Dad Poor Dad by Robert T. Kiyosaki
The Blessed Life by Robert Morris
Suze Orman's Financial Guidebook by Suze Orman

5

Doing Life
Together

HOW TO NAVIGATE FRIENDSHIPS

A friend is a present you give yourself.

ROBERT LOUIS STEVENSON

WE'RE ALL IN THIS TOGETHER

I have to admit, I've never really understood the *High School Musical* phenomenon. I remember high school . . . and it certainly did not include breaking out into spontaneous song with the star athlete and cheerleader in the school cafeteria.

But I will give props to one song from the film. It's called "We're All in This Together." Here's why I like it: because it's true.

We are all in this together. Being human is not an individual, isolated experience. It's corporate. It's social. It's communal.

God puts it this way at the very beginning of the Bible: "It is not good for the man to be alone" (Gen. 2:18).

The great South African civil rights activist and Christian leader, Desmond Tutu, has written and delivered numerous speeches on this very subject. In his words, "We can be human only together."

Christian author and pastor, Eugene Peterson, who paraphrased and created *THE MESSAGE* version of the Bible, wrote, "We need community to complete our humanity."[1]

You and I were made to flourish and find fulfillment in healthy, genuine relationships. Without them, we will never experience the fullness of God's love for us and will never have the support we need to live out His extraordinary plans for our lives.

We weren't created to solve all of life's problems on our own. We need each other! We really are all in this together!

We need one another's wisdom and experiences. We need mentors who encourage us to become more like Jesus and enjoy the abundant life He has for us. We need friends to cheer us on when we face the larger-than-life challenges that come our way.

Life truly can become a grand, beautiful adventure when we have healthy friendships. This chapter is all about giving you the tools you need to find, grow and strengthen great friendships . . . the kind of friendships that bring levels of joy to your heart you didn't know were possible!

WHERE MY FRIENDS AT?!

We have talked to many women who faced crises, whether financial or health-related or marital, and felt all alone; or worse, they expressed that they got into the situations they were in partly because of the influence of poor friendships in their lives.

In conversation, they usually reveal how hard it has been for them to find quality friends they could rely on and trust.

Maybe you feel the same way. Maybe you have been betrayed by a friend in the past and now find it hard to trust. Maybe you just moved to a new city or started at a new school and are having a hard time meeting people. Maybe you never put much thought into choosing friends and have just sort of defaulted to having close friendships with the people you happen to spend the most time with.

We need to ask you a few questions.

Do you want great, life-giving, exciting friendships?

Do you want friendships that encourage, inspire and challenge you?

Do you want friendships that help you wholeheartedly follow Jesus and pursue His plans for your life?

Do you want friendships that endure and are able to overcome the many storms life will bring?

If you do, the good news is that God wants the very same things for YOU! He created you for relationships—a thriving, loving relationship with Jesus and thriving, loving relationships with other people! He wants you to experience the wonder and happiness found in genuine, healthy friendships!

The first step toward developing quality friendships is deciding to *be the type of friend you are looking for.*

We can only expect from others what we are willing to give. In many areas of life, we tend to attract the qualities that we ourselves are exuding.

What qualities do you wish for in your close friends? A good sense of humor, an adventurous spirit, a good listener, a passion for Jesus . . . ?

Take a few minutes to come up with your own list of qualities. Then reflect and pray about which of these traits you currently have, and where you can grow and become a better friend to those around you . . .

TEN QUALITIES OF A GREAT FRIEND

1. She knows how to laugh and have a good time!

2. She listens well.

3. She doesn't hold grudges.

4. She is kind to others.

5. She is generous.

6. She refrains from silly gossip.

7. She is confident in her own skin.

8. She always tells the truth.

9. She has an authentic and growing relationship with Jesus Christ.

10. She dreams big and pursues God's purposes for her life!

STEP OUT OF YOUR COMFORT ZONE

One of the best things about being part of our local church is the diversity of friendships it has brought us. We both have friends of all ages, backgrounds, shapes and sizes . . . and our lives are better for it! Each friend adds a new, vibrant hue that colors our life experience! Our world gets brighter and larger every time we step out of our comfort zones and invest in friendships with people who are different than we are! (It's also a great preview of what heaven will be like!) Here are some types of friendships to pray for and pursue in your life:

1. **Friends with DIFFERENT personalities.** Are you the type that would rather talk with one person for 45 minutes at a party than chat it up with everyone in the room? Chances are you will have an opportunity to develop a friendship with someone who is the

life of the party. It's like she always carries confetti in her purse!

It's easy to feel more comfortable with people who think like we do, but if we only connect with people who have similar personalities, then we will be missing out on friendships that draw the very best out of us. Plus, life quickly becomes boring when we surround ourselves with people just like us!

2. **Friends of a DIFFERENT age.** We can gain a great deal of wisdom by hanging around an older woman who has a genuine faith in Jesus. She has weathered a few storms, and we need to hear how she did it! Are you married? Spend some time with someone who has been married for more than a minute . . . and still likes her husband! Are you trying to start a business? Learn from a woman who has successfully built her business from scratch. Make sure to connect with women who can encourage and help you as you navigate different seasons of life.

Now, remember what we talked about back at the beginning of this book? No matter what your age is, you are an OLDER woman. You may still be trying to wrap your mind around this idea, but it doesn't need to be depressing. ☻ Right now, someone who is a few years younger than you are could use your advice and support. Have you graduated from college? I guarantee there is a younger woman who is pulling out her hair trying to study for exams. She needs YOU. Have you successfully paid off your student loans without signing away your firstborn? There's a younger woman who is in debt up to her eyeballs. She needs YOU. There's a young woman who just got her heart broken and doesn't know how she can ever love again. Perhaps you've kissed a few frogs before marrying your prince. That heart-broken woman needs YOU. Make sure to reach out and encourage the younger women in your world. You can be the friend you wish you had when you were her age.

3. **Friends from a DIFFERENT culture.** We have Latino friends. We have Asian friends. We have African-American friends. We have Caucasian friends. We have multiracial friends. Our friendship world is a melting pot, and we love it! Because of our friends, each of us has been exposed to more cultures, traditions and ways of doing life than we ever thought possible!

The apostle Paul wrote, "In Christ's family there can be no division into Jew and non-Jew, slave and free, male and female. Among us you are all equal. That is, we are all in a common relationship with Jesus Christ" (Gal. 3:28, THE MESSAGE). Jesus never intended for us to remain segregated. Through faith in Jesus, we discover what it means to live in racial harmony with one another. If we are ever going to bring lasting change to our world, that racial harmony must be more than a poetic, romanticized ideal. It has to affect how we do life in a personal way. We must be honest about our prejudices and hurts . . . and choose

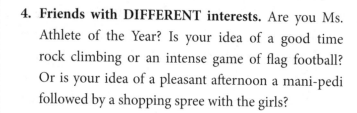

to overcome them with reconciliation and grace. When we embrace friends with different last names, languages, skin tones and traditions, we show the world that through Jesus it is possible to love one another!

4. **Friends with DIFFERENT interests.** Are you Ms. Athlete of the Year? Is your idea of a good time rock climbing or an intense game of flag football? Or is your idea of a pleasant afternoon a mani-pedi followed by a shopping spree with the girls?

Whatever your interests are, make sure to build friendships with people whose interests are *different*. I (Nicole) love indie rock and alternative music . . . and I (Holly) love the sound of new country! A good friend of ours loves classical music and operas. We've had some great and hilarious conversations about music! She's even schooled us on what different operas are about. (She explains them like they're movie plots, and throws in a couple of explosions to keep our attention.) We now know a thing or two about operas! Who knew?

Our world becomes larger when we open ourselves to the differing interests our friends have! Every now and again, we even become smarter because of them! ☺

FRIENDSHIP CIRCLES

Not everyone you meet will end up being your BFF. Some will be people you routinely see at church or in your apartment complex—people you stop and say hi to when you run into them. Others will become friends you hang out with more regularly. A few will become the kind of friend you call when you just broke up with your boyfriend or he popped the question or your baby just said his first word. These are the friends who know more about us than anyone else does . . . and who love and respect us more than anyone else does.

But how do we know who falls into what category of friendship? How do we figure out who should stay acquaintances and who should gain entrance into the deeper levels of our trust and confidence? Below are three different friendship zones, with brief descriptions of qualities friends in each zone should display. Think about your current friendships and make sure you are placing people in the right friendship zones. There may be some friends who need to be relocated to another zone . . .

Zone 1:
Your Closest Friends

- Display a genuine love for Jesus
- Inspire and challenge you in your faith
- Give you biblical advice
- Hold you accountable when needed
- Have earned trust over time
- Celebrate and support you
- Have integrity in decision-making
- Have fun doing life with you!
- Are a real friend to your future!

Zone 2:
Friends To Hang With

- Have similar values as you
- Demonstrate qualities that are trustworthy
- Make responsible decisions
- Easy to get along with
- Are considerate of others

Zone 3:
Acquaintances

- Spend time with you every now and again
- Fun to be around
- Have similar interests

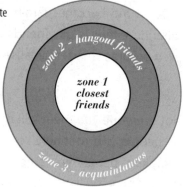

WARNING SIGNS OF TOXIC FRIENDSHIPS

1. **She is possessive.** In healthy friendships, the other person isn't jealous of other friendships you have. In fact, a friend should encourage you to broaden your friendship circle!

2. **She makes no effort.** It's disappointing, but sometimes we want a friendship more than the other person does. If you are always there for her, but she's never around for you, there's a problem. The effort made in friendships should be reciprocal; both parties should invest the time and energy to care for one another.

3. **She doesn't share many of your values.** Our values shape our actions, which ultimately shape our lives. If two friends don't share similar values, then inevitably their lives will head in different directions. It's important to have friends who are different from us, but when it comes to our closest friendships, we need to have mutual values. Make sure your closest friendships are with women who have a genuine faith in Jesus and are pursuing His plans for their lives.

4. **She compares herself to you.** Stay clear of the comparison game . . . because no one ever wins! Avoid comparing your weight, your salaries, your opportunities, or your talents and abilities. Comparisons only breed insecurities and jealousy.

5. **She can't keep her mouth shut.** If you are friends with someone who is always gossiping to you about other friends, you can be sure she is gossiping about YOU when you aren't around. People who are careless with their words are not people you can trust. Be around

people who speak highly of others and who refrain from contributing to or listening to hurtful gossip.

6. **She holds grudges.** No one's perfect. We all make mistakes. We say the wrong thing or forget a birthday. Make sure your friends are people who can address hurts quickly and forgive. No one likes to be continually reminded of something they did years ago or feel like there is a record being held against them by those they love. Cultivate friendships where people are mature in handling conflict and moving past hurts and miscommunications.

7. **She never lets you know what's really going on.** Emotionally mature friendships consist of two people who can honestly and respectfully share their feelings. Over time, they let their guards down and allow each other to know when they are going through difficult times. When someone is overly guarded, she excludes you from opportunities to be a genuine friend to her.

8. **She lacks character.** A friend who lies to avoid consequences or steals from the cash register or consistently flakes on your plans is NOT a good friend. You may care about this person, but you can't save her or fix her by being a better friend. They only way someone can change her character is by making the choice to

do so herself. We experience a lot of heartbreak and disappointment when we try to change people or expect them to give what they are unwilling or unable to give.

9. **She is inconsiderate.** Good friends appreciate and affirm each other. They value each other's efforts and the time given to the friendship. When someone doesn't communicate gratitude, she diminishes the other person's value as a friend. A friendship that consists of one friend always demanding or expecting another person to do something for her is just plain TOXIC.

10. **The friendship is boring.** The longer we know someone, the easier it is to fall into a rut. We eat at the same restaurant and order the same meal. We talk about the same things. We go to the same movie theatre and see the same type of romantic comedy. Traditions are comforting, but make sure to create new and fresh experiences with your friends. Take up a new hobby together. Visit a museum. Plan an adventure together.

FRIENDSHIP BOOSTERS

1. **Saying "thank you."** Maintain a level of gratitude toward your friend. Saying a simple "thank you" when she buys you a coffee or offers to pick up your kids from school goes a long way. Drop your friend a note or send her a thank you card sharing just how grateful you are for her friendship!

   Communicate that you don't take the friendship for granted and that you truly appreciate your friend!

2. **Celebrate each other!** Each of your friends is uniquely wired with a different personality, traits, background and interests. Celebrate your differences while focusing on your similar values! Don't secretly wish your friend were more like you. Maybe your friend is a detail-minded organizer, and you are a fly-by-the-seat-of-your-pants free spirit. Don't let that frustrate you. Be happy you have a friend who can bring a little organization to your fun spontaneity!

   No one likes to feel merely tolerated in a friendship. Your friends want to be celebrated! Applaud their uniqueness and learn to complement one another's strengths and weaknesses.

3. **Cheer each other on!** Is your friend studying hard for an exam? Did she just get engaged? Is she trying to overcome a bad habit or lose a few pounds? Is she working hard at getting out of debt?

Be her biggest cheerleader! Assure her that she's got what it takes and that you are there to support her however you can. Be willing to go out of your way to show that you care and that you've got her back! That may mean you hit up the gym again or find things to do together other than perusing the mall.

I (Nicole) remember when Holly was diagnosed with breast cancer a few years ago. The diagnosis began a dramatic journey on which she learned more about how to eat right and avoid toxic behaviors that jeopardize good health. She said goodbye to processed foods filled with sugar and chemicals, and she embraced a healthier, organic diet. She changed her soap, lotions, shampoos, and even her deodorant to natural products. She invested in water purifiers and began taking more raw vitamins and shots of wheatgrass than I knew were humanly possible to consume!

Even though I loved my donuts and soda and lard-infested refried beans and oh-so-yummy bacon . . . I loved my good friend and mentor even more. I couldn't do everything for her; in fact, there was a lot I couldn't do for her that I wish I could (for one, zap the cancer away!). But, one thing I knew I could do was walk alongside her on her health journey. So I, along with a few other friends, also gave up the unhealthy and ridiculously tasty foods for salads and wheatgrass and raw almonds.

Holly has been cancer-free for a few years now! Woohoo! Praise Jesus! In addition, both of us have discovered a much healthier way of taking care of the bodies God gave us!

You never know where being a friend's biggest fan will take you. It might mean changing habits or letting go of what's comfortable, but I guarantee it's an adventure worth taking!

4. **Laugh a lot.** There's nothing quite as sweet to the soul as a good laugh with a friend! One of my (Holly's) best friends started to become my friend because one day we found ourselves laughing at the same situation. Another friend of ours had a very public mishap with a glass door that still makes us laugh so hard that tears stream down our faces if we just think about it! And still another friend makes up the most ridiculous songs about random everyday events just to make us laugh! With some friends, we share inside jokes that have been going on for years! Make sure not only to

talk about the serious stuff, but also to have fun with your friends. Everyone needs girlfriends they can let their hair down in front of and just be girls with!

5. **Listen.** You never stop learning about people if you listen hard enough. Make sure to make time to be the person your friend can talk to when she needs someone to listen to her. When you really actively listen, you discover how to pray for and offer support to your friend. You also learn about her hopes, dreams, passions and fears. If you listen long enough, you will find out things you never knew, like:
"I went skydiving once."
"I backpacked through Europe."
"I was adopted."
"I studied to be an engineer before changing majors."
"I've always been a bit fearful in this area."
"I was abused as a child."
Listening unites hearts more than talking does. Maybe your friend does not need to hear your opinion right now. Maybe she just needs you to listen.

FRIENDSHIP KILLERS

1. **Being too busy.** We lead very busy lives, and sometimes, in our busyness, we sacrifice quality time spent with

friends. If we aren't careful, our friendships can get put on the back burner. Friendships are crucial to our happiness and success in life! As your life gets fuller, make sure to continue to invest in quality friendships, even if that means grabbing coffee at the airport during a layover or catching up over Skype after the kids go to bed!

2. **Taking life too seriously!** Remember to laugh with your friends! There are going to be moments and seasons of life that bring challenges with them . . . from surviving final exams to navigating the responsibilities of a new promotion to working through marital conflicts to overcoming an illness to raising a family or losing a loved one. Just because moments are stressful or overwhelming doesn't mean we can't enjoy a good laugh with a friend. In fact, it's our ability to laugh in the face of adversity that gives us the courage to move forward when it would be a lot easier—and feel a lot better—to call it quits!

Proverbs 17:22 tells us, "A cheerful heart is good medicine." Medical science agrees. Sharing a good laugh with a friend provides numerous benefits. According to licensed massage therapist, Leslie Guerrero Collins, laughing:

- Lowers blood pressure
- Increases vascular blood flow and oxygenation of the blood

- Gives a workout to the diaphragm and abdominal, respiratory, facial, leg and back muscles
- Reduces certain stress hormones such as cortisol and adrenaline
- Increases the response of tumor- and disease-killing cells such as Gamma-interferon and T-cells
- Defends against respiratory infections—even reducing the frequency of colds—by immunoglobulin in saliva
- Increases memory and learning
- Improves alertness, creativity and memory[2]

3. **Jealousy.** Nothing kills a friendship faster than jealousy! When we fail to deal with the insecurities in our own souls, we inadvertently sabotage the best of friendships!

Avoid destructive mind games in which you compare yourself to your friends. When we become jealous of someone else's appearance, talent, opportunity and achievements, we lose the ability to fully love and support our friends. Be confident that God made you wonderfully unique. You are an original, so why try to live as a copy of someone else?

4. **Impatience.** There are no overnight best friends. Think of your closest friendships as being prepared in a crock-pot—simmering for hours and acquiring an

irresistible taste—not in a microwave that pops out a frozen TV dinner in less than three minutes!

The best friendships require T-I-M-E. Don't force a level of intimacy right away; instead, take the time to really get to know someone and allow the friendship to develop into something significant and refreshing!

5. **Disrespect.** When we become too familiar with our friends, it becomes all too easy to forget to communicate honor and respect to one another. Great friendships consist of people who are celebrated and valued. Make sure your words and actions demonstrate kindness, love and respect.

SHIFT HAPPENS

When I (Nicole) was in the second grade, I met my first true girlfriend—my very first BFF. Her name was Jolene. We met in the playground at St. Joseph's Catholic School. We both hated our ugly school uniforms and thought MC Hammer pants were legit! We agreed that Thor Jaramillo was the dreamiest second grader in all of elementary school. We passed funny notes during math class about how weird Father O'Flanagan was. We shared our Fruit Roll-Ups and Cheetos with each other at lunch. We stayed up all night at our sleepovers playing "Truth or Dare" and giggling over boys and silly ghost stories.

Jolene had muscular dystrophy, which left her confined to a wheelchair. In true schoolgirl fashion, we pimped her wheelchair out with Lisa Frank sparkly stickers! Jolene rode around in some serious style! When her electric wheelchair was in the shop for repairs, I would wheel her around our school. I would even run her around our grass field so she could experience what it was like to play goalie in a soccer game. (Granted, we didn't block that many goals, but we had a lot of fun trying!)

Jolene and I were inseparable. She had my back . . . and I had hers. And boy, could we laugh together! I never laughed as hard as I did around Jolene!

One day, toward the end of our fourth grade year, Jolene broke the news to me that her family was moving. One month later, I gave her a homemade goodbye card (with lots of glitter glue and dolphin and puppy stickers on it), and we hugged for the last time. I watched as the U-Haul truck drove off into the distance, taking with it the best friendship any little girl could ask for.

I learned an important and painful lesson that day: Not every friendship will last a lifetime . . . and that's okay.

Some people are in this race with us for the full marathon; others will join us for a mile or two. Some friendships are built for a lifetime; more often than not, friendships shift as seasons in our life change.

It takes wisdom and grace to allow friendships to evolve, and to provide room for friends to grow and change as life goes on.

Friends transfer to out-of-state schools.

They get married.

They move to different neighborhoods.

Their careers take off.

They start families.

Their values and priorities change.

Over time, some close friends may turn into acquaintances. Sometimes, this takes place because of a change in life circumstances (like a move), and sometimes it happens as our values change—we simply "grow apart." As disappointing as this can be, it's a normal part of life. We have to willingly and graciously release people, while always remaining grateful for the role their friendship has played in our lives in seasons past.

SOCIAL MEDIA ETIQUETTE

Back in the day, communicating with friends meant grabbing a cup of coffee at the local coffee shop or chatting on your home phone while folding laundry. Well, those days are long gone! Now we can connect with friends through e-mails, text messages, instant messaging, Facebook, Twitter, Pinterest, Skype . . . to name just a few! With social media comes a whole new list of do's and do-not's. Below are some tips on social media etiquette to help you genuinely connect with friends and avoid some potentially awkward moments along the way!

1. Avoid criticizing someone else, famous or not. Not everyone needs 2 know what u think about Lindsay Lohan's haircut.

2. Stay positive. Posting "My world is falling apart" as an update because a network canceled your favorite TV show may be a little much!

3. No need 2 get political. Express views that r going 2 bring people together . . . not cause a greater divide on hot topics.

4. Please limit photos of your pet 2 once a week. 'Nuff said.

5. A photo that u look cute in, but your friends are making weird faces in . . . doesn't need 2 b posted. & they don't need 2 b tagged either!

6. Do not social media-stalk the cute guy u just met. It's 2 soon 4 u 2 know his every move!

7. Check out the Facebook page of a friend u r getting 2 know or someone u r starting 2 date. U may b surprised! But no stalking! ☺

8. Good rule of thumb: Before posting, ask yourself, "Would I want my grandma 2 view this?"

9. Keep work or school hours 2 actual work or study, & enjoy social media (including checking Facebook) on your lunch break or your own time!

FUN WAYS TO SAY, "LOVE YOU, FRIEND!"

1. Make a "Why My Friend Is So Awesome" list and leave it in her purse for her to find in the middle of the day.

Reasons why Lucy is awesome
1. She loves monty python movies
2. She is a great listener
3. She only eats the green m&m's
4. She is a great daughter to her parents
5. She knows the whole theme song to Fresh Prince of Bel-Air
6. She is super smart
7. Her faith in Jesus inspires everyone around her
8. She gives the best hugs
9. She has a secret crush on Conan O'Brien
10. She always knows what to say to make her friends laugh

2. Watch her favorite movie with her (for the hundredth time) after she's had a long day. Bonus points if you bring her favorite dessert to share!

3. Give her a ride to the airport, even if it's at 4 A.M. Yikes!

4. Offer to plan her birthday party with a theme that's totally her!

5. Surprise her at work with her favorite latte.

6. Drop off some saltines, ginger ale, chicken soup, and your copy of *The Notebook* at her place when she is stuck at home with the flu.

7. Help her with things that come easily to you but are torture for her: redecorating a room, creating a spreadsheet, buying the perfect black dress . . .

8. Listen to her vent over the phone about her hard day, and offer her encouragement and prayer!

CAFE LATTE

MORE, PLEASE!
(Additional reading)
God Chicks by Holly Wagner
Relationships: How to Make Bad Relationships Better and Good Relationships Great by Drs. Les and Leslie Parrott
Boundaries by Dr. Henry Cloud and Dr. John Townsend
A Garden of Friends by Penny Pierce Rose
Everybody's Normal Till You Get to Know Them by John Ortberg

6

Love Life

HOW TO WIN AT ROMANCE

*Love sought is good, but given
unsought is better.*

WILLIAM SHAKESPEARE

WORST PICK-UP LINES EVER!

If a man ever says **ANY** of these things to you with a straight face, please make sure to run in the opposite direction! Then, after you've made your getaway, make sure to have a good laugh with your girlfriends! 😊

1. You must be a thief, because you've stolen my heart.

2. Did it hurt when you fell from heaven?

3. Hey, I've seen you before . . . oh yeah, in my dreams!

4. Baby, you're so sweet, you put Hershey's outta business.

5. Hi, my name's Right . . . as in your Mr. Right.

6. God told me you are the ONE.

7. Do you believe in love at first sight, or should I walk by again?

8. Do you have a map? Because I keep getting lost in your eyes . . .

9. If you were a sandwich at McDonald's, you'd be called McGorgeous!

10. Are your legs tired? 'Cuz you've been running through my mind all night long!

TEN THINGS NOT TO SAY ON A FIRST DATE

1. **"That reminds me of my ex-boyfriend . . . "** (This is not the time to talk about your romantic history!)

2. **"So, when do you see yourself settling down, getting married and having kids?"** (Avoid conversations that lead him to believe you are already picking out the china!)

3. **"I was just wondering . . . how much money do you make exactly?"** (T.M.I., way too soon.)

4. **"Do you have any ibuprofen with you? I have horrible cramps!"** (This is not your girlfriend you are talking to!)

5. **"I was praying, and God told me you are THE ONE."** (That just sounds WEIRD.)

6. **"Do I have something in my teeth?"** (Remember, you are a lady. If you have questions about your appearance, that's what the restroom mirror is for.)

7. **"Let's talk politics! What are your political views?"** (The first date is not the place to debate.)

8. **"It's so great to finally get asked out on a date!"** (And try to leave out any possible references to past Friday nights with Ben & Jerry and the latest romantic comedy.)

9. **"Are you going to open that door for me, or do I have to do everything myself?"** (No one likes a nag.)

10. **"Have you ever thought about getting your eyebrows waxed?"** (Keep all grooming and makeover ideas to yourself.)

TEN THINGS NOT TO DO ON A FIRST DATE

1. **Pile up the garlic.** (Avoid foods that will make your date wish your fascinating conversation were taking place on Skype instead of in person!)

2. **Let loose with your bodily functions.** (Yes, we all get gas, but that doesn't mean we should ask our date to pull our finger or let out a belch after packing down that cheeseburger. Gross!)

3. **Become someone else**. (He asked you out because he likes YOU. You will have some shared interests . . . and some differing ones. You don't have to agree on everything, and you don't need to change your interests just because you like a guy.)

4. **Do all the talking.** (Ask questions. Listen. Make sure that your conversation is two-sided and engaging.)

5. **Text on your phone the whole time.** (There's nothing more annoying than trying to have a meaningful conversation with someone who is too busy texting, checking emails, and posting Twitter updates to pay attention. It's just plain rude.)

6. **Stay out too late.** (Take your time getting to know someone. Even if you are having a great time, it's always a good idea to call it a night at a reasonable hour. Definitely avoid being alone late at night. Like Grandma says, "Nothing good ever happens after 11 P.M.!")

7. **Overanalyze everything.** (It's just coffee. You are getting to know each other. Don't try to figure out if he's the ONE. Take the time to get to know someone, and have fun!)

8. **Forget the other half of that dress at home!** (If you want to be treated like a lady, make sure to dress like one.)

9. **Share too much too soon.** (No one needs to know your whole life story right away. For sure avoid a play-by-play of your dating history. TMI!)

10. **Insist on paying for everything.** (If he asked you out on a date, he wants to be a gentleman! Allow him the opportunity to be chivalrous.)

FOUR WAYS TO LIVE SEXUALLY PURE

God's very best for our lives is to experience the gift of true sexual intimacy inside of marriage. When we choose to honor God with our sexuality, we position ourselves for great blessing and emotional health in both our present dating lives and our future marriages.

Living sexually pure doesn't just happen . . . it takes commitment and intentionality on our part. Below are some thoughts on *avoiding going too far too soon* . . .

1. **Purchase a chastity belt.** (I'm sure you can get a great deal on one on eBay.)

2. **Insist on your father chaperoning all your dates.** (Dad's stink eye will keep

your date on his very best behavior. If he brings his shotgun along for the ride, even better!)

3. **Don't shave your legs.** (Enough said.)

4. **Live stream your dates to your closest friends.** (It'll be your very own reality show, but without the making out in hot tubs.)

Okay, that list was just for fun! But here are *some godly, smart ideas for living sexually pure while in the dating scene . . .*

1. **Set clear boundaries early on in a dating relationship.** (If the man you are dating doesn't share your desire to value purity, then he simply isn't the right guy for you!)

2. **Avoid certain settings.** (You don't need to share the same bed or be alone watching a movie on the couch late at night. Choose to spend the majority of your time in public, safe settings.)

3. **Check in with your friends.** (Make yourself accountable to those close to you. Have them call to find out how a date went. Allow them to ask the tough questions, and be willing to answer honestly.)

4. **Learn from others.** (Seek out the advice and support of women who have successfully navigated living sexually pure, and who have made great decisions in dating.)

PROTECTING THE HEART
Above all else, guard your heart,
for it is the wellspring of life.

PROVERBS 4:23

Your heart is valuable—so valuable, in fact, that it should not be given away to every bidder. You are a daughter of the Most High

King, and you are precious in God's sight. Jesus is passionately in love with you . . . so much so that He gave His very life to be with you!

Your heart ought to be protected by wisdom. Make sure that as you get to know and date someone, you make choices that will guard your heart.

One mistake women commonly make in dating is giving their hearts away too freely and too quickly. Make sure to take the time to really get to know the person you are dating.

Don't feel pressured to share the most intimate desires and memories of your heart with someone you barely know. Those aspects of your heart should be reserved for someone who has proven himself trustworthy.

Trust is developed over time.

How does he handle conflict? How does he respond to correction? How does he manage his finances? How does he deal with loss or challenges? How does he treat those closest to him? How does he manage stress?

These are things that can only be discovered over T-I-M-E. Make sure to give more than enough time to really get to know someone before investing your heart in a serious relationship.

We should maintain a slow pace not only emotionally, but also physically. Slowing down physically doesn't just mean abstaining from sex. It also involves being aware of how physically intimate we are early in a relationship. Make sure that your physical interactions—from holding hands to hugging to kissing—develop over time. When physical affection moves too fast, it gives a false sense of closeness that can backfire later on, causing needless heartbreak and confusion.

DRAMA-FREE BREAKUPS

Breaking up is the not-so-fun part of dating. We all know what it feels like to give or receive the "let's just be friends" talk. Awkward, right?

Just because it's uncomfortable doesn't mean it has to be heartbreaking. Through wisdom and humility, we can avoid some of the bad-breakup pitfalls. We recently sat down with Philip Wagner (author, pastor, and the best husband ever!) to get a few tips on achieving drama-free breakups. Here's what he had to say:

Philip Wagner: First off, it's important to keep in mind that not every relationship deserves a "dramatic" breakup.

A simple conversation could be what the relationship calls for. There is a difference between a serious relationship and having gone out on a couple dates. If you've gone out on one or two dates, not getting a call *is* breaking up. But after three or four dates, it's appropriate to have "the talk."

Us: Is it okay to text someone to break up?

Philip Wagner: No. In our world of cell phones, e-mails and texts, it's easier than ever to stay in touch with someone . . . but please, don't use those devices as a way of avoiding confrontation. If you liked a guy enough to kiss him and have a relationship with him, then the very least you can do is honor that connection by ending it in person—face to face. Bottom line: Using technology to break up is cruel and shallow.

Us: Is there a right time or a wrong time to break up?

Philip Wagner: There is never a perfect time, but it's good to be thoughtful about what is going on in the other person's life. You don't want to put it off too long, but if your boyfriend is already going through a difficult time—say he lost his job yesterday, or a family crisis came up—it can wait a week or two. If

there's a special occasion like a birthday or Christmas
. . . again, it can wait a week.

Us: How long should the conversation last?

Philip Wagner: Give the person a fair amount of time
to process the breakup. You probably want to deliver
the news and then get the heck out of there . . . but
don't be in such a hurry. It's really unfair to tell him
without giving him adequate time to process.

Us: What if he tries to talk you into changing
your mind?

Philip Wagner: That happens sometimes. You might
have to endure some tears, hear about some frustrations, or even bear some accusations out of hurt . . . but
talking about it is the right thing to do. It's important
to give him the chance to ask questions and feel the
sentiment behind your words. If he gets upset, cries
or even gets angry—don't try to stop him. Guys are
allowed to have and express feelings. Keep in mind,
you've been thinking about the breakup for a few
days; he only heard about it a couple minutes ago. But
if at any point you feel threatened, or he gets overly
aggressive, leave immediately and let him know you
are willing to talk later, when he has calmed down.

Us: Are there certain things that shouldn't be said
during a breakup?

desires and feelings before making decisions. He should demonstrate respect in his treatment of you and others around him, as well as in how he talks to and about others.

Someone who really respects you will honor the purposes of God in your life! He will support you and encourage you to pursue wholeheartedly the great plans God has for you, and won't be intimidated by your dreams for the future!

3. **A man who is protective about you and your feelings.** He should be considerate of you and do his best to care for and support you. Under pressure, he should demonstrate an ability and willingness to look out for you. This means that he conducts his dating relationship with you in a way that is protective of your emotional and spiritual well-being. He should date you in such a way that it doesn't jeopardize you, your family life, your friendships, and most importantly, your relationship with Jesus.

4. **A man who serves others.** In today's culture, it is pretty easy to become self-focused. Make sure to partner with someone who can see beyond his own needs and is committed to addressing others' needs. Is he serving in your local church? Is he quick to help out you and his friends? Is he generous with his

time and his resources? Great marriages are developed when both husband and wife are committed to serving each other. Look for someone who is actively serving others now.

5. **A man with vision.** He should have direction for his life and a strong desire to make a real difference in the world. A lot of people have dreams for their futures, but the man you are dating should have more than a dream . . . he should be taking real steps toward those dreams! Ultimately, you want to be in a serious relationship with a man who is passionately and ambitiously pursuing God's will for his life!

HE'S NOT YOUR GIRLFRIEND

You don't have to be a rocket scientist to realize that men and women communicate very differently. For one, we women tend to have more words in our daily quota than men ever will! We also tend to connect more easily with people through communication. It's how God wired us.

It may be true that men need help learning how to communicate their feelings, but even with that help, they will likely never communicate like women!

That's a good thing. God made men and women different to complement each other.

If we are going to have meaningful relationships with men, we have to learn to communicate in a way that men understand and that makes them feel valued.

 In other words, we need to remember that our boyfriends aren't our girlfriends! If we try to talk to men like we do to our girlfriends, we will find ourselves running into a lot of cement walls in the communication department.

With that in mind, here are a few ways to improve communication with your boyfriend:

- **Use fewer words.** Men tend to be direct. They will have an easier time actively listening to the 3-minute description of your day at work than the 30-minute version.

- **Ease up on the subtleties.** Dropping hints is an art form for women. That's not the case for men! Don't expect them to know what you're thinking. Instead, be clear about what you are asking of them or feeling.

- **Realize that your delivery matters.** It's not just what you say, but how you say it. Your tone will communicate either honor and respect or disrespect and frustration. Make sure to approach discussions with a tone that communicates that you value him, even if you are disagreeing about something.

- **Show your appreciation.** Thank him for specific kind and admirable things he has done, and make sure to let him know how those things made you feel. Men want to know that they aren't just tolerated, but celebrated! Encourage his efforts to care for and support you. When you are your partner's biggest cheerleader, you help him grow as a man of character and strength.

- **Do more listening.** Get to know his interests. Understand how he is feeling and how you can support him. Ask questions about him as you continue to date. Let him know you want to keep learning more about him. When you find yourself in a conflict, fight fair. Actually listen to his side of things and discover his perspective.

MORE, PLEASE!
(Additional reading)
GodChicks and the Men They Love by Philip and Holly Wagner
Date . . . or Soul Mate? by Neil Clark Warren, Ph.D.
Boundaries in Dating by Dr. Henry Cloud and Dr. John Townsend
Your Knight in Shining Armor by P. B. Wilson
The Purity Principle by Randy Alcorn

7

Tying the Knot

BUILDING A MARRIAGE THAT LASTS

There is no more lovely, friendly, and charming relationship, communion or company than a good marriage.

MARTIN LUTHER

CINDERELLA LIED!

I (Holly) loved Philip. He loved me.

Then we said, "I do."

Like Cinderella, I thought that was all it took to get to happily ever after—love and a wedding ring.

Uhhh . . . she lied.

Thinking that marriage is as simple as love, a wedding ring, and the right house is about as naive as thinking that all you have to do to get great abs is want them and buy a cute workout outfit! Sadly, great abs come after lots of crunches, Pilates and diet control.

Just like marriage.

Well . . . maybe not the Pilates . . . but definitely the work.

Don't worry—it is not a life sentence of hard labor! It is work to bring enjoyment!

But yes . . . building relationships is a lot of work.

Period.

I don't know anyone who has been married very long who will not attest to that.

Great marriages are not genetic. They don't happen just because you want one or hope to have one. If that were true, everyone everywhere would have a great marriage. The desire for a healthy marriage is really only the first step on a long list of steps. Sadly, many couples don't make it very far down the list.

It's good to remember that struggling marriages don't just happen either.

There are a lot of reasons for divorce.

Communication breakdown.

Personality differences.

Sexual frustration or unfaithfulness.

Money problems.

Unresolved issues of the past.

It can't just be your spouse that is the problem (although there are days when I am convinced he is . . .). Sometimes we think that if we were just married to someone else, then our problems would be solved.

Not so.

Sixty percent of second marriages end in divorce too.[1]

I have heard that divorce statistics for third and fourth marriages are even higher.

Maybe at the core of all of these numbers is a lack of preparation. Most of us spend more time planning for the wedding than we do for the marriage.

How much time do we spend on the selection of wedding invitations . . . flowers . . . meals . . . a wedding dress . . . ? We agonize over how many bridesmaids to have . . . where to hold the ceremony . . . our honeymoon plans . . . and so on and so forth.

I am not saying that you shouldn't plan your big day . . . but really, if we just spent as much time preparing for the commitment of marriage as we do for our wedding day, then our marriages would start off much healthier.

We expect our physicians to have gone through years of school and residency in order to be good at what they do, yet most of us expect to have a strong marriage without ever learning how. Wouldn't it be great if all universities required students to take a Marriage 101 class? In the long run, that class would probably prove more useful than the calculus class I took! But even for those of us who missed the Marriage 101 class, there is hope!

For those of you who are planning a wedding . . . how about working on these things too . . .

Is your passion for Jesus the same?

How will you handle finances?

What are your expectations in terms of husband/wife roles?

Do you both want children?

How do you handle disagreements?

How much will your in-laws have to do with your marriage?

What will you do during leisure time?

Are you both equally committed to a church?

FIGHTING THE "YOU COMPLETE ME" SYNDROME

In the movie *Jerry McGuire,* Tom Cruise's character says to the love of his life, "You complete me." Now, that certainly sounds romantic, and like the other women watching the movie, we probably all said "*Awwww!*" when we heard it. But honestly, that is nonsense.

We shouldn't be looking for someone to complete us.

You are not some fragmented being looking for a man to fill the gaps. God didn't create you as a half. A healthy relationship is when two wholes come together . . . so the goal is for each of us to be whole before joining our life to someone else's.

When God told Adam that it wasn't good for him to be alone (see Gen. 2:18), the woman was created to bring partnership. She was created to add to his life, not take away from it.

Solomon said that two are better than one (see Eccles. 4:9).

Doing the math, we know that $1 + 1 = 2$.

By contrast, $1/2 + 1/2 = 1$, which is not better than one. Two whole people can engage in a mutually dependent relationship—with

honest, open and vulnerable communication and accountability—while encouraging and urging each other further and
deeper into the purpose of God.

Two halves united together will typically experience false intimacy
laced with veins of co-dependency, secrets, hiding, miscommunica-
tion and fear. When it comes to each other's purpose and destiny . . .
well, it is very hard to encourage your mate to become who they are
meant to be in God, when you aren't even sure who you are in Him.

You are designed to bring help and companionship to
the relationship.

Together, you and your husband will accomplish far more
than either of you could alone.

A positive self-image is vital, but remember that my ability to
like myself does not come simply from thinking that I am wonderful. It comes from knowing that God thinks that (see Ps. 139:14).

I am His masterpiece (see Eph. 2:10).

His one-of-a-kind creation.

The deepest needs of my soul can only be met by my Creator—
and they will be if I have an honest and real relationship with Him.

We have to quit asking our husbands to meet needs that only
God can.

Neediness demands. Having a need, asks.

Most of us fall into one of the following categories:

---

1. **Independent** (we think we can do everything on our
    own—or at least, we try to)

    Not good, because we are designed to do life together.

2. **Dependent** (fully relying on someone, as an infant would a mother)

Not good, because God is the only one who can be our All-sufficiency. Our spouses cannot fill that role.

3. **Interdependent** (confident in ourselves, and yet needing others to fulfill our purpose)

Good, because we were designed for reciprocal relationships that are rooted in God.

SEVEN RULES FOR FIGHTING FAIR
(These work for any relationship . . . not just marriage!)

Wouldn't it be easier if all of life were like the climate control in a car? The car we have has dual controls, so I can make it cooler or warmer on my side of the car, and Philip can have his side how he wants it. I can even warm up my seat, and he can make his cool. Pretty awesome! Sometimes I wish life could be full of "his and her" everything, but it isn't. Most of the time, the conflict we experience in marriage arises because we are not willing to give up what we want.

I have a friend who was raised in a family whose way to resolve any conflict was to fight it out. Just fight until you win. These were not necessarily physical fights, but definitely verbal fights that got louder and louder. One person always had to win, and the other was made to feel totally wrong. There was either complete domination or complete submission—no compromising or meeting in the middle.

Surely this is not the best way.

Then I have talked to people who were raised in families where one or both parents backed down from anything resembling a confrontation—they would just give in, totally avoiding any conflict whatsoever. One of my friends who grew up in this kind of environment said that this method of dealing with conflict kept the peace for a while, but eventually there would be an explosion.

That way can't be good either.

There are right and wrong ways to face and resolve conflict.

I am not a big fan of boxing, but I do know that there are rules in boxing. There are rules in karate. There are rules in wrestling. I am not sure about the WWE or Lucha Libre (made famous in the movie *Nacho Libre*) . . . but I think that, even in those matches, there are a few basic ground rules.

Rule #1: The first step toward resolving conflict is to make sure that you yourself are at peace with God.

It sounds so basic, but we were created to have a relationship with Him, and our ability to connect with people comes out of our relationship with God. I just don't think that we will ever have peace with people if we haven't made our peace with God. Sometimes conflict occurs because we are expecting people—in this case, our husbands—to meet needs that only God can meet. As amazing as your husband is—and he is amazing—he is not your Savior. He has nothing with which to save you.

Rule #2: Ask God how much of this problem might be your fault.

Before you attack or accuse or blame, check yourself out. Jesus said that before we worry about that little piece of sawdust in somebody else's eye, we should remove the tree trunks from our own eyes (see Matt. 7:3). We all have tree trunks in our eyes sometimes. We can all get so focused on the weaknesses and faults of the other that we forget we have shortcomings of our own. The reality is, some part of the conflict is my fault, and the responsibility for that part of the problem is 100 percent mine. I have to own that.

So now, occasionally I will ask myself questions like, *Am I being oversensitive? Am I being insensitive? Am I being ungrateful or too demanding?* Oftentimes, if I am honest, the answer to one of those questions is yes—which means that I have to take responsibility for what I have contributed to the conflict.

Rule #3: (This is the tough part.) Apologize for your part of the problem first.

Get great at saying, "I'm sorry."

Not, "I'm sorry, but . . ."

Just "I'm sorry for being oversensitive." Or too demanding . . . or whatever.

Maybe, just maybe, you are wrong in this instance. I am sure he needs to apologize, too. He undoubtedly has a tree trunk in his own eye. But you can only deal with you, so I am saying be 100 percent responsible for your part.

Apologizing does not mean that the issue is over; it just means that there is now the right atmosphere for solving whatever the conflict might be.

Rule #4: Trying to see an issue from the other's point of view is important.

It is not always easy, because the only perspective from which we naturally see life is our own. A number of years ago, Philip and I were looking for a house.

This was when I was still living under the illusion that all men knew how to fix things . . . or could manage people who knew how to fix things. We walked into a house that was for sale. It was the funkiest house ever, and I just loved it. It had a tree growing right in the middle of it. The previous owner had begun some renovations, laying the groundwork for what I thought would be the most amazing house.

As I walked around the house, I said things like, "We could put this here, and do that there. In this room we could do this." As Philip walked through it, he saw all the work that would need to be done—none of which he had any idea how to do. In his mind, he saw months of sawdust, hammers and chaos. I got frustrated with him as he let me know we were not going to live in that house. I said things like, "Why do we always have to do things your way? Why can't we have a house like this?"

I remember walking off by myself and really trying to see the situation from his perspective. He wanted a home—a peaceful home. He had no idea how to create a peaceful home out of this half-finished building. I came to recognize and understand the stress that even the thought of living there gave him.

So we walked away from that house that needed lots of work . . . and eventually moved into a beautiful home that only required us to unpack our boxes and mount a lamp. Perfect! Working hard at trying to see the issue from his point of view helped resolve that particular conflict.

It's amazing how well this approach works—not only with husbands, but also with friends.

Work hard at trying to see issues from your loved one's point of view and watch those conflicts begin to resolve.

Rule #5: You will need to pick a time to resolve the issue.

Timing is key. For instance, on the way to his birthday party is probably **not** the time to let your husband know that he could lose a few pounds. (Wish I could tell you I learned that from a book!) Now, the issue may have been a fair one to bring up, but the timing was not good. If his mom just got diagnosed with Alzheimer's, it's probably not the time to tell him you think he should read a book on parenting. Again, the issue may be a reasonable one to bring up . . . the timing is just wrong.

Is it late at night?
Has he had a long day?

Is he at work?

Maybe those would not be the best times to start a difficult conversation.

If you are trying to resolve conflict with a friend . . . consider the timing as well.

Has she just been in the hospital with one of her parents?

Is her child having a crisis?

Is her house flooded?

You get the idea.

We need to be sensitive to whether or not this is the right time to bring up the issue. The goal is to resolve the problem at hand, not create another one.

Rule #6: Picking the right place is also important. Running out the door on the way somewhere is probably not the place to resolve anything. Because neither one of you will feel like you are heard, and you will feel like you need to hurry through the process. The place to work out an issue is away from the telephone and other distractions.

The bed is probably not the place to work out the issue either, because any man left horizontal for long will start snoring! (This will just cause another issue that will need to be resolved!) Besides, a couple's bed shouldn't be a place of conflict. It should be a place for intimacy. You don't want to bring a fight there.

Taking a walk can be a great place to resolve issues. Or over coffee at Starbucks. Or sitting by the beach. Or hiking in the woods. Or on a park bench. You pick a place that works for you.

Rule #7: Words matter. There are some verbal weapons that Philip and I have agreed never to use against each other. For example, we have decided that no matter what kind of conflict we get into, we will never use the word "divorce." Ever. If divorce is not an option, then we realize that working things out is the only solution.

Think about the damage you may cause before you launch that verbal missile. Sadly, sometimes my method is *Ready . . . Fire . . . Aim.* Not good! Reckless shooting can cause damage that is impossible to fix. Words cannot be taken back . . . only forgiven.

I love M&Ms, especially the peanut ones. Back when I used to eat that kind of stuff, I could polish off a bag really quickly . . . in about 35 seconds! It only took

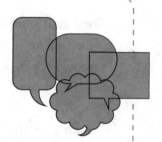

35 seconds to consume a bag full of fat and sugar . . . and it would take about 30 minutes of exercise to work off all those calories—not to mention the hours that my body would require to get rid of the toxins I had ingested.

This is like a verbal missile . . . we can throw one at our partner in a matter of seconds, but it may take years to work off the damage.

Besides "divorce," Philip and I try to refrain from using words like "never" or "always"—because they are rarely true. "We *never* do anything I want to do!" "You *always* ignore me!" "You *never* think about me!" "You *never* say that you love me!" Nobody "always" or "never" does anything, so be careful about using these absolute words.

To these seven rules, add the basic ones you probably learned in kindergarten: No yelling. No pushing. No hitting. No kicking. No biting. No slamming doors.

CLASS IN SESSION: QUESTIONS TO ASK

Whether preparing for marriage or seeking to deepen your relationship with your husband, it's always important to ask questions.

Questions are a great way to get to know someone (and to continue to learn about someone you already know well).

How about you? Are you asking questions?
Try these:

"What is your biggest fear?"

"What do you want our life to look like in five years?"

"If you had a million dollars, what would you do with it?"

"What are two things you love about me?"

"If money were no object, where would you like to go on vacation?"

"What are you looking forward to?"

"What makes you feel the most alive?"

Over the years, the questions might change, but we should still ask them. The answers might change, too. Because the truth is . . . both you and your husband are mysteries that will never be completely solved.

A stale marriage occurs when no one cares enough to ask questions. When we quit learning about each other.
Dr. Robin Smith, in her book *Lies at the Altar*, suggests 276 questions that should be asked before marriage . . . and asked again during marriage. They should be answered truthfully . . .

not how you think your partner wants you to answer them. After all, it is truth that sets us free!

If you are dating and you don't have the time to ask the questions, then you don't have the time to get married.

Here are a few of the questions Dr. Smith suggests:

- Are you working in your chosen profession?

- How many hours a week do you work?

- Do you prefer urban, suburban or rural settings?

- Do you think of your home as a cocoon, or is your door always open?

- If you had unlimited resources, how would you live?

- Do you have any debts?

- When was the first time you felt that you were in love with another person?

- Do you exercise regularly?

- What do you like or dislike about your appearance?

- Do you want children?

- Have you ever been alienated from your family?

- Do you have a best friend?

- Are you serving in church?

- What is your idea of a fun day?

- Do you enjoy traveling?

- Do you like to cook? Eat?

- Are there household responsibilities that you think are primarily male or female?

- Are you a morning person or night person?[2]

Being a perpetual student is crucial. (Not that you need to remain in college forever—please don't.) Please continue to learn new things . . . about life and your spouse . . . and then do the work necessary to put what you have learned into practice.

No matter how long we have been married, we all need to remain students in our marriages.

Why is it that we often spend more time and effort becoming better at our jobs or careers—which may or may not last a decade—than we do learning about, and becoming better at, marriage?

Being a wife is a role you will have for many years, so dedicate yourself to learning and growing in it.

We all learned in biology class that the way to tell a living  organism from an inanimate one is by observing any change. After a time, if there is no growth or change, the object is considered to be dead.

The same is true with you and me as individuals and as part of a couple.

We must grow.

As individuals, we must be willing to learn new things and think new thoughts. If we are thinking only the same old thoughts, we won't make it through life the way we are supposed to. We need to meet new people, read new books, take on new challenges, and set new goals. Basically, we need to be lifelong students.

As part of a marriage, I had to grow in a few ways. Primarily, I had to truly become a student of Philip—not only in recognizing his personality strengths and weaknesses, but also in learning his likes, dislikes and needs. From the simple to the more complex—from remembering his favorite food to knowing what he needs when he is hurting—I had a lot to learn. Then, I had to be willing for him to change his mind . . . which meant I had to learn new stuff all over again! The tricky thing for me was learning about him . . . not to change him . . . but to know him.

Some people come crying to a counselor: "He's not the same person I married!" Well, probably not . . . and neither are you. Our tastes, interests and emotional needs change over time. That's what keeps life and relationships interesting, and why we have to continue to be students.

Maybe he needs time to process most things.

Or maybe he likes the computer and television on when he is reading. Perhaps he doesn't like human interruptions when he is studying.

Maybe he is not a big fan of surprises.

Or perhaps he takes his time when making decisions.

Maybe he doesn't like interjections when he is talking. (Maybe he actually calls them interruptions.)

Maybe he reads multiple books at the same time, not always completely finishing any of them.

What if the first thing he wants to do in the morning is turn on his computer?

Do you know that he doesn't like long meals in fancy restaurants?

Now, what if you are completely the opposite in every one of those areas? That can make a marriage challenging! If we're honest, sometimes deep in our hearts, we wish our husbands were more like us . . . and that's not good! Because it means that you have stopped studying who he is, and instead are focusing on who you want him to be.

TEN WAYS TO LOVE YOUR HUSBAND

1. **Be kind.** Most of the time, we are kinder and more polite to strangers and acquaintances than we are to our spouses. It should not be that way, but often it is. Little acts of kindness can go a long way toward creating intimacy.

2. **Demonstrate respect.** You are not his mother, so don't talk down to him or nag him. Interrupting him communicates disrespect (at least, that is what Philip tells me!). So, let him finish his sentences . . . no matter how good you think your ending would be!

3. **Get some sexy lingerie.** Enough said, really.

4. **Occasionally be the sexual aggressor.** He likes/needs to feel that you want him. Don't just be the passive one. Mix it up!

5. **Go with him to a game/sporting event.** He really does want your company. It is not about whether or not you like sports—just doing something with him shows your love. (But you are a smart woman, so surely you can learn a thing or two about the sport while you're at it!)

6. **Kiss him.** I'm not talking about the quick "don't mess up my lipstick" kiss, but the "stop and grab his face" kiss. Even if you don't have time for it to lead anywhere ☺ . . . kissing is such a great connector!

7. **Listen without interrupting.** Yes, I know this one is hard . . .

8. **Encourage him.** Say something encouraging to him. He probably hears negativity all day long from others. What can you say that would be encouraging? What has he done well? Be his biggest cheerleader!!

9. **Say nice things about him in front of others.** This is huge . . . and communicates love in a whole other way.

10. **Show support for his dreams.** Come alongside him and support him. Life has a way of deflating our dreams. Let him know that you are with him and believe in him.

WHAT YOUR MOMMA DIDN'T TELL YOU ABOUT SEX

Great sex is not about how many people you can have intercourse with, but rather the intimacy that occurs in a marriage when two committed people join hearts and bodies. This kind of intimacy grows over the years.

Sex should be fun. We should both experience physical pleasure and touch each other emotionally at a deep level. The average person thinks that Christians are uptight and sexually repressed simply because we have convictions we believe should guide us. But emotionally and sexually healthy Christians experience passionate, uninhibited, hot, laugh-out-loud, heart-stopping and jaw-dropping sex!!!

INGREDIENTS FOR GREAT SEX

1. **Developing good communication.** We have to be willing to discuss our thoughts, fears and feelings. We have to be willing to talk about what we like and what we don't like. And we must be willing to listen without being insecure or rejecting the desires and concerns of our mates.

2. **Honesty.** Honesty is another tool. It's important that we ask (and truthfully answer) questions like . . . "What have I done that you like?" . . . "What have I done that you don't like?" . . . "What makes you uncomfortable?" . . . "In what ways can I touch you that would be arousing?" Questions like these can go a long way toward building understanding and unity.

3. **Being willing to learn, change and grow.** It takes work to have a great sex life. (Or maybe instead of thinking of it as work, we should see it as an investment in our marriage!) If you want to have a better sex life than you do now, you're going to have to change. There is more to learn about sex . . . yes, even for you. Sometimes we act like we know what we're doing, but how would we know if we've never discussed these intimate issues with our spouses?

4. **Keeping a sense of humor.** The best way to break tension is to laugh—not at each other or at the attempts to please . . . but just at the humorous situations that can arise. Relax. Playfulness is part of a great sex life. You can't take yourself so seriously. You have to laugh a little and play a little. This is an enjoyable part of life. You get to learn. You get to practice again and again. Sometimes you get it right and sometimes . . . not so much . . . but you get to try it again tomorrow!

5. **Creativity and imagination.** Eating the same thing for dinner every night would quickly get boring, no matter how good it tasted. In the same way, your sex life might get a bit humdrum if you do not apply your God-given creativity to it.

In today's culture, to promote "creativity," couples are sometimes encouraged to bring pornography—via movies or the Internet—into the bedroom. This is NOT the kind of creativity we mean. Bringing someone else into the bed, even if only on film, will eventually undermine the work you and your husband are doing to become one.

There are plenty of other ways to be creative—just the two of you. Whether it is turning the music on and dancing in the bedroom, or you wearing a sexy

> dress to catch his eye . . . the ideas are endless. We are not going to tell you how to be creative . . . just that you need to be. Whatever ideas you come up with should be things that both of you are comfortable with and enjoy.

It is possible in today's society to build a strong marriage. It really can be done. That said, there will be seasons in a marriage that are more difficult than others.

The season when you have young children who seem to take up all of your time. Don't lose sight of the marriage.

The season when you want children, but can't seem to get pregnant. Don't lose sight of the marriage.

The season of trying to work around two careers, school and a family. Don't lose sight of the marriage.

Philip and I have been married for 27 years, and there were moments in the early years when I wanted out. My bags were packed, and I was leaving. All I can say is: I am so glad I didn't. We really are enjoying the sweet years now. I am more in love with him than I ever have been. So don't give up. Really.

MORE, PLEASE!
(Additional reading)
GodChicks and the Men They Love by Philip and Holly Wagner
Love and Respect by Dr. Emerson Eggerichs
The Triumphant Marriage by Neil Clark Warren, Ph.D.
Creating an Intimate Marriage by Jim Burns

8

Modern Family

HOW TO MAINTAIN A
HEALTHY HOUSEHOLD

*Before I got married I had six theories
about bringing up children; now I
have six children and no theories.*

JOHN WILMOT, EARL OF ROCHESTER

A few years ago, I (Holly) visited Seaside, Florida, which has to be the most perfect-looking town I have ever seen. People in this master planned community, whether visitors or residents, rode bicycles along the perfectly groomed sidewalks . . . to the perfectly clean Starbucks, to the perfect-looking stores, to the perfectly designed school, to the perfectly adorable post office, to the perfect ice cream parlor, to the perfectly beautiful chapel, to the perfect-looking grocery store, to the perfect restaurants, to the perfectly sandy beach, and then back to their perfect-looking homes.

As someone coming from the city of Los Angeles, which is far from perfect-looking, I found this experience to be quite novel. Riding around on my bicycle in this perfect town, I felt like I was on a movie set. In fact, I was. Seaside, Florida, was the community used in the filming of the movie *The Truman Show*. If you have seen the film, you'll recall that it tells the story of a man who was unaware he was living in a totally controlled environment.

However, unlike Truman, we don't live in a bubble.

Our families must figure out how not only to exist, but also to thrive, in the real world, with all of its distractions and complications. Most of us do not live on some remote desert island where we get to focus entirely on one another 24 hours a day. Nope. We have to work out our marriages and our families with all the trappings that come with life in the twenty-first century.

How do we do that and not lose sight of each other?

PAST, PRESENT . . . FUTURE!

We do bring our pasts—good and bad—into our marriages. Each of us enters adulthood with a different background, and those backgrounds will have an effect on our marriage, often feeling like a third person invading our present.

My friend Priscilla Shirer (I call her "my sista from anotha mista") was one of the speakers at our GodChicks conference in 2008. She told a great story that has stuck with me. She and her husband, Jerry, went to minister to a local church. When they arrived, a little exhausted from the weeks leading up to this visit, they were grateful to settle into their hotel and looked forward to getting some rest.

However, they were awakened in a panic around 11 P.M. by the sound of a train whistling past their room. After their near heart attack, they fell back asleep . . . only to be awakened again by the same sound at 1 A.M. . . . and then again at 5:30 in the morning. So much for resting!

When a woman from the church arrived the next morning to drive them to the meeting, Priscilla gently mentioned that the loudest train on the entire planet had kept them up throughout the entire night.

The girl's face turned white as a sheet. She began to apologize profusely and then explained that the people who had been living in the town for years could no longer even hear the train as it went by.

I'd like to suggest that many of us are the same way. We get so used to the voices of our pasts whistling around in our minds that we don't even notice them anymore. We can live with depression, insecurity, jealousy, self-loathing, lust or pride for so long that we no longer recognize their daily impact on our lives.

When another person enters our environment, the voice we have learned to live with is incredibly loud to our partner and may continuously disrupt his rest . . . like the train disrupted Priscilla and Jerry's.

In marriage, hidden issues will come out of hiding. In the light of another's perspective, we will be forced to face our problem areas. Because our spouses don't share our exact struggles, things we have learned to ignore or accommodate will sound like a roaring train to them . . . this is the third person from the past invading our present.

Maybe we had parents who loved us and loved each other, so we are confident in relationships. But there are a lot of us who have been hurt and betrayed . . . and aren't quite so secure in building relationships.

Maybe you experienced years of abuse and are now on a healing journey . . . but it is a journey . . . and your husband will have to be patient while you walk it out. There will be times when your past will interfere with your present. That can be frustrating, and you both have to remain focused on what you are building together.

Maybe he was raised by a single mother and really has no idea what a husband . . . much less a father . . . should do. When you marry him, you are committing to encouraging him on that journey . . . and joining him in working through the frustrations that come with it.

Maybe he expects a home-cooked meal because that's how his mom did it . . . but you have never even been in a kitchen. Maybe you expect him to fix whatever breaks around the house . . . but he has never even held a hammer. Our pasts, along with the expectations that come from them, will enter into the reality of our marriage. So be prepared to deal with them together.

Often our pasts will include a relationship or two (or more). Philip was not the first person to ask me to marry him. He is just the only one to whom I said "I do."

So, like most of us, I came into my marriage with a past. Not a sordid one, because the truth is I only dated great guys. I never spent any time with any man who did not treat me with respect and kindness.

You know that saying that you have to kiss a lot of frogs before one becomes a prince? Not true . . . I kissed no frogs. I wasted no time with frogs. Honestly, I only have great memories of the men I dated before I met Philip.

But that can be a problem, too. In the first few years of our marriage, whenever Philip would make me mad, my head would be full of thoughts of a past boyfriend whom, in that moment, I could only remember as being perfect. I would think, *I should have stayed with _____. He wouldn't be treating me this way.* Also not true. I had said no to that guy for a reason.

We can't prevent our pasts from having an influence on our marriage. But it is crucial that we watch where our thoughts lead us. Keep your focus on today. Stay engaged in this relationship that you are building.

HOME FOR THE HOLIDAYS?!

Some of you love the thought of Christmas approaching. You delight in the anticipation, the shopping, the meals and the family time. Others of you dread the whole season, wishing the calendar would quickly turn from the day before Thanksgiving to January 2. Most of our feelings about Christmas come from our memories of childhood Christmases.

Here's the thing.

You are not a child anymore. If you have great memories of Christmas, it is because someone made your Christmas great. Now you are the grownup. It is your turn to make Christmas great for someone else.

If you have painful holiday memories, then it is now your turn to create new ones.

Be careful about getting sentimental.

Be careful about wasting time wishing your memories were different.

Going to visit your family for Christmas can be a good thing . . . and it can be a painful time.

If going to see your family only brings you pain . . . why go? If you keep hoping that your dad won't get drunk this time, or your mom won't constantly berate you, then maybe you should stay away. Or at least keep your visit brief.

As a grownup, you get to make your own traditions.

If you are married, you have a new family . . . and you get to create your own holiday memories.

FIVE HOLIDAY TRADITIONS TO CONSIDER

1. Attend a candlelight service

2. Have a special Christmas breakfast

3. Read the story of Jesus' birth before you open gifts

4. Invite friends to Christmas dinner

5. Go see a movie Christmas night

FOR THOSE OF YOU WITH CHILDREN: TWELVE WAYS TO MANAGE LIFE AND PICK UP KIDS FROM SOCCER PRACTICE ON TIME

1. Post a calendar somewhere in your house so that everyone knows who is going where.

2. Trade babysitting with other parents.

3. Keep dinner simple. Especially if both parents work outside the home, this can be a challenging hour. But it doesn't have to be. The point is to have a meal together . . . not to impress your gourmet neighbor.

4. Get school clothes and lunches ready the night before.

5. Do a lot of laughing. For instance, when your third-grade son tells you that his science project is due tomorrow and he hasn't even started it . . .

6. Get up earlier in the morning. Even a few extra minutes will help because something always comes up. Rushing around and that feeling of "running late" cause stress for everyone.

7. Limit the number of teams and after-school activities your kids are involved in. They can't do everything at the same time . . . and neither can you.

8. Carpool with other families.

9. Plan the days of the week that the house gets cleaned, or on which day which part gets done.

10. Plan a laundry day . . . or two or four or even six! ☺

11. Plan meals in advance, maybe a week at a time, so that trips to the grocery are minimized and advance preparations can be made. If it is a freezable meal, then make double and freeze one.

12. Forgive yourself when you don't get it right!

SIX ORGANIZATIONAL TIPS (SO YOU DON'T END UP ON *HOARDERS!*)

1. Have a landing strip. This is the bowl or tray that you put everything in when you come home. That way you are not always looking for your keys, phone and other pocket-sized belongings.

2. Clean as you go. Really. Makes all the difference.

3. Everything in its place.

4. If your house is currently an organizational nightmare . . . start small. One room at a time. You can do it!

5. Use a calendar. Either the paper kind or an online version will work . . . as long as you remember to use it!!

6. How many things do you really need to collect??? Most of them just become "dust catchers."

EIGHT WAYS TO CLEAN YOUR HOUSE QUICKLY ('CUZ GUESTS ARE COMING OVER!)

1. Take out the trash.

2. Clean the mirrors and windows.

3. Get dirty dishes out of the sink.

4. Make your bed.

5. Do something with that pile of paper.

6. Vacuum the common areas.

7. Do a quick wipe-down of the bathroom.

8. Light a candle.

JUST A REMINDER FOR THOSE OF YOU WITH CHILDREN . . .

Your children are not the center of the home.

My children are a blessing.

Most of the time.

It has certainly been work raising them, and there have been moments along the way when I wondered how I would get through certain parenting phases . . . or if my kids would survive them! The miracle of it all is looking at their faces and seeing some of me, some of Philip, and mostly just them. They are wonderfully unique individuals with their own purposes in God.

For many of us, children are part of our lives as we work out our marriages. We might want to ship them off to Siberia sometimes, but we don't . . . although I now know people who live there, so if you are interested, we have connections! ☻ Of course, we invest tremendous amounts of time, energy and affection in our kids—and that's a good thing. The problem is when our children become the center of our marriage.

From birth to 18 years old is 6,570 days (well, it is if you don't count leap years). This is roughly the amount of time your children will be with you on a daily basis. Obviously, our children remain our children forever, but the daily input will last for about 6,570 days. If Philip and I are blessed to have a 60-year marriage (just 33 more years to go!), we will have been married for 21,900 days.

6,570 days.

21,900 days.

Do the math.

Assuming all goes as we hope it will, the time our children spend living with us is much shorter than the span of our marriage, which is why it is not in the best interest of the relationship to make our children the center of it. They are a vital part, but not the center.

I made this mistake with my son, Jordan. After he was born, I did not leave him—even for a few hours—for many months. He was the center of my world. His needs took priority over Philip's. His cry was louder and more demanding, so I accommodated him. What ended up happening was that my marriage wound up on the back burner. This certainly wasn't a conscious decision—it just happened as I looked to meet my child's needs instead of my husband's. Eventually I started feeling more and more disconnected from Philip.

I had some ground to make up.

Fixing the problem was as simple as realizing a few things. First, I needed to get Jordan on some kind of schedule, so that he fit in with our family instead of running it. There are some great parenting resources out there that can help with this. It is so important! Your children are a blessing from God . . . not to distract you from His purpose, but to join you on the journey.

Secondly, I realized that I needed to go on a date with my husband. We needed to spend some hours together as a couple. Jordan would be fine.

Over the years, we have learned that regardless of the ages of our children, we need time as a couple. Time away from the kids. Time to remind each other that we got together for relationship, and not just the work of a marriage. Often, if we don't take that time, our communication can simply be:

"Who's cooking dinner?"

"Who's picking up the kids?"

"Did you sign the permission slip?"

"He forgot his lunch—can you take it to the school?"

This is all necessary communication, but intimacy requires just a bit more!

Do your homework to find a good babysitter, and then go out to dinner or go on a walk. It doesn't really matter what the activity is—just that it's something where you reconnect on a regular basis.

We have also made it a practice to have not only family vacations, but also Philip and Holly vacations. When our children were younger, we might just be gone for a few nights, and then come back and get the kids before embarking on our longer family vacation. But eventually, it got to be that Philip and I would spend a week together somewhere . . . just the two of us. Then Paris and Jordan might join us. But that week alone with Philip would remind me why I married him! We needed that time away as a couple.

I have talked to some couples with young children who say they would love to go out, but their children cry when they leave . . . and that makes it too hard. I understand that. I remember how difficult it was initially to leave our children in the hands of a babysitter, no matter how qualified the sitter was. But let me tell you what going out on a date teaches the children. It teaches them that the husband-wife relationship is a very high priority in the family. It teaches them that Mommy and Daddy love to spend time together. The best thing you and your spouse can do for your children is to love each other.

We are to love our kids. We want the best for them. But making them the center of the family universe is not in their best interests. Nor does it serve our world to have a generation of young people who think the world revolves around them. It will certainly not serve your marriage well either.

I also found we had to be careful about how many activities Jordan and Paris got involved in. I have loved watching them both play various sports over the years. But I have tried to limit it to one at a time. Otherwise, Philip and I would be so busy keeping up with their schedules that it would be tricky for us, in our already very full lives, to find time together.

Another thing to remember is that it's important for parents to present a united front. Do not let your children, or their desires, drive a wedge between you and your spouse. If you disagree about the way something should be handled with the kids . . . driving, curfew, spending the night away from home, whatever . . . don't disagree in front of them. Go discuss the issue behind closed doors, and then present whatever decision you come to together to your children.

Really, parenting is the process of teaching and training your children to leave your home and begin lives of their own. That might sound strange, but it is true. Our job is to equip our kids to leave us well.

(Just as a confession . . . I am already working on my apology to the woman who marries my son. I failed. While he is one of the smartest, most compassionate and fun-loving young men I know [that's the part I did right!], he has no idea how to do laundry or clean anything. Maybe there is some sort of crash course I can send him to!)

> Therefore a man shall leave his father and mother and be joined to his wife, and they shall become one flesh (Gen. 2:24, NKJV).

Children are supposed to leave, and parents are supposed to stay. Thus the marriage should be at the top of the chart. Navigating life with children is fun, but it is also hard work. Don't let the work of it cause you to lose sight of each other.

TEN THOUGHTS ABOUT PREGNANCY

1. **Pray!** There is nothing more important than praying for your new baby, your relationship with your spouse, and the transition into parenting. God is the creator of life and the One who will give you peace and comfort in this exciting and challenging season. Pray, pray, pray!

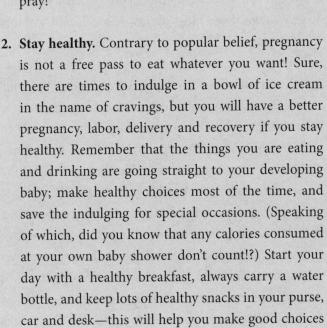

2. **Stay healthy.** Contrary to popular belief, pregnancy is not a free pass to eat whatever you want! Sure, there are times to indulge in a bowl of ice cream in the name of cravings, but you will have a better pregnancy, labor, delivery and recovery if you stay healthy. Remember that the things you are eating and drinking are going straight to your developing baby; make healthy choices most of the time, and save the indulging for special occasions. (Speaking of which, did you know that any calories consumed at your own baby shower don't count!?) Start your day with a healthy breakfast, always carry a water bottle, and keep lots of healthy snacks in your purse, car and desk—this will help you make good choices

throughout the day. Continue to exercise (talk to your doctor if you are unsure about what you should and shouldn't do).

3. **Get connected with other moms.** We are not meant to do life alone, especially when raising children! Find other moms with whom you can connect, share advice (and clothes!), swap tips, and pray. Join a new moms' group so you can share the season you're in together. It's equally important to find moms with older kids to get a different perspective. If you don't know those moms, look for older kids whom you would love to see your baby emulate one day—take those kids' moms to lunch and ask lots of questions!

4. **It's not all about the baby.** It may seem like your whole world is focused on your baby right now, but make an effort not to completely succumb to babymania. I'm sure your friends who don't have kids are very excited for you, but they probably don't want to hear every detail of your latest OB appointment. Just sayin'. Plus, your pregnancy is a great time to focus on your dreams and passions as a mother and as a daughter of the King. Fulfilling your own purpose will help your kids discover theirs. You may need to make a few changes in your life in those first years of parenthood, but don't lose sight

of your God-given purpose in the midst of diapers and midnight feedings. Stay connected beyond your baby—keep serving at church, read books that have more than five words on a page, go out on a date with your husband, or have a baby-free girls night. Ask someone to keep you accountable on this one, because it's very easy to get caught in the baby bubble!

5. **Educate yourself.** Unfortunately, babies don't come with manuals! It is up to you to educate yourself about your pregnancy, delivery and parenting options. Read, learn and ask questions. Even if all your friends did something one way, do your own research and decide what is best for your family. There is a lot of good (and bad!) information out there, so be sure to look at a lot of different resources—no one is responsible for your pregnancy and baby except for you (and your husband).

6. **Trust your instincts.** God has given you everything you need to be an excellent mother. Isn't that amazing?? Go to Him every day (see #1) and ask Him to give you the peace, patience and understanding to make great decisions for your child. When something just doesn't seem right, trust that the Holy Spirit is the primary source of your capabilities as a mother—stop and listen.

7. **Assemble a good team around you.** Thankfully, there are many resources available to you during pregnancy, delivery, recovery and parenting. Choose your support team carefully—doctors, midwives, doulas, nurses, lactation consultants, birth educators, pediatricians and whomever else you wish to involve. Make sure you feel comfortable with the people who will be helping you bring this new life into the world. You will be so happy to have a team you trust during this very emotional and precious time of life.

8. **Include your spouse.** Let's be honest, there are a lot of elements of pregnancy and new babies that just freak some men out. You may have a husband who wants to make every decision with you, or one who is completely confused and overwhelmed by the whole thing. Make sure you are including him and valuing his opinion. It might seem easier to make decisions on your own or with your mom, sister or girlfriend. But if you shut out your husband now, don't expect him to jump into Super Dad mode overnight. Establish yourself and your husband as a parenting team early on, and make sure he knows how valuable he is.

9. **Be thankful.** Come from a place of gratitude, thanking God every day for the blessing of being able to carry His creation. This attitude will change your pregnancy. Women who live in a place of thankfulness

have healthier pregnancies and a better transition into motherhood. Of course, there are moments (morning sickness, anyone!?) that are not comfortable or fun, but complaining constantly won't help and can be hurtful to the many women who are not able to get pregnant. Focus on the prize at the end of your discomfort—a sweet baby!

10. **Don't compare.** This is your pregnancy, not a competition. It's so easy to compare weight gain, baby development, parenting choices, nursery decor, and a hundred other things. Allow yourself to enjoy your pregnancy journey for what it is for you, not what it is compared to your friend's pregnancy. Don't waste your time on jealousy or competition; be confident in who God created you to be and you will enjoy your pregnancy so much more!

SEVEN WAYS TO COMMUNICATE WITH YOUR CHILD

According to author Deanne C. Haisch, M.A., if getting your child to do something feels like an impossible task, it may be because of the way you are asking. The instructions we give to our children must be spoken in a way that they will understand. Here are some helpful hints on how to give your kids instructions that will make both you and your child more successful.

1. **Get your child's attention.** Make sure you have your child's attention before you give a direction. Doing this will help your son or daughter know that you are speaking to him or her. Call your child's name, make eye contact, or turn off the light. Also, try to put yourself within about three feet of your child so you can speak at a normal volume and in a calm voice.

2. **Be clear and concise.** Make sure your instructions are short and to the point. A good guide is one word per year of life (for example, instruction for a two-year-old might be "shoes on," while you could tell a five-year-old to "go get your shoes on"). If you use too many words, your children will have difficulty in knowing what is expected of them. The instruction should also be free of vague words.

3. **Give one instruction at a time.** Giving multiple instructions to your child can overwhelm him or her.

4. **Be realistic.** Give your child instructions that you know he or she can actually follow.

5. **Be positive.** Tell your child what you want him or her to *do* rather than *not do*. If you only describe a negative behavior ("don't run"), you leave the door open for your child to some other types of behaviors that you don't want (skipping, hopping, sliding). However, if

you give a positive direction ("please walk"), it closes
the door on your child doing other options.

6. **Don't ask, tell.** Always try to tell your child in a firm
   but pleasant voice what you want him or her to do.
   Again, don't say something like, "Will you not run
   in the hallway?" as this might indicate to your child
   that he or she has a choice in the matter. Instead, say,
   "Please walk in the hallway."

7. **Reward compliance.** Let your child know when
   he or she does a good job following your instructions. The more you praise your child, the better the
   chances are that he or she will follow your directions
   in the future.[1]

TEN INEXPENSIVE WAYS TO ENTERTAIN YOUNG CHILDREN

1. Bubbles!

2. Play in the dirt with spoons and bowls.

3. Large cardboard boxes.

4. Paper airplanes.

5. Hopscotch.

6. Turn on the music and dance!

7. Homemade pizza (they get to put whatever they want on theirs!)

8. Water sprinkler.

9. Make a tin-can telephone.

10. Go read books at the library.

GET PLANTED!!!

The righteous will flourish like a palm tree, they will grow like a cedar of Lebanon; **planted in the house of the Lord, they will flourish in the courts of our God.** *They will still bear fruit in old age, they will stay fresh and green.*

PSALM 92:12-14 (EMPHASIS ADDED)

The Bible is pretty clear. If we want our lives to flourish—and I would imagine most of us do—we must be planted in the house of God . . . in church. Planted. Not just attending. But planted, with roots going down, taking in nutrients, and leaves sprouting, giving off oxygen.

Planted. Learning, growing and serving.

Planted. Not moving from church to church.

Planted. So that people know you.

Planted. So that people can hold you accountable to living the God-life.

Planted. So that when life is hard, people know how to pray for you.

Planted. So that when life is good, people celebrate with you.

Interestingly enough, the Bible does not say we will flourish if we have a great job, buy a great house, or live in a great neighborhood. No. It says our life will flourish if we are planted in the house of God. All of the good stuff—including a strong marriage and healthy family—comes out of being planted in God's house.

My life revolves around being planted in the house of God. I don't just clock in and out, as if my attending church is an obligation or is doing God a big favor. No. I am committed to these people in my world. We are not just "church friends." We call it "doing life together." We are every day, every season kind of friends.

The theme song of the old sitcom *Cheers* basically says that we all want to go to places where we are known and where people are glad to see us. That's what happens when you are planted in God's house. You are known and valued.

Maybe you are experiencing such pain in a relationship right now that loneliness is overwhelming you. You and I were created for relationship, so when there is a disconnect, we feel lonely and isolated. I have good news:

God sets the lonely in families (Ps. 68:6).

He brings the lonely, which is often you and me, into the family and house of God . . . to connect and to do life with people!

Connecting into a life-giving church is one of the best things you can do for yourself and your marriage.

Because I am planted in God's house, I have surrounded myself with people who are committed to making a difference on the planet. We are determined to build healthy homes because we realize that as our own homes and families get stronger, we become better equipped to minister to others in our world.

And that's why we are here! To bring light into dark places. Our churches and our families should be beacons of light, guiding those who are frustrated, hurt, lost and confused to the place where they can receive help and refreshing. Sometimes one of the best things you can do is take your eyes off your own pain for a moment and focus on helping other hurting people.

MORE, PLEASE!
(Additional Reading)
*Clueless: 10 Things I Wish I Knew About Motherhood
Before Becoming a Mom* by Kerri Weems
Making Children Mind without Losing Yours by Dr. Kevin Leman
Organizing from the Inside Out by Julie Morgenstern

9

Moving Forward

OVERCOMING HURTS OF THE PAST

You are responsible for your life. You can't keep blaming somebody else for your dysfunction. Life is really about moving on.

OPRAH WINFREY

EXCESS BAGGAGE

Excess baggage. It's expensive. It's heavy. It tends to get in the way of perfectly good legroom or hog all the space in an overhead compartment. No one particularly likes it . . . mostly because it slows everyone down.

Then there's the excess baggage of the heart: those less-than-perfect experiences of the past that have a way of weighing us down on our way to the future . . .

Betrayals . . . Insecurities . . . Rejections . . . Failures . . . Heartbreak . . . Fear . . . Abuse . . . Addictions . . . Shame . . .

A word was spoken in anger. A parent was too busy working to notice a need. A father abandoned the home. A friend betrayed our trust. A boyfriend unexpectedly ended the relationship. A business deal didn't go as planned. A few bad decisions left us wallowing in guilt and shame.

It doesn't matter whether we were raised in a strong Christian home with loving parents or in a harmful, dysfunctional home (or, like many of us, somewhere in between). Regardless of our experience, one thing is certain: We each have our own excess baggage of the heart. And what we do with it matters.

Quite honestly, this type of baggage is far more dangerous and costly than a couple of extra carry-ons at the airport. Overweight luggage may slow us down just enough to miss a connecting flight, but untended wounds of the heart have the potential to slow us down just enough to miss out on our God-given destiny.

I (Nicole) had more than my share of excess baggage as a 19-year-old first stepping through the doors of what has since become my church home (Oasis Church).

You see, I grew up in a home with two funny, smart and hard-working parents who frequently told me they loved me . . .

. . . They just didn't always show it in the best possible way. They had some excess baggage from their own childhood experiences, and all that baggage left them unable to create the healthiest environment for my older sister and me.

My father was an alcoholic until I was 10 years old. This caused constant tension, which often erupted in the form of my parents fighting and threatening each other with divorce. My father, feeling disrespected in his own home, would regularly lash out at my mom. Though I couldn't articulate it at the time, I now realize that my mother was both verbally and emotionally abused by my father on a regular basis.

These of course were things we never discussed outside of our home. Even within the family, we struggled to give voice to our feelings. My sister and I often found ourselves (from a very early age) looking after the emotional well-being of both of our parents. In many ways, this left us confused about what healthy and loving relationships looked like.

By the time I reached my late teens, I had discovered my voice in my home—it was loud and it was angry! Years of bitterness and resentment toward my father came out in a number of full-on, hold-nothing-back fights. We really duked it out! In the end, neither of us emerged the victor of those emotional boxing matches. We both lost. We lost our relationship.

For about two years, we lived under the same roof, but hardly spoke a word to each other. Our conversations began and ended with one of us saying, "Pass the salt" at the dinner table.

I never realized until then just how painful silence could be.

When I left home and moved to Los Angeles to pursue an acting career, I couldn't get away fast enough. I wanted nothing to do with my father. The more distance I could put between myself and my family, the better!

I had surrendered my life to Jesus when I was 12 years old. I accepted His salvation and pursued His plans for my life.

None of that changed the fact that I was an emotional mess when I first became a part of my local church 10 years ago. I was broken by the wounds of my childhood, and I was relationally isolated and afraid. I didn't know how to connect with people. I didn't even know how to identify people who were safe to connect with. I was extremely guarded and preferred to find

love in how well I performed than in healthy, Christian friendships and relationships.

Talk about baggage!

I'm so thankful for the healing journey God has taken me on as a young woman! He has been faithful to heal my wounds and bring joy and strength to my relationships! God has also done MIRACLES (some suddenly, but most of them years in the making) in my family! My father overcame his addiction to alcohol. My parents have done the hard work of saving their marriage and are happily married to this day! I now have a loving and healthy relationship with my father!

God has taught me how to let go of my past and my hurts, and He can do the same for you! Jesus gave His life for us so that we might become healthy and whole. God doesn't want any of us to live our lives hurting and alone. You and I were fashioned and created for so much more!

My prayer is that as you read this chapter, you will have the courage to hand over your excess baggage to Jesus and learn how to pursue a whole and healthy heart! The truth is that you and I weren't meant to carry excess baggage, and Jesus is the only One strong enough *to* carry it. You may have to unpack some of those nicely kept but unbearably heavy issues of the soul—and that can be painful—but I am confident that as you open the hurting places of your heart to Him, you will begin to experience what it means to live light and free!

> Come to me, all you who are weary and burdened, and I will give you rest. Take my yoke upon you and learn from me, for I am gentle and humble in heart, and you will find rest for your souls. For my yoke is easy and my burden is light (Matt. 11:28-30).

WHO'S SAFE?

When I (Nicole) was four years old, my family moved to 8th Street, where we lived in a beige house at the end of a cul-de-sac. That house became more than a house; for the next 10 years, it was home. Similarly, 8th Street became more than a residential street; it served as the setting for my many adventures with my two neighborhood friends, Rick and Brandon.

It was my mom who first encouraged me to go introduce myself to Rick and Brandon. She saw me watching them through my bedroom window as they played outside. They were playing catch, and I desperately wanted to join them.

For two days, I continued to watch them. That's how long it took me to work up the courage to leave my safe bedroom viewpoint and awkwardly ask if I could play with them.

I hated being the new kid in the neighborhood.

I was afraid they would laugh at me and tell me I couldn't play with them because I was a girl. To my surprise, we exchanged names, and by the end of the week we were all best friends.

For the next eight years, we were inseparable. We dreamed dreams together, laughed together, and occasionally fought with one another. We always had each other's backs, and we each believed we were the best friends anyone could ever ask for.

I'll admit we occasionally even got into a little mischief together. ☺

Our parents used to call us the Three Musketeers. We were too little to really understand the reference, but we understood that it meant something special . . .

We understood that our friendship was something special.

We each eventually moved away from our childhood neighborhood, and our adventures together came to an end. In fact, it's been 16 years since we've seen one another.

But I will be forever grateful for Rick and Brandon and the childhood memories we shared.

As I've gotten older, I've realized that friendships and relationships don't come that easily. It takes more than a week of playing catch on 8th Street to become best friends. We

have to work a bit harder to create truly special relationships. A key part of the process is figuring out which people are safe to develop relationships with.

It can be hard to recognize who the safe people are, especially if, like me, you were not always exposed to safe people in your home growing up. But healthy, Jesus-centered relationships are ones where both you and the other person are **safe.** Below are two lists to help guide you. While reading over these lists, you may want to think and pray about how you can become a safer person and ask yourself how you can actively choose to invest in relationships with safe people.

TEN QUALITIES OF SAFE PEOPLE

1. Safe people have authentic, growing relationships with Jesus and are pursuing His plans for their lives.

2. They are able to engage in healthy conflict, speaking truth in love and working through differences.

3. They are accepting of others and show grace to those around them.

4. They have great relationships with other friends besides you and encourage you to have great relationships with other friends besides them.

5. They have values similar to yours.

6. They are quick to forgive.

7. They avoid gossip and bad-mouthing others.

8. They are eager to serve and help others.

9. They are generous with their time and resources.

10. They want to learn and grow in all areas of life.

TEN QUALITIES OF UNSAFE PEOPLE

1. Unsafe people have a hard time admitting when they are struggling with something or going through a tough time.

2. They are defensive and receive advice as criticism.

3. They are overly critical of others.

4. They consistently fail to follow through with what they said they would do.

5. They blame others instead of taking responsibility for their own actions.

6. They are envious of others' successes and frequently compare themselves to others.

7. They get jealous of other friendships you are investing in.

8. They lie to avoid consequences and conflict.

9. They have a hard time respecting and honoring those in positions of authority.

10. They try to influence and encourage you to do things that will negatively impact your relationship with Jesus.

THE F-WORD: FORGIVENESS
Without forgiveness, there's no future.
ARCHBISHOP DESMOND TUTU

Archbishop Tutu knows what he's talking about. The only way to move forward and embrace the grand purpose and destiny God has in store for each of us is to forgive those who have wronged us in the past.

Now I know that for many of us, this concept of forgiveness is a hard pill to swallow. In fact, some of you reading this may be contemplating stapling this section of the book together and never looking at it again!

Many of you are thinking . . .

"Well, you don't know what he did to me."

"You've never had those harsh words spoken to you."

"What they did is just too cruel to forgive."

You are right. I don't know what you've been through . . . and I am deeply sorry that you have been wounded and hurt by those you've trusted. Something I do know is that our heavenly Father is head over heels in love with you, and He is not for a minute okay with the wrongs that have been done to you!

I also know that what's even worse than the pain of our pasts is what happens to us when we allow that pain to plague our presents and sabotage our futures.

Unforgiveness is a trap. It keeps us chained to pain and disappointment, and unable to freely embrace the abundant life that Jesus came, died and rose from the dead to give us.

Unforgiveness is also like a cancer that spreads in our souls. It taints all of our relationships, ambitions and experiences with bitterness and resentment. It's the worst kind of disease, with the capacity to destroy any of our hopes for the future.

I (Nicole) will never forget hearing a woman share her story at a GodChicks night many years ago. I was 19 years old and fiercely loyal to the idea of never forgiving my father for what I had experienced in my home growing up. I was completely bitter and angry and determined to keep as much distance as possible between my father and me. Of course, these are the sorts of thoughts I didn't articulate to my Christian friends. In fact, I made it a point not to talk about my feelings toward my dad with anyone, mostly because I knew how ugly and unkind these feelings really were.

Instead, I had made a choice in my heart not to speak to my father. For a little while, I kept that resolution.

But that all changed as I sat listening to this courageous woman share the story of abuse she had been exposed to in her home as a child. She shared about how a real relationship with Jesus had brought healing and hope to her life. She described this healing journey as a process, and said an important step in that process was FORGIVENESS. She recognized that she had to forgive her mother and father for what had been done to her when she was a child. She encouraged all of us to make the strong, hard choice to forgive those who had wronged us.

I thought, *Forgiveness?! You've got to be kidding me! I am never going to forgive my dad! He should be asking me for forgiveness, and until he does, I'm not even going to entertain the thought!*

But no matter how hard I tried to fight it, by the time she reached the end of her story, I knew that as much as I hated the idea of forgiveness, it was what God was leading me to do . . .

I kicked and screamed in my heart over the idea. I cried and prayed all the way home that night. I remember praying, "This is too hard, God. I can't do it. How am I supposed to forgive him? Why would You ask me to do something this hard? Don't You love me?"

I truly believe this was our loving and wonderful heavenly Father's response to me: "I do love you. More than you could ever know. It's because I love you that I want you to forgive. I want you free, and you won't be free without forgiveness."

That night I called my father. We hadn't exchanged words in a very long time. In fact, I was surprised that he took my call. I suppose he was just as surprised that I had called in the first place.

I clenched the phone in my hand so tightly that my knuckles turned white. My hands wouldn't stop shaking. I struggled to control my voice as it cracked and swayed under the weight of confined tears.

To my dismay, and by God's grace, I listened as these words poured out of my mouth: "Papi, I just wanted to call to tell you that I love you. And I am sorry. I want to ask for your forgiveness, because for so long I have been angry and bitter toward you. That's not right of me. I want you to know that I love you, and I am deeply sorry my love has been in question."

Then came an awkward silence that seemed to last forever. It may have been the longest pause of my life.

My father finally spoke. I could hear the tears in his shaking voice as he told me that he loved me, and that it was he who was sorry for all that had taken place.

It wasn't a long conversation that night. But some things don't have to be everlasting to be eternal.

My relationship with my father wasn't supernaturally repaired in one night. It had taken years for the brokenness to be formed, and it would take years for it to fully mend. But a bridge of reconciliation that I never imagined possible was built over the act of FORGIVENESS.

Perhaps even more miraculous was the shift that had taken place in my heart. It was as if a chain wrapped around me had burst open. I was beginning to understand the personal freedom that comes with forgiveness. Once I experienced this type of freedom, I resolved never to willingly allow myself to be chained and weighted down by unforgiveness again.

Forgiveness unlocks purpose and destiny. It allows us to run freely toward our future. It replaces skepticism with hope, and bitterness with love. Forgiveness is not an emotion. If you stop and think about it, you'll realize that forgiveness is never anything we naturally feel like doing.

No, forgiveness is a choice. It's a choice we have to make over and over again. We may have to choose in our hearts to forgive someone a hundred times before the pain of the wrong loses its sting.

In fact, Jesus addressed this very point with His disciples:

> Then Peter came to him and asked, "Lord, how often should I forgive someone who sins against me? Seven times?"

> "No, not seven times," Jesus replied, "but seventy times seven!" (Matt. 18:21-22, NLT).

It is worth noting that forgiveness is not an invitation to allow someone to continue to harm us. I am so thankful that I was able to reconcile with my father and rebuild a loving relationship with him. For some of us, that may not be an option. There is a difference between forgiving someone and putting yourself in a harmful situation. You may need to seek the advice and support of your pastor or another Christian leader to help you navigate a particular situation. Remember, forgiveness is something we freely give, but trust is something that is earned.

Whether or not relationships are made new, our perspective on life certainly is. Forgiveness unleashes the God-given potential for greatness that lies within each of us. My prayer is that you will have the courage to embrace the type of freedom only accessible through FORGIVENESS. After all, you were made for far more than a life confined by past hurts.

DIRTY MINDS

Usually this phrase is associated with crude jokes, and it is often followed by someone adding, "Get your head out of the gutter!" Though impure thoughts are certainly one element of a less-than-squeaky-clean mind, there are all kinds of thoughts that pollute our brains as they run through them!

"I'm not pretty enough."

"I'm not smart enough."

"I'm a loser."

"If people knew the real me, they would reject me."

"God is angry at me."

"I'm going to end up all alone."

"Something bad is going to happen—I just know it."

This is not the way God thinks about us. He loves us, and His thoughts toward us are good and loving!

A key to overcoming our past hurts is to recognize these types of filthy thoughts and throw them in the trash! Then, to make sure these thoughts stay in the dumpster where they belong, we must discover and focus on what God thinks about us!

We purify our minds when we get rid of negative thoughts and replace them with God-thoughts!

The great news is that we don't have to wonder what God thinks about us! He makes His thoughts clear and accessible to us through His Word. So grab your Bible, read, and let God's Word perform a deep cleaning of your mind!

WHAT GOD REALLY THINKS ABOUT YOU...

...YOU are the loved-beyond-measure daughter of the King.

God put his love on the line for us by offering his Son in sacrificial death while we were of no use whatever to him (Rom. 5:8, THE MESSAGE).

My choice is you, God, first and only. And now I find I'm your choice! You set me up with a house and yard. And then you made me your heir! (Ps. 16:5-6, THE MESSAGE*).*

...YOU are precious and valuable to God.

Are not five sparrows sold for two pennies? And [yet] not one of them is forgotten or uncared for in the presence of God. But [even] the very hairs of your head are all numbered. Do not be struck with fear or seized with alarm; you are of greater worth than many [flocks] of sparrows (Luke 12:6-7, AMP).

. . . YOU are beautiful in the sight of God.

Gabriel greeted her:
Good morning!
You're beautiful with God's beauty,
Beautiful inside and out!
God be with you (Luke 1:28, THE MESSAGE).

. . . YOU are wonderfully made.

When I look at the night sky
and see the work of your fingers—
The moon and the stars you set in place
What are mere mortals
that you should think about them,
Human beings that you should care for them?
Yet you made them only a little lower than God
and crowned them with glory and honor (Ps. 8:3-5, NLT).

. . . YOU are never alone; God is always with you.

He [God] Himself has said, I will not in any way fail
you nor give you up nor leave you without support. [I
will] not, [I will] not, [I will] not in any degree leave
you helpless nor forsake nor let [you] down (relax My
hold on you)! [Assuredly not!] (Heb. 13:5, AMP).

... YOU are not defined by your past, but you are now a new creation in Christ Jesus.

Therefore if any person is [ingrafted] in Christ (the Messiah) he is a new creation (a new creature altogether); the old [previous moral and spiritual condition] has passed away. Behold, the fresh and new has come! (2 Cor. 5:17, AMP).

... YOU have a hope and a future in Jesus.

For I know the thoughts and plans that I have for you, says the Lord, thoughts and plans for welfare and peace and not for evil, to give you hope in your final outcome (Jer. 29:11, AMP).

... YOU have a special purpose and destiny.

We are assured and know that [God being a partner in their labor] all things work together and are [fitting into a plan] for good to and for those who love God and are called according to [His] design and purpose (Rom. 8:28, AMP).

... YOU can do all things through Jesus who gives you strength.

I know how to be abased, and I know how to abound. Everywhere and in all things I have learned both to

*be full and to be hungry, both to abound and to suffer
need. I can do all things through Christ who strength-
ens me* (Phil. 4:12-13, NKJV).

SUIT UP!

Overcoming past hurts is no small task! In fact, it's a battle of the
mind—perhaps the greatest battle you will ever face.

A soldier goes to battle suited up for a fight! You won't find her
engaging the enemy in a summer dress and some flip-flops! She
enters the war zone with a helmet, a bulletproof vest, camou-
flage, boots, and a deadly weapon.

When it comes to overcoming our pasts,
we too need to dress the part! The Bible
describes this very outfit in Ephesians
6:13-17:

Therefore, put on every piece of
God's armor so you will be able
to resist the enemy in the time
of evil. Then after the battle you
will still be standing firm. Stand your
ground, putting on the belt of truth and
the body armor of God's righteousness. For shoes, put
on the peace that comes from the Good News so that
you will be fully prepared. In addition to all of these,
hold up the shield of faith to stop the fiery arrows of
the devil. Put on salvation as your helmet, and take the
sword of the Spirit, which is the word of God (NLT).

Determine to overcome the wounds of your past! Stand your ground! Take back what the enemy of your soul has stolen! Defeat every insecurity, fear, doubt and worry you are attacked with! Your victory begins the moment you decide to suit up!

THE PERFECT SMILE

She dresses with strength and nobility, and she smiles at the future.

PROVERBS 31:25, GOD'S WORD

Life is made up of moments—so many, in fact, that we would never be able to remember them all. Some memories seem a bit random, while some memories we wish we could forget. Others we simply treasure . . .

The moment we held that diploma in our hand. The moment we first saw our groom as we walked down the aisle. The moment our boss told us all our hard work didn't go unnoticed, and we got the promotion. The moment we said yes to the nervous but adorable guy who just asked us to coffee. The moment the doctor confirmed we were pregnant.

These are the types of moments that have a way of leaving big smiles on our faces. In fact, some of us are grinning ear-to-ear just thinking about them!

The same way we smile at these special moments in our pasts, God wants us to smile at our futures. He doesn't want us to be afraid of what might happen—or worried about how it will all turn out. If you are like me, then perhaps some experiences from your past have left you skeptical of your future. You may believe that something bad always ends up happening. Maybe you are convinced that people close to you will end up hurting you, rejecting you, or abandoning you.

When we entrust our lives to Jesus, we discover that His plans for us are good! We can walk confidently into the future, because we know that He is with us, leading and guiding us each step of the way! We don't have to live in fear that our pasts will rewrite themselves in our futures. God has His very best in store for us! That's not to 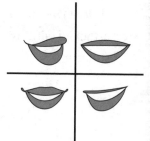 say there won't be any more challenging moments. There will be. That's an inevitability we can't avoid. But when we follow Jesus, we can live in the certainty that we can overcome any and every challenge that comes our way! And we can always anticipate that when it comes to following Jesus, the best is yet to come!

Are you able to smile at your future? Do you trust that Jesus has His very best in store for you as you daily follow Him? What fears and doubts from your past are stealing your joy about the future?

Choose today—and every day—to trust Jesus with what's to come! Go ahead and show off those pearly whites! ☻ Your best days lie ahead!

LOOK AROUND

When it comes to our own hurts, it's easy to develop a bit of tunnel vision. The emotional aftermath of a painful experience can feel all-consuming. If we're not careful, our own pain can blind us to the needs of those around us.

God not only wants us to notice the needs of others, but He also positions us to lend a helping hand. When you and I reach beyond our own pain to lift someone else up, we discover strength we didn't know we had! As crazy as it may seem, God uses our simplest acts of service to bring healing and purpose to our hearts.

Here are a few ideas for serving others as you embark on healing the wounds of your past:

1. Begin serving in your local church and discover how you can use your unique gifts and talents in God's house!

2. Share your story with someone who is struggling in an area you have overcome. By sharing what Jesus has done in your life and what you have learned, you can be the encouragement someone else desperately needs!

3. Volunteer at a homeless shelter or other nonprofit organization with which your local church partners.

4. Be a "big sister" to a younger woman in your world, cheering her on and giving her advice as she navigates seasons of life you have already walked through.

5. Take the time this week to ask a friend, family member or coworker how they are really doing. Listen and see if there is any way you can be of help or support to them.

CALL FOR BACKUP

I (Nicole) love cop shows. I used to watch them religiously with my dad. I would then reenact my favorite scenes with my next-door neighbors, Rick and Brandon.

Brandon always insisted on being the detective. (Everyone wanted to be the detective because, well, he was the hero, but we let Brandon have his way because it was the only way we could get him to play.)

Rick was always the bad guy.

I rotated parts depending on what the script called for. Sometimes I was the hostage. Sometimes I was an accomplice.

But my absolute favorite was when I got to play Detective Brandon's backup.

He would call on me when things got crazy—when shots were being fired, and everyone was dodging bullets. He would call in for backup . . . which when you're nine years old, basically means yelling the phrase "backup!" in between making fake gunshot noises and imagining bullets flying out of your gun-pointed-hands.

I loved being my friend's backup. It meant I got to be part of the action. I helped save the day. Together, we caught the bad guy and made the world a safer place.

It's been close to 20 years since I played a game of "cops and robbers," but that doesn't mean I haven't been called in for backup over the years.

Providing backup and calling for backup are parts of developing a healthy life. When we lose jobs or have marital problems or struggle to know whether or not to end dating relationships or try to lose weight and get in shape, we need friends and mentors to be our backup—people who can encourage and inspire us in our faith.

When a friend or family member is navigating a divorce or overcoming an addiction or working on the ability to communicate respectfully or dealing with the loss of a loved one, we get to be backup for them, ready to support them the best way we can. The truth is that we need each other. We will never overcome the hurts of our pasts on our own. We were created to do life together. Sometimes that means being willing to call for backup . . . Together we can catch the culprit who seeks to destroy our souls, and we will make our world a much better place!

FIVE WAYS TO SILENCE CRITICISM

The apostle Paul certainly experienced his share of criticism. Most leaders do.

The person out front is always the easiest to criticize. Paul had a way of dealing with criticism that he passed along to his protégé Timothy:

> Don't let anyone look down on you because you are young, but set an example for the believers in speech, in life, in love, in faith and in purity (1 Tim. 4:12, TNIV).

One of the difficulties Timothy had to overcome was his youth. The word translated "young" or "youth" is the Greek word *neotes*, which can describe anyone of military age, up to age 40. The Church usually liked its leaders to be people of maturity. Timothy was certainly younger than Paul, and many would watch him with a critical eye. Paul explained to Timothy that the only way to silence criticism was through his conduct. This is hard advice to follow . . . and yet, it's the only possible way.

Timothy was challenged to be an example—and so are we. Fighting with our critics never accomplishes much, so let's just commit ourselves to living exemplary lives. In what ways?

In speech. Words are powerful. The apostle James tells us that in many ways, our words set the course of our lives (see Jas. 3:3-8). What kind of speech is coming out of your mouth? In the heat of the moment, what words are you uttering? Do they honor God? Are they building faith in the hearers? Are they kind? Defensive? Arrogant? Do you feel the need to have the last word? Are you talking too much?

In conduct. How are you behaving? Would you want someone imitating your behavior? Are you leading a disciplined life? Or is there an area that is a bit out of control? Are you kind? Hospitable? Gracious? Forgiving? Do you demand your own way? Are you willing to take second place? Or do you need to be in front? Are you serving anyone or anywhere? WWJD . . . really?

In love. This word is *agape*. One of the definitions is "unconquerable benevolence." If we have *agape*, then no matter what anyone does to us or says about us, we will seek nothing but their good. Ordinarily love comes from the heart, but this kind of love comes from the will. This is the kind of love that refuses to get bitter, never hates, always forgives, and cares for others no matter what they have done. This kind of love, according to Bible scholar

William Barclay, will take the whole of our nature and strength of character to achieve. To silence our critics, we will need to love like this. How are you doing in this department?

In faith. This word in the Greek is *pistis* and implies an absolute conviction that God is Creator and Jesus is Messiah. This word also means loyalty—a loyalty that defies circumstances. Do you trust God when things aren't going the way you planned? Can you remain loyal in the middle of the battle? Are you really trusting God with your life? Your money? Your relationships?

In purity. As Christians, we have committed ourselves to lives of purity. Regardless of how bad our pasts may have been, once we begin to walk with Jesus, we are committing to a different way of life. Our sins have been washed away, and we are as white as snow. Now we have to walk that out. We won't do it perfectly— we will mess up from time to time and need to ask for forgiveness—however we must turn from our old ways and pursue His way. We have to have a different standard of behavior, of self-control and discipline. Pure lives. Pure motives. Pure hearts. Do you think the world will really have any use for Christians until we can be committed to living according to the standards of Jesus Christ?

We all experience criticism; perhaps some of it is justified, and I would imagine some is not. Regardless, the way we will silence it is by being committed to living the way Paul challenged his spiritual son, Timothy, to live.

MORE, PLEASE!
(Additional reading)
Safe People by Dr. Henry Cloud and Dr. John Townsend
Undaunted by Christine Caine
Scars and Stilettos by Harmony Dust
Battlefield of the Mind by Joyce Meyer
How People Grow by Dr. Henry Cloud and Dr. John Townsend

10

It's All About Jesus

HOW TO GROW IN YOUR RELATIONSHIP WITH GOD

You will find as you look back upon your life that the moments you have really lived are the moments when you have done things in the spirit of love.

HENRY DRUMMOND

THE MOST IMPORTANT DECISION
YOU'LL EVER MAKE

People make hundreds, if not thousands, of choices every single day. Yikes! That's a lot of decisions! What to wear, what to eat for lunch, which classes to take, whether to say yes or no to that cute guy asking you out on a date, which freeway to take for a shorter commute on the way home . . . As young women, we also have a significant number of *really important* decisions to make. Where to go to school, what career to pursue, to whom to say "I do," when to start the small business, when to start the family, whether or not to forgive, how to invest our finances . . .

Even though these are all very important decisions, there is one decision that is even more significant. It is the decision that will determine the course of your life from here into eternity.

It is the most important decision you'll ever make.

We've all contemplated making this decision before. We've asked ourselves, *Why am I here? What's the point of everything? Do I serve a greater purpose? Is there a real God? If there is, what is He really like? How does He explain the state of the world today?* And perhaps the most personal question of all: *How does God feel about me?*

Jesus offers this answer to our questions: "For God loved the world so much that he gave his one and only Son, so that everyone who believes in him will not perish but have eternal life" (John 3:16, NLT). *THE MESSAGE* puts Jesus' words this way:

> This is how much God loved the world: He gave his Son, his one and only Son. And this is why: so that no one need be destroyed; by believing in him, anyone can have a whole and lasting life. God didn't go to all the

> trouble of sending his Son merely to point an accusing finger, telling the world how bad it was. He came to help, to put the world right again (vv. 16-17).

The great news is that Jesus gives us an answer to our questions: God, our heavenly Father, loves us . . . and He has great plans and purposes for us!

In fact, God loves you so much that He gave His one and only Son, Jesus Christ, for you! The Bible says Jesus, fully God and fully man, came to earth from heaven and lived a blameless life. He willingly allowed Himself to be beaten and crucified on the cross so that you and I might have authentic, intimate relationship with God. On the cross, He became the sacrifice for our sins, our mistakes and our failures. Not only did He die for us, but three days later Jesus also rose from the dead! He conquered sin AND death to offer us a new start with God!

Jesus did all this because God passionately loves you and wants you to experience life with Him—eternal life. He wants nothing more than to have a real relationship with you! He created you with eternity in mind! He wants to be with you and care for you—in this life and in heaven—but the only way to experience life with God is through faith in Jesus.

Perhaps, you have never made the decision to open your heart and life to Jesus—to turn from your own way of doing life and instead choose to accept Him as your Lord and Savior, and begin following Him. Perhaps, at one time you made this decision, but honestly, now you feel very far from God.

Today—this moment—is your opportunity to make the decision to follow Jesus! It is the best decision you will ever make, and you can make it right now!

Simply believe in your heart that Jesus is your Lord and Savior, and pray this prayer inviting Him into your heart:

God the Father, thank You so much for sending your Son, Jesus, to pay the price for my sins—a price I could never pay. Thank You for loving me so much that Jesus died on the cross and rose from the dead for me. I accept Your love. I accept Your forgiveness. From this moment on, I am a new person—a follower of Jesus Christ. I accept Jesus as Lord and Savior of my life. Let Your Spirit lead me and guide me as I follow You all the days of my life. In Jesus' name, amen.

Congratulations! All of heaven is throwing a party for you right now! You just made the most important decision of your life!

WELCOME TO THE FAMILY
You are a member of God's very own family . . . and you belong in God's household with every other Christian.

EPHESIANS 2:19, TLB

I (Nicole) grew up in a large family. One older sister may not seem like a large family, but our house was often filled with additional relatives—cousins, aunts, uncles, grandparents and even great-grandparents.

We weren't exactly what you would call a "reserved" family. "Loud" and "crazy" would be more accurate words to describe our family functions. There were always a lot of laughs, a ton of food, and an occasional brawl that somehow seemed to end with more laughter and new memories. I told you—loud and crazy! ☻

Maybe you can relate. Or maybe you had a quiet family . . . or a distant family . . . or a dysfunctional family . . . or a loving family . . . or an all-of-the-above family.

As Christ-followers, we are also included in another family— the family of God. Through faith in Jesus, we have become sons and daughters of the most high God, adopted as His very own. That makes each of us siblings in Christ. We are now a part of God's family—or as the Bible calls it, the Church.

The Church isn't a building; the Church is something far more magnificent. It's you and I united together to worship Jesus and spread the great news about His love.

We are part of something much larger than we can see or comprehend. We are among the countless many around the world who, for more than 2,000 years, have been (and are now) called the family of God!

You may not have realized it until now, but your family just grew a whole lot!

The Bible describes this family, when united together, as the showcase of God's glory to a fallen world. It is through His Church that Jesus brings love and hope to the hurting, dying and broken all around us. It is through His Church that people hear the good news of Jesus and His love for each and every one—the kind of love that cares for the orphan and the widow, and provides shelter for the homeless, freedom for the addicted, joy for the suicidal, healing for the brokenhearted, and justice for the oppressed! The loving and united Church provides the kind of Christlike love that transforms lives for all eternity!

Here's the best part . . . YOU! You are a part of this family—a unique and important part! God gave you specific talents, abilities, passions and experiences, and they are to be shared in His Church for His purposes!

No one can replace you in this family of God! You are one of a kind!

You may never have set foot in a church before . . . or maybe it's been a very long time since you have. Maybe your idea of church is a stuffy place full of critical or hypocritical people. Maybe you've even been deeply hurt by an experience at church. (We're truly sorry for that.) Maybe church is something you never really connected with or thought much about.

But you need a place where you can connect with other genuine Christ-followers, so make the bold decision to find a church you can call home! It may take some time and effort to find a local church you can be a part of, but as you pray and take the steps to find *your* church, the Holy Spirit will lead you to the right spot for His blessing!

As we noted previously, Psalm 92:12-13 tells us, "The righteous will flourish like a palm tree, they will grow like a cedar of Lebanon; planted in the house of the Lord, they will flourish in the courts of our God." And Hebrews 10:24-25 encourages us to "think of ways to motivate one another to acts of love and good works. And let us not neglect our meeting together, as some people do, but encourage one another, especially now that the day of his return is drawing near" (NLT).

The Bible promises that when we plant ourselves in a healthy local church home, our lives will flourish, and our faith will be encouraged. When we connect with the family of God and become contributing members, we discover and fulfill the great purposes God has for each of us!

So whether you've never attended church before or you are currently a part of a great local church, make sure you commit to being an active member in God's family! You were never meant to do life alone . . . you were created to be a part of the family of God!

IT'S TIME TO TALK!

Think about the people closest to you. They're the people you make time to talk with, right? You swap stories about your days over a cup of coffee. You laugh over memories shared at the dinner table. You talk for hours on the phone with your friend from college.

You have meaningful conversations with the people you love. Your ability to communicate is one of the things that keeps your relationships strong and exciting!

The same could be said about prayer. When we consistently pray, we are building a great relationship with Jesus!

Prayer isn't as complicated as we might think it is. Prayer is simply talking and listening to your heavenly Father. You can pray when you wake up, on the way to work, before a big meeting or a hot date , or before you head to bed to catch your beauty sleep. You can pray by yourself, with family, with friends, or even with someone you just met! You can pray in your room, in your car, at the office, at church, at the dinner table, or at the grocery store. You can pray for 5 minutes, you can pray for 20 minutes, or you can pray for an hour. When you pray, you can say, "Thanks!" You can praise God! You can ask for His help. You can believe for miracles. You can seek direction and guidance. And you can listen to discover God's will for your life.

When we pray, God hears us, and He responds . . . but the only way to get answered prayer is to *pray*! ☻

When we pray, not only do we invite God's blessing, but we also get to know our Savior more, which is the greatest gift of all. Through prayer, we deepen our relationships with Jesus!

Make time to pray every day, and build the relationship with Jesus you were born to have!

> The earnest (heartfelt, continued) prayer of a righteous man makes tremendous power available [dynamic in its working] (Jas. 5:16, AMP).

THE BIBLE: YOUR NAVIGATION SYSTEM

Of all the books I (Holly) have read, none has shaped my life as much as the Bible has. The interesting thing about the Bible is that while much of it contains stories about other people and other events, it is very personal. Too many people, perhaps, keep their Bibles on the shelf and never allow God to speak to them through the Scriptures.

God's Word is His voice. My time with God always involves reading His Word. As I read the Bible, it is as if God is inviting me into His very

big world and opening up the possibility that His world can become my own. It is not a question of how much I read, but rather of how I let His Word shape my day. Some days I read several chapters, while other days I focus in on just a few verses.

God will probably not speak to you in an audible voice or use skywriting or a message in a bottle to give you direction. He will speak to you through His Word.

His Word is your map for living. It is your GPS. It is your navigation system. When you are taking a road trip and plan on arriving at a specific destination, you probably don't just point your car in any direction and go. No, I imagine you have a plan. Well, God's Word is your plan for life. Without it, you will never arrive where you want to go. It is very easy to get lost on the highway of life . . . but not if you are using His Word as your guide.

HOW TO GET THE MOST OUT OF YOUR BIBLE READING

1. Pick up a **Bible Devotional** to start each day with. Devotionals focus on a short passage of Scripture and provide creative ways for you to reflect on what that passage means. After reading only a couple of pages, you will have begun your day with the Word of God as your guide.

Get ready to be-schooled list

1. BibleGateway.com for commentaries and translations

2. Rick Warren's Bible Study Method: 12 Ways You Can Unlock God's Word

3. Great Lives from God's Word Series by Chuck Swindoll

4. Bad Girls of the Bible by Liz Curtis Higgs

5. The Jesus I Never Knew by Phillip Yancey

6. The Bible Jesus Read by Phillip Yancey

7. Bible Studies by Beth Moore

8. Life Application Bible

2. Find a Bible verse to help you with a situation you are facing right now. (Maybe you can use one included in this book.) Write the verse on an **index card** and carry it with you in your purse or stick it on your bathroom mirror. Make sure to read it a few times a day. Think about what this verse means for your life, and how it changes the way you think about God, yourself, others, and even your circumstances.

3. Pick a verse that stood out to you in your Bible reading and **memorize** it. It will strengthen your faith and give you new words to pray and focus on!

4. Have you ever wondered what God thinks about something??? Why do some people seem to be happier in life than others? What does God really think about money? How does God want me to treat that annoying co-worker? ☺ Does Jesus really forgive me for *everything*? Try a **topic study** and get the answers you are looking for (and discover new questions to be asking along the way!). Simply use a basic concordance (many Bibles have one located in the back) or try out the Topical Index or Keyword Search functions on www.biblegateway.com. Look up or type in a basic topic to get started. You can narrow your search to a particular book or portion of the Bible (such as the New Testament), or you can search the entire Bible. I recommend using the *New International Version* or

New Living Translation for a topic search. If you're not sure where to start, you could give one of these topics a try: patience, joy, obedience, friendship, courage, discipline, forgiveness, giving, healing, integrity, kindness or thanksgiving. Some studies may take an hour or so. Others you may continue exploring for a week, or even a month, in your daily time of reading the Bible.

5. Read a **psalm** or a **proverb** a day as part of your daily Bible reading. The psalms are beautifully written prayers and songs of praise and worship to God that help us develop a passionate, loyal love for Jesus. The proverbs are a collection of wise sayings that give us clear and practical direction about how to live life God's way.

6. Read through a **Gospel** in a month by reading a chapter a day. The Gospels—Matthew, Mark, Luke and John—are written accounts of the life of Jesus found in the New Testament. They include His teachings, His miracles, His interactions with His disciples and others, His death and His resurrection. As we learn more about Jesus, we ultimately discover more of the heart of our heavenly Father toward us!

7. Check out **study companions** to accompany you in your Bible reading. There are resources that assist you

in different types of Bible study; commentaries that offer additional insight to your Bible reading; and books that further explore themes, characters and historical context in the Bible.

8. Have you ever wanted to read the whole Bible cover to cover??? Find a **Bible Reading Plan** online, and decide to read the New Testament or the entire Bible in a year. By reading only a few chapters a day, you'll be able to complete the Bible in just a year's time!

9. Purchase a **journal**, and take notes while reading the Bible. Write down verses that stand out to you. Jot down thoughts about God, yourself and others that are sparked by what you read. List action steps you are going to take based on what you found in the Bible. You can even write out prayers to God that a particular part of the Bible inspired you to pray. Every month or so, take 30 minutes to read what you've written in your journal and reflect on all the great things the Holy Spirit is showing you and doing in your life!

10. Read a chapter of the Bible in three or four **different translations**. Compare verses that stand out to you. This is a great way to gain a fuller understanding of what you are reading. You can find various translations of the Bible available for free at www.biblegateway.com.

Bible Translation Formula:
New International Version (standard)
+ THE MESSAGE (modern paraphrase)
+ Amplified (lots of words)
+ New American Standard Bible (standard) =
AWESOME TIME SPENT IN THE BIBLE

11. **Find a consistent time and place** to read your Bible every day as part of your time spent with God. Give yourself enough time to really connect with Jesus. Transform your space into a distraction-free zone (no TV, no phone calls, no interruptions). This may mean waking up early or finding a secluded spot during your lunch break or locking yourself in your bedroom with a "DO NOT DISTURB" sign for your roommates to read! ☺

12. **Pray!** Pray before, during and after reading your Bible! Pray before, thanking God for sharing His thoughts with you through the Bible. Pray during, asking the Holy Spirit to give you understanding of the verse or passage you are reading. Pray after you are done reading, asking God to make it personal for you! Ask the Holy Spirit to show you how you can realign your thoughts to the thoughts of His that you have just discovered in the Bible . . . and how you can practically apply what you have just read to your situation or circumstances!

TWELVE PRETTY AWESOME THINGS JESUS DID (AND WHAT THEY TELL US ABOUT GOD)

1. **Jesus declared He was the Son of God and the only way to eternal life** (see John 14:6-7). God sent His Son, Jesus, to provide salvation for each of us. Jesus was more than a good man or a great prophet; He was—and is—the Son of God. It is only through faith in Jesus that we are able to have a genuine relationship with God and receive eternal salvation.

2. **Jesus preached a different way of life** (see Matt. 5-7). God wants to teach us how to live: how to love one another, how to forgive, how to manage our finances, how to worship God, and how to discover our purposes. His way for your life is the best way for your life! By following the direction for your life that He gives in the Bible, you will begin to live out the great life God has planned for you!

3. **Jesus ate with tax collectors and sinners** (see Mark 2:15-16). God doesn't expect us to be perfect before we can be in relationship with Him. He forgives us and accepts us as His children no matter what we have done! God desires an authentic relationship— one in which we are accepted and loved as we are!

4. **Jesus turned water into wine** (see John 2:1-11). God loves to have a good time! He wants us to live with joy and celebration regardless of our situations or circumstances.

5. **Jesus healed the sick** (see Matt. 12:15). God does not want anyone to be physically or emotionally sick. He doesn't punish us with sickness and His desire is to heal us!

6. **Jesus cast out demons** (see Matt. 8:16). God is all-powerful—more powerful than the enemy of our souls—and He has given us freedom and healing from hurts, bad habits and addictions.

7. **Jesus multiplied a couple of tuna fish sandwiches to feed thousands** (see Matt. 14:13-21). God provides for us, both spiritually and physically. When we trust Him with our resources and finances, He miraculously provides for us and always meets our needs!

8. **Jesus calmed storms and even walked on water!** (see Matt. 8:23-27 and Matt. 14:25-27). God is not a distant God who leaves us

to figure things out on our own. When the storms of life come our way, we can pray to God! When we do that, we can rely on His power and strength to give us peace, wisdom and provision for whatever storm we are facing!

9. **Jesus defended the cause of the poor and marginalized** (see Matt. 5:3 and John 8:7). God is a God of justice, and He cares for the hurting and marginalized. He is moved with compassion for the poor, the sick, the ignored and the abandoned. He desires that you and I each do our part to care for and fight for those who are experiencing injustice in our communities and in our world.

10. **Jesus died on the cross for our sins** (see John 3:16 and Mark 8:31). God has offered each of us salvation through Jesus. On the cross, He paid the price for your sins, mistakes and failures, and it is through faith in Him that you are saved. You can't earn God's love; He gives it freely!

11. **Jesus rose from the dead!** (see Luke 24:6). God is more powerful than death itself! As believers in Jesus, we no longer have to fear death—because we are confident that we are heaven-bound!

12. **Jesus gave us His Spirit to continue His work!** (see Matt. 28:18-20). God sends His very Spirit to reside

in our hearts when we believe in Jesus. His Spirit gives us the power to experience His great love for us and to live out the great purposes He has for us as His children.

GOD'S WORD FOR YOU . . .

Healing. "Jesus turned and saw her. 'Take heart, daughter,' he said, 'your faith has healed you.' And the woman was healed from that moment" (Matt. 9:22).

Peace. "Don't fret or worry. Instead of worrying, pray. Let petitions and praises shape your worries into prayers, letting God know your concerns. Before you know it, a sense of God's wholeness, everything coming together for good, will come and settle you down. It's wonderful what happens when Christ displaces worry at the center of your life" (Phil. 4:6-7, THE MESSAGE).

Courage. "There is no fear in love; but perfect love casts out fear, because fear involves torment" (1 John 4:18, NKJV).

Strength. "But those who hope in the Lord will renew their strength. They will soar on wings like eagles; they will run and not grow weary, they will walk and not be faint" (Isa. 40:31).

Hope. "'For I know the plans I have for you,' says the Lord. 'They are plans for good and not for disaster, to give you a future and a hope'" (Jer. 29:11, NLT).

Joy. "I'm singing joyful praise to God. I'm turning cartwheels of joy to my Savior God. Counting on God's Rule to prevail, I take heart and gain strength. I run like a deer. I feel like I'm king of the mountain!" (Hab. 3:18-19, THE MESSAGE).

Forgiveness. "If we confess our sins, he is faithful and just and will forgive us our sins and purify us from all unrighteousness" (1 John 1:9).

Love. "And I am convinced that nothing can ever separate us from God's love. Neither death nor life, neither angels nor demons, neither our fears for today nor our worries about tomorrow—not even the powers of hell can separate us from God's love. No power in the sky above or in the earth below—indeed, nothing in all creation will ever be able to separate us from the love of God that is revealed in Christ Jesus our Lord" (Rom. 8:38-39, NLT).

OOPS! MY BAD! NOW WHAT???

You blew it. Big-time. . . . Or maybe not big-time, but enough to feel bad about it. You did something you shouldn't have. You lied to someone who trusts you. You talked behind your boss's back. You gossiped. You went too far with your boyfriend on your last date. You gave in to an addiction you thought you had overcome.

Or maybe it's something you didn't do. You didn't tell the truth when you had the chance. You didn't defend the person you witnessed being teased. You haven't extended forgiveness to the one who wronged you. You didn't leave that party or club when you should have.

Well, here are two pieces of good news: God doesn't love you any less, and you are not alone.

That's right. God loves you. Period. You can't add to His love, and you can't diminish it. Nothing you do or don't do changes the way God feels for you. John 3:16 tells us that "God so loved the world that He gave His only begotten Son, that whoever believes in Him should not perish but have everlasting life!" (NKJV). Talk about GOOD NEWS! God proved just how much He loves you, and to what lengths He would go to be with you. He was willing to sacrifice His own Son, Jesus, on the cross for you! It's through faith in Jesus that we each get in on this life of love that God has for us!

Our failures and our mistakes don't change that. They don't change the way God feels and thinks about you or me! Nothing ever will!

Be assured, you are not alone. There are no perfect Christians roaming the planet. They certainly aren't sitting next to you at church this Sunday, even if you think they are. We all make mistakes. Romans 3:23 tells us, "For everyone has *sinned*; we all *fall short* of God's glorious standard" (NLT, emphasis added). We all need God's grace and forgiveness . . . and He is faithful to give it!

So when we make mistakes, what do we do? Well, we certainly don't sweep them under the rug. We don't shrug our shoulders and just forget about it. Neither do we have to feel overwhelmingly guilty and undeserving of God's love.

When we make a mistake (the Bible calls this "sin"), here are a few easy steps we can take to move past our big "oops-moment." I call them "The 4 Rs of Moving On."

1. **Recognize** that the Holy Spirit, out of love, is convicting your heart about something you have done or thought (or something you have chosen NOT to do or think) that doesn't honor God.

2. **Rely** on forgiveness. Psalm 86:5 promises us, "O Lord, you are so good, so ready to forgive, so full of unfailing love for all who ask for your help" (NLT). Ask God genuinely for forgiveness, and trust that He is quick to forgive you!

3. **Repent.** To "repent" simply means to turn from an old way and embrace a new way. Turning from an old way of doing something may mean changing habits and influences. (The Bible calls this "avoiding temptation.") It also means that you are willing to share your mistake with a mature follower of Christ. (The Bible calls this "confessing your sins one to another.") By telling this person about your "oops-moment," you invite her encouragement, support and accountability to grow and move past a mistake that is now in your past.

> **4. Realign** your thinking and attitude to God's will for your life. (The Bible calls this "renewing the mind.") Discover in the Bible what God says about you and about the particular area in which you are growing. Choose to believe what God says about you, rather than base your understanding on your past or even your present circumstances!

FAN VS. FOLLOWER

Have you ever attended a large sporting event? If you're a sports fanatic or married to one—or even if you ever attended a high school football game—then you know that being a fan can be a lot of fun! You get to wear team colors and jerseys; shout and wave foam fingers; give out a lot of high fives; participate in "the wave"; consume more than the normally recommended amount of hot dogs, soft pretzels and nachos; and create hilarious and unpredictable memories with friends and family. You get to pick and choose your favorite players, critique athletic performances, and argue with a referee's call. Fun, right?!

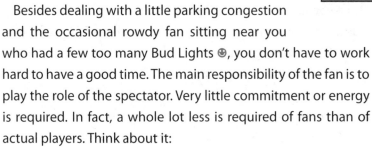

Besides dealing with a little parking congestion and the occasional rowdy fan sitting near you who had a few too many Bud Lights ☺, you don't have to work hard to have a good time. The main responsibility of the fan is to play the role of the spectator. Very little commitment or energy is required. In fact, a whole lot less is required of fans than of actual players. Think about it:

Fans sit on the sidelines.	Players get in on the action of the field.
Fans critique.	Players contribute.
Fans' enthusiasm is easily swayed.	Players' passion is immovable.
Fans show up to games when it's convenient.	Players show up prepared for every game.
Fans aren't on a team roster.	Players work as a team under the direction of the coach.
Fans don't break a sweat.	Players train to win.
Fans buy T-shirts.	Players bring home championship trophies.

You get the idea.

While being a fan can be fun when it comes to sporting events and concerts, it's not exactly the kind of life Jesus had in mind for us when He issued the invitation: "Come, follow me, and I will make you fishers of men" (Mark 1:17).

Jesus never intended for us to be *fans*; instead, He calls us to something much greater—to be His *followers (players on His team)*... Luke 9:23-25 tells us:

Then he [Jesus] told them what they could expect for themselves: "Anyone who intends to come with me

has to let me lead. You're not in the driver's seat—I am.
Don't run from suffering; embrace it. Follow me and I'll
show you how. Self-help is no help at all. Self-sacrifice is
the way, my way, to finding yourself, your true self. What
good would it do to get everything you want and lose
you, the real you?" (THE MESSAGE).

What Jesus is calling us to is life not as a fan but as a true
follower. We were never meant to be spectators of faith, but
active players winning for God's kingdom.

Refuse to spend your life on the sidelines! Get on the field and
live out the God-adventure set in place for you before the beginning of time! Make Jesus the number one priority of your life!
Pursue Him at all costs! Each and every day, make the powerful
choice to be a true follower of Jesus! Only then will
you discover the life you've always wanted to live!

THIS LITTLE LIGHT OF MINE . . .

"This little light of mine, I'm gonna let it shine." (Sing it
with me if you know it! ☺ "This little light of mine, I'm
gonna let it shine. This little light of mine, I'm gonna let it
shine, let it shine, let it shine, let it shine!"[1]

If you ever went to Sunday School as a kid, chances are you've
heard this gospel song. It's a song sprinkled with nostalgia. It's
the kind of song you could watch a freckled two-year-old with
pigtails sing on YouTube. It's guaranteed to stir up warm and fuzzy
feelings in even the most disgruntled and grumpy individuals.

But the message in this song is far more significant than simply
offering a trip down memory lane or a sense of innocence in the
world today.

Instead, this song speaks to a great mandate that you and I have been given by Jesus Himself! It's a call to a life of meaning and mission . . .

Listen to Jesus' words from Matthew 5:14-16:

> You're here to be light, bringing out the God-colors in the world. God is not a secret to be kept. We're going public with this, as public as a city on a hill. If I make you light-bearers, you don't think I'm going to hide you under a bucket, do you? I'm putting you on a light stand. Now that I've put you there on a hilltop, on a light stand— shine! Keep open house; be generous with your lives. By opening up to others, you'll prompt people to open up with God, this generous Father in heaven (THE MESSAGE).

To quote another translation, Jesus calls us "the light of the world" (v. 14, NIV)! We are meant to shine brightly—so brightly, in fact, that the darkest places are exposed to God-colors! Our light is meant to reflect the Light of the world, our Savior Jesus!

We shine brightest when we love and show value to others. When we pick up a coffee for a coworker, when we help a friend move into a new apartment, when we buy groceries for a neighbor who is experiencing financial strain, when we forgive the ex who betrayed us, when we speak highly rather than poorly of someone when she or he is not around—well, it's in these simple, daily acts that we truly SHINE!

We become a light that causes the people in our world to pause and take notice; whether or not they know God, they are drawn to the illumination of our lives. It is then that we get the opportunity to share with others what Jesus has done in our lives. We simply

tell our stories—the stories God is author-
ing in our lives . . . what He has saved us
from, how our lives have changed since
embarking on a relationship with Jesus,
and how we continue to experience His
love and grace.

When we shine, things change—or
more accurately, people change. People
are introduced to the heart-transforming
love of Jesus! Ultimately, when we shine, we aren't
shining our own light, but the light that comes from Jesus
Himself living in our hearts! We are merely reflectors of God's
miraculous and magnificent light! It's through the Holy Spirit at
work in us that we have the strength and courage to shine!

Don't hide. Refuse to live timid. You were born to shine!
Shine! Shine in your family! Shine in your school! Shine in your
workplace! Shine in your community! Shine in this world! It's
waiting to be lit with God-colors by YOU!

MORE, PLEASE!
(Additional reading)
He Chose the Nails by Max Lucado
GodChicks Awakened by Holly Wagner
Rick Warren's Bible Study Methods by Rick Warren
The Jesus I Never Knew by Philip Yancey
Lord, Teach Me to Study the Bible in 28 Days by Kay Arthur
The Life You've Always Wanted by John Ortberg
Too Busy Not to Pray by Bill Hybels

ENDNOTES

CHAPTER 1: WHY AM I HERE? HOW TO DISCOVER YOUR GOD-GIVEN PURPOSE

1. Thom S. Rainer, *The Unchurched Next Door* (Grand Rapids, MI: Zondervan, 2003), p. 24.

2. "11 Facts About Dropping Out," www.dosomething.org/tipsandtools/11-facts-about-dropping-out (accessed February 2012).

3. "A Generation At Risk," www.rainbows.org/statistics.html (accessed February 2012).

4. "The Need" www.generositywater.org/the-need (accessed March 2012).

CHAPTER 2: ONE OF A KIND: HOW TO CELEBRATE YOUR UNIQUE STYLE

1. "Hair Color," http://www.my-virtual-makeover.com/hair-color.html (accessed April 2012).

2. Viktoria Love, "A Fashionistas Guide—Emergency Wardrobe Kit," April 30, 2011, http://viktorialove. com/2011/04/30/a-fashionistas-guide-emergency-wardrobe-kit/ (accessed April 2012).

CHAPTER 3: HEALTHY LIVING: HOW TO LIVE LONG AND LOOK GOOD

1. Susan Goodwin, "Why is Omega 3 Good For You?" http://ezinearticles.com/?Why-is-Omega-3-Good-For-You?&id=4505704 (accessed December 2011).

2. "6 Health Benefits of Black Beans," May 29, 2011, http://www.healthdiaries.com/eatthis/6-health-benefits-of-black-beans.html (accessed December 2011).

3. "All the Health Risks of Processed Foods—In Just a Few Quick, Convenient Bites," http://www.sixwise.com/newsletters/05/10/19/all-the-health-risks-of-processed-foods----in-just-a-few-quick-convenient-bites.htm (accessed December 2011).

4. Adapted from "The Six Thousand Hidden Dangers of Processed Foods (and What to Choose Instead)," October 18, 2007, http://bodyecology.com/articles/hidden_dangers_of_processed_foods.php (accessed December 2011).

5. Kathleen M. Zelman, MPH, RD, LD, "The Skinny on Fat: Good Fats vs. Bad Fats," November 1, 2007, http://www.webmd.com/diet/features/skinny-fat-good-fats-bad-fats? (accessed December 2011).

6. Ibid.

7. Shelley Levitt, "6 Secrets to Gorgeous Skin," August 18, 2011, http://www.webmd.com/healthy-beauty/features/tips-for-gorgeous-skin (accessed January 2012).

8. Mayo Clinic staff, "Exercise: 7 benefits of regular physical activity," http://www.mayoclinic.com/health/exercise/HQ01676/ (accessed December 2011).

9. Eric R. Braverman, M.D., with Dale Kiefer, B.S., "Combating Age-Related Brain Deterioration," *Life Extension Magazine*, http://www.lef.org/magazine/mag2011/oct2011_Combating-Age-Related-Brain-Deterioration_02.htm (accessed December 2011).

10. Mayo Clinic staff, "Stress relievers: Top 10 picks to tame stress," http://www.mayoclinic.com/health/stress-relievers/MY01373/ (accessed December 2011).

11. Joseph E. Pizzorno, Jr., and Michael T. Murray, *Textbook of Natural Medicine*, 3rd ed. (St. Louis: Churchill Livingstone, 2006), vol. 1, pp. 701–708.

12. "Brain Basics: Understanding Sleep," National Institute of Neurological Disorders and Stroke, http://www.ninds.nih.gov/disorders/brain_basics/understanding_sleep.htm (accessed January 2012).

13. "Aging Alters Sleep and Hormone Levels Sooner Than Expected," University of Chicago report, August 15, 2000, http://www.uchospitals.edu/news/2000/20000815-soma.html (accessed April 2012).

14. Jordan Rubin, *The Great Physician's Rx for Health and Wellness* (Nashville, TN: Thomas Nelson, 2006), p. 150.

15. "Myths, Truths and Looking Good," *20/20*, February 18, 2005, http://abcnews.go.com/Health/2020/story?id=512095 (accessed April 2012).

16. "Sleep position gives personality clue," *BBC News*, September 16, 2003, http://news.bbc.co.uk/2/hi/health/3112170.stm (accessed January 2012).

17. Melinda Smith, M.A.; Lawrence Robinson; Joanna Saisan, M.S.W.; and Robert Segal, M.A., "How to Sleep Better," December 2011, http://www.helpguide.org/life/sleep_tips.htm (accessed February 2012).

18. *The Great Physician's Rx for Health and Wellness*, p. 45.

19. Don Colbert, M.D., *The Seven Pillars of Health*, (Lake Mary, FL: Siloam, 2007), p. 12.

20. F. Batmanghelidj, M.D., *You're Not Sick, You're Thirsty!* (New York: Warner Books, 2003), pp. 225-226.

21. *The Great Physician's Rx for Health and Wellness*, p. 47.

22. Ibid., p. 154.

23. Ibid., pp. 154-155.

CHAPTER 4: WHAT'S IN YOUR WALLET? HOW TO MANAGE FINANCES

1. Dave Ramsey, *Dave Ramsey's Financial Peace University* (Brentwood, TN: The Lampo Group, 2008), p. 71.

2. Ibid., p. 72.

CHAPTER 5: DOING LIFE TOGETHER: HOW TO NAVIGATE FRIENDSHIPS

1. Eugene H. Peterson, *Five Smooth Stones for Pastoral Work* (Grand Rapids, MI: Wm. B. Eerdmans Publishing Co., 1980), p. 192.

2. Leslie Guerrero Collins, L.M.T., "Relax with Laughter," http://absolutelyrelaxedaustin.health.officelive.com/RelaxwithLaughter.aspx (accessed February 2012).

CHAPTER 7: TYING THE KNOT: BUILDING A MARRIAGE THAT LASTS

1. Margaret K. Scarf, "Remarriage Is More Fragile Than First Marriage," in *The Bonus Years of Adulthood*, *Psychology Today*, January 12, 2009, http://www.psychologytoday.com/blog/the-bonus-years-adulthood/200901/remarriage-is-more-fragile-first-marriage (accessed April 2012).

2. Dr. Robin L. Smith, *Lies at the Altar* (New York: Hyperion, 2006).

CHAPTER 8: MODERN FAMILY: HOW TO MAINTAIN A HEALTHY HOUSEHOLD

1. Deanne C. Haisch, M.A., LMHP, "Giving Good Instructions to Children," parenting.org from Boys Town, http://www.parenting.org/article/giving-good-instructions-children (accessed February 2012).

CHAPTER 10: IT'S ALL ABOUT JESUS: HOW TO GROW IN YOUR RELATIONSHIP WITH GOD

1. Harry Dixon Loes, "This Little Light of Mine," www.hymns.me.uk/this-little-light-of-mine-favorite-hymn.htm (accessed February 2012).

ALSO BY
HOLLY WAGNER

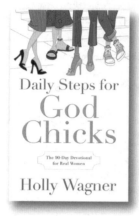

Daily Steps for GodChicks
ISBN 978.08307.42059

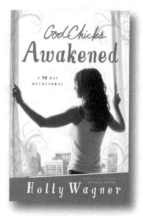

GodChicks Awakened
ISBN 978.08307.57503

GodChicks and the Men They Love
with Philip Wagner
ISBN 978.08307.52386

Warrior Chicks
ISBN 978.08307.44800